The Hall of Doors

The Chain of Living Fire: Book 3

Phillip M. Locey

Elisahd Books

DURHAM, NORTH CAROLINA

Book Layout © 2017 BookDesignTemplates.com
Cover Art by Soheil Toosi

The Hall of Doors / Phillip M. Locey. -- 1st ed.
ISBN 978-1-947579-13-2

This book is dedicated to the dedicated –
all the people who stick with it, whatever *it* is,
even when the hill is steeper than you ever
thought it would be.

"Knowledge is a cursed gift, isn't it? Ah, if one could simply choose to un-know things, our people might be spared tremendous strife."

–TRIGILAS EVERMOON, FATHER OF SPELLS

PLANAR RELATIONSHIPS

within the COSMOS

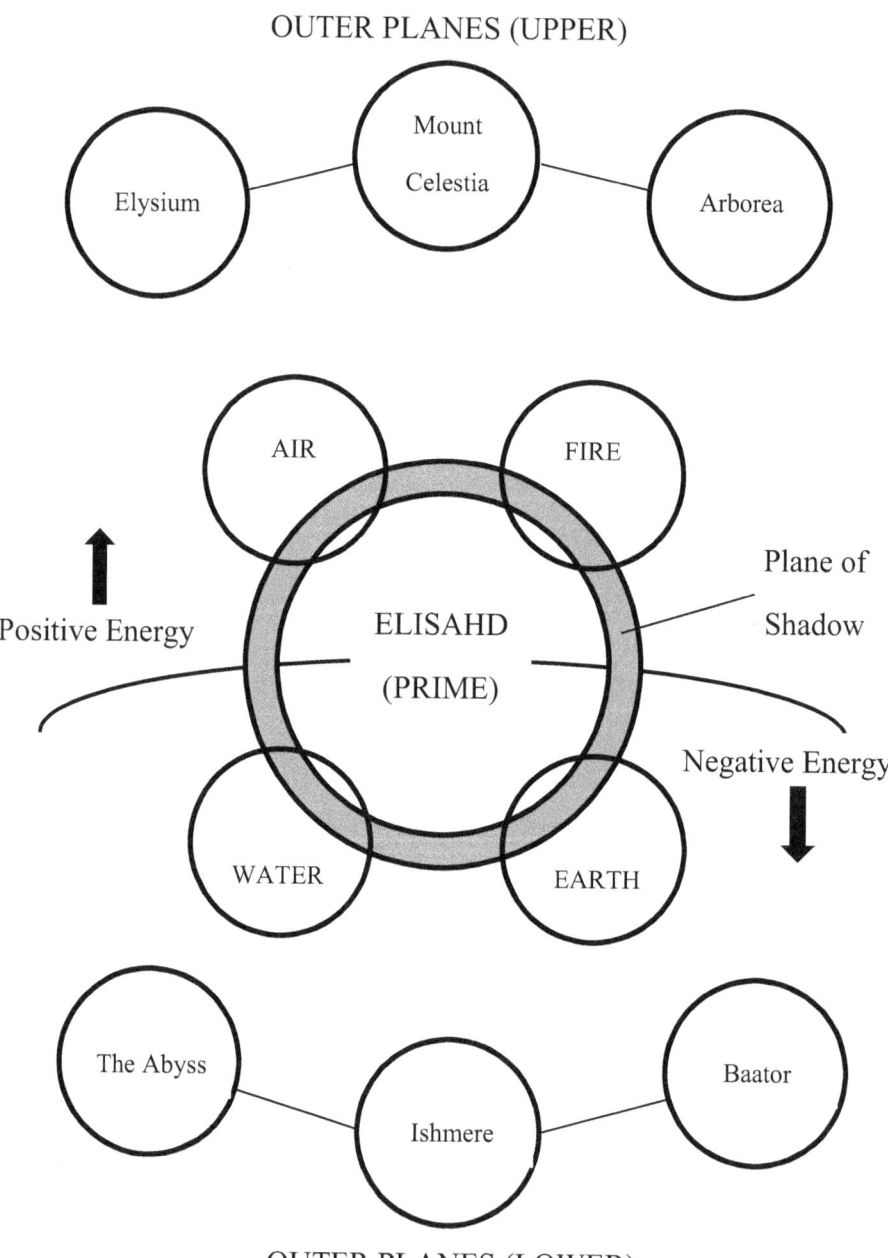

OUTER PLANES (UPPER)

Mount Celestia

Elysium

Arborea

AIR

FIRE

Positive Energy

ELISAHD (PRIME)

Plane of Shadow

Negative Energy

WATER

EARTH

The Abyss

Ishmere

Baator

OUTER PLANES (LOWER)

Contents

Chapter 1

The Long-Forgotten

"Who's going in first?" Thaelios asked. He figured taking the initiative to frame the question exempted him from the task itself. The hot, desert sun warmed his back, and while the cool of the darkness ahead was beckoning, the specter of the unknown was not.

"I can't see a thing," Dyphina said, stretching her neck toward the threshold yet not daring to step across.

Phaerim patted Saffron's shoulder. "Good thing we have a fire-singer with us then, eh?"

"Yes, give me a moment," she responded. "We need something to burn." Saffron and the rest of the group briefly checked, but Thaelios knew almost all their belongings were now buried like the rest of Ancient Tarmuth. Nothing remained to ignite save their clothing, or perhaps the pages of his master's spellbook, but those were clearly too valuable.

"Cauzel cast a spell that made his dagger glow," Be'naj offered to him in Eladrin once the fruitlessness of their search became obvious. "If you have his book, maybe you could duplicate it?"

"Ah, yes, why didn't I think of that?" Thaelios's left side still caused considerable pain, and he kept his arm tucked against it for protection. Cradling the spellbook in his right arm, he extended it to Be'naj. "Would you mind holding this so I can find the incantation?"

He'd noted that Cauzel's arcane writings were exceedingly organized, first by function and further by complexity, so it didn't take long to locate a simple spell entitled 'Radiance.'

"What are you two discussing?" Saffron asked.

"Sorry. I was just suggesting a spell I'd seen Cauzel use might be a solution," Be'naj answered while Thaelios continued reading the instructions. "Could we borrow your dagger?" she asked Phaerim.

He seemed hesitant to relinquish the only weapon the group possessed, but ultimately didn't refuse. Thaelios accepted it from Be'naj and recited, "*Lucemi*," as he held the pommel. A grin of satisfaction broke across his face as white light sprang from the metal, providing a soft glow.

He handed the dagger back to Phaerim, who nodded repeatedly at the outcome. "Would you like to lead the way?" Thaelios asked, and Phaerim's face fell as if he realized he'd been tricked into something he should have seen coming.

"I don't mind …" Be'naj offered, closing the spellbook and returning it to Thaelios while extending her empty hand in Phaerim's direction.

After seeming to weigh the risks of walking in first against being unarmed, he mumbled something and headed into the high stone corridor. Thaelios cradled the book under his right arm and followed, figuring he could see further than the human in their wan light, anyway. Dyphina came next, and the others filed in behind.

Phaerim's tentativeness supplied ample opportunity for Thaelios to assess their new environment. They entered a long hallway that extended beyond the reach of the dagger's white glow. Two pairs of wooden doors awaited only a few long strides ahead on either side of the corridor, though at their creeping pace, they would take many steps to reach. The dry air of the sealed Hall of Doors had kept the wood in excellent condition, while its staleness supplied a heavy, dusty smell.

Dyphina's hand pressed against his back, and as he looked over his shoulder, Thaelios saw the women had all compressed in tight formation in an effort to remain within his spell's aura. He felt cramped with Phaerim creeping just ahead of him and nowhere to go.

"This is ridiculous," he said. "The Hall has been sealed for centuries, and we're all too old to be this scared of the dark." Despite his words, Thaelios felt uneasy. While nothing could have reasonably survived such a duration of entombment, he couldn't account for whatever magical experimentation may have taken place in the mighty Trigilas's laboratory.

"Do you want to lead, then?" Phaerim asked without turning his head. He'd nearly reached the first door, and the shuffling of feet on worn stone was the only sound beyond their voices so far.

Thaelios would have considered it, but given the distracting pain and bound status of his left side, putting him in front didn't make sense. "Let's have a look at the doors," he replied instead. His curiosity regarding anything to do with the Father of Spells was enough at the moment to ignore the constant prickling of his eroded flesh.

Yielding to his suggestion, Phaerim turned to the right and lifted the glowing pommel of his dagger closer to the nearest portal. Thaelios gazed upon the colorfully painted door, whose tones were muted in the pure white light. Chips of missing paint marred the forest motif of the surface design, creating an effect similar to the aftermath of a locust swarm. Eladrin runes scripted at eye level declared the name: Erdelain.

"What about the one next to it?" Thaelios asked. Phaerim moved the light over to the adjacent door, which looked plain in comparison. Though it appeared stained and mostly smooth, there were no letters or designs upon it. Without being asked, Phaerim shifted to the opposite side of the corridor, and Thaelios followed to study the mirroring doors. The one across from the ordinary door was similarly devoid of decoration, but his heart leapt into his throat when he viewed the portal opposite Erdelain's.

Faded runes, aligned over a majestic mountain background, announced this as the room of none other than Trigilas himself. A gasp from Dyphina suggested she understood the discovery's significance as well, and Thaelios's mouth went dry as he struggled with whether or not to set down Cauzel's spellbook to free his hand for the door.

Dyphina recognized his plight and reached toward the painted surface to assist. "Should I open it?" she asked, though Thaelios now noticed all the doors lacked latches.

He nodded, failing to generate the saliva necessary to speak.

"Perhaps I should go first?" Saffron offered, her earlier reticence banished by the presence of illumination. Dyphina shrugged and Saffron squirmed past, switching places. As soon as her fingertips met wood, a sharp tinkle like the ringing of a wind chime sounded and the door swung open.

They all took a step back at the unforced movement, but once the door stopped and no further effects manifested, Phaerim crept forward, carrying light into the room. The spacious chamber was furnished like personal living quarters combined with a study. It was nearly square, with one corner abbreviated by a diagonal wall.

A still-made bed lay against the wall to the door's left, its top blanket shredded by insects or the ravages of time. A carved, oaken desk sat opposite, and in its chair was...

"Shecclad, grant us shelter!" Be'naj said from behind as Thaelios passed the spellbook back to Dyphina and stepped closer.

A robed body occupied the seat, but its head was obscured, slumped forward on the desk. Phaerim brought the dagger only marginally closer, but it was enough for Thaelios's keen eyes to see. He reached out slowly and lay a hand on the figure's shoulder. Thaelios knew the person had to be long dead, but his pulse beat as if expecting a different revelation. He grabbed hold and pulled back, twisting the slack body until its face popped upward.

Phaerim jumped when it did. "For the love of—" He closed his eyes and turned away.

Sockets once belonging to large, eladrin eyes gaped up at Thaelios as the skeletal remains creaked at his disturbance. The fleeting thought that he might be looking at the decayed body of the greatest Shaper who ever lived passed through him... the he remembered that Trigilas had died well before the Hall of Doors was sealed. One of his apprentices must have taken over residence in his quarters.

Behind Thaelios, the others filed into the room, spreading out now that they were free of the corridor. He let go of the skeleton's shoulder and it shifted to equilibrium.

"There's another one," Saffron said.

Thaelios turned to see a second skeleton lying on the floor near the wall opposite the door, marking a gap of vertical shadow, perhaps a hand-span in width. "What is that?"

Be'naj reached the spot first, but kept her feet clear of the corpse. She put her hand into the darkness. "The air's cooler." She grabbed hold of one side of the gap and pulled, stretching the shadow wider. Everyone drew nearer as she did.

Dyphina was closest and stretched to peek around as the stone seemed to slide into itself. "It's some sort of passage – there are stairs."

Giving the dead scholar at the desk a wide berth, Phaerim carried the light across the room. Thaelios followed on his heels. Once closer with better illumination, he saw that Be'naj had opened a hidden door in the midst of the stone wall. His skin tingled in excitement at the thought of what secrets the Father of Spells had deemed fit to hide in a disguised chamber.

"Do you suppose what we're looking for might be down there?" Be'naj asked, stepping over the eladrin remains to stare further into the shadows.

"What exactly *are* we looking for?" Phaerim asked. "Besides a meal, of course. If I don't get some food soon, my stomach's going to eat me."

"To save the Eladrin, we have to pass through a series of portals," Be'naj answered, staring down the stairs into the darkness.

Thaelios expounded, for Be'naj seemed to have lost her focus, "The Hall of Doors supposedly housed gateways to other planes for the purpose of Trigilas and his apprentices conducting magical research."

Be'naj took two steps down the secret stairs, her wings folded tightly to squeeze through the opening, then immediately backed out, nearly tripping over the corpse behind her. "I don't think we should go this way."

"Is something wrong?" Saffron asked.

"My skin started itching, and I've felt that before – at the Shaper's mansion in Zeblon." Be'naj rubbed her forearms with her fingertips, worry evident on her face.

"Do you think it's magically trapped?" Thaelios shared her concern, but still felt enticed by discovery.

"I don't know," the half-Aasimar responded. "Before, it was when that fiendling drew near."

"Sirran?" Saffron interjected. "Did he do something to you?"

Be'naj walked further from the disguised door, distracting her eyes by inspecting the contents of a bookshelf opposite the foot of the bed. "I don't think so. It was more like his presence itself affected me. I just think we should leave those stairs alone."

"That's a good enough reason for me," Phaerim added, crossing to Be'naj's side of the room to provide more light.

Thaelios frowned at the summary rejection of exploration, but peeled his attention from the shadowed crevice when he heard Be'naj exclaim, "Look at the binding on these books!"

She pulled one off the shelf, an expulsion of dust coming with it as the ancient text separated from its peers for the first time in centuries. Be'naj carried the tome to the bed and blew more dust out of its textured cover. Sewn into the binding of tanned animal hide were designs in dyed, iridescent cloth. They depicted rainclouds releasing a deluge on the dark world below, while above the clouds sat a bright, heavenly sky. Shiny, silver lettering announced the title: *Gradations of Immortality.* "It's still in excellent condition."

"Probably a preservation enchantment," Thaelios said, squirming between Saffron and Dyphina to get a closer look.

Saffron crouched by the bookshelf and trailed a finger down the edge of a couple spines. "I wonder how much forgotten knowledge is resting on this single shelf..."

"I'm sure there's plenty," Phaerim quipped, "but unless it's going to help conjure a plate of venison, can't it wait until we've either found a meal or one of these portals? Hells, I'd probably even settle for just watching you read in a room that doesn't have dead Eladrin draped over the furniture."

Saffron stood. "You're right. Curiosity can wait until our basic needs are met. We should continue exploring the halls. Maybe we'll find some food stores with a preservation enchantment on them."

"Can't argue with that," Dyphina echoed, holding her stomach as the reminder of food caused it to complain anew. She leaned over the bed and set Cauzel's spellbook overlapping Trigilas's tome.

When Thaelios shot her a look, she shrugged. "It gets heavy. It'll be here when we come back – it's not like those other books have walked off in the last few centuries."

"What if there's a trap or other mischievous magic we need to overcome?" he objected.

Dyphina cocked a hip to the side and placed her hand upon it. "And you think you're going to be able to break an enchantment placed by the greatest Shaper ever to walk the forests of Elisahd? She rolled her eyes and followed Saffron, who was exiting into the hallway with a hand on Phaerim's shoulder.

As the light from the dagger receded beyond the doorway, Be'naj tucked her arm around Thaelios's uninjured one and interlocked elbows. "Come, there are more great things to be discovered," she offered in Eladrin. After glances back at the bed and secret stairway, Thaelios sighed and joined Be'naj in leaving Trigilas's room.

They caught up to the others soon, for they'd reached an intersection of corridors, and the light didn't extend far enough to illuminate an end in any direction. More doors were visible along the walls in the perpendicular hall, but after they'd regrouped, Phaerim kept straight. "I wonder how many poor souls met their end down here," he asked no one in particular.

A dozen slow paces forward, the corridor opened into a spacious hall, complete with a vast table running across their view. Thaelios was last to enter what must have been the dining area, and after peering right and left, he guessed there were enough seats in place for at least a score of Shapers to have eaten simultaneously in the days of Trigilas.

Across the table, a wide circle was cut out of the floor, three-fourths of it surrounded by an iron railing. To either side of the circle were tight rows of close-set doors, extending the length of the table. Beyond the open space at the head and foot of the table, Thaelios could just make out more doors in the uneven walls at the edge of the light.

"What was that?" Dyphina cried from the rear, her voice's urgency claiming everyone's attention, though Thaelios hadn't heard a single other sound disturbing the dry air. "Something touched my face."

"Sorry," Be'naj apologized. "I think my feathers must have brushed against you."

"Phaerim, we should check those doors," Saffron said, ignoring the distraction. "If this was where they ate, maybe those held their food stores."

While the others eagerly skirted around the edge of the wooden furniture, lured by the hope of quelling their hunger, Thaelios remained still, his eyes fixed on the dark circle. As the light moved away with his companions, its receding coincided with faint whispers tickling his ears.

"Did you say something?" he asked, shifting his gaze and nearly shouting so the others could hear.

"What?" Dyphina called back.

He realized almost immediately they hadn't been the source as the voice was distinctly Eladrin, and he heard it again as his friends peered back at him.

"*Khilterel pelenari,*" it whispered. "*Yelen quentireth guriel.*"

"Did you hear that?" Thaelios responded, narrowing his eyes to penetrate the darkness in search of the speaker.

"What's going on?" Saffron asked.

"Shhh." Thaelios held up his hand as multiple voices repeated the message.

"I hear it, too," Be'naj said.

"Hear what?" Saffron demanded, irritation setting in.

"Look, up at the ceiling!" Be'naj pointed upward.

A handful of slowly moving streams of light coursed through the air near the top of the room, stretching like caterpillars, disappearing and reappearing after each body-length slide.

"Phaerim, cover the light for a moment." As the pommel of Phaerim's dagger went dim underneath his shirt, Thaelios saw the iridescent streams more clearly, glittering like ethereal bands of silver across the black space overhead. Now that everyone else was frozen in wonderment, he could hear them more clearly: several voices overlapping but repeating the same phrases.

"*Khilterel pelenari. Yelen quentireth guriel.*"

"What are they saying?" Phaerim asked.

Be'naj answered before Thaelios could think of a more palatable translation, "*You are unwelcome. His hunger protects our secrets. You are unwelcome.*"

Almost instantly, Phaerim uncovered the light. "What in the Nine Hells is that supposed to mean? Whose hunger?"

Thaelios never took his eyes off the shimmering entities, who grew dimmer with the competing illumination. "It's an ancient dialect. The words may have different shades of meaning. Maybe we can communicate with them." He stepped closer to the table and rested his hand upon it, feeling the need to be further grounded.

"We did not intend to trespass. We come in peace. We are eager to share in your wisdom," he stated in Eladrin. Instead of a reply, the silvery streams circled the ceiling and started floating away into the darkness beyond the further end of the table.

"Where are they going?" Phaerim asked. "What did you say?"

"I know I'm half-fey," Dyphina added, "but this is a little eerie, even for my taste."

Thaelios tried calculating the possibilities of danger in his head, but if he didn't act quickly, he might lose sight of the lights. "I want to see where they lead." He followed with quick steps, hoping the others would join him.

Jogging to keep up, he was vaguely aware of Phaerim's trailing glow as he advanced further into shadow. After reaching the end of the dining hall, Thaelios turned left and started down another long hallway with doors on either side. The spectral lights continued whispering as they moved away, but too faintly for him to decipher.

Finally, they stopped at the end of the corridor, their dim illumination just enough to expose an arched doorway beneath where they hovered. Thaelios halted, now that the chase was over, waiting for his companions to catch up.

"Thaelios, the dagger is starting to wane," Phaerim announced as he drew level. The others packed into the flickering halo of the dagger's radiance, their breathing harried from the brief spurt.

"You may need to re-cast the spell," Dyphina observed.

Thaelios remained fixated on the door at the hall's terminus, however. "What do you think's behind it?" he asked, taking slow steps forward again.

"Shouldn't we address the light situation first?" Saffron asked firmly.

Thaelios looked over his shoulder at the sound of her voice, but just as he did, the dagger's aura gave out completely. He swiveled back to look at the door and, sure enough, the lights started moving again, this time out of view down an adjacent hallway to his left. He instinctively took two steps to follow, so as not to lose their haunting glow, when Saffron's voice halted him again.

"Thaelios! We need to see!"

When Thaelios turned back toward his fellows, the darkness was complete. Even a few steps away, he could see nothing of them. "Alright, alright." Cauzel's spellbook was still on the bed in Trigilas's quarters where Dyphina left it, and Thaelios closed his eyes to remember what he knew was a simple incantation. Before he could recall the words, however, the sounds of ragged breathing from his party was pierced by Be'naj's panicked voice.

"What is *that*?"

Thaelios opened his eyes, a moment of confusion passing until he knew where to direct them. A continuous, rough gasping sound drew his attention back down the hall where the shimmering lights had passed from view. In the blackness, two points of red shone from where the gasping grew into horrible bursts like choked-off screams.

"It's coming closer!"

"Cast the spell, Thaelios!"

The red lights accelerated toward them, bounding up and down like a rowboat on the roiling waves of an ocean. The words just on the tip of his tongue evaporated into the smoke of Thaelios's dismay. He heard singing as he turned to flee.

"Move, move!" Phaerim urged as Thaelios collided with another body, sending a fresh surge of pain through his injured side. Cries, rapid steps, and a nearby thud filled his ears as they all scrambled to navigate the hall in complete darkness.

A blossom of red fire suddenly bloomed into existence a few steps ahead of Thaelios, lighting up Saffron's palm and the features of her face as she leaned forward to blow on it. He halted and turned to follow the flame as it launched past him, casting a pale glow along its route.

Phaerim was rising from the floor between Thaelios and their pursuer, having tripped in the tangle of legs. The blossom streaked past him and collided in a burst of red against the body of a demonic aberration.

The creature's face seemed all teeth, other than its luminescent red eyes. It had a jumble of legs, all ending in massive, clawed paws, some of which were set on the floor while others pressed against the wall. The only thought Thaelios could conjure before the light dissipated in a sizzle of magic and bestial snarls, was that the thing chasing them looked like the twisted offspring of a hairless panther and some giant insect.

With all light gone, Thaelios scrambled to escape, guessing as best he could which way to go. Perhaps he could barricade himself inside one of the many doors they'd passed. That idea fled as Phaerim screamed in pain behind him. Thaelios swiveled toward the sound, promptly slamming into one of the high-backed chairs surrounding the great table.

He tumbled to the ground in a heap, banging his head on the way down. Oddly, the jarring blow came with a burst of clarity, as he suddenly remembered the single word of the Radiance spell. He needed an object to cast it upon, and the only thing within reach was the chair. "*Lucemi.*"

Illumination sprang from the furniture, and Thaelios grasped it with his good hand to pull himself up.

"Over here, down these stairs!" Be'naj yelled. She was at the back of the room, leaning against the metal railing that protected three-fourths of the descending circular stairwell. With her white wings spread wide, she seemed a beacon of safety even though Thaelios knew she was unarmed.

Dyphina streaked from the shadows to hustle down the stairs while Thaelios staggered around the end of the table, cradling his left arm with his right. When he reached the protective railing, he spared a look back to find what had become of Phaerim and Saffron.

"Keep going!" Be'naj ordered. Phaerim hobbled closer, drastically favoring his right leg, and Saffron had picked up a chair to fend off the creature. Thaelios saw it grasp an entire chair leg in its mouth before his view was obscured by Be'naj's wings as she hurried to assist Phaerim.

Deciding the best thing he could do was clear out of the way, Thaelios navigated the twisting stone stairs, his heart in his throat and his mind desperate to think of a solution to their danger.

Once his head descended past the edge of the floor, the world became dark again. Keeping his right hand on the central column, he followed the petal-like extension of stairs until the ground leveled off beneath him. He heard snarls and the sound of splintering wood from above, then the effort of Be'naj leading Phaerim down the stairs. Thaelios backed away from the base to make room.

"Dyphina, are you there?" he asked.

"I'm here," she responded, her breath labored.

"We've got to think of a spell to keep that thing from following us."

A sudden wail assailed Thaelios from the top of the stairs as Saffron came spilling down them. Looking up, the glow of the lit chair provided just enough brightness to reach the lip of the stairwell. The beast peered over the edge from one angle then another, though it made no attempt to descend.

As his eyes adjusted to the pervasive darkness, Thaelios distinguished Be'naj helping a winded Saffron to her feet, while Dyphina tended to the reclining Phaerim. The creature continued vocalizing a repertoire of disturbing cackles and yelps, though as Thaelios watched and listened, they grew quieter and less frequent. Finally, the beast retreated, its whines replaced by the winces and exhalations of his friends.

"Hold still so I can get a better look," Dyphina commanded, though there was no bite in her voice. "Thaelios, can you give us some light?" she asked more sharply.

"Are you hurt?" Be'naj questioned Saffron as Thaelios knelt beside Phaerim.

"You've still got your knife," he noted, reaching over to place a hand upon its pommel. "*Lucemi.*" White radiance once again issued from the dagger's hilt, almost shockingly bright under the circumstances, though Thaelios knew it was no more brilliant than a torch.

"There's blood on it," Saffron said, drawing closer.

Phaerim's face was beaded with sweat, and Thaelios spared a glance at his companion's wounded thigh. "That doesn't look too bad," he lied.

Phaerim snorted a laugh in spite of himself, following immediately with another wince.

"We need something to cinch his leg…" Dyphina looked around in vain.

"The bandages were with the camels," Be'naj replied, her face crestfallen.

"Tear my sleeve, Saffron." Dyphina lifted her right arm parallel to the floor. Saffron grasped the sleeve near her shoulder and ripped the cloth from it. At least they had been bundled in their warmer clothes when the sandstorm hit.

"You should probably wash the wound, first," Saffron mentioned as she handed the makeshift bandage to Dyphina.

"With what?" Phaerim croaked. "We've only got a few swigs of water left in my bladder, and we're not wasting it on my leg."

"I've seen a bite wound like that before, and it ended up getting infected," Saffron retorted. "You don't want to lose your leg altogether."

"Of course I don't," he snapped. "But what good will my leg be to any of us if we die of thirst in the next few days?"

"Saffron's right." Thaelios had to butt in, feeling a little responsible for the injury. "Given how little water we have left, we're going to have to find more to sustain us anyway. We might as well treat your wound now and put our efforts into replenishing supplies."

In the silence that followed, the women all nodded and Phaerim rolled his eyes, silently giving in. Thaelios turned his back as Dyphina and Saffron tended the wound. Though he heard more tearing of cloth and groans from Phaerim, his eyes assessed their new surroundings.

He was standing on a curved dais that formed a semicircle against the north wall, centered by the spiral stairwell. Obsidian walls framed the rectangular room that easily stretched a dozen paces across. Four smooth gaps, more than wide enough to walk through, had been designed into the walls – one each on the western and eastern sides, and two on the southern. Curiously, however, an even wider hole had been smashed through the center of the southern wall, surrounded by debris from its annihilation.

While still in Phaerim's grasp, their source of light was too far to provide much detail, but the obvious devastation made Thaelios uneasy. He yearned to know what lay beyond this room, though the possibilities were admittedly frightening.

"There you go," Dyphina said at last. "That's likely the best we can do until we find more supplies. At least the bleeding has slowed."

Saffron joined Thaelios to look upon the ruined section of wall. "Thankfully that creature didn't pursue us down here," she noted, folding her arms across her chest. "Do you think that's because it's afraid of whatever did *that*?" She nodded toward the rubble.

Thaelios shook his head. "I think this place is going to provide more questions than answers."

Saffron nodded, the truth of his statement offering no comfort. "We may not survive another attack, but we need to find food and water. Phaerim needs to be stitched, and fresh bandages wouldn't hurt. I'm going to look around to see what I can find. Someone has to. I want you to watch after the others; use whatever magic you can to help."

Thaelios glanced at her, though she was still staring into the darkness. He didn't know what to say, but felt ashamed for his relief that she'd taken the decision from him. Finally settling on "Be careful," he placed his hand on Saffron's arm.

She turned to him and forced a smile. "Would you mind casting another light spell for me?"

"Unfortunately, casting the spell anew cancels any previous ones."

"Oh." She looked down at Phaerim and the others. "Would you mind sitting together in the dark for a while?" she asked.

Dyphina snorted, "You must be jesting."

Saffron shrugged. "It's either that or come with me, and clearly Phaerim shouldn't move more than he has to."

"I could retrieve one of those chairs to burn," Be'naj offered.

"Don't be ridiculous," Dyphina objected. "That beast is probably waiting in the corner to grab you."

"We'll get by, Saffron." Phaerim grimaced as he extended his dagger toward her. "You should take it."

That seemed to be the final word. No one offered additional arguments, given Phaerim was currently the most vulnerable. "I'll cast it again anyway," Thaelios said, "to make sure it lasts longer."

After refreshing his *Radiance* spell, Thaelios sat on a step of the spiral stairwell, letting his chin sag. Though not complex magic, the successive casting left him weary.

"That's odd," Saffron said from the far side of the room.

Thaelios lifted his head to see her pressing a hand against the air in front of one of the designed gaps of the wall, to the right of the pulverized section. When she brought the light closer, the previously unseen surface shone like glass.

Shifting her grip on the dagger, she pushed with both hands against the air, but couldn't penetrate it. "Some sort of invisible barrier."

Thaelios perked up, but continued simply watching as she slid right of the room's corner to try another gap. This one she passed right through, and Thaelios could tell from the reflection of the light that the dark stone walls were nearly as thick as Saffron was tall.

She drifted beyond view, though he could still hear her footsteps echoing and catch the glow of her light as she explored the space beyond.

"What do you see?" he couldn't help asking.

Be'naj stood and took tentative steps toward Saffron, though she looked hesitant to cross the threshold into the next room. "Are you in danger, Saffron?"

"I'm safe enough."

Thaelios could barely hear her reply, and the light was all but out of view. "She'll be alright, Be'naj. Saffron can handle herself." He wondered if his words sounded as hollow as his confidence in them.

Several long moments passed with only the sound of his companion's breathing to keep Thaelios company. At last, the light returned, and with its brightness, Saffron.

"What did you find?" Thaelios asked.

"Nothing to eat, I'm afraid. One of the walls was nearly taken up by a flat square of blackness, like a huge painting. The surface seemed to be in motion, though almost imperceptibly. A raised basin sat in one corner, etched with a pentagram. A great wheel was mounted on the wall opposite the painting, divided into sections. Glyphs marked each one, though I couldn't read them."

Thaelios was fascinated by Saffron's description. "I might be able to decipher the writing … if you think it's safe."

Saffron nodded and shrugged, then looked to Be'naj. "Are you okay watching the others?"

"I'm not a child!" Dyphina protested.

Be'naj bit her lower lip, but nodded in return.

"It should only take a moment," Saffron assured her, ignoring Dyphina.

Thaelios gestured back toward the adjoining room. "Lead the way." He followed Saffron into a chamber nearly as large as the one they were just in, though more square. Just as Saffron described it, Thaelios immediately made for the mounted wheel. He lightly grasped the edge – metallic and cold. Applying a bit of pressure, he was able to turn it, though it groaned heavily. A triangle at the top of the circle remained in place, pointing down to the selected section as they rotated.

He brought the wheel to a stop to read the designations, which were thankfully scribed in the same ancient dialect of Eladrin he guessed the shimmering lights above had spoken. "*Nirvana*," he translated aloud. "*Elysium, Mount Celest—*"

"There's light coming from above!" Be'naj called out in Illanese from the next room. "Who's there?"

Saffron abandoned Thaelios, rushing back to the others and taking the light with her. He followed but couldn't keep up, his injury making it painful to run. When Thaelios returned through the gap, he saw a young human woman halfway down the staircase, holding a lamp and peering at Saffron, who'd stopped beside Be'naj.

"Nazee Saffron, ibit shurul?" the woman said.

"Rhazine?" Saffron responded, taking another step toward the stairs. "Khalem ufaari nuhut?"

The woman tucked her lantern closer to her body and hurried down the remaining steps, the heavy pack on her back bobbing as she descended. She was beaming widely and started spouting sentences in Begnari so quickly that Thaelios didn't know how Saffron could possibly keep up.

He hadn't paid much attention to the prisoners they'd freed, due to his injury, but Thaelios surmised this must be the daughter of the Wolfspider. He couldn't imagine what she was doing here, though she seemed pleased to have arrived.

Saffron got in a few words of her own, but seemed surprised when Rhazine almost leapt upon her in an embrace, her lantern swinging precariously around Saffron's back. When they separated, she turned to face the rest of the group. "Everyone …" Saffron said, "you may remember the young woman we rescued from the slave caravan, Rhazine."

Rhazine continued smiling and waved upon hearing her name. She was thin, with straight, dark hair and a complexion slightly lighter than Saffron's.

"How did she get here?" asked Phaerim.

"Apparently, after leaving the oasis, instead of heading for her intended new village, she cut north and came upon our tracks," Saffron answered. "She simply followed until she caught up."

Be'naj wore a frown to oppose Rhazine's countenance. "What about the sandstorm?"

Saffron translated and Rhazine expounded.

"She was sheltered when it blew in, and found our animals afterward at a watering hole. Sheen survived after all!" Saffron's excitement at the news failed to inspire her fellows. "She was worried she might have lost our trail, but kept on the same course and eventually picked it up again."

"Anything useful in that pack?" Phaerim butted in.

Saffron gestured to her backpack as she asked Rhazine a series of questions. Those ended with the girl nodding and unburdening her load. She withdrew a brown sack, full of biscuits, which Saffron sampled and passed around.

Thaelios's mouth watered as soon as he smelled the morsels, bland as he knew they were. Everyone took a break from talking while they stuffed their mouths, and soon Saffron was passing around Rhazine's full waterskin as well.

When he had swallowed his portion, Thaelios's inquisitiveness caught up with him. "How did she get down here safely? Is the beast no longer menacing the corridors?"

Saffron used her tongue to clear out some stuck biscuit from her teeth, then asked Rhazine his question. "She has no idea what I'm talking about. She found the abandoned halls to be a little unnerving, but assumed we were down here somewhere. She didn't encounter any beast."

"So what do we do now?" Dyphina asked. "The snack was nice, but Rhazine doesn't have enough food to keep us fed for long. Are we going to keep looking around down here in the dark until something else attacks us, or cut our losses and get the sleeping skunk out of here?"

Be'naj exhaled loudly in disbelief. "What about our quest to save the Eladrin? Cauzel believed in it, too." She looked from Dyphina to Saffron, hoping for support.

"I don't think we should abandon it, by any means," Saffron responded. "But it's clearly going to be difficult for Phaerim to continue. Thaelios and I are injured as well, and we have no weapons to defend ourselves."

Be'naj looked surprised, as if Saffron had just assaulted her.

"Perhaps Rhazine can lead us back to Sheen and the camels," she continued, "and we can find an outpost to regroup. Once we've healed and gotten more provisions, we can always return …"

"What if we can't?" Be'naj snapped. "What if the door seals again and we have no way to disable the Dampening Stone a second time. Cauzel warned the cancellation spell wouldn't be permanent."

"Maybe we should vote on it," Dyphina offered. "What do you think, Thaelios?"

All eyes turned to him, and Thaelios stroked his chin as he considered the arguments. He certainly wished to explore Tarmuth further and uncover the ancient lore Trigilas had undoubtedly left behind, and there was no guarantee they could enter the Hall of Doors again. Was he willing to die for that knowledge? Saffron was right: they were lucky to have escaped that menace the first time without weapons, but they were also taken by surprise. If he'd only held onto Cauzel's book, he might find a spell that could destroy it …

"I vote we stay."

Dyphina and Saffron sighed and started to protest.

"At least until we finish exploring this level," he added. "Saffron and I found what I believe might be a magical gate. If I'm able to find a way to activate it, it could be the quickest way to safety."

"Or the quickest way to eternal doom. How do we know where it might lead?" Dyphina asked.

"Well, there was a wheel that I think might determine the destination—"

"I vote we leave as well," Phaerim interrupted, his voice calm but firm. "My leg actually feels like it's getting worse."

Dyphina knelt beside him to assess. "You've got a fever," she said, placing the back of her hand on his sweat-beaded forehead.

"What about Rhazine?" Be'naj asked. "What does she think we should do?"

"She does *not* get a vote," Dyphina snapped. That seemed to be the cue for everyone to start arguing all at once.

"Enough! Enough!" Saffron finally yelled, bringing the room to silence. "We've got two sources of light now. Thaelios and I will continue exploring this level, and if we don't find anything useful for getting us out of here, we'll all exit the front door together and do what we can to come back when we're better prepared. Agreed?" She gazed from face to face, and everyone reluctantly nodded save Rhazine, who had no idea what she'd said.

Saffron instructed the young woman to remain with the others, then she and Thaelios headed for the smashed section of wall, once he'd recast *Radiance*. Saffron stepped over large chunks of rubble while he navigated around them. They entered a vast hall with two rows of sculpted support columns flanking a long, elliptical dais in the center of the room. So large was the chamber, their meager light did not reach the other walls or ceiling.

Without words, they walked toward the dais, taking in the enormity of the space. Dark and silent, the hall's air hung heavily. Thaelios had the impression of intruding upon a history he could not fully fathom. He noticed Saffron's boots left footprints in a layer of dust as they drew near a pedestal, erected in the center of the dais.

"What do you think it is?" she asked as they reached the gilded, rectangular display.

Part of a fractured stone tablet lay upon the flat surface, and though curious, Thaelios felt palpable revulsion to the object, understanding innately that it should not be touched. "Those runes are written in Infernal," he said, tracking down the dozen words forming a list on the tablet. Each one was cut off at the fracture line to remain incomplete.

"You read Infernal?" Saffron asked.

Thaelios shrugged. "I went through a phase in my adolescence where I thought the Underworld was exciting. Thankfully, I grew out of it."

"So what does it say? I think I am starting to feel ill." She turned away and took a step back from the pedestal, bending slightly at her waist.

"They are names, I think. Truenames, if I had to guess. I'm not going to read them aloud." Thaelios retreated as well. "Look, there are gaps in the walls to either side. Perhaps we should try a new room." He headed right and Saffron followed, clutching her stomach but not yet retching.

When he reached the gap in the smooth, stone wall, he bumped into an invisible barrier. He reached out and tested the blockage with his palm. It was as if the air itself was solid. "Force walls," he mumbled to himself. He looked over his shoulder at Saffron, who was walking fully upright again. "This is advanced magic. I surmise there's a password to get through."

"Do you know it?" she asked.

Thaelios sighed, turning back to the barrier. "Of course not."

"Then I guess we should try the other one, no?" Without hesitating, Saffron turned on her heel and traversed the width of the spacious hall, her light merely a dim halo staving off centuries of undisturbed darkness. Up the steps of the dais, then across and down again, giving the pedestal a wide berth, she finally reached the gap in the opposite wall. There, she held still for Thaelios to catch up.

This time he reached out, anticipating another wall of force, though the gap was vacant. Tentatively, with his arm still extended, he stepped forward into the room. Similar to the one they'd been exploring when Rhazine arrived, it was square, with a patch of black void further darkening the wall to his left. Hanging on the wall across from it was another wheel, partitioned, with each section bearing writing. In the middle of the space was a pedestal that supported a metal basin.

Thaelios lowered his arm and waited for Saffron to advance with the light before peering into the basin. Also etched with a five-pointed star, this one bore dark stains that he guessed could have originated from blood. His stomach started churning as he hesitantly approached the wheel to read its script.

"*Gahanna, The Abyss, The Nine Hells, The Grey Wastes...*"

"Those don't sound very appealing," Saffron responded.

"No, they do not," he agreed.

"You said earlier you thought these might be the planar gates. Any idea how we might use them?"

Thaelios shrugged. "It's logical enough that the wheels are used to choose the desired destination, but whether they even work in both directions is a mystery to me. My studies are nowhere near advanced enough to have reached theories of extra-planar travel."

Saffron nodded, considering the black square mounted on the far wall.

Thaelios stepped in behind her. "I have the unfortunate suspicion that these basins play a role, though whether as magical conduits or just vessels of superstitious sacrifice, I wouldn't wager."

"Well, what now?" she asked. "If we don't know how to use them, they aren't doing us much good."

Thaelios sighed. He was having a series of unfortunate realizations. "Though I'm not fond of it myself, the course that makes most sense regarding the gates is to return to Trigilas's chamber and see if there's any useful lore there. Of course, that means evading that creature somehow."

Saffron nodded somberly. "Rhazine seemed to manage it. Perhaps something we did the first time around roused its attention..."

"That could be. Either way, whether to leave Ancient Tarmuth by the front door or one of its portals, it appears we're going to have to head the same direction."

"Let's get back to the others," Saffron suggested. "If I have any sense of it, this light is going to fade soon anyway, and I'd rather not have to navigate in the dark."

They returned to the stairwell and their companions. Be'naj seemed especially relieved to see them return, though she embraced Saffron and not Thaelios. His explanation of their predicament received a few groans, but after Saffron passed the news along in Begnari, she and Dyphina helped Phaerim to his feet while Rhazine collected her backpack and lamp.

"Try to be as quiet as you can," Saffron instructed before leading the way up the stairs, carrying Phaerim's dagger with a freshly cast *Radiance* upon it. Thaelios followed, feeling drained, and the others came behind, Rhazine and her lamp last. They advanced slowly to account for Phaerim's difficulty, especially managing the stairwell, and Saffron waited in the dining hall until they'd all emerged.

Thaelios's eyes strained in the darkness, but he couldn't catch any sign of movement from the heavy shadows. They wove a path around the end of the long table, much louder than he would have liked. He was prepared to cast his *Mirrored Image* spell at the first sign of danger, hoping to at least confuse the beast with more options if it moved to attack them.

Saffron had just reached the central corridor leading to Trigilas's quarters when Thaelios heard the voices return. Looking up, he saw the shimmering ribbons of light flowing across the ceiling.

"*Have you seen the relic? Do you know our secrets?*" they asked in Ancient Eladrin.

Everyone had stopped moving at the intrusion, and Thaelios was unsure whether to attempt answering their query. He had just opened his mouth when they seemed to come to their own conclusion.

"If you have seen, there is but one way to leave..." The ribbons changed direction and surged through the air down the passage they were about to enter. At the end of it, two dozen paces away, Thaelios saw a shallow rectangle of light, coming from the outside door.

"Go!" Thaelios shouted with a sudden sense of panic, worried what the cryptic words portended. Saffron started jogging down the corridor, obviously concerned at his tone. Thaelios followed but couldn't keep up with her stride without severe pain from his side.

She was over halfway down the hallway when a grinding sound coincided with a vanishing of the lit rectangle. "No!" Saffron yelled, sprinting the rest of the way to confirm their fate. From behind, Thaelios saw the silvery ribbons change direction and advance upon him before turning to evacuate down a side passage.

He looked back to Saffron once they disappeared from view. She answered the question in his mind before he asked it.

"It's sealed shut!" She struggled to pull back the massive stone door, even using the dagger to pry at it, but it would not budge.

"Run, run!" Be'naj's urgency snapped Thaelios's attention behind him. Dyphina was soon passing him on her way to Saffron, then Phaerim too, cursing in pain as he limped by.

"Not this way, it's blocked," Saffron directed.

"The beast is back!" Be'naj confirmed from further down the corridor as Rhazine and her swinging lamp reached Thaelios.

"Into Trigilas's room!" he shouted, having already planned on the destination.

They hurried into the Shaper's quarters, one at a time but with amazing efficiency. Be'naj followed Thaelios as the last one in, but before she could close the door, the snarling creature grasped both sides of the frame with two of his many paws and lunged forward to bite. Be'naj kicked it hard under the chin, momentarily stunning it.

"Down the stairs!" Saffron yelled before slipping past the others to aid Be'naj, flipping the dagger in her palm.

Thaelios didn't stay to watch, grabbing the books on the bed with a stab of pain and waiting his turn to descend the steep and narrow, secret stairs. He heard horrible snarls and a battle-cry from Saffron, then glanced back just long enough to see her slash her blade across the beast's eyes.

With Phaerim ahead of him, Thaelios stepped over the wasting skeleton at the top of the stairs and descended, fighting the urge to push past the slower human to escape. He hadn't made it all the way down before a log-jam completely prevented his progress.

"Go! Why aren't we moving?" He gave in and started pushing, groaning at the ache in his side and drawing protestations from Phaerim and Rhazine in front of him. His force moved the pile of bodies forward, however, and he'd just spilled into a five-sided room when he felt Be'naj pressing in behind him.

Looking up, he realized why the others had stopped. Within a wide circle of white powder on the floor was a glowing red pentagram, and standing in its center was an eight-foot tall humanoid with ruddy skin and horns on its head, draped in gold-embroidered, black clothes. It calmly stroked its barbed chin, then opened its mouth to speak.

"Now this is interesting. Can you understand me, Silver-skin?" it said in Infernal. "Are you the one I've been waiting for?"

Chapter 2

The Way Through

Thaelios's jaw dropped. Frozen for a moment, he spun around once his feet recovered and headed back to the stairs, though Be'naj blocked the passage.

"If you do understand me, I can do you no harm. I am forbidden from it," the room's giant resident continued.

Shutting his eyes and fighting to suppress his fear, Thaelios faced the speaker. No one else uttered a word or even moved a muscle as far as he could tell, their flight from the beast seemingly forgotten. He'd vaguely registered that Saffron was present and unhurried, which must mean their previous threat was under control.

Say something, Thaelios. He tried to conjure a response in Infernal, but his mind scrambled all memory of forming words in the language.

"Even if you are mute, it has been ages since I've had visitors, so I suppose we'll have to devise some way for you to amuse me." The ruddy-skinned speaker pressed his palms together and started tapping his fingers.

"I, I understand you," Thaelios finally managed to say.

"Oh you do?" The creature's eyes widened. "Wonderful. Then your hour has begun, and I am almost a free fiend. I shall assist you with knowledge, but only until the glow of this symbol has faded." It pointed to the floor, where the red light of the pentagram was slowly erasing as it traced the figure. "Until then, ask what questions you will."

Thaelios was shocked. He looked to his companions, who were now all staring uneasily at him. This would be much easier if they could all understand, he thought. "I don't suppose you can speak Illanese, or even Eladrin?" he asked.

"I am capable of communicating telepathically with any linguistic creature, under normal circumstances," it answered. "However, I am currently bound by the stipulations of my imprisonment, which means I may only speak aloud in my native tongue, and only to a full-blooded Eladrin. Quaint, isn't it?"

"What sort of trick is that?" Thaelios asked, trying to buy time while he determined the best course.

His host sighed, then shook his fiendish head. "If I was capable of bringing you harm, I can think of little that would grant me more pleasure. But, I have not moved against you, have I, nor from this Summoning Circle? Since you are apparently the Chosen, I'm sure you're clever enough to work it out."

The insult actually made Thaelios feel better. "Do you have a name?"

The seemingly bound Outsider drew back his lips in a menacing expression that could have passed for a smile. "I see you *are* clever, indeed. Of course the one who trapped me here discovered my Truename, but you may call me M'thenzor, arch-devil of Malbolge. Since we are being polite, you could share your appellation if you wish…"

Thaelios didn't see the harm, but knew that didn't mean there wasn't any. "That won't be necessary," he answered. He turned to Dyphina and Saffron, who had managed to squeeze past him into the open room, and spoke in Illanese, "He is a fiend who claims to be sworn to answer my questions, though only in Infernal. We should not speak each other's names. Are there any questions you'd like me to ask him?"

"What is that creature that attacked us, and why does it not follow beyond the stairs?" Be'naj demanded while scratching the skin of her arms. She had stayed back in the shaft containing the secret stairs until coming forth to speak, and spread her wings once she had the room to do so.

"My dear Celestial – would that I could slay you myself," M'thenzor decreed. "It has been an Age since I've bathed in the blood of your kindred." He looked from Be'naj to Thaelios. "You keep poor company, Silver-skin. But no matter, I shall be free soon enough."

"You understood her?" Thaelios asked.

"Of course. I said I was only permitted to speak Infernal – that doesn't mean I can't hear perfectly well."

"So?" Thaelios raised his eyebrows. "What's the answer?"

"How should I know?" M'thenzor scoffed. "I've been trapped in this Circle for centuries. We are in the Hall of Doors, however. That fool Trigilas and his minions entreated with scores of beings from the nether realms. I am still here, after all. There could be others, and there's no telling what laws and stipulations they are bound by."

"Ask him how to use the Portals," Saffron said once the fiend was finished.

Thaelios nodded, never removing his gaze from the creature's face. "Can we use the Planar Gates to leave, and if so, how do we control where we end up? Also, what is your home plane?"

"Why, planning to come visit?" M'thenzor's face screwed up slightly after his comment, as if uttering it brought discomfort. "I've already told you, but I traveled here from the sulfurous wastes of Malbolge, if you must know. You can depart Tarmuth through its Gates, though not without cost.

"Each portal is generally attuned to a group of planes that share the most basic characteristics of the cosmos, relative to your Prime. There is a wheel corresponding to each portal that provides choices for more specific locations, though those realms themselves may be infinite."

Thaelios nodded, having already guessed as much.

"However," M'thenzor continued, perhaps intuiting the level of his acquired knowledge, "you will first need a key to activate any of those portals, and it rests in another dimension itself."

"What?" Surely he'd caught the fiend in a lie. "How are we supposed to retrieve the key from another plane if we need the key in order to travel to another plane in the first place?"

"A hidden chamber, mirrored to this one, can be reached through the Summoning Vault, where lies the Tablet of Broken Names. Follow the stairs in the secret room to a lone portal. Passing through will take you to the realm of the key."

"And how do we activate that portal, if the key is on the other side?" Thaelios wondered if the hellish denizen was talking in circles purposefully to run out his sentence without truly helping.

A grin spread across M'thenzor's face. The gesture held a definite suggestion of malice. "That is the part I sincerely regret having to miss. There is a basin near the gate. Opening the portal requires that the heart of a willing sacrifice be placed in the basin."

Thaelios felt as though all his insides were about to drop out. "You're not serious," he said sternly.

M'thenzor simply nodded, the horrifying smile still stretched across his face.

"That's sickening. Who would devise such a mechanism?"

The devil shrugged. "Someone who did not want Planar Gates to be used on a whim. It seems extraordinarily prudent for a mortal if you ask me."

Thaelios shook his head, unamused. "I didn't." He glanced at his companions, who had taken seats on the floor but looked eager for an explanation of his conversation. How would he tell them this? "Then what?" he directed toward M'thenzor. "How do we use the key once we have it?"

"It is dimensionally anchored to its resting spot, and will return there an hour after its removal. You place it into the basin within the room whose gate you intend to use and simply step through to the selected realm. You may even come to visit me in the Nine Hells, if you wish. I'll keep a seat warm for you, Silver-skin."

"How do I know you're telling me the truth?" Thaelios asked. He desperately wanted at least part of the fiend's instructions to be a fabrication.

"I suppose you don't, but that means nothing to me. I am answering your questions as I must, but whether you act on what you learn is beyond my caring."

Thaelios looked down at the diminishing outline of the pentagram – more than one side of the star had already vanished. He turned to his friends again. "He's told me how to activate the portals. Is there anything else you'd like me to ask?"

The light on the dagger in Saffron's hand blinked out, though Rhazine's lantern still burned. The shifting of shadows seemed sinister, given their company. While the others were thinking, something popped into Thaelios's head. "Did Trigilas himself trap you here? If so, for what purpose? Surely not to merely answer my questions a thousand years later…"

The smile drained from M'thenzor's face. "Aye, Trigilas summoned me. I only hope his spirit has survived long enough for me to claim my vengeance once released." The devil winced again following his declaration. "Your 'Father of Spells,' as I heard him called, was insufferably insolent, though admittedly brilliant as well. He sought magical knowledge from whatever sources he could, and I turned out to be one of them. Through all our dealings, I never discovered how he manifested my Truename… He was obsessed with banishing the Juda-cai from your realm, and I had much to teach him on that matter."

"The Juda-cai? So you mean the god's Avatars did in fact walk upon Elisahd?" Thaelios never believed the stories as a child, though his interactions with Cauzel had started to change his mind.

"Oh yes," M'thenzor confirmed. "Though the Juda-cai are not your gods any more than I. They have walked upon many worlds. Or, their Avatars have, for they possess no bodies themselves."

"What do you mean?" Thaelios asked.

The fiend looked down at the pentagram, then back at Thaelios, who thought he saw the devil roll his eyes. "The Juda-cai live in a realm called Ishmere, where nothing is solid. Therefore, they have no bodies."

"How? What?" Thaelios couldn't figure out exactly what he wanted to ask. Perhaps this line of questioning wasn't the most useful given their predicament. "Is there any magic you can teach me before you leave?"

"Oh, an ambitious one, after all? How surprising. I almost never get that request." M'thenzor flinched again, dipping his shoulder slightly. His voice had lost some of its calm and he spoke more quickly when he resumed. "I can't answer that very well without knowing what you already know. Are you even a Shaper? I suppose one of you must be, for I noticed your little light spell expire. Come to think of it…"

The arch-fiend suddenly lifted his arms perpendicularly and clenched his clawed fists, grimacing. A pair of previously unlit braziers along the wall behind M'thenzor leapt alive with purple flame, and the devil laughed.

Dyphina, closest to them, squealed and stood upon their ignition.

"So, you have disabled the nearby Dampening Stone." M'thenzor looked at Thaelios with what he interpreted as newfound respect. "You must possess a modicum of skill, then. I can tell you it won't last long, though. The Heart of the Abyss churns in such stones, and your mortal magic will only affect them temporarily. Once its powers return, you will be unable to open the portals."

"What?" Thaelios had not calculated such a complication. The sacrifice stipulation seemed bad enough.

"Don't you think the other mortal Shapers trapped here would have simply used the portals to escape were they able?" The devil seemed in good spirits again. "Don't worry, I am still limited by Trigilas's binding and cannot use my magic to harm you." He looked down at the pentagram, which Thaelios noticed was losing its third edge.

"Now you tell me?" Thaelios huffed and located Saffron, switching to Illanese. "We can use the Planar Gates to leave, but must do so before the Dampening Stone becomes active again and may not have much time."

Saffron peered at the stairs. "What about the beast roaming above? Did you learn of a way to defeat it? I'm not sure I can best it with merely a dagger."

"He didn't even know what it was, so I don't think he's going to be much help with that," Thaelios responded. "I grabbed Cauzel's spellbook, though. Maybe there's something useful in there. Give me a moment to look." Fighting the rising panic induced by their time constraints, he extended his arm, which cradled both his mentor's spellbook and the tome from Trigilas's bookshelf. He passed the latter to Saffron, hoping to project the very calm slipping from him grasp.

"What are you searching for?" M'thenzor asked, leaning forward but unable to pass the circle of salt around him.

"Something to keep us safe from whatever bit Phaerim," he replied, still scanning the book's contents. Several rapid heartbeats passed before Thaelios registered that he'd just stated his companion's name aloud.

"And what was it that bit Phaerim?" the fiend asked. Thaelios heard the smile in his voice. "Can you describe it to me?"

Thaelios glanced at his friend, who was none the wiser. From the strain on Phaerim's face, he seemed to still be struggling with the pain from his injury. He chose not to respond to M'thenzor. He kept skimming through pages while Saffron prepared the others to move again.

After several minutes of hasty cross-referencing, Thaelios discovered a promising lead: a protection spell, intending primarily to ward against mental possession, also reported to prevent physical contact from beings not native to the plane of the casting. "Is there another exit from this room?" Thaelios asked in Infernal, raising his eyes to meet those of the looming fiend. "Other than the stairs?"

M'thenzor's mirth had once again dissipated, perhaps intuiting that Thaelios had come upon a solution. "There is not. Trigilas wanted to keep me all to himself – for as long as he could, anyway."

Thaelios nodded. "Gather around, everyone," he said in Illanese. "Saf—" he caught himself, nearly using another name, "could you ask our Begnari friend if she has some salt stowed in that pack?"

"Certainly," she replied before relaying his request.

Excited to see Rhazine nod, Thaelios buried his nose in Cauzel's book to make sure he understood the nuances of the incantation while she retrieved the necessary ingredient. When he was confident in his grasp of the instructions, he asked everyone to join hands in a tight circle. After packing the books into Rhazine's backpack, he sprinkled salt around their circumference, then ducked under arms to stand in the center as he recited the spell.

Once finished, he held his breath, waiting to see if the Dampening Stone was still neutralized. Satisfaction welled inside him when he saw a white vapor rise from the circle of salt in a curtain around them. It evaporated almost immediately, but Thaelios was sure it'd worked.

"Keep holding hands, but you're going to have to trust me," he announced. "As long as we're in contact, the beast won't be able to touch us, but the protection will break if you force aggression upon it first. If we remain calm, we should be able to simply walk on past." Thaelios left out the part where this would only work if the creature was indeed from another plane.

"So, what now?" Dyphina asked.

"Up these stairs, then back to the other stairwell," he answered.

"And that's going to get us through the portals?" Even with her wings folded, Be'naj had to stretch her arms to keep hold of her neighbors.

"One thing at a time."

"You still haven't told them what's coming," M'thenzor mentioned from behind. "I think Phaerim deserves to know you're marching him off to his death."

"Nobody said that," Thaelios snapped back in Infernal. It was true, though – the hardest part was yet to come.

"We'll have to go slowly," Phaerim said, as if on cue.

They broke their circle with Thaelios taking Phaerim's hand and bringing up the rear. Saffron led, climbing the steep stairs back to Trigilas's quarters, with Rhazine's lamp extended in front of her.

"I hope you're right about this, Thaelios," she said as they ascended one deliberate step at a time, for Phaerim's benefit. After the infuriatingly awkward process of climbing the narrow passage sideways, with hands occupied and a crippled member, the group reached the level ground of the main floor.

All was quiet – the beast was nowhere to be seen, though Trigilas's room was in disarray. Furniture had been toppled, and what was left of the bedding was shredded. Saffron peeked out the door into the corridor beyond, and whispered that all was clear.

Soft-footed as they could, the party snuck down the passage toward the dining hall and the spiral staircase. Saffron led the living chain, and all Thaelios could see from the back was the illumination of the lantern, interrupted by the vague forms of bodies passing between him and the solitary light source.

Though he'd been unconsciously waiting for it, Thaelios still jumped when a hungry snarl erupted from the cross-passage ahead of him. Dyphina was the most exposed and screamed as the beast lunged toward her.

"Don't let go!" Thaelios reminded her, though he couldn't really tell what was going on. The progression of bodies and light stopped.

"What's happening?" Saffron yelled. "Is everyone okay?"

"Dyphina?" Thaelios asked, his own voice nearly drowned out by the aggressive vocalizations of her attacker.

"She's fine," Phaerim answered for her. "It can't touch her."

"Let's keep moving," Dyphina finally said, her voice higher-pitched than normal.

They shuffled forward again, and once Thaelios reached the intersection, he saw glowing red eyes lighting up the beast's alien features as it paced from one side of the hallway to the other, little more than an arm's length in front of him. Its teeth were thin and pointed like needles, overlapping the rim of its mouth. The skin of its face looked shiny and hardened – as the spell seemed to prove, it was obviously not of this world.

It followed Thaelios as he cleared the side-passage, gurgling its desired menace and keeping his nerves on edge. He hoped the spell maintained until they'd gotten below, or he'd be the first one to fall.

Before long, they turned to wind around the long table, and Thaelios checked the ceiling to see if the shimmering ribbons were keeping watch. Only darkness hovered above, and he was glad when they began their descent. Once on flat ground again, he felt confident telling his companions they could separate. Phaerim had been limping severely during their journey and dropped to the floor as soon as they'd all let go.

Rhazine's lamp seemed to be growing dimmer, and Thaelios wondered if she'd brought more fuel. The increased darkness seemed to remind everyone of their weariness, for both Saffron and Dyphina stifled yawns. Thaelios couldn't say for sure how long it'd been since he'd last tranced.

"How are you holding up?" Thaelios asked Phaerim. His friend's eyes looked sunken and sad.

"Not great," he replied. "My leg stings something awful."

"You probably need to rest," Be'naj contributed. "We all do."

"You may be right, of course, but we can't afford to," Thaelios countered. "Not yet." He raised his voice so that everyone took notice, "We have to activate the portal before the Dampening Stone prevents us. If not, we may be buried down here as sure as the Cult of Broken Names."

Saffron exhaled noisily through her nose. "All right, then, what do we do next?"

"That devil said that the key we need to use the Planar Gates resides in an extra-dimensional space. We've got to find that doorway first, and he said the way there was hidden in the Summoning Vault."

Saffron shook her head. "You Eladrin certainly love hiding things, don't you? Alright, lead the way before this lamp goes out. Unless, of course, you'd like to give us more light?"

Thaelios frowned. "I'd prefer to save my strength if it's all the same. That protection spell exhausted me. I don't want to drain myself further in case we have dire need of magic."

Saffron pursed her lips and nodded. "So be it. Let's get moving, then."

At her urging, Be'naj and Dyphina helped Phaerim stand, and they followed her through the rubble-strewn gap in the southern wall. Thaelios fell in line, preoccupied with figuring out how to deliver news of the price they would soon have to pay.

This time, they steered clear of the dais and its gilded pedestal, keeping to the left of the columns as they traversed the enormous hall. "Spectacular," Be'naj said, extending her wings in the wide open space and staring toward the ceiling as she walked.

"Where do you think it is?" Saffron asked as they reached the other end of the room. A golden cupboard rested against the far wall, bearing three vertical, textured doors.

Thaelios was curious about its contents but wasn't sure he should open it. "Supposedly the chamber mirrored the one M'thenzor was in, so it should be behind the eastern wall …"

"M'thenzor?" Be'naj asked. "Is that the name of the fiend? He made my skin itch awfully bad."

"Is it better now?" Saffron asked, rubbing the half-Aasimar's upper arm.

Be'naj nodded and smiled, leaving Thaelios to roll his eyes and walk over to investigate the wall. Its black stone was flecked with small patches of grey and smooth to the touch. Phaerim leaned against one of the columns, just on the edge of Thaelios's peripheral vision, while the others milled about somewhere behind.

"Saffron, could you bring the light closer?" he asked. Keeping his focus on the wall, he searched for signs of irregularity as the glow of the lamp drew closer. He ran his fingertips along the cold surface, hoping to find creases that might betray a door's presence.

A metallic clang sounded behind him, followed by Dyphina's voice. "It's locked."

Thaelios looked over his shoulder and saw that she was referring to the golden cabinet. "Then it should probably stay that way," he said, returning his attention to the wall. Finally, his fingers felt a slight vertical ridge in the stonework, though the darkness prevented his eyes from discovery. "There!" Satisfaction relaxed the tension in his shoulders momentarily, though it returned as he realized it meant the fiend had been telling the truth.

"You found something?" Be'naj asked. "I don't see it."

Thaelios followed the line of the crease up and over, confident it belonged to the outline of a door. "It is very well made. Now, how do we open it?" He took a step back from the wall to change his perspective. It still looked massive, and dark, and blank.

"How did the one upstairs work?" Be'naj asked after the passing silence failed to yield answers. "The door to the stairs?"

The obvious missed opportunity felt like a slap to Thaelios's brain. "I don't know," he answered after mentally chiding himself. "It was already open when we entered the room."

"Well," Dyphina said, wandering over after abandoning the cupboard. "Either it's magical or there should be a mechanism of some sort."

Thaelios hoped for the latter. If it was opened by magic, they might be guessing at passwords until the next moon-cycle. Although the Dampening Stone would probably end their chances well before that, he thought darkly. "She's right. Everyone, look around and see if you can find a lever or button hidden somewhere. It would probably be nearby."

After a translation from Saffron, Rhazine joined the rest of the group in spreading out and searching the walls and floor close to the secret door. Only Phaerim stayed put, confining his half-hearted search to the pillar he'd been using to support him.

"Maybe it's over by the cupboard," Dyphina mentioned before wandering back that direction. "Ugh, it's too dark this far from the lamp. Can't you cast that spell again, Thaelios, or at least give me the spellbook and let me try?"

"That's not a bad idea," he admitted. He started toward Rhazine, who had the books in her pack, when Saffron sidled up to him.

"You don't think the way in might have something to do with that tablet on the pedestal, do you?" she whispered.

He had to consider the possibility, though his intuition still screamed that they shouldn't disturb it. "I doubt it," he replied, feeling dishonest. "That's too far away." He'd reached Rhazine and got her to stop moving, but had trouble opening the pack with one hand while it was on her back. "Could you help me?" he asked Saffron.

"I found something!" Phaerim shouted, his voice cracking with dryness.

Thaelios turned in his direction, but the lamp was now too feeble to show more than his outline. He could hear movement, though, the soft grate of sliding stone coming from the wall where he'd been standing.

Everyone hurried over, denying him the chance to retrieve Cauzel's book. Even Phaerim limped that way, the sounds of his struggle to move still clear in the blackness. Sure enough, a rectangle of even deeper darkness now interrupted the smooth surface of the wall.

"We still need more light," Thaelios reminded them.

"Right." Saffron handed him the nearly extinguished lamp and dug out the spellbook from Rhazine's pack. Swapping with Thaelios, she held the lamp closely overhead as he flipped through the pages to the desired heading.

Casting a spell required more than just the right words. He made room for Dyphina to slide in beside him so she could read, for she needed the full instructions in order to succeed. Physical ingredients, if there were any, the correct phrasing and emphasis of the triggering words, and directions for the sequencing and flow of the spell's energy all had to be absorbed. Beyond that, the practice of initiating the internal magical spark to begin harnessing the *sahd* was not easy to master, and nearly impossible without the innate talent to do so.

"Alright, I think I've got it," she said after reading over the page. "Can I have the dagger?"

Saffron slipped it from her belt and presented the hilt to her friend.

Dyphina touched the pommel and recited, *"Lucemi."* The expansion of white light, though not overly bright, was still shocking in comparison to what was left of the lamp.

"Congratulations," Be'naj said with sincerity.

Dyphina beamed. "I could have done it a long time ago if someone had been sharing." She gave a sideways glance at Thaelios, but had a playful twinkle in her eye.

"Let's get going," he said, cognizant of their diminishing window. The room was similarly shaped to the Summoning Chamber where the arch-devil was trapped, but the center of the floor was cut out to reveal stairs heading further down. Saffron went first as usual, and after what seemed like at least twice their previous depth of descent, the ground leveled.

They were no longer in an eladrin-made structure, however. The walls were hewn rock, rouch and uneven. The floor had collected a layer of sand, but was solid underneath. The tunnel was wide enough for two to walk abreast, and after ten paces it curved around a full one-hundred eighty degrees, leading them back at least as far as they'd come.

It curved again, only half as much, but then abruptly ended in a wall of stone. An arm's length from the wall, however, on a knee-high block of stone, was another metal basin, similar to those they'd seen in the Hall of Doors.

"Do you think there's another hidden door?" Saffron asked, already reaching out her empty hand and moving it along the uneven rock surface.

The time had come for the full explanation of their predicament, but Thaelios was still having trouble thinking how to phrase the awful requirement. He cleared his throat. "I think it's another portal," he said, looking at the basin. "And, according to M'thenzor, passage requires a sacrifice."

"What sort of sacrifice?" Dyphina asked, her uneasiness clear by the way she drew out the words.

"Unless it's a trick," Thaelios replied, "and your guess there is as good as mine, the doorway to the Planar Key will only open if one of us willingly kills themselves." He trailed off toward the end, his final words barely more than a whisper.

Saffron had heard him plainly enough. "What?" She laughed the word uncomfortably, shaking her head. "That's ridiculous."

Thaelios shrugged. "I agree. But, it's what I was told. He professed to be unable to deceive me, but that could all have been some elaborate deception of its own."

"How do we decide?" Dyphina mumbled.

"No one is killing themselves!" Saffron wailed. "We've kept each other alive through too much to end things in such a way."

"That's not what I meant! How do we decide if the fiend was lying?" Dyphina clarified. "Thaelios was the only one who could understand it."

"True, but what do we do if we think he was trying to mislead us? We have no other way out." Phaerim's voice was still croaky, but calm.

"And probably not much longer before we can't use magic anymore." It hadn't escaped Thaelios's notice that the lamp had gone out. He took a closer look at Rhazine, who seemed dismayed at what probably sounded like arguing while continuing to stand silently to the side.

Saffron put her back to the tunnel wall and slid to the ground. "I know we can figure this out, we just have to stay calm and think."

An uneasy silence descended. Thaelios glanced from person to person – none of them appeared to be making progress toward an alternate solution. He imagined that, like him, they were probably struggling with the hope that someone else would volunteer to do the hardest thing, as horrible as the thought was.

Dyphina made eye contact with him, though the others had all been looking at the ground. He knew trickery was part of the very nature of fiends, though he felt like M'thenzor was being honest. His head went in circles, thinking that if Trigilas had bound the devil, there must have been conditions. And yet, perhaps all of that was just a ruse by the devil to trick a mortal into committing suicide. Wasn't that scenario just as demonstrative of a fiend's nature? How could Thaelios not second-guess any conclusion he reached?

"Anyone come up with something?" Phaerim finally asked. All their eyes moved to him, though no one said anything. "I didn't think so."

Saffron's tone was obstinate. "We can search every brick of this building for more secret doors. There could be one that leads out of the Hall of Doors altogether." She stood as if ready to begin searching.

"One that the Eladrin who built it didn't know about?" Thaelios pointed out. "If such an exit existed, don't you think those poor souls who were trapped here centuries ago would have used it?"

Saffron grumbled and stiffened her hands. "This can't be all we have!" she exclaimed, jostling the basin with her boot so it spun noisily on its pedestal.

No one reacted for a long moment, so Thaelios broke the silence. "Should we draw lots to be fair, then, or try and reason this out further?"

Saffron shot him a stare sharper than the dagger in her hand. "Reason it out? That would require this making any sense in the first place."

"Saffron, I would gladly give my life for you," Be'naj said, taking her hand. Then, she looked around the tunnel. "But I think Shecclad was speaking to me for a reason, and since that's why we are here in the first place, I think I need to go on in order to receive his guidance."

"Whoa," Phaerim took a turn. "Like you said, Be'naj – you're the reason why we're here. Maybe that makes it your responsibility to get us out, no?"

"She's the only one of her kind, Phaerim," Saffron said, squeezing Be'naj's hand. "There is no way I'm letting her kill herself. I would die twice before that happens."

"What about the new girl?" Thaelios thought it was worth mentioning. She was only there because she couldn't follow directions, and beyond the contents of her pack, he couldn't really see how she was useful to their quest. "You haven't even explained to her yet what's going on."

"I'll do it," Dyphina mumbled.

Thaelios was still waiting for Saffron to translate when the half-fey's words registered. "Wait, what? When did you learn Begnari?"

"I said I'll do *it*." Dyphina pointed her thumb toward the basin. "We're running out of time, and we're all dead if we don't open this gate, so I'll do it. Thaelios is better at magic anyway – you don't really need me. Give me the dagger, Saffron."

"No, Dyphina, that's not true." Saffron let go of Be'naj's hand and placed both of hers on Dyphina's shoulders. "We do need you." Their eyes locked and Dyphina's lips began trembling.

"Yeah, that's not going to happen," Phaerim said from where he'd slid to the floor. He held a small vial between his finger and thumb. "A little left-over from the Wolfspider's stores," he said, manipulating the vial with his fingers before pulling out the stopper. "I guess you'll all owe me one, then." He put the vessel to his lips and tipped it back.

"Phaerim, what are you doing?" Dyphina screamed through her first falling tear.

"Phaerim!" Saffron echoed. "We haven't decided … you can't just …"

"The poison's probably enough to stop my heart, but give it a moment to do the job." He hissed as if a delayed, bitter taste had just washed over his palate. "I was only going to slow you down, anyway."

Dyphina dropped to her knees and took Phaerim's hands in hers. "Why did you do this?" She started weeping in earnest and rested her forehead against his.

A lump rose in Thaelios's throat and his eyes prickled annoyingly.

"You're beautiful, Dyphina." Phaerim's voice was still calm. "I hope you remember me."

"Phaerim," Saffron repeated as she shook her head, her voice sad, her expression one of defeat.

He glanced up and smiled, and Thaelios could see wetness forming around his eyes. "Find your ways home." Phaerim closed his lids and breathed harshly through his nose three or four times, then became still.

Dyphina slid onto her backside and covered her face with her hands as sobs wracked her body.

Thaelios wasn't sure she'd be able to handle it when he told her they'd have to cut out Phaerim's heart …

Chapter 3

Return from Sepathia's Lair

Though they'd talked much of the way, Annoxoria wasn't sure Thuvian truly understood her better by the time they'd reached the edge of the swamp. She'd succeeded in acquiring one of his sister's scales, but at what cost? Her stomach had been pierced by Sepathia's stinger, her fingers were throbbing in pain from her climb up the Nightwing's lair, her lover had risked his life coming to save her, and she wasn't even sure the transformation was going to work. Izefet had clearly set her up.

At least his treachery was now in the open; however, it came with new worries. "We need to be prepared for anything when we reach the castle," she said. "Izefet and the Aasimar will have had free reign of the castle for days, and we've no idea how deeply they've infiltrated. We may have to retake it by force."

Thuvian growled. "I am not losing my hard-earned throne to some accursed outsiders."

Annoxoria nodded, glad to hear his resolve, but expecting nothing less. She concentrated on blocking out the pain enough to focus her magic and conjured a shadowy steed for them to ride.

"How does it fare over terrain?" Thuvian asked as he boosted Annoxoria onto its back. "With Sepathia on the hunt, we should avoid the road."

"Certainly," she replied, leaning to make room for Thuvian to mount. He knew the woods of Ifelian even better than she, and she was too weary to navigate in her compromised state. Her mind wandered to other matters as she grasped her lover's waist and closed her eyes. She had to believe the wards on her private rooms within the castle were still intact. If she ended up losing any of her research or enchanted collection to Izefet the Damned, the rampage to come was going to make the Xithany Cataclysm seem like a child's tantrum.

They rode west, into the rising sun, and the journey allowed Annoxoria plenty of time to seethe. Her embarrassment at being outmaneuvered mixed with anger at being betrayed and the disappointment of her dream remaining beyond reach. It was a potent combination that eventually hardened into resolve. She would make the Name of the Beast pay and use the Living Fire to become the graceful harbinger of death she knew she was meant to be.

As the last of the overnight frost melted from the ground, they crossed the Ifelian Corridor. Thuvian slowed their pace periodically to check for signs of Sepathia's minions following them, but so far, naught had been discovered. An added benefit of their spectral steed was that it left no tracks.

They pushed hard, but shortly after reaching the root of the mountains and turning south, they stopped to get some rest. Both needed sleep, but Thuvian insisted on keeping watch and took the first shift. He checked the dressing of Annoxoria's stomach wound, which was stained red at the source but no longer spreading, before allowing her to lay down. "We still need to properly clean it," he said, his countenance grim as usual. They would only get a couple hours of sleep each before moving on, and she was too tired to argue or pretend she was strong enough to ignore treatment.

Annoxoria felt better after resting, even though her body craved more. Some of her anger, at least, had slipped away. "Thank you for coming after me," she whispered to her lover as he slid into her still-warm bedroll.

"I will always come for you," he stated. While his tone was devoid of tenderness, she knew he felt it. "Wake me if there is need." A few moments later he was snoring, and she envied his ability to still his mind.

As Thuvian slept and what was left of the morning matured into afternoon, she worried more about coming reprisals. Surely Sepathia had returned to her lair by now and found Annoxoria missing. Would she guess that her half-brother had snuck in and stolen her prey? Could she smell the lingering traces of his presence? Would she pursue them immediately or wait for night to fall again? Mighty as Thuvian was, getting caught in the open by a Nightwing was a serious threat. Perhaps they should plan on how to face such an occurrence …

Annoxoria's brain didn't stop, cycling through dangerous thoughts until Thuvian awoke. "Do you think your sister is looking for us?" she asked as soon as he'd risen.

Thuvian yawned and stretched his muscular arms. "Undoubtedly, but that's why we're keeping under the trees." Unfortunately, besides the firs, many had lost the majority of their foliage.

The day never seemed to have warmed much as the sun remained shrouded by a persistent layer of clouds. As her Lord rolled up the bedding, Annoxoria rummaged through her pack for food. "What are we going to do if she finds us?"

Thuvian looked at her intently, first at her face then down to her stomach, but completely ignored her question. "I'm famished and tired of trail rations. There is a hunting post nearby, stocked with some cured meat. We should not suffer too much from a slight detour."

She nodded and pushed the plain fare back into her pack. She knew Thuvian well enough to realize he'd not given an answer because he saw no choice in it. He would die before allowing Sepathia to get the better of him.

Annoxoria summoned a new nether horse for them, and in little more than an hour, the pair entered a clearing with a crude, but stable, wooden shelter. Shelves within the refuge were stocked with knives and other tools for stripping and preparing carcasses, and jars of salt and herbs for curing.

Thuvian unblocked and lifted a heavy hatch in the floor, revealing an underground chamber used for storage. He retrieved dried meat and frost-packed leafy vegetables that had been picked in season from the wired-in garden behind the shelter, while Annoxoria scavenged the shelves for a pot and wooden spoon.

"There's a stream a hundred paces east if you'd like to get water while I start a fire," Thuvian suggested. "Don't wander any further."

In the castle, they had servants prepare their meals, but Annoxoria knew he enjoyed feeling self-sufficient when out in the wild. She did as asked, knowing he'd take care of the cooking once she returned. His apparent lack of concern about Sepathia put her more at ease, and she had to agree they'd be in more danger come sundown. Until then, she decided to try and relax.

She picked her way through the shallow banks of dead leaves until she came to a creek. The water was biting cold, but moving well. Squatting to dip her pot caused uncomfortable pressure on her abdomen, so she pressed her empty hand against the wound. Her vessel was halfway full when Annoxoria heard the snap of a branch. Looking up in alarm, she spotted a wild boar approaching from the far side of the stream to drink.

She kept still, assuming the creature had not yet noticed her. The boar rooted in the mud along the bank of the creek with its nose, and Annoxoria decided to risk standing since her legs were cramping.

The boar rose to attention at her movement, turning its head to get a better look. Annoxoria was certain the animal could cross the shallow water without trouble, large as it was. Would casting a spell scare it away or provoke an attack? While contemplating her next move, she heard the low *thwap* of a bowstring from behind.

An arrow struck the boar in its upper shoulder, triggering its flight response. It bolted east, away from the stream, and Annoxoria turned to see Thuvian jogging toward her, a longbow in his left hand. Switching back to the feral swine, she watched it head for a swath of undergrowth, then collapse onto its side.

"Better still," Thuvian said as he reached her. "We'll have fresh meat. Our luck must be changing."

He didn't seem at all concerned for her safety, and she wasn't sure how to take that. "Do we really need a whole boar for one meal?" she said, shifting the weight of the pot in her arms.

"Probably not," he replied, "but the forest provided, Nox." Thuvian propped his bow against the trunk of a nearby tree and leapt across the water. The black scales of his back shimmered in the forest-filtered sunlight, so shiny they looked wet, as he made his way to his kill.

Distracted by envy of the massive curved horns jutting from the side of his regally shaped skull, Annoxoria decided to leave it alone and head back to their campsite. Her lover's fire-making had been interrupted by the arrival of the boar, so she set the water near the already positioned logs and looked for a reasonable place to sit. Even if she'd wanted to get her hands dirty, the pain in her stomach was flaring and all she craved in the moment was getting off her feet.

Thankfully, Thuvian carved up the animal out of her view, and she'd apparently dozed off while leaning back against a large rock, because the hiss of water coming to a boil roused her. "How late is it?" she asked, the clearing noticeably darker than when she'd sat down.

"The bleeding started again," Thuvian answered, nodding toward her. "You need more rest."

Annoxoria glanced down at her bandages, which appeared sticky, but she couldn't tell the relative freshness of the blood. "What about your sister? Won't a fire give away our position if she's on the hunt?"

"We'll eat soon, then have to move, yes. But I want you still for as long as possible."

He was so hard to read, but sounded concerned. This both warmed and worried her. "That smells good," she finally said, desiring to change the subject. "How did you know about this place? And who else knows?"

"I've got a few shelters like this within a day or two of the Castle. My hunting partners or I visit every few weeks to check on supplies and keep it stocked. Makes sure we have something to eat, even if the trip's not successful." Thuvian stepped toward their modest fire and lifted the simmering kettle from the flame by the spit. "The change in diet was just a luxury. We really came here for the bow."

Annoxoria appreciated how Thuvian seemed to always think a step or two ahead. It reassured her, even though she knew a single bow would be of little use against a full grown Nightwing. She waited patiently as he poured his meaty broth into a wooden bowl and handed it to her. The warmth of the steaming bowl felt good in her hands while reminding her just how hungry she was.

She sipped at her meal, consisting of chopped green onions in addition to chunks of boiled boar flesh. Thuvian crudely fished bits of meat out of his broth with his scaled hands, oblivious to her judgement. Her back felt cold, propped against a rock, but she decided to finish her dinner before moving closer to the fire.

They ate in silence, save for Thuvian's slurping, and once he stood, Annoxoria slid toward the flames to soak up what warmth she could before they had to be on their way. She knew her lover had no trouble seeing, even in near-dark, and trusted he'd be able to navigate regardless of nightfall. What she hadn't counted on was the rumble of thunder coming from the north as she stretched her hands to the fire.

"Foul weather headed our way," Thuvian said as he positioned the longbow beside Viper's Kiss across his back. He dumped the pot of uneaten broth on the fire, then scattered the smoldering logs with his foot. "We should try to stay ahead of it. Are you feeling well enough to ride?"

She nodded – she wasn't going to be a burden. At least, not more of one than she could help. They climbed atop her summoned steed once more, and Thuvian had them traveling south again as the wind picked up.

The temperature fell fast, and the breeze that streaked across Annoxoria's face as they wove through the wild woods held a bite. Twilight arrived as the unseen sun dipped behind the Wyvernwatch Mountains, and she couldn't help looking to the sky to see if the shadow of death was hovering over them. With her face upturned, the first drops of cold rain landed upon her cheek. This is not the recipe for a pleasant night, she thought.

Thuvian kept his eyes ahead, watching for obstacles, checking landmarks, and steering their steed. He didn't flinch when a boom of nearby thunder shook the trees around them.

Rain descended harder, picking up until it drove down in sheets that oscillated with the wind.

Annoxoria's leather garments were quickly soaked, and she squinted to keep water from rolling off her forehead into her eyes. Maybe the rain would at least make it harder to spot them from above? That wouldn't make much difference if she ended up freezing to death before morning. She was already shivering, and it was only going to get colder.

She was having trouble keeping a tight grip around Thuvian's waist. His scales were slick, and her strength was failing. Annoxoria put one hand to her bandaged stomach and it came away stained red, though all traces of blood were quickly rinsed clean by the rain. Perhaps she needed a surgeon worse than she thought.

Her consciousness became fuzzy and Annoxoria drifted repeatedly to the verge of passing out. More than once, she caught herself slipping out of the saddle and had to clutch at her Lord to keep from falling. They rode well into the night, though she'd lost any certainty of time. The rain finally passed, and after what seemed like another hour, Thuvian brought their steed to a halt.

"We're drawing near the pass," he said, sliding down from the saddle in front of her, then catching her as she started to slip from the shadowy mount. "Nox, are you still with me?" he asked, a tinge of panic stressing his tone.

She was so cold, she wanted to stay curled up in his arms forever, the heat of his broad chest spreading into her skin. "Mmm," she responded, but her lids were closed and she was floating on the night wind as the squishing of Thuvian's soles into the muddy earth counted out his steps in a rhythmic lullaby.

Then the world moved around her again and Annoxoria's bottom pressed against the wet ground. Thuvian released her and she sank back against the rough trunk of a thick pine. This certainly wasn't the castle, so why were they stopping? Thuvian's clawed hands cupped her face and she forced her eyes open.

"We're almost home, my Lady, but I need to leave you here while I scout ahead. We're near the valley, which is exactly where I'd set an ambush if I was my sister. I need to make sure it's safe to proceed. Sepathia knows we have to cross this way to reach the castle."

Izefet knows it as well, Annoxoria thought. She nodded her understanding, though she was freezing and didn't want to be left alone. She closed her eyes again, savoring the warmth of her lover's hands upon her cheeks. An instant later they were gone.

Annoxoria shivered and looked down at her stomach. The front of her bandage was solid red, and she pressed her hands against the wound, hoping the pressure would help preserve whatever blood remained. While the rain had now passed ahead of them, the forest canopy was dripping with the remnants of the storm – the air still heavy and wet.

Thuvian had already disappeared into the maze of soggy pines, and the last traces of ambient radiance were only enough for her to see outlines in the dark beyond a few feet. Annoxoria closed her lids and worked on steadying her breath while she awaited her beloved's return – dying now on the forest floor was unacceptable.

Her forked tongue darted out to taste the air, something she avoided in Thuvian's presence. With night so near, however, it would be a comfort to at least get a glimpse of what her eyes couldn't see. If she could only catch Thuvian's lingering remnants, it might help her remain calm.

But she tasted something different. Something unclean. Her eyes shot open and she strained to spot whatever matched up with her new sensory input. She used her tongue again, penetrating the wet air repeatedly as panic rose within. A fog was rising, she could barely see, and every quickened beat of her heart sent blood pulsing into the wound she continued clutching.

A scratching noise, like claws stripping pine bark, drew her attention ahead and to her left. She faced the source, only to have it answered by a hissing laugh from somewhere behind her. She swiveled again, but footsteps sliding against wet needles called her back to the front.

"Thuvian?" she whispered harshly, nearly certain it wasn't him. A dark, human shape, tall but smaller-framed than her Lord, stepped into view from behind the trees, the contrast of the fog against its skin her only aid against the falling blackness. It approached slowly, assuredly, and Annoxoria heard the sound of steel being drawn.

She drew up her knees and pushed her free hand against the damp pine straw beneath her, attempting to rise. As she did, the hissing from behind returned, only this time mere steps away. Annoxoria's back slipped against the trunk as she flinched, dooming her to the ground.

This second creature loomed over her, and even in the dark she spotted filed teeth as it pulled back its lips. It was a Thrall of the Nightwing, grey and scaled, leering at her with a downturned dagger in its hand.

Annoxoria knew she was finished. She didn't possess the concentration necessary to call upon her magic, nor the strength to physically resist. She shook her face reflexively after a large drop of water struck her forehead. Her movement coincided with a series of rapid, rhythmic thuds, like the hooves of a charging stallion.

The glowing blade of Viper's Kiss sliced straight through the midsection of the more distant Thrall, just beneath its ribcage. It spiraled to the ground, and the one standing above her snapped its neck to assess the oncoming threat.

Perhaps calculating his own physical inferiority, the Thrall hissed and flung his dagger at Thuvian. The Lord of Nightwing Castle ducked and brought up one end of his double-bladed weapon just in time to redirect the hurled projectile into the pines.

The Thrall turned and bolted back into the darkness from whence it came. Thuvian snarled and gave chase, sparing a glance at Annoxoria as he passed. Her predicament must have changed his mind, for shortly after disappearing beyond the nearest trees he abandoned pursuit, circling back to her side.

The wounded Thrall was regaining his feet, somehow still alive. Annoxoria could make out his silhouette, holding his injured abdomen with one hand while brandishing a curved sword in the other. Thuvian stiffened his posture above her, his menacing shape outlined in the icy glow of his enchanted blades as he advanced on the defiant enemy.

A whirl of light and the clang of steel against steel hinted at the action she could barely see. They parried several of one another's blows until Thuvian, the quicker and stronger, delivered an arcing swing the Thrall couldn't account for. He toppled to his knees, defeated, and Thuvian ended it with a definitive thrust to the grounded Thrall's chest.

He turned back to Annoxoria, who had barely moved since Thuvian arrived, and scanned the forest with his draconic sight. Satisfied, he replaced his weapon in its harness and dropped to a knee to lift her. Returned to his arms, she welcomed his warmth again, only now aware of how frigid she'd become. She shivered as he carried her.

"Two more were overlooking the base of the pass," Thuvian stated, though her chattering teeth hadn't produced a question. "I dispatched them with arrows then returned as quickly as I could. You're safe now, Nox – I won't leave you again."

Annoxoria *felt* safe, at least from any outside threats, but she wasn't sure it mattered. She had no doubt her lover would carry her all the way back to the castle if he had to, she simply wasn't sure she'd still be with him. The cold and the pain were retreating to an absence of feeling, and she had the sensation that her spirit was retreating from her body as well. She could see herself hanging limply in Thuvian's arms, as if watching from above, and it was the strangest experience.

"Wake up," she ordered herself. "Open your eyes!" But her body didn't respond, and she was starting to float higher …

Retrieving the Key

Be'naj wasn't sure how to process what she just saw. She could read Saffron's quiet sorrow, but Dyphina seemed as if the loss might break her. The half-fey held Phaerim's limp body against her chest, which shook under an avalanche of sobs.

"Was there no other way?" Be'naj asked Saffron quietly, trying not to disturb Dyphina's grief. She glanced at Rhazine, who stood mutely, appearing more scared than anything.

Saffron raised her brows while shaking her head slightly. "Someone had to die to let us through the gate, but that's if you believe the fiend."

Was that devil from the summoning room behind this? Thaelios was the only one who could converse with him, and Be'naj wasn't sure how impressionable the eladrin Shaper was. Had he been able to discern between the truth and a convenient diabolical trick? "Thaelios," she called, continuing in their native tongue. "What exactly did the fiend tell you about opening this portal?"

Thaelios hesitated before answering her question, "M'thenzor said that, in order to open this portal and retrieve the key to the Gates in the Hall of Doors, someone would have to willingly surrender their life." He swallowed. "And then we'd have to place their heart into the basin."

Be'naj couldn't find her voice for a moment. "That's … barbaric," she finally sputtered.

"I agree, and I'm not sure it's wise to mention it aloud with Dyphina in her current state, but time is running out."

"So you believe everything the devil said?" Be'naj wanted to know if Thaelios was too concerned with pursuing knowledge to accurately appraise the costs.

Thaelios sighed. "Phaerim already took his life, and macabre as it may be, he won't miss his heart now."

"What about his *sahd*, Thaelios? You think Phaerim's spirit will achieve peace if we defile his body?" Be'naj felt her ire swell and took a deep breath, mindful that Thaelios was not one of the tormentors of her youth, though he seemed cold enough now to resemble them.

"What would you have us do, Be'naj?" Thaelios answered. "We, the living, are going to end up trapped in this tomb unless we make tough decisions. Should we squander Phaerim's sacrifice by not completing the ritual?"

"What are you two arguing about?" Saffron interjected.

Be'naj balled her hands into fists and set them against her hips, then rotated to face Saffron. She saw Thaelios's point, but didn't want to admit it so quickly. "Thaelios says there's more to be done," she said, switching to Illanese.

Saffron turned to the Eladrin. "More? What does that mean?"

The apprehension in her voice dealt Be'naj a tiny pang of guilt, but she figured the least Thaelios could do was deliver the news himself. His eyes darted her way first, his thin lips pressed hard against one another, before he answered.

"Obviously," Thaelios started, "Phaerim's death is a tragedy." He looked down at his companion's lifeless body to find Dyphina's tear-streaked face peering up at him. "But as you've no doubt noticed, no portal has opened merely because of his demise."

Seeing Thaelios squirm with everyone's attention upon him, Be'naj felt bad again. This wasn't his fault, after all. He just happened to be the only one who'd studied the Infernal speech. "We have to place Phaerim's heart in the basin," she cut in. "It's the only way to get us out of here."

Thaelios looked at her over his shoulder, but she was more concerned with Saffron's reaction. "Give me the dagger," Be'naj urged softly, holding out her hand. "You shouldn't have to be the one to do this."

Saffron stared at her without moving. "All right, everyone, back out of the tunnel," she finally said. "Time to get up, Dyphina." Saffron crouched and took hold of Dyphina's upper arm, helping her to her feet. She seemed hesitant to release Phaerim, but Saffron's grip was firm and she didn't resist.

Be'naj glanced at Thaelios, who merely shrugged before supporting Dyphina with his untethered hand. "I said I'd do it, Saffron."

Saffron ignored her. "Rhazine, ishuari fat-al." She cocked her head back toward the way they'd entered, and the girl eagerly joined Thaelios and Dyphina in their departure.

"You've got the only light, you know," Thaelios mentioned over his shoulder, though it didn't keep him from moving.

"Then you'll be standing in the dark. I'll make it quick," Saffron added before finally meeting Be'naj's gaze. "This is for me to do, Be'naj," she said, just above a whisper. "Please go with the others. The hourglass is emptying."

Be'naj wanted to protect Saffron from any pain, but realized the woman was stronger than anyone she'd ever known. Strong, like she aspired to be. Not wanting to demean that strength, she placed a hand on Saffron's shoulder and nodded.

Once they were far enough back in the tunnel that only the faintest glow of the dagger reached them from around a bend, Be'naj heard the sound of tearing cloth. She didn't want to hear what was next, so she decided to distract herself and the others with a question. "So if we do find the key to these portals, where do you think we should go? And how do we find our way home?"

"Those are both important questions," Thaelios answered, seeming eager for a distraction as well. "Do you have any insights from your trance-vision? Without further knowledge, I think it sensible to at least choose from the Upper Planes. What do you think, Dyphina?"

Thaelios still supported the woman with his arm around her back and a hand cupped to her ribcage, though her form sagged.

Even in the dark, Be'naj swore she could almost *feel* Dyphina's beauty, now that she took the time to notice. Her skin tingled, but unlike her itching response to the devil's presence, the fey-aura seemed to increase her sensitivity.

Dyphina sniffled but didn't provide an answer to Thaelios, so Be'naj filled the silence. "Shecclad's gift has not provided any guidance past this point, yet I pray further instruction will come. I would like to visit Mt. Celestia, which Saffron says is the home realm of my father. Until now, I never imagined I'd have a chance to. I am eager to meet the Sky Lord himself, though I know not where the gods reside."

"Hmm, both destinations would be immeasurably intriguing," Thaelios agreed. "Perhaps we should see what Saffron has to—"

"It's open!" Saffron yelled from the far end of the tunnel. "Come quick, everyone, the portal is open!"

"Let me take her," Be'naj offered as she claimed possession of the slumping Dyphina. "It's going to be all right, my lady. You will find grief can help sustain you." She let Thaelios and Rhazine clear the way before following at a slower pace. Dyphina's feet started cooperating after a few steps, allowing Be'naj to look up.

As they drew nearer the light, she saw that the flat rock face across from the basin was now reflective, it's surface rippling like a pond settling after a rainstorm. She caught a glimpse of red, streaked inside the metal bowl, then looked to Saffron's hands. They held irregular stains despite her attempts to wipe the blood clean. Searching the floor, Be'naj found Phaerim's body in the corner, legs and arms folded to conceal his wound.

"Do we just, step through?" Saffron asked.

"Perhaps we should join hands, in case it only works once." Thaelios reached out to Saffron, who looked at the blood on her hand before taking his. She, in turn, straightened three fingers of her right hand to Be'naj, keeping the lit dagger gripped by her thumb and forefinger.

Be'naj claimed it, then linked with Dyphina, who hesitantly joined with Rhazine. Thaelios stepped forward once their line was complete and passed through the shimmering rock as if it were a curtain of water. The rest followed.

On the other side, Be'naj emerged into a snow-covered forest glade. The shroud of night blanketed the sky, but white snow reflecting silver moonlight provided ample illumination. She looked up, noting that the black veil revealed no stars. She likewise felt no wind, and though the air held a slight chill, it was not enough to warrant the white dusting that had painted the trees and floor of the wood.

Everyone released hands and spread out to investigate. Whatever Be'naj had been expecting, this was not it. A calmness pervaded the area, but it also seemed less than real. It was as if this space wer some dream-like approximation of a memory whose details couldn't quite match the truth.

When she scooped up a handful of snow, it evaporated within ten heartbeats, not even leaving a pool of melt-moisture behind. After walking about twenty paces to her right, Be'naj bumped into an object she couldn't see. It looked as if the forest continued in front of her, but when she reached out, an invisible wall contained her – she'd reached the edge of wherever they were.

"Supplies!" Dyphina yelled out from a copse of trees beyond the far edge of the glade. "I found food." Those were the first words Be'naj had heard her utter since Phaerim took his life, and they were welcome.

Everyone rushed to see what Dyphina had found, even Rhazine. Stuffed between the thick trunks of a pair of snow-dusted oaks were two wooden chests, broad and already open. The powder formerly covering their lids lay in crumbly piles on the snow behind them.

One of the chests seemed stacked full of folded clothes, enough outfits to dress perhaps a dozen Eladrin. The other box was packed with foodstuffs: crackers and grains and leaf-wrapped filets of smoked fish, already neatly sliced, among others. No trace of rot or spoilage tainted the food, even though many of the items were perishable. Be'naj lifted a strip of game fowl to her noise and sniffed – it smelled fresh, as if prepared within the hour.

She was about to ask Thaelios if he thought the food had been protected by magic and was safe to eat, but Saffron and Dyphina were already chewing mouthfuls. She shrugged and followed suit, biting into the bird meat and savoring the taste of the first cooked meal she'd had in what seemed like a week.

Be'naj had just devoured her handful of cooked fowl when Saffron stepped close, drinking from a metal canister. When she'd finished her swig, she handed the container to Be'naj and wiped the moisture from her lips.

"It's pure water, cold as a mountain stream." Saffron smiled as Be'naj tipped the canister back to take a drink. The blood was gone from Saffron's hands.

"Where are we?" Be'naj asked after she'd quenched her thirst. "Don't get me wrong, I certainly prefer this to that crypt we were in, but everything about it is odd. It feels like we're in a place beyond the normal world."

"I believe we very much are," Thaelios interjected. He sifted through the collection of available clothes until finally lifting a sapphire tunic with silver filigree around the sleeves. "My guess is, this is an extra-dimensional space. A pocket dimension, existing outside of normal time and physical location. The magic required to Shape one is well beyond me, but I've read about them. Trigilas certainly would have been able to pull one off."

"So, the Shapers who lived here probably created this place to hide the key? Then why stock it with other supplies?" Be'naj asked.

Thaelios clawed his old shirt over his head and slipped on the fresh tunic. "Probably so it could be used as a sanctuary as well. Powerful magic often serves more than one purpose."

Saffron kneeled beside the chest and took over searching for a new outfit. "I'm glad they did, whatever the reason. This food is certainly a blessing … I should have Rhazine refill her pack before we leave." She conversed in Begnari with their adopted companion as she looked through the clothes.

The crunch of Dyphina's boots heralded her approach from behind, and Be'naj offered her the water canister. "I see you've found something new as well." The soiled grey tunic she'd been wearing had been replaced by an embroidered emerald top. Given the clothes were intended for the slighter-framed Eladrin, what was meant as a loose smock ended up hugging her frame, revealing her womanly shape. "How are you feeling?" Be'naj added, afraid her stare might be misinterpreted.

"I've been better," Dyphina admitted. "But I'm not going to let Phaerim's sacrifice go to waste. We need to see this through." She took a long drink of water, and Be'naj once again noticed the effect the half-fey's proximity had on her skin. How had she not noticed during their time in the desert? Always near Saffron, perhaps she'd never spent much time this close to Dyphina.

"Has anyone seen this key we're supposed to retrieve?" she asked after swallowing.

"Not yet," Saffron answered from her spot by the chest. She'd removed her slave tunic as well, exposing the bare skin of her back as she worked her arms through the long sleeves of a ruby-red shirt. "It doesn't appear to be here with the other supplies, but we should fan out and see if we can find it."

Be'naj found it impossible to turn away, and when Saffron turned to face her, she found the new clothing accentuated Saffron's curves as well. Suddenly, despite the ambient chill of the snow-crusted glade, Be'naj felt quite warm. "I'll go this way," she offered, using the excuse to spin around and hide her embarrassment. Only, the image of Saffron's body was still clear in her mind. What was worse, her memory called up a clear picture of Saffron naked, bathing in the starlit pools of Skywatch Haven.

Not now. She had to focus on something else. "Did the fiend mention what this key might look like, Thaelios?" What if it was buried in the snow? If that was the case, they might be looking forever.

"He did not," Thaelios responded, somewhere off to her right. "But it's likely magical and would only have to rest in the basin, so it need not look like the traditional key to a door."

"Of course!" Dyphina exclaimed. "It *would* be magical."

Be'naj kept her eyes on the ground in front of her, unsure why that fact seemed such a revelation to Dyphina, but then she heard her chanting in Eladrin, which was not her primary tongue. "What is she doing?" Be'naj asked Thaelios in their native speech.

He sighed. "Using her wits, along with one of the first cantrips Cauzel ever taught us."

"What's that?" Be'naj didn't like missing out on what appeared obvious to others.

"She's cast a spell so that she can spot any latent magical auras. Any object carrying an enchantment will bear a glow in her sight."

"Oh." Be'naj straightened and turned to watch Dyphina on the hunt. "That does seem helpful to our situation."

"Indeed."

The two of them remained still as Dyphina advanced through the snow, step by step, turning her head from shoulder to shoulder. "There it is!" she announced after a few moments, jogging directly for the twisted trunk of an elm.

Be'naj and the others followed, drawing near in time to see Dyphina extracting her hand from a hollow in the elm. In it was a steel-colored, metallic ball, nearly spherical, with a band of gold bisecting its surface. Four symmetrical grooves were carved equidistant to one another near its pole. Be'naj stared at the key, wondering if it should be responding to the half-fey's touch in some way instead of simply resting peacefully in her palm.

"You're sure that's it?" Saffron asked.

"What else could it be?" Dyphina responded. "I haven't seen anything else give off such an aura."

Thaelios cleared his throat. "Now that we've got the key, we ought to discuss our plan for when we leave this place. According to M'thenzor, we'll only have an hour to use the key before it returns here. Be'naj started the conversation earlier, and suggested we visit Mount Celestia."

Be'naj opened her mouth to defend her choice, but Thaelios kept talking.

"While I can see some of the merits of visiting such a realm: safety, her familial curiosity, and the possibility of finding useful allies in our quest, I also highly question whether that would be our final destination. If there is a plot against the Eladrin here on Elisahd, it hardly seems like the threat lies anywhere in the Upper Planes."

"All right, just slow down for a moment, Thaelios." Saffron raised her palms as if they could actually impede the momentum of his speech.

Be'naj was still having trouble looking at her friend without focusing on the beauty of her physical form. "The fact is," she started talking to keep her mind occupied, "the message I received from Shecclad during my trance has been suggestive of truths up until this point. But I have no idea where to look next for an answer." She made eye contact with both Dyphina and Saffron to drive the point. "Without further clues, we'd only be guessing at the source of the threat anyway, and I don't think any of us wants to end up ill-prepared on one of the nether planes."

Dyphina nodded. "That makes sense to me."

"Palomar and his Aasimar brethren were invaluable in the struggle against the King-priest of Chelpa. He perished, but we could certainly use friends of the same ilk." Saffron was addressing Thaelios, but stole a look at Be'naj and nodded faintly as well.

Thaelios stood with his hand upon his chin, appearing to mull over the information.

"Celestials may very well have knowledge we can use and possibly point us in the right direction," Saffron continued, stacking the measure in her favor.

The glassy look in Thaelios's eyes passed and he lifted his head to acknowledge Saffron. "Agreed. Mount Celestia it is."

"Excellent. That's acceptable to all?" Saffron received nods from Dyphina and Be'naj.

"What about Rhazine?" Be'naj asked, though she doubted the girl was in any position to weigh-in intelligently on such an outcome.

Saffron waved dismissively. "I'll tell her. We should fill her pack with rations before we leave, anyway. Are you sure you don't want a change of clothes, Be'naj?"

Be'naj's face flushed warm again. "I may take a spare tunic, but I've got to make some … adjustments before I could wear it."

Saffron's mouth dropped slightly at her oversight, and she struggled to recover. "Of course. Just … let me know if you need any help with the alterations."

"I will." Be'naj smiled and walked over to the clothing trunk while Rhazine and Saffron picked through the food supplies to select what was best to pack.

Selections completed, the five of them stood hand-in-hand opposite the shimmering portal. Thaelios cast a new light spell upon the dagger, both to renew its radiance and assure that the Dampening Stone wasn't functioning once again. It worked, so they appeared to still have time.

"I wish we'd brought Phaerim's body with us," Dyphina said. "This seems a better place to rest than that stone tunnel."

Be'naj squeezed her hand and they each stepped forward, returning to the carved passage beneath the Hall of Doors.

"We should not delay," Thaelios said. "There's no telling how much time we have. It can't be long."

Dyphina stared at Phaerim's still form, which had been tucked against the far rock wall. While everyone else broke, Be'naj clung to Dyphina's hand and silently wept with her. She felt a surge of kinship reflecting on the fact that, even with different ancestry, they shared the bond of coming from mixed heritages.

Saffron claimed the dagger and took the lead, pressing toward the stairs and the secret door that fed back into the Hall of Doors. "This way," she said as she hurried by the stone pillars. The light of Thaelios's spell briefly highlighted the gold cabinets before plunging them back into shadow.

They passed through the shattered portion of the marble wall, making their way across the dais that marked the stairs, and into the adjoining room. A great wheel hung upon the wall, names scrawled in Eladrin upon its divided surface. Thaelios approached it and turned the mechanism until the triangle hanging from top-center rested squarely in the section labeled, "Mount Celestia."

"All right, Dyphina, place the key in the basin on that pedestal," Thaelios instructed before joining the others in the center of the room.

When she set the sphere into the metal tray, the key's surface came to life with a bluish light, and the dark patch of wall opposite the wheel started to hum. Slowly, it changed from a void of fathomless blackness to something lighter. The radiance grew until it appeared to Be'naj like she was looking out of a window over a jade green valley, and into a beautiful, cloud-strafed sunrise.

"Is that where we're going?" Dyphina asked the room, though no one seemed to have the words to respond. The view was striking, and Be'naj felt a twinge in her heart as if a piece of it that had been absent her entire life had just been found.

Chapter 5

The Slopes of Mount Celestia

S tepping through the portal in the Hall of Doors felt different to Be'naj than entering the pocket dimension Phaerim had sacrificed himself to open. Whereas that resembled passing underneath a waterfall and simply emerging instantaneously on the other side, this was clearly a journey. Her body felt like it was made of rope and was being stretched and twisted. An elongated, half-minute of helplessness left her on her knees and gasping for air once her senses returned to normal.

Looking back, she could not see any sign of a Planar Gate, but her friends were around her, similarly spent, and that was a relief. Her recently returned breath was nearly taken again as she rose to absorb her new surroundings. She stood in the realm she'd viewed through the portal-window, though its reality exceeded her previous glimpse.

A sun rested a short jump above the horizon, and though its brightness seemed muted, the air was filled with a warm white light. She and her companions had been deposited on a wide path, paved with pale stones. A dart's throw to her left, the ground dropped away to a steep decline. In the valley that sprawled below, a mixture of green vegetation and shining lights that sparkled like jewels peeked out at her from between passing clusters of thin, wispy clouds.

Far off to the right, the mountainside rose. Its stones were green as if blanketed by a layer of soft moss. Be'naj followed the slope with her eyes but noticed that low-lying clouds obscured everything more than a hundred feet above. The current lateral position of the sun, however, prevented the clouds from obscuring its radiance.

"This is where you're from, Be'naj?" Dyphina asked. "It's amazing!"

Be'naj shook her head, but felt herself smiling. "I've never been here before." She unfurled her wings, whose feathers seemed somehow fuller. "Shall we see what lies up the path?" She led the way, noticing the gradual incline of the paved trail in the tendons of her ankles. Though it also descended behind them, going forward and up seemed right.

They'd only progressed a short way when Be'naj stopped in her tracks. A pair of male humanoids flew around the bend of the mountain toward them, their pearl-like skin even more luminescent than hers. Their wings were broad and mostly white, though the tips of their outer feathers were brightly colored, matching the creatures' hair: one brilliant gold, the other a royal purple.

"Hold where you are, travelers. What brings your kind to the slopes of Mount Celestia, and by what means have you journeyed here?"

The voice Be'naj heard was in her head! The lips of their welcomers had not moved, and the pair alighted a dozen paces ahead, their great wings folding behind their backs as they landed.

"Palomar, is that you?" Saffron cried from behind. Be'naj turned to see her rushing past, a look of sheer wonder on her face.

"Saffron min Furasi! Child of Fire, it is a gift to be reunited! Praise the wisdom of Hiruth Jeshu."

"May His light shine forever," the original voice followed.

Saffron and the gold-haired angel embraced, the taller creature's reach lifting Saffron to her tiptoes.

"That is quite the bruise on your arm," Palomar commented after they'd separated.

Saffron waved off his observation. "Come, you must meet my friends!" She grabbed his palm and dragged him toward Be'naj.

"You know these mortals, Palomar?"

"This one at least, Jubilex. We strove together against the King-priest of Chelpa during my time of banishment." Palomar allowed himself to be led within a few paces of Be'naj, where

Saffron released him. *"Wonders of the Mount, what do we have here?"*

Be'naj looked away, embarrassed by the sudden scrutiny.

"This, Palomar, is my friend Be'naj," Saffron answered. "We met in the forests of Ifelian, and I believe her father to be Aasimar."

Be'naj forced her eyes back to Palomar's so as not to appear rude. "Hello. Your wings are magnificent!" She knew she sounded stupid, but couldn't think of anything else to say.

"It is my great pleasure to meet you, Be'naj. I must admit, I find myself more surprised than you look."

"Can you *all* speak with your minds?" she asked.

Palomar nodded. *"All Aasimar can, yes. In fact, most natives of the Higher and Lower Planes share such an ability. It allows us to communicate with those from other realms."*

"I thought you were dead, Palomar," Saffron cut in, a tear streaking down her left cheek.

She was still smiling, though, so Be'naj tried to calm her quaking heart.

The golden-haired Aasimar placed a hand gently on Saffron's shoulder. *"I did die, Lady Saffron. On your world. And there, I cannot return for a hundred and one years. The Silver Chord of Immortals can only truly be severed on their home plane, however. If we perish elsewhere, our spirits simply return to our native realm."*

"Well," Saffron said, sniffing and wiping her cheek, "I'm glad to see you again. I didn't get to say 'goodbye,' and so much has happened since you left."

"So much, indeed. It looks as though your other friend is injured as well." Palomar nodded in Thaelios's direction. *"Why*

don't you finish introducing us and tell me more about why you're here, while I escort you to the Celestial Fountain?"

Saffron agreed and presented the rest of her companions. As they followed Palomar and Jubilex up the road, Saffron caught their hosts up on the circumstances that had brought them here.

Be'naj watched closely as Saffron and the Aasimar interacted, noting her obvious affection for the one named Palomar. Perhaps it would be helpful to learn more about their connection. Maybe she could seek his advice later on how to further develop her own relationship with Saffron. Be'naj was certain she wanted something beyond friendship, but didn't want to do anything that might push her away.

After listening to Saffron talk for a quarter of an hour as they walked, Be'naj noticed the scenery ahead had changed. Great stone buildings, polished white and enhanced with designs of precious metals, peppered the hillside. It became clearer as she gained perspective from the receding slope that an entire city was built into the face of the mountain. Its structures extended upward beyond the visual limitation of the clouds, with the road continuing higher in a series of switchbacks.

A waterfall poured out of the mountainside beneath a many-columned temple, or at least that's what Be'naj assumed such a magnificent structure must be: dedicated to the gods. A large pool collected the run-off at the base of the falls, and near its front, a series of artful fountains sprayed the clear water into smaller basins. She realized that she wasn't the only one staring in amazement, noting that Saffron had ceased her story-telling.

"Come, all who are thirsty, but especially Lady Saffron and Thaelios. You should drink from the fountain." Palomar extended an arm toward the pools, then headed over while the

others fell in behind. A stand with four metallic posts, each pointing in a different direction at various heights, held drinking horns, suspended by leather straps. Palomar chose one, dipped it in the water beneath the nearest fountain, and handed it to Saffron.

She accepted the horn with a look of uncertainty, but when Palomar nodded, she lifted it to her lips and drank. Be'naj watched with wonder as the bloom of yellow and purple on Saffron's exposed shield arm blended back to her normal, light brown pigmentation. Saffron exhaled after her drink as if she'd been holding her breath for a while. She smiled up at Palomar, then dipped the horn back into the water for more.

Saffron started to pass the vessel to Thaelios, but realized it would be easier for him to drink if she held it. "You have to taste this, Thaelios. The aching all over my body just vanished!"

Thaelios drank eagerly as she tipped the horn back, spilling some around the edges of his mouth. "Oh, sorry," Saffron apologized, leveling the horn.

Be'naj took a few steps closer as Thaelios wiped his lips with the back of his hand, curious to witness the extent of the fountain's healing ability. The Eladrin's injuries were well beyond Saffron's, after all. Before her eyes, even the melted skin outside the boundaries of his bandages regrew and smoothed itself. Thaelios, a look of astonishment on his face, used both hands to unwrap the linen from his arm and torso … it was as if the ghost's spell had never struck him!

"That's incredible!" Thaelios looked to Palomar, beaming. "Thank you, a thousand times thank you! I feel whole again." He turned to Be'naj next, still smiling, and tore the makeshift sling from his left arm before locking her in a sudden embrace.

She wasn't sure how to respond, but tentatively placed her arms around him just as he pulled away. "I suppose I shouldn't pass up a drink," she said, suddenly curious if it healed more than just physical wounds.

"Certainly, Be'naj." Saffron dipped the horn into the pool once more and carried it to her.

Be'naj accepted the horn and brought it to her lips, but a loud voice boomed in her head, startling her before she could swallow the first mouthful.

"Intruders are not permitted to drink from the Celestial Fountain!"

Be'naj reflexively closed her mouth, spilling some of the water across her chin. She lowered the horn and looked toward Palomar, though the voice was distinct from his and, given it was telepathic, could have come from anywhere.

Palomar turned to the open street ahead, and Be'naj followed his attention to an especially imposing Celestial. Standing more than twice her height, the figure wore shining silver armor and bore two separate pairs of long, narrow wings. He advanced on her with a menacing stride.

Rhazine, who'd remained silent and unobstrusive since their arrival, shrunk further behind Saffron for protection.

"Arinome," Palomar's calmer tone interjected as he raised a palm, halting the giant's approach. *"These are mortal guests, not intruders. Hiruth Jeshu himself, may His light shine forever, bade me greet them."*

"Why was I not informed of their arrival?" Arinome tilted his head downward, possibly to look Be'naj and her companions over, but his great, golden-plumed helm concealed his eyes. *"And this one... how can this be? She is half-Celestial. Who*

sired you, my lady? Do you owe your mortal blood to mother or father?"

"Be at ease, Arinome. Her father's identity is unknown to her, though I shall take them to Hiruth Jeshu, may His light shine forever, and He will know the truth." Palomar turned to Be'naj and spoke Illanese from his mouth, though the words in her head had been Eladrin. "I am sorry if you've been alarmed. Arinome takes the defense of Mount Celestia seriously, that is all. You are safe."

"Is he another kind of Aasimar?" Saffron asked. "He's huge!"

"I am a Seraph, mortal woman, and I can hear you speak. You are a human, are you not?"

Saffron straightened. "I am. We come from Elisahd, looking for assistance against agents of evil."

"And what do mortals know of true evil? Have you ever traveled to the depths of the Abyss, or struggled against the thousand fires of the Nine Hells?" Arinome gripped the pommel of the enormous sword sheathed at his hip.

Be'naj didn't like the idea of a supposed protector bullying Saffron. "Evil grows first in the heart, brave Seraph. It can live anywhere when people forget to embrace compassion."

"And all Celestials have taken oaths to combat evil, as I'm sure Arinome is aware," Palomar interjected. "Please, Lady Saffron, continue with your plea."

Saffron made eye contact with Be'naj and then cleared her throat. "Be'naj can explain our particular quest better, but the rest of us have all spent time as captives to the Dread Lich, Hadrian No More. He is a creature of Undeath, and anyone who deals in slavery qualifies as evil in my ledger."

"I agree with Saffron," Be'naj said. "There is evil we know, and I fear, even more that we have yet to uncover. I received a trance-vision from the Sky Lord, Shecclad. It warned that my people, specifically the ruler of my nation, were marked for death by 'The Name of the Beast' – some sort of diabolical cult, from what Cauzel deduced."

"He is—was, our mentor," Thaelios butted in, gesturing to himself and Dyphina.

"*I am sorry you were deprived of your freedom.*" Palomar spoke to all of them but was looking directly at Saffron. "*Were you successful in finding your sister?*"

Saffron nodded. "She is well… Be'naj saw her most recently. She is helping Baron Rogan search for his son."

"*These are not the concerns of Mount Celestia,*" Arinome's booming tenor filled Be'naj's head. "*Palomar, Jubilex, I leave the mortals under your care. Make sure they do not cause mischief.*" The great Seraph's wings began vibrating up and down, different in their movement than her own. He leapt upward with surprising grace, continuing higher until completely disappearing into the hanging mists.

"*I am sorry for that,*" Palomar apologized. "*What Arinome lacks in courtesy, I assure he more than makes up for in valor. I would gladly hear the rest of your tale, but to keep you from repeating it, perhaps we should go before Hiruth Jeshu and let Him hear?*"

"*May His light shine forever,*" Jubilex added.

"*He would have to give His blessing for us to intercede on your behalf, and His knowledge and wisdom far outstrip any counsel I could give.*"

Be'naj looked to Saffron and they both nodded, which was enough for Palomar to start leading them up the road. Be'naj stole a quick sip before replacing the drinking horn, and found that the water removed even small, physical aches that she'd not been aware of. Her heart, however, remained unsure of how to capture Saffron's.

Palomar's voice snapped her attention back from staring at Saffron's dark hair, wishing she could run her comb through it. *"Be'naj, you said you received your vision from the Sky Lord ... is that one of the Juda-cai?"*

Be'naj looked back to Saffron in confusion, hoping for help, but her friend was ahead of her and didn't notice. "I'm not sure what you mean. Shecclad is god of the Sky and Mastery. He relishes excellence in all endeavors."

"I see. My apologies, I momentarily forgot about the differing perspectives of our two worlds. What mortals on Elisahd often refer to as 'gods,' we know as the Juda-cai. They are beings who reside in a strange realm called Ishmere. I was just wondering if your vision was at all similar to Jaiden's connection with Criesha."

Saffron flinched at Palomar's final words, and she finally looked back at Be'naj as they walked. "Uh, Be'naj grew up with this gift, didn't you?" she said.

Be'naj nodded, wondering why her friend was suddenly acting strange. "I have received visions since I was young." A thought suddenly struck her as she recalled one of Palomar's earlier explanations. "Palomar, if my father was indeed an Aasimar, and he died on my world, would his spirit also return to Mount Celestia?"

Palomar paused at the turn in a switchback, allowing those in the rear of their procession to make up distance. Though Be'naj saw other Aasimar walking within the city and flitting from place to place on their angelic wings, her party had yet to cross any on the paved path. She wondered if they were being purposefully avoided.

"*I suppose he would,*" Palomar finally answered. "*Though I am honestly puzzled at your very existence, Be'naj. I have never known of a union between Aasimar and mortal, but Hiruth Jeshu surely would.*"

Be'naj expected to hear, "May His light shine forever," issue from the mind of their second Aasimar companion, but it didn't come. When she looked around, she noticed that Jubilex was no longer part of their caravan.

"May His light shine forever," Dyphina stated after a few breaths, apparently also missing the refrain.

"What would happen to Be'naj's spirit?" Thaelios asked. "Would it travel to Mount Celestia, since she's half Aasimar?"

"*I don't have the answer to that question, unfortunately. Though I wish her a long, joyful life with those who make her happy.*"

Be'naj looked to Saffron, who she found already staring at her, and felt her heart melt. They continued up the slope, reaching a thin blanket of clouds, which they passed through. The mist was palpable, but didn't leave her feeling damp. When they emerged above the foggy layer they were very near the huge temple, nestled into the mountain above the head of the waterfall.

A number of Aasimar stood in pairs or larger groups upon the temple's wide, white steps, and they turned in unison to consider the newcomers. Their hair and wingtips struck a palette of colors to shame a rainbow. Be'naj saw several of them nod, though none intruded with telepathy.

"Jubilex went ahead to announce our arrival, so we should be expected," Palomar said.

"I have one more question before we enter, Palomar." Saffron came to a stop at the base of the steps and appeared as if what she had to say wouldn't be easy for her. "You said that all Celestials took an oath to fight evil, yet obviously they don't all keep it. Illicurus comes to mind. I want Be'naj to have an honest understanding of her parentage. Given the splendor of your home," she opened her arms to the beauty around them, "it would be easy to come away with a singular view of Celestials as perfection incarnate. However, I believe an Aasimar may have aided our slavers in the Wyrmsmoke Mountains when we were trying to escape. Jaiden Luminere could never account for Illicurus or his band after the war with the King-priest. Have you received any tidings on the whereabouts or actions of your brethren on Elisahd?"

Palomar's face appeared strained, almost sad. *"My own past with Illicurus is complicated, for sure, and I think I understand what you're getting at."* He turned to face Be'naj. *"None of us are infallible, and you should always follow your own conscience, even if it dictates a different path than those around you. Such things aren't always easy, of course. But I do believe my kind – our kind – strive to do what is best for others as often as we can, even though the reasons behind our actions may remain invisible, or the actions themselves counter to what those we help would choose for themselves."*

He turned back to Saffron. "*I am sorry to hear that not all of my kin who were punished on your world have taken to heart the lessons we were sent to learn. I have been given no word on the actions of the Aasimar I left behind, though Hiruth Jeshu, may His light shine forever, is bound to have more knowledge of this than his humble servant. Our audience with Him will no doubt be illuminating for you in many regards.*"

Palomar tilted his head toward the great open doors at the height of the steps. "*If you are ready, we shall go seek your answers.*"

Be'naj reached out her hand, and without words, Saffron took it. Their hands clasped once again as they approached the threshold of yet another door to the unknown.

Chapter 6

May His Light
Shine Forever

Thaelios could hardly believe his luck. Only a couple of days earlier, he'd gotten to peruse the personal bookshelves of the greatest Shaper who ever lived, and now he was about to enter the seat of power of an Upper Plane. It was a lot to absorb.

He vowed to never again take his health for granted, too. With the pain of his debilitating injury washed away, he felt invigorated and ready to accomplish anything. He allowed his companions to walk ahead of him up the steps to the temple doors, using the moment to crystalize the image of his surroundings. The façade of the temple embedded in the cliff face was massive, a feat of engineering surely added by magic. He noted that the street they'd been walking continued past the temple steps, leading further up the mountainside, switching back a great distance above his head. What more was there to see?

The telepathic communication of these Celestials was a fascinating development. The Aasimar's thoughts must somehow translate into understandable language inside each of their minds. Rhazine must've felt especially glad to finally be included in at least one end of the conversation. It was her choice to show up and follow a group of strangers, though, so Thaelios didn't feel too badly.

Each Aasimar's colorful head contrasted the surrounding polished white stone and muted emerald hues of the receding mountainscape. He wondered, as he finished scaling the final step to the doorway, if there was any social meaning derived from the pigmentation.

The inside of the building was cavernous. Stairs led to wide landings, elevated above one another in a series of levels. Upon some, Thaelios could just make out what appeared to be shelves with cubbies holding scrolls of parchment. More Aasimar, as well as a couple of Seraphs, many of whom were reading from the scrolls, populated the temple floors.

Palomar led the way to an inner sanctum of sorts – a closed-off space, barred by golden doors. Jubilex waited by the entrance, and the two Aasimar seemed to hold a private conversation.

Finally, Palomar turned toward the mortals. "*Hiruth Jeshu, may His light shine forever, awaits you beyond these doors. I wanted to warn you to shield your eyes, for His brilliance can be blinding. You will not be able to look at Him directly, but it is not considered rude to turn away, so fear not for decorum.*

"He knows a great many things and holds a great deal of power, but that does not mean He wields or shares it indiscriminately. If you ask for something and He declines, please, do not press Him on it." Palomar took a moment to look at each of them. Thaelios nodded. *"Well, then,"* the Aasimar added, *"I hope you find much of what you're looking for."*

Palomar and Jubilex each grabbed a vertical handle of a door and pulled them open, the task appearing to require a good deal of effort. A flood of light poured out of the room, making it impossible to see what lay within. Shielding his eyes with his hand, Thaelios followed the others in.

Once the doors were shut, however, the bright light vanished. Palomar had come with them and was still squinting and turning his head away from the center of the room. Be'naj was likewise staring at the floor and using both hands to shield her eyes. Like himself, Saffron, Dyphina, and Rhazine had no such issues with the room's radiance, which Thaelios found comparable to a sunlit courtyard in spring.

"Welcome, mortal travelers." While clearly telepathic, this voice vibrated like a plucked harp string, speaking to Thaelios in every language he knew, simultaneously. The effect was a bit jarring, though remarkably didn't impede his understanding. *"I am Hiruth Jeshu, Lord of the Near Summit of Mount Celestia."*

The chamber they'd entered had a high, domed ceiling, plated with gold, but was not extensively wide. There were no windows, leaving Thaelios to deduce that the source of the ambient light was somewhere within the room. A massive Seraph stood beside a throne, its identity concealed by armor.

Seated in the gilded chair was a lithe humanoid, no larger than a tall Eladrin. The creature's skin was black as onyx and polished smooth. Its eyes were large and gold, with irises just like Thaelios's people. It wore a stylized golden tabard, marked with inky runes. Could this have been the being that just spoke?

Thaelios wasn't aware of how long the silence stretched until Saffron broke it. "Lord Jeshu," she bowed deeply from the waist, "Thank you for gifting us with your time. I am Saffron min Furasi of Begnasharan. My friends and companions, Ladies Be'naj and Dyphina, as well as Thaelios, hail from Ifelian. We are joined by Rhazine of Zeblon, a newcomer to our company."

"*You are all welcome,*" the vibrating voice responded. None of the Celestials seemed to be moving, leaving Thaelios uncertain of who the speaker truly was. He certainly couldn't account for any blinding light, though Be'naj still shielded her eyes.

"*I am not often surprised, but I admit your arrival here was not foreseen. The power to travel from one Plane to another is rare, especially among mortals. I suppose I put this all into motion by sending my own subjects to your world.*"

"I cannot speak to that, my Lord, but it was dire circumstances that led us here." Saffron glanced at Be'naj, seeming concerned that she could not look up at their host.

Thaelios took the opportunity to continue the narrative. "We were trapped in the buried city of Ancient Tarmuth, and Planar Gates were the only available means of escape."

"*Ah, I see Trigilas the Intrepid has a hand in this, even though his body has withered. He was one of your people, Thaelios, if I am not mistaken – the first resident of your world*" to ever set foot upon the Mountain. Centuries have passed since that day."

"Yes. The site was once Trigilas's magical laboratory, according to what I've read."

"*I am pleased you were able to find a way out of your predicament, but I sense that was not the only factor leading you to my realm.*" The onyx creature turned His eyes to gaze upon Be'naj, convincing Thaelios that he must be the speaker.

"You are correct, Lord Jeshu." Saffron resumed as the group's mouthpiece, having stepped closer to Be'naj. She lay her hand upon the half-Aasimar's shoulder. "I counted myself a friend of Palomar's while he visited Elisahd, and my interactions with the Aasimar led me to suspect that one of them may have fathered Be'naj, for she grew up without knowing one."

Hiruth Jeshu lowered His eyes. "*I have heard Palomar's accounts of his time upon your world. I was pleased to welcome him back into the fold following his return to the Mountain. He mentioned you specifically, Fire-Singer, and his stories bring you honor. I was saddened to learn that not all of the Lost have yet made amends, though I hope to be reunited with them someday.*

"*As for the young Be'naj, let me assure you of your place among the Celestials. You are welcome to remain for eternity, should you choose to stay.*" Hiruth Jeshu's gaze shifted ever so briefly to Saffron before returning to Be'naj. "*But I expect you won't. Most rightfully cherish what they know above uncertainties, even if those exceed in potential. You are indeed one of our children, Be'naj, regardless of half your blood being mortal.*

"While I have never sent a Celestial to Elisahd – for those who were punished had been stripped of their divinity – even mortals have access to magic that can summon citizens of the Outer Realms. Occasionally, one of my people is magically compelled to grant aid to a Summoner for a limited duration. One such occurrence must have resulted in an unsanctioned union, for your parentage is without question half-Aasimar. Rest assured, I will discover your progenitor in due time."

"That would be beyond my expectations, Lord Jeshu, but I thank you." Be'naj's voice was directed at the floor, and Thaelios couldn't stop wondering why their experiences were so different. It clearly had something to do with Celestial blood, given Palomar's similar state. Did that allow them to see a different spectrum of light than those with mortal blood?

"What hasn't been mentioned yet is that we're currently on a quest – one for which we are woefully short on information. Such knowledge would be an even greater boon, if you are able to help us." Be'naj finally shut her eyes so that she could lift her head.

Hiruth Jeshu stood from His golden chair and took a few steps closer, prompting the statue-like Seraph to come to life as well, uncrossing his thick arms and leaning slightly forward. It certainly looked like the Celestial Lord was not comprised of flesh, though He had familiar musculature. His skin, if that's what it was, seemed more similar to sanded wood, or perhaps polished stone, for its surface gleamed.

"Tell me about this quest, Be'naj."

Even with Be'naj's eyes closed, Hiruth Jeshu's proximity necessitated her raising a hand to cover them. "I received a riddle as part of a prophetic vision," she began, going on to recite the rhyme. "Most of the elements within have been revealed, though we've not yet traveled through three planar portals. It may be we have further to go, or perhaps we made an error coming here. Either way, we need to discover the nature or whereabouts of the Name of the Beast in order to confront them. And it sounds like we only have until the end of the season, for winter had started on Elisahd before we left."

"In this, I may be able to assist you. For uncounted ages, those who serve the Mountain have waged war against the hordes of the Abyss. Palomar, in fact, knows this well, for he has fought to protect the Ulimar near the Abyssal Rift on many occasions.

"The Name of the Beast sounds like something from the mind of an Abyssal, or at least someone aligned as such. Their nature is Chaos – they thrive on it, and often fittingly refer to it as the 'Beast.' The Name of the Beast therefore is Chaos, and this cult you mentioned may be doing everything it can to sow despair and confusion in your world. They likely worship some demonic force or even receive instruction from some denizen of the Abyss."

Thaelios felt his prior enthusiasm and sense of wonder drain from him. This did not sound like good news at all. He envisioned having to face dozens of those creatures that wounded Phaerim, in order to set things right.

"I think we have to go there – to the Abyss," Be'naj said, though Thaelios was deep enough in thought that he barely heard her.

"What are you, crazy?" Dyphina cried. "Why would we want to go there?"

Be'naj turned toward her. "I'm not saying we all must, but I think I do." She shook her head, slowly. "I believe we have to pass through other portals, and I think that's where we're going to discover who is behind the plot against the Eladrin. I just *feel* it. It's hard to explain."

Hiruth Jeshu's voice once again entered Thaelios's mind. *"I'm sorry to have to say it, but if there are demons directly involved, the danger is likely more widespread than just one culture. They likely won't stop until they've turned your Plane into a second Abyss, or something very close to it."*

"I will go with you," Saffron directed to Be'naj, "if that's what you choose."

Dyphina waved her arms across one another. "Hold for just one moment. We don't even know how to get home, let alone to the Abyss. Unless Lord Jeshu can send us?"

Thaelios joined his mortal companions in looking to the golden-eyed, onyx Celestial. Ultimately, this was the issue that mattered most to him – how were they going to return home, if Hiruth Jeshu could not facilitate the journey?

"I can send those in my presence to any of the Prime planes, though I do not do so lightly with my own people, given that I cannot bring them back. However, I would gladly send home those not of this world, if that is your wish."

Thaelios looked to his peers. "I have to say, that sounds pretty good to me."

Dyphina nodded.

"What about saving the Eladrin, Thaelios?" Saffron questioned. "Don't you want to discover the nature of the threat and possibly how to stop it?"

Palomar took a step closer from the door. *"For those who decide to journey to the Abyss, I will defend you – if my Lord allows it."*

Saffron placed her palms together and bowed in the Aasimar's direction. "Thank you, Palomar. Thaelios, Dyphina, I would feel better if we were not separated, but I understand there's danger ahead. Whatever you choose, I think Rhazine should remain here where it's safe, until we return."

"You have my consent to enter the Abyss, Palomar, in order to protect those of good intent. But do not let your zeal for redemption place you in unnecessary danger. You have already made your penance."

"What say you, Thaelios? Dyphina?" Saffron was not giving up easily. "Shall the apprentices of Cauzel Blackfeather honor his last endeavor?"

This last plea stung. Thaelios owed most of his magical knowledge to his dead mentor. Traveling the outer planes was an experience beyond what most Shapers could ever hope for, and if he could help save his own people from danger, he'd end up a hero ...

"You really have to do this, huh?" Dyphina asked, reaching to touch Be'naj's forearm.

She shrugged, but kept her eyes closed. "If not us, who? My god wants me to follow this path, and my intuition tells me the answers lie through more portals. Hiruth Jeshu seems to think the root of the cult lies within the chaos of the Abyss."

"May His light shine forever," Palomar added, still shielding his eyes.

"All right, then," Dyphina continued, turning to Saffron. "I'm not leaving you two."

Saffron smiled widely and lunged forward to catch Dyphina in an embrace. "Thank you," she whispered into her ear. "And what about you?" she asked Thaelios, arms still wrapped around the half-fey.

"I suppose the trip is worthwhile. Having an Aasimar escort *does* make me feel better about it."

"Thank you, Thaelios." This time, the gratitude came from Be'naj.

"Wonderful," Saffron said, finally releasing Dyphina and standing straight. "Palomar, we would like for our companion, Rhazine, to remain on Mount Celestia until we return for her. She is not prepared for such a voyage."

Dyphina laughed uncomfortably. "Are any of us?"

Saffron shot her a look. "Is that acceptable?"

Palomar tilted his head. *"We will find a place for her to reside, nearer to the base of the Mountain. We have to enter its roots to cross the Abyssal Rift, anyway."*

"When can we leave?" Be'naj asked, though Thaelios didn't understand her hurry. He wouldn't mind taking a few days to soak in more of the environment and hospitality. If their waters alone could heal, what other wonderful mysteries might await his discovery?

"If everyone now feels strong, we can leave forthwith. Just let me summon a few companions to quicken our way down the slopes."

After thanking Hiruth Jeshu again for His insights, they left the inner sanctum and waited outside on the steps of the temple while Palomar rounded up a few more Aasimar.

"Is everyone ready?" he asked, stepping behind Saffron and looping his arms under and around hers.

"Wait, are we flying?" Be'naj asked, a smile fighting its way to her lips.

"*It's faster than walking, and it's a long way down, my friend.*"

With that, each Aasimar took hold of a mortal and launched into the air, soaring toward the drop of the slope.

Chapter 7

The Abyssal Rift

Be'naj couldn't believe she was getting the chance to fly, even if it wasn't with her own wings. What followed was more like a controlled dive; wind pushed furiously past her face, whipping through her hair as she pierced a layer of thin clouds. Their vapor felt cool and damp, but whatever moisture her skin accumulated was whisked away by the wind.

Beneath her, the valley opened up and came into view. It appeared to be mostly primordial forest, a gloriously green textured carpet with spatterings of white and gold settlements. The slanted rays of the sun kept her skin warm despite the cool, rushing air.

On either side, Be'naj's friends fell in similar states of wonder, wrapped securely by their stoic Aasimar hosts. The trees drew persistently closer and she felt in her bones that it was time to level off, but the dive continued. Green filled her vision, and her heartbeat quickened as they hurtled toward the canopy. Be'naj instinctively raised her forearms to shield her face, not understanding why the Aasimar were willing to let them crash.

Just before striking the trees, however, the air around her burned with golden energy as if she were wrapped in an invisible bubble forcing itself against radiant resistance. A vague sense of passing through the trees flashed by in the span of an eye-blink as the air surrounding her was consumed by color.

Be'naj never felt a brush or scrape as they stabbed through the dense green of the living forest. They simply continued their descent as if it were all an illusion, once again falling through open sky, a new ground far below. She wished *she* were capable of telepathy to ask her carrier what was going on, as the raging wind made speech useless. She had to trust the Aasimar knew what they were doing.

Tucking her head, she saw the slope of a mountainside flying past. Had their descent somehow begun anew from near the peak? This time, as she fell further, the plane beneath distinguished itself as a great blue lake, shimmering in the light of a sun that retained its horizontal orientation.

They had been diving for some time, and tears streaked across her face, forced from her eyes but quickly drying along her tightened skin. As they neared the water, Be'naj found herself holding her breath, readying for the plunge, but once again they simply passed through as if nothing were real beyond the wind and their fall.

Three more times they were greeted by new terrain below, traversing the ground each instance like a fleet of ghosts, searching for a new haunt. Finally, when Be'naj was questioning whether they'd actually visited Limbo instead of Mount Celestia, doomed to fall for all eternity, the Aasimar spread their wings, jerking them upright.

Be'naj felt like her stomach repositioned into her throat, but relief washed over her when it appeared they were finally going to land. Her guide set her lightly on her feet, though her knees buckled at the reintroduction of her own weight. They'd ended up in a quaint village with ample gardens and doors painted in vibrant colors. The people had luminescent skin like the Aasimar, but no wings, and a few had gathered outside their homes during Be'naj and her friends' arrival.

"*Mortals?*" an unknown speaker entered her mind, "*on Mount Celestia. What does it mean?*"

"*Do not be concerned, my friend,*" Palomar responded as he landed. "*We are here under the authority of Lord Hiruth Jeshu, may His light shine forever, and won't tarry long.*"

"I was curious about those words, Palomar," Thaelios said, brushing his clothes with his hands as if he'd collected debris during their trip. "You and the other Celestials seemed to find Hiruth Jeshu's countenance almost blinding, but that was not my experience."

"*May His light shine forever,*" one of the other Aasimar added.

Palomar's lower lip protruded and he cocked his head sideways. "*What did you see, if I might ask?*"

"He looked, well, almost Eladrin, though his body was smooth and dark like polished obsidian."

"I saw a woman of astounding beauty, whose hair constantly changed as if to match the rapid passing of seasons," Dyphina cut in. "I thought you were all crazy, not referring to her as 'she.' What did you see, Saffron?"

"I, I saw a figure in metal armor, ornate and proud, though I suppose it could have been a man or a woman. It had wings like Palomar's, with a halo of fire circling its head. Was I the only one to see that?"

"*Astounding,*" said Palomar. *"And you were all able to look directly at Him?"*

"Not I," Be'naj offered. "He was surrounded by such a bright aura that I could only look long enough to see some movement from within."

"I noticed the two of you were having problems raising your eyes," Thaelios said, "and it struck me as interesting to not have the same experience."

"I have never known a mortal to stand in the presence of my Lord before. Perhaps He purposefully altered His appearance for your benefits. I trust that Hiruth Jeshu, may His light shine forever, has His reasons.

"From here we will travel on foot to the Rift, my friends. Before we do, we must visit the armory and make sure Rhazine is taken care of."

"I imagine she's frustrated, being surrounded by people she does not understand. But I cannot translate everything; it's exhausting" Saffron lamented.

"Fortunately enough, the Ulimar who live here also use telepathy, and all Celestials are able to interpret the speech of

others, if not verbally speak it. She will be able to converse at her leisure while we're away."

Palomar thanked and dismissed the other Aasimar, who took flight and headed up the Mountain. He led Be'naj and the others further into the village, knocking on the door of a modest abode, where they were greeted by an Ulimar named Grennald. The two held a private conversation, at the end of which Palomar bowed deeply and Grennald made room for them to enter his home.

"Welcome, friends of the Mountain," he projected at large. *"Palomar saved me from a demon invasion years ago, and I am in his debt. I would happily host whoever wishes to stay, until he returns to fetch you."*

Be'naj smiled and nodded, feeling awkward while Saffron and Rhazine held a spirited conversation in Begnari. She assumed Rhazine had been able to catch Palomar's half of previous conversations, but this was the first time the situation was being fully explained to her, and Rhazine seemed less than pleased.

Whether she'd seen things beyond even the imaginings of her peers, she was still a child. It would be unfair to put her in the kind of danger Be'naj assumed they may be seeking out, and in the end, Saffron scolded her into capitulation.

"Rhazine will be glad to help with chores, or whatever service you deem appropriate in exchange for your hospitality," Saffron announced while the sour-faced Begnari girl bit her lip and cast her eyes downward. That settled, Saffron kissed Rhazine's forehead and gave her a tender goodbye. Saffron took over her pack, and the others patted Rhazine's shoulder or clasped her wrist awkwardly, one-by-one, waving as they left her behind.

From there, Palomar led them down a narrow street away from the center of the village. Curious Celestials continued to stare and follow their progress, but all kept their distance, not wanting similar attention.

They headed toward the base of the Mountain, a large, open field with trampled grass stretching before them. A collection of low, rectangular buildings came into view as Be'naj drew nearer, and a mixture of Ulimar and Aasimar congregated around them.

"This almost looks like a military camp, Palomar," Saffron said, a note of concern tinting her voice.

"*Yes. When the hordes of Yugoloth and Tanar-ri spill forth from the Rift, this is where the fighting begins. Usually, we're able to contain them nearby, but sometimes there are too many and they infiltrate the nearby villages.*"

"You're saying that demons are able to penetrate Mount Celestia?" Be'naj asked.

Palomar's golden locks shook as he nodded, for he did not bother turning. "*Only this layer, if we do our duty. There is a Planar Rift within the roots of the Mountain that cannot be sealed, even by the Celestial Lords. While it doesn't lead directly to the Abyss, it joins a demi-plane adjacent to the Abyss, known as the 'Doomwait,' where demons can also gather. We have the distinct advantage when fighting on our own turf, but we'll never match the sheer numbers of the enemy.*"

"That sounds horrible," Dyphina said, and Be'naj had to agree.

"It is an unfortunate reality that the struggle against evil is never-ending. There ..." He pointed toward a nearby structure whose door was flanked by two armed Aasimar. *"We're almost to the armory."*

Though the same slanting sunlight shone everywhere else on Mount Celestia, a heavy shadow hung over the field, sown into the air by centuries of battles. The dimness, in turn, created a tension that something horrible or violent might erupt at any moment. Currently, only Celestials on watch occupied the field.

Palomar nodded to the Aasimar flanking the doors of the armory, and whether he communicated telepathically or not, they each pulled open a heavy panel at the group's approach. Inside was much brighter than where Be'naj stood, and entering the building showed her why. The armory was a wide, open hall filled with racks of armor and stands of weapons. The metal of the armor shone with a bright polish while the blades glowed with their own white light, pale but steady.

"This is amazing!" Be'naj said. Having trained with eladrin swords for much of her life, she had an appreciation for finely crafted weaponry. "What makes the blades glow like that?"

"Some of the more powerful denizens of the Abyss are resistant to mundane weaponry," Palomar explained. *"Celestial weapons are all crafted with the essence of this plane infused into them. The Celestial Light is greatly feared by demonkind."*

Be'naj stepped closer to an array of arming swords and reached out. "May I?' she asked, looking back at Palomar before touching one.

"Certainly. We are here to arm ourselves against the darkness. You may each take a weapon of your choosing. Unfortunately, I don't think any of the armor would fit."

Be'naj took hold of the hilt in front of her and lifted the sword from its rack. It felt lighter in her hands than the weapon she'd lost in the sandstorm, but perhaps only because she hadn't held such weight in days. The blade was unequivocally more beautiful. She walked a few paces deeper into the armory to give herself room, then swung the sword in various arcing sweeps. The Celestial steel left motes of white light in its wake as it sliced through the air, and Be'naj could scarcely believe she was receiving such a precious gift. "I will wield this in the cause of justice, I promise," she spoke aloud to no one in particular.

When she turned back to the group, the others had claimed weapons as well, even the slender Thaelios. He'd chosen a dagger; Dyphina, a curved blade nearly twice the length of her fellow apprentice's. Saffron executed jabs with a spear, a slightly oversized shield balancing her left arm, while Palomar fastened a breastplate of bright alloy around his chest.

Be'naj exhaled, feeling braver than she had in a while, ready to do battle with whatever awaited them in the Abyss. "We are going to succeed, I can feel it."

Saffron smiled, then straightened and placed the butt of her spear against the floor.

"*Are we ready, then?*" Palomar asked as he buckled the harness of a greatsword over his shoulder and between his wings.

"As ready as can be expected," Dyphina answered, her tone failing to mirror the confidence Be'naj felt.

"*Then we should head to the Abyssal Rift. Learning not to linger will serve us well once we've left the safety of the Mountain.*"

Be'naj and her troupe followed Palomar through the war camp, which ended close enough to the Mountain that its slopes swallowed her entire field of vision. A huge, roughly triangular cave opening gaped like a misshapen mouth in the rock. Palomar continued toward it.

"Is this the Rift?" Saffron asked within a few steps of where the shadow deepened into true darkness.

"No. This is merely the tunnel to it. You can use your weapons to see by." Palomar didn't seem to need his.

Saffron's spear tip was already naked, but Be'naj breathed easier when Dyphina unsheathed her sword to add its light. She looked up as they passed from open sky into a world of cavernous stone. She couldn't spot a ceiling, but the air underneath it felt dead. The unseen weight of the entire Mountain loomed above her – it created a sort of pressure, if only in her mind. She unfurled her wings for a moment, just to be sure she still had the room to do so.

Their path wasn't completely straight, but it was hard to tell direction, given she couldn't see any landmarks except the worn, rock floor beneath her. "How far does it go?" she finally said, her voice sounding small in the still, heavy air.

"We are not far," Palomar answered.

Sure enough, as soon as his thought was expressed, Be'naj heard a slight humming. She assumed it came from ahead, since she hadn't heard it prior, but it was impossible to be sure. A dim, blue glow came into view a spear's throw beyond Palomar, allowing her to make out the contour of a jagged stone wall rising from the floor. As she continued closer, a crackling joined the hum, and the light grew to outshine their weapons once they rounded the corner.

Before her, a scar of energy – indigo and black battling one another in a chaotic dance – marred the rock face behind it. Cracking and popping like a cauldron of captured lightning, the scar was more than three times Palomar's height and even wider across. Be'naj didn't have to ask: *this* was the Abyssal Rift. Just being within sight of it made the tiny hairs on her arms stand at attention.

"We're supposed to go *into* that?" asked Thaelios.

"*If you're still resolute on reaching the Abyss, then yes. It is a serious thing, I know, and you should have fair warning about what to expect – which is to say, anything.*" Palomar turned his winged back to the Rift, which silhouetted him in a wreath of dark energy. "*As Hiruth Jeshu said, may His light shine forever, the Abyss is strongly aligned with Chaos, but also Evil. Things won't necessarily make sense to the ordered mind. Don't waste time trying to figure out what appears incongruous.*"

"Is everyone there an enemy?" Be'naj asked, tightening her grip on her sword's hilt.

"*Potentially, but that doesn't mean you should attack indiscriminately. Not every creature is hostile by nature, even if they can't be trusted. We're not entering the Abyss directly, after all. The Rift will take us to a demi-plane where many beings from the Outer Planes travel, though often on their way to the Abyss. Do not place faith in anyone not with you now, no matter how beguiling an offer of friendship.*" Palomar placed his hands on his hips and spent a moment considering them.

"*Be'naj and I will stick out with our Celestial heritage. That will make us both targets and rightly feared. Your weapons will give you away, too, if their light is laid bare. Bluffing anyone with suggestions of alliance will be a difficult strategy to execute. Any questions before we enter?"*

Be'naj's head swam with them, but she knew most could only be adequately answered through first-hand experience. She placed her faith in Shecclad and her friends to help her manage whatever came next. *I have friends,* she realized, looking around their small group. That was certainly new, and something she wouldn't have dreamt of a season ago. "I'm ready," she said, since no one else seemed eager to speak.

"Then follow me into the Rift, and I'll see you in the Doomwait." Palomar made an "X" with his arms across his chest and stepped into the scar of energy, vanishing with a loud crackle.

"I don't know that I'm ready for this," Dyphina said as soon as the echo of the Aasimar's departure faded. "I want to help, but ..."

"We will be there with you," Saffron comforted. "You will be protected."

"Yes, Dyphina. And you don't want to pass up the chance to rub this adventure directly in Illiana's face when we get back to the Perch, do you?" Thaelios winked at her, drawing out a smile. As if to show there was nothing to worry about, he stepped into the Rift and disappeared.

Be'naj swallowed hard; Dyphina's hesitation had summoned up the severity of the moment, but Thaelios's unexpected courage solidified that she couldn't abandon course now. She stepped forward to fully commit, then realized the wisdom in making sure the other's doubts were conquered first. "Dyphina, are you ready?"

"I'm ... I'm not sure."

Be'naj was thinking of what she might say next, but Saffron beat her by shifting her spear to her shield hand, then grasping Dyphina's. "Come, we'll step through together," she said, looking straight into the half-fey's eyes. Dyphina was half-human, too, Be'naj reminded herself. That was a connection she and Saffron would never share. Be'naj bit her tongue, watching as the women's hands tightened around one another.

Saffron looked back at Be'naj and dipped her chin, causing a few strands of dark hair to fall over her eye. "I'll see you on the other side." Saffron smiled and then stepped forward, leading Dyphina into the Rift. They vanished in a pair of offset *pops* of entropic energy.

Be'naj was alone in the darkness, under the immeasurable weight of Mount Celestia. She hadn't bothered to unsheathe her weapon; the discordant Abyssal Rift was bright enough for her to still see the fingers at the end of her hand, though they looked like someone else's. The dark light turned her normally pale skin a hue of blue like the first hour of nightfall.

Memories of the severe loneliness she felt during her long exile washed over her. Muscles locked in place, preventing her from following Saffron into the Rift. Be'naj shut her eyes and clenched her hands into fists. "No, this is real," she announced to the darkness. "Saffron cares for me, and I won't leave her. I won't give up."

Opening her eyes, she waited for the tightness in her arms and legs to relent, subdued by her will. She exhaled deeply and put one foot in front of the other, entering the hungry portal …

This time, she felt like she was expanding from the inside out. Her body stretched and swelled, while the cacophony of crackling energy popped against her skin. Strobes of flashing darkness overwhelmed her senses. The passage was not instantaneous – a strange sort of momentum pushed her forward, though she had no landmarks to reference actual travel. She closed her eyes to reduce the onslaught of stimulation. The noise stopped suddenly, and Be'naj opened her lids to find her friends near her once more.

"That wasn't so bad, all told," Thaelios mused, patting himself down as if making sure he was still whole.

They were no longer underground, but it was still dark – not absolutely pitch as it had been in the tunnel beneath the Mountain, nor even as dim as a moonless night, but a uniform grey like when the sun is hidden by a solid blanket of rainclouds. Looking up, Be'naj could find neither atmosphere nor the heavens beyond. What passed for sky was simply a boundless expanse of depressing smog. The Abyssal Rift still hummed and crackled behind her, casting its bluish-black light.

"Ellingle once told me of a semi-cooperative sage that resides on this plane. He spends much of his time in a tavern, chronicling, and will sometimes assist travelers with information for like payment. I suggest we start there." Palomar spread his wings and leapt into the air, rising to hover a few body lengths above the ground as he scanned the horizon in every direction.

He pointed before descending, and while Be'naj followed the direction of his finger with her gaze, the pervasive haze prevented her from distinguishing anything more than the vague aura of distant lights.

"Sounds good enough for me," Saffron said. She held her spear in front of her like a lamp pole, though its light didn't extend far in the thick air. She walked side-by-side with

Palomar. Be'naj took up the rear, listening for signs of danger and regularly peeking over her shoulder. The ground was firm but unnaturally flat and didn't seem to consist of dirt or stone. No grass or plants grew, either; the terrain was simply grey and featureless.

"Ellingle said that a collection of dwellings had risen up not far from the Rift, and I'm fairly sure that's what lies ahead. The locals refer to it as Anarchiapolis, *but she thinks that's mostly in jest. It is not a true city. The tavern the sage typically haunts is there – a place called 'The Three Branches.' It shouldn't be far."*

Given the environment, it was difficult to track the passage of time, but in what seemed like less than an hour later, Be'naj heard sounds from ahead. The light had grown brighter, too. The noises were repetitive. Creepy grinding of metal, shuffling of leather, chopping of wood, but no voices. Were they nearing a village occupied by ghosts, where all the tools functioned without need for labor, and carts meandered through the streets without being pulled?

The lights turned out to be torches, and as they drew nearer, Be'naj could make out the flames of a few. Those further away remained orange halos blurred by the haze. The torches hung in sconces on the sides of buildings constructed from an indeterminate material. No obvious signs of timber or mortared stone revealed their nature, and while clearly solid, the shapes of walls and doors were irregular and haphazard.

"Remember, Be'naj: our wings will announce our heritage well before we ever engage in conversation." The reminder came unbidden, and she wondered if Palomar shared it only with her, for he gave no physical indication of attention.

As soon as they passed the first row of structures on the outskirts of Anarchiapolis, Be'naj's mind was bombarded by outside thoughts. A dozen conversations, all at once, danced in and out of her head like an impressionist changing voices every few words.

Be'naj clasped her face in both hands and saw that the others, save Palomar, were experiencing similar distress. Thaelios had covered his ears, and Dyphina shrugged and squirmed like a slug bathed in salt.

"How do we stop it?" Saffron asked Palomar. "Can we shut them out?"

Palomar looked at her calmly, then assessed the others. He opened his mouth and sang; the sound was instantly soothing, though different from Saffron's lulling tone. His voice was more like warm honey, dripping over Be'naj's mind, blocking the extraneous noise with its viscosity. "*There,*" he said when he was through. "*It's only temporary, but that should keep telepathic thoughts not directed at you from being heard. I'm used to such things.*"

"Thank you." Be'naj felt much more at ease and able to focus on deciphering the strange environment. Not far off, shapes moved in the alleyways between buildings, and Palomar headed toward the activity.

"*Keep your eyes open for 'The Three Branches' and possible danger as well,*" he said. Be'naj did her best to obey, though her eyes kept returning to Saffron. Palomar walked straight through a cross street, and his head swiveled left as he cleared the corner, drawn momentarily toward something he then chose to ignore. Dyphina winced and made a sound of disgust when she reached the same spot, then hurried forward closer to the Aasimar.

Curious, Be'naj turned left when she reached the intersection and stopped. A couple of hulking creatures stooped over a third who was strewn out on a flat-topped cart. The ones on their feet had short legs and one massive, ape-like arm paired with a second, shriveled appendage. They had monstrous faces, bat-like wings for ears, and short tails that looked like two clawed fingers, moving independently.

Disturbing as their appearance was, what they were doing shocked Be'naj more. The hands of their muscular arms sifted through the entrails of the creature on the cart like a bowl of warm noodles. It was also not human, Eladrin, or anything she was familiar with, and its head still rolled from side to side on an elongated neck.

The creatures turned to Be'naj, drawn by her stare, and her hand instinctively grasped the hilt of her sword. Before she drew, though, Saffron clasped her shoulders and pulled her away from the street. "Come, Palomar found it," she said, sustaining eye contact until Be'naj nodded.

Around the next corner stood a slanted, multi-story building. A pair of lit torches graced the two sides within view, illuminating what looked like the gnarled limbs of an old tree, springing from the outer walls. Dangling from chains that hung from these three branches were the severed heads of apparent humans – or something close. Their faces were grotesque in death, eyes and mouths wide as if the horror of their demise was purposefully captured and preserved.

A massive door, reinforced with iron bands, gaped open on the closest side. The sounds of a large gathering drifted out from it. An assortment of odd creatures milled about the exterior, many of whom took glances in their direction, taking particular notice of the Aasimar's arrival. Palomar gave no outward sign of concern, but projected behind him without turning, *"Come along and stay tight."*

Be'naj crowded forward with the others and they pushed into "The Three Branches," close on Palomar's heels. The interior bustled with activity. Tables had been placed inefficiently across the floor, forced to wind around haphazardly placed walls. The design of the structure, if there had indeed been any, was anything but orderly. The tables were nearly all occupied and patrons smashed together at the long, crooked bar that dominated the left side of the room.

What exactly the patrons were defied Be'naj's knowledge. Some looked similar to one another, but the assortment was still widely varied. Horns or barbed appendages appeared common enough, along with rough or scaled skin of red and brownish hues. They uttered crude-sounding phrases in languages that grated harshly on her ears. Her skin had started to itch, and Be'naj felt extremely uncomfortable.

The noise level dropped considerably once the denizens noticed their group. Many stopped to stare, granting a wide berth to Palomar as he cut through the standing crowd near the bar.

"Telepathy doesn't seem to work here – or they're all ignoring me," Palomar said in Illanese as he circled back to face the mortals. With his brilliant armor, white skin, and golden hair, he stood out like a lantern in a dark wood. His wings created a buffer around them as the natives backed away, seemingly unwilling to make physical contact. "I don't suppose any of you speak Abyssal?" he asked dismissively, scanning the room for someone who might be able to help.

"Actually," Thaelios spoke up, "I do know a little, though it's even worse than my Infernal."

"Seriously?" Dyphina asked, not sounding impressed.

"Thaelios, you are a marvel!" Saffron exclaimed.

He shrugged. "Studying useless languages got me through my seventies, what can I say?"

"That's wonderful," Palomar said. "Can you ask if someone can point us to Ivaldi? And it might help if Be'naj and I move on first so it doesn't look like you're asking on our behalf." He reached over and took Be'naj's hand, which soothed some of the itching. Palomar pulled her deeper into the bowels of the tavern, leaving the rest behind. She looked back at Saffron, concerned at their separation. "Do not fret, we won't go far," he said quietly, and she worried less when they stopped moving while still within view.

She watched Thaelios engage one of the less dangerous-looking fiends, who still looked the Eladrin up and down like he was a potential meal. The creature's gaze also caught the Celestial light of Saffron's spear, and he eventually responded, pointing over the heads of the crowd toward a far corner of the tavern. Thaelios thanked the creature and took Dyphina's arm, leading her toward the others as he whispered into her ear.

"The fiend says the sage has a regular table in a corner of the second floor. He didn't like that I was associating with Celestials, but I told him I'd just hired you as bodyguards." Thaelios looked over his shoulder as he talked, checking to make sure no one was eavesdropping.

"There are stairs over there," Saffron pointed out. What Be'naj had thought to be a slanted column supporting the ceiling turned out to include a set of steps, each a different length and height.

Thaelios led the way, and she wondered if his confidence was due to his ability to communicate with the locals. She hoped his tongue wouldn't get them into more trouble than was already likely. Be'naj climbed the stairs ahead of Palomar, who went last, keeping a buffer between them and the other patrons.

The second floor was narrower than the first, and by the time Be'naj had cleared the final step, Thaelios was approaching a fiend sitting alone in a booth near the corner. It nursed a frothy brew in a ceramic mug.

"Urzgwak thun coomtak Ivaldi?" Thaelios asked.

A ridge of triangular bones bisected the face of the creature, and its eyes, split by criss-crossing pupils, held a wildness Be'naj had never seen before. It opened a fanged mouth, cursing in Abyssal as it scurried to get out of its seat. Saffron reacted fastest, jumping in front of Thaelios to brandish her spear at the fiend. Catching sight of the Celestial light, it growled and hissed but resisted standing.

"I don't think he's the one you're looking for," a voice from two booths over said in Eladrin. It belonged to a humanoid in a green, wide-brimmed hat that obscured his face. He held a feathered quill in one hand and a ledger sat open on the table in front of him. Books and parchment were stacked and spread across the majority of the surface.

Saffron backed Thaelios away from the aggressive fiend, and the whole party shifted in the direction of the speaker. Be'naj stepped up to the edge of his table and placed her hands upon it.

She scanned the documents but couldn't read the writing, and the stranger's hat prevented her from establishing his identity.

"How is it you speak Eladrin in such a place as this?" she asked.

"I don't," he responded, setting his quill into an inkpot and leaning back. "Well, not exactly," he amended. "I'm subject to an enchantment that allows my speech to be interpreted by any who hear my voice, and allows me to understand any language in return. A necessity, when one deals in information." Finally, he raised his head to look at her. He seemed to be telling the truth, for he was certainly not one of her people.

A patch covered one eye, though the iris of the other was red. His nose was upturned like a hog's, with wide nostrils, and short tusks protruded from his lower lip. "I am Ivaldi, Sage of the Doomwait," he said. "Sorry to have not met your expectations, but I don't see the point in maintaining the mystery. My cause is enlightenment, after all."

"Oh, pleased to meet you, sir," she said, surprised at both his appearance and straightforwardness. "My name is Be'naj, and these are my friends."

"What are you saying, Be'naj?" Saffron asked.

She realized she'd been speaking in Eladrin and switched to Illanese, figuring it made no difference to the sage. "I'm sorry, I was just introducing myself."

"I haven't seen an Aasimar in 'The Three Branches' in a hundred tremor-cycles," Ivaldi said, glancing past her to Palomar. "You must really be in need."

Thaelios stepped closer, no doubt looking to put some distance between himself and the fiend two booths down. "You said that you were 'subject to an enchantment.' Does that mean you're a Shaper?"

The hog-nosed sage turned to Thaelios and gestured an invitation to the open bench across from him. "I know some magic, among other things," he said once the Eladrin had accepted the seat.

"So you have seen an Aasimar before?" Palomar asked. He looked over his shoulder at the fiend in the corner who was still cursing and muttering. When the creature spotted Palomar's eyes on him, he fell suddenly silent and returned his gaze to his mug.

"I have," Ivaldi answered. "A Plane-walker, named Ellingle. Courteous lass. Traded in some useful information. I assume that's why you're here, risking all this unwanted attention?"

"It is." Saffron nudged Dyphina into the booth, beside Thaelios, and slid in after her, handing off her spear to Be'naj. "We need some information about a cult, back on our world. They go by 'The Name of the Beast,' and we have reason to believe they may have ties to the Abyss. Have you ever heard of them?"

Be'naj was a little surprised Saffron opened up so readily about their mission, but realized she'd probably calculated that spending time in such a place was far more dangerous than mentioning a cult operating on Elisahd, which most of these creatures had probably never heard of.

"A direct one," Ivaldi answered. "Excellent. Dispensing with pleasantries will return me to my work faster. However, my friend, not even one as benevolent as I gives away his work for free …"

Dyphina scoffed. "You'd make us pay for information?" She looked sideways at Palomar. "Don't you think we have ways to get what we want out of you?"

"Dyphina!" Be'naj exclaimed. The half-fey shrugged.

Ivaldi cleared his throat. "Do not worry. What I ask in this case is something that means more to me than it will to you."

Saffron leaned forward, resting her forearms on the table. "And what might that be?"

"Three of your friend's golden feathers," he answered.

Saffron's head drew back as if she'd heard him wrong. Be'naj was confused as well – why would this stranger want Aasimar feathers?

Palomar stood straight, arms crossed over his chest. "How do we know your information is good?"

"Yes," Saffron added, "what assurance do we have that you're not just trying to swindle us?"

This time, the hog-nosed sage shrugged and tilted the green hat on his head. "You can afford it either way, I suspect. But I do have a reputation to uphold. Given that I trade in information, lying doesn't serve me well."

"Very well," Palomar agreed. "I will give you the feathers – after you've told us what you know." After a brief silence, he added, "I also don't lie."

Ivaldi snorted a laugh. "I suppose we're trusting one another, then. *That* may be a first for 'The Three Branches.' So be it." He set his hands on the table and interlaced his fingers. "As it happens, there was a Cambion – a half-fiend – in this very tavern, two tremor-cycles ago. She was recruiting Plane-walkers for a project she called 'The Name of the Beast.' Said she'd set up camp at the Tanar-ri assembly grounds for any berks interested in joining."

"Do you remember her name?" Be'naj asked.

"And how long is a tremor-cycle?" Dyphina added.

"She went by the moniker, 'Excaliana,' and tremor-cycles vary, but it was not so long ago. She's likely still there, unless she got exceptionally lucky in her recruitment." Ivaldi looked calm. He was either telling the truth or an adept liar.

"Can you direct us to the Tanar-ri assembly grounds? Are we likely to find Tanar-ri there?" asked Palomar.

Ivaldi shrugged. "I can tell you the way, sure. As to their current occupation – that depends, as always, on the current plans of the Lords of the Abyss."

The Aasimar seemed perturbed, reaching down and plucking three feathers from different places along the edge of his wings. Be'naj felt a pinch of vestigial pain, flashing back to her own assault during her adolescence.

"Here is your payment. I think we've taken enough of your time," Palomar said as he handed over the feathers.

Ivaldi took them and quickly tucked his prize into a pocket inside his robes. He started explaining the directions to where they could find Excaliana, but Be'naj wasn't paying attention. She felt ill and her itching had returned, and now her wings were experiencing a thousand tiny pricks, born from her memory. All she wanted was to get out of 'The Three Branches' as soon as possible.

"Are you all right, Be'naj?" Saffron asked as she scooted from the booth and reclaimed her spear.

"Oh, yes, I'm just sick of the crowd."

"I agree. The company leaves much to be desired, though even outdoors, this Plane is no prize. Still, you'll feel better once we're free of these strange folk." Saffron put on a smile, but Be'naj could not find the energy to mirror the gesture.

She led the way back downstairs, giving a slight push to a spiny fellow blocking her path at their base. She felt the crowd's eyes on her, and the itching only worsened. She found herself holding her breath and didn't release it until she'd squirmed past numerous fiends and escaped the cramped confines of the tavern. Be'naj bent over, hands on her knees, and exhaled deeply, not even sure whether her friends had kept up.

Chapter 8

The Recruitment

The gibbering, Abyssal voices in her head had returned, and Be'naj felt like she was going to vomit. Already bent at the waist, she wanted to curl up on the ground and enter a restful trance until everything else was pushed away.

"Come now, this is not the place to show weakness."

Be'naj heard Palomar's voice and felt hands around her midsection, guiding her up the alley, though she was not fully aware of her surroundings. There was walking and turning, and strange noises, and itching, and the world was spinning, though she knew somewhere in the back of her mind that this wasn't her world.

Whether mere moments or hours later, Be'naj wasn't sure, but eventually, relative calmness returned. She sat cross-legged on the unnaturally flat ground, yet to open her eyes. Soft, murmuring voices floated to her ears, and she worried that lifting her lids might somehow upset her solace. She stretched a hand to the ground, which was surprisingly cold, then felt a soft touch against the crown of her hair.

"Be'naj, are you feeling better?" It was Saffron's voice, and Be'naj smiled at the sound.

"My skin isn't itching anymore," she realized, supposing they must have gained some distance from the fiends.

"That's good," Saffron replied. "You had me worried."

Be'naj opened her eyes to look upon the dark-haired beauty. The bright red of her form-fitting eladrin tunic stood out against the uniform grey of the Doomwait, and Be'naj felt an overwhelming desire to hold her close, to feel Saffron's tanned skin against her own, to reassure herself that as long as this woman was around, Be'naj couldn't be anything but okay.

She settled instead for, "I am better, thank you."

"I'm glad," Saffron said, sitting cross-legged across from her. "We've been talking and think we've come up with a plan, but only if you're feeling up to it."

Be'naj looked past Saffron, whose spear lay across her lap, providing a halo of white light around them. The others were difficult to distinguish in the dim, hazy environment, but she saw shapes moving perhaps a dozen paces away. "Of course." She dared to reach out and take hold of Saffron's hand. "I want to put a stop to this cult."

Saffron intertwined their fingers and nodded. "I'd hoped you'd say that, because this next part is going to be up to you and me. We're going to try and trick Excaliana into giving us the information we're looking for … by posing as possible recruits to her cause."

Be'naj shook her head but didn't let go of Saffron's hand. "What about the others? Why just the two of us?"

"Palomar can't go," she replied. "He said if there are Tanar-ri nearby, they will spot his Celestial aura and attack without question. Likewise, if they *are* plotting to destroy the Eladrin, having one show up might raise suspicions, so Thaelios is out. I would do it by myself …" Saffron paused as she looked over her shoulder, "but the rest of them decided it was too dangerous for anyone to go alone."

Be'naj spread her wings. "Won't I have the same problem as Palomar?"

Saffron shook her head. "He said that, since you were born on Elisahd, they would only see you as mortal. Sure, your appearance may create questions, but we came up with an idea to handle that." She stood and, keeping hold of Be'naj's hand, helped her to her feet.

They rejoined the group. "Dyphina is good with enchantments, and she found one in Cauzel's spellbook to alter your features enough that you might pass. Isn't that right, Dyphina?" Saffron asked.

"I – I think it'll work. You'll certainly be in disguise."

"*Are you sure you're up for this, Be'naj?*" Palomar asked. "*They'll be using telepathy, so I won't be able to block that out for you again.*"

Be'naj flooded with worry, but wasn't about to let Saffron do this on her own. "I'll be fine," she said, trying to sound sure.

"Given we can't completely hide your wings, you're going to pose as one of the Fallen – a corrupted Celestial. Chances are, this 'Excaliana' has never seen one, so given that you don't have an aura, she just may buy it. Saffron and you will have to claim to be Plane-walkers, wanderers looking for work and not bound to the Outer Planes. Ivaldi said that's what she was after, so odds are, she needs someone who is free to travel back to Elisahd."

Saffron took over. "We'll go along with whatever she needs, but ask enough questions to learn what we can about The Name of the Beast." She handed her spear to Dyphina. "Trade with me for now? I need a sheathed weapon to hide the light." Dyphina unfastened the short, curved sword from her belt and passed it to Saffron.

"You know where we're going?" Be'naj asked Saffron.

She nodded. "I heard the directions the sage gave, so as long as he wasn't lying …"

Be'naj exhaled. "Then I guess Dyphina should cast her spell."

Everyone kept quiet as Dyphina flipped through Cauzel's tome, searching for the dog-eared page. Using the light of Saffron's spear, which she handed off to Thaelios, Dyphina began reciting the incantation.

Be'naj didn't feel anything extraordinary, but watched as the skin on her arms changed. The veins carrying her blood turned black and stood out against her pale flesh, which tinted grey as if turning to stone. She stretched her arms, then glanced over her shoulder at her wings. Their white feathers had turned coal, reminding her of Cauzel's raven familiar.

"Your hair is dark, too," Saffron commented, no doubt catching Be'naj's reaction as Dyphina finished her spell. "Darker than mine."

"Yes, that should do nicely," Thaelios said. "I mean, your skin looks really off-putting."

"Thanks?" Be'naj said. "How long will this last?" she asked Dyphina.

The half-fey shrugged. "Maybe an hour, our time. I have no idea how many tremor-cycles that comes to."

"Let's not waste any, then," Saffron said.

"Yes, you should get going. Good luck to you both. Take care of each other, and we'll be waiting for you back by the Rift."

Be'naj and Saffron exchanged quick hugs with the others, then Saffron led them into the dimness. The pale torches of Anarchiapolis could barely be seen in the distance to their left, imparting a minimal sense of orientation.

"We'll stay away from the locals for as long as possible," Saffron stated after they'd left their friends far back in the haze.

"Agreed." Be'naj knew she'd have to try and cope with the inevitable itchiness once they encountered more fiends. She was supposed to be a Fallen now, and didn't imagine they had any such reactions to incarnate evil. "I'm not used to lying, Saffron. I hope I don't ruin things."

"Don't think of it like that," Saffron said. "We're not really lying, we're just playing a part. We're actors. Have you ever seen a drama performed on stage? My father took me and my sister to watch a traveling troupe from Tarirtown, once. I liked the costumes, but I think the masks scared Dhania." Saffron let out a stilted laugh at the memory.

"No, I've never seen anything like that," Be'naj said, her concerns unalleviated.

"Don't worry. I have some experience with the cult and can do most of the talking, if you prefer."

"That may be for the best."

Saffron took an angle a little left of parallel to the settlement so they would eventually intersect. "If we're supposed to be Plane-walkers, we should probably not act too surprised by any strangeness we see. No doubt there will be plenty in a place like this."

As the lights grew closer, Be'naj's pulse quickened. *You're not you*, she told herself. *You're not really you.*

Just as the flames of the nearest torches became distinguishable, Saffron shared a few last words. "Remember not to unsheathe your sword unless absolutely necessary. Its light will give us away. If we get speparated, find your way back to the Rift. If you can't, head for the Three Branches so we can find you."

No sooner had Saffron finished her sentence than Abyssal speech entered Be'naj's head, *"We're going to gut those berks when we find them."* The words were startling in their suddenness, their tone suggesting the promise of violence was legitimate. Be'naj froze as a pair of shapes, squat but wide as bears, cut across their path close enough that she could see their outlines clearly through the haze.

Saffron took her hand and pulled her to the right at a jog, then forward again. Buildings came into view, and more voices started filling in the silence. Be'naj tried to block them out so she could think.

"We're looking for a huge set of steps leading downward," Saffron said aloud, answering Be'naj's unvoiced question. They slowed their pace, still pushing forward but keeping right when necessary to make their way around the crooked structures that sprung into view. A loud series of *pops* suddenly filled the air overhead, followed by cruel laughter in Be'naj's mind. She tilted her head upward to make sure nothing was falling, but couldn't see anything. The itching returned and she raked her nails across the foreign, grey skin of her arms. It offered no reprieve.

"Over there!" Saffron cried, pointing ahead before once again pulling Be'naj along with her.

A formidable, rectangular tower rose several stories into the air, though how far it continued was impossible to determine. To the right of its base, extending into the haze further than Be'naj could make out, were steps, each at least as wide as she was tall, cutting downward into the darkness.

Once they'd reached the top of the steps, she noticed that the haze did not descend with them, and she could see their terminus. Perhaps forty paces down, the steps ended in a vertical wall of dark fog. The veil was more substantial than the general haze of the Doomwait, appearing almost solid. She saw a disturbance in the wall, which became a large humanoid insect, twice her height, emerging from the fog. It carried a barbed spear and shield and started climbing the steps with long strides.

"Do we have to go down there?" Be'naj asked, panic draining all the moisture from her mouth. She couldn't believe what she'd gotten herself into. What she'd gotten Saffron into.

"No," Saffron answered. "The stairway leads to the Abyss itself. This is just our landmark. Come on." She took Be'naj's hand again, following the line of the top step across the width of the great stairway. A dozen paces later she released it so they could pick up speed, jogging to cut ahead of the creature ascending the steps.

Finally, a second tower came into view, marking the far side of the stairway. They leaned against its cold surface to catch their breath. "The assembly grounds are just beyond," Saffron said. "Are you ready?"

Be'naj nodded. For the moment, at least, her mind was devoid of fiendish voices. She stood straight, stretched her arms, and wriggled her fingers. Time to get into character.

Saffron scooped her long hair over her shoulders and exhaled, then proceeded with a rigid gait. A tall pavilion came into view, and to the left of it, a tiered depression in the ground, stretching beyond the edge of sight. Saffron led them under the pavilion, where rows of table-like protrusions rose from the otherwise featureless floor, and stopped. Several rows inward, at a protrusion marked by a stone-grey banner, a pair of strange creatures appeared to be absorbed in telepathic conversation.

The banner was emblazoned with the pattern of a black clawed hand, encircled by unfamiliar runes. One of the creatures standing beneath it had feminine, almost human features to go along with scaled, green skin, pointed ears, and two pairs of arms. Each set acted independently of one another: one hand pointed at the parchment rolled out between the creatures while another held the owner's chin. The second pair signaled impatience: one hand fidgeting with the belt around the creature's waist while the other tapped its fingers on the edge of the tabletop.

The creature she communicated with was similar in height, but with the traditional number of appendages. Its skin was black, armor-like. It leaned on a polearm, butted against the floor. Its head appeared hollow, with a flame inside that glowed red through its mouth and eye holes. Neither of them had looked up, so Saffron advanced with slow steps and Be'naj followed, staying within arm's reach.

Finally, the four-armed woman noticed them. "*And what do you berks want that's important enough to interrupt me?*" The fire-mouth seemed to give his attention as well, though it was difficult to tell.

"Are you Excaliana?" Saffron asked, her voice remarkably steady. "The one recruiting for a job?"

All four muscular arms undulated simultaneously, which Be'naj found eminently distracting. "*I am,*" she said. "*And where does such a mismatched pair of Plane-walkers come from, eh?*"

"Where we come from doesn't matter nearly as much as where we're going, does it?" Saffron replied. "I'm Tanaz. What kind of payment are we talking about?"

"*The payment will depend upon your degree of success ... but what about this one?*" Excaliana peered over Saffron's shoulder at Be'naj. "*Are you some sort of defective Erinyes? My skin's itching, but you don't look quite like any Celestial I've encountered. What's the story with those wings?*"

Panic flashed through Be'naj and she nearly turned to run. Why hadn't she considered the itching? She thought back to her brief encounter at the Circle of Twelve's mansion and the tiefling who'd casually mentioned it. It never sank in that it may work both ways. Saffron had turned to face her – they didn't know anything yet. All she had to do was stick with their story.

"I used to be a Celestial, but denounced my heritage." She made sure to speak in Illanese and not Eladrin. "Couldn't stand suffering all those rules."

Excaliana stared hard like she was deliberating. *"What's your name?"* she finally asked.

Saffron hadn't used her own so Be'naj didn't want to, either, but she hadn't invented one. All she could think of was how her wings reminded her of Cauzel's familiar … "Nokia," she said, hoping she hadn't taken too long to respond.

"So, Nokia and Tanaz, what sort of skills do you possess that might make you useful?"

"All sorts of things might be useful, depending on the circumstances," Saffron countered. "Why don't you tell us what the job is, and we can tell you how our talents would benefit your cause?"

Two of Excaliana's hands rubbed together while the other arms folded behind her. She glanced at the creature standing beside her, who remained silent as far as Be'naj could tell, though he could have been communicating with only his partner. *"Well, obviously, the reason I need Plane-walkers is because the job takes place on one of the Primes, and it's too complicated trying to send fiends back and forth. I will be joining my brother there shortly—"*

"Your brother?" Saffron interrupted.

"Yes, my twin," Excaliana continued, boring her unsettling golden eyes into Saffron. *"Izefet awaits my arrival at a place called Rinn-Rhulian, but some of his allies on the Prime have proven … unreliable. The job is to assist him in bringing those*

allies back into line, and if necessary, helping to eliminate anyone that may try to stop him from entering the site."

"And where will you be during this endeavor?" Saffron asked.

"*I must finish serving our matron here before I can travel to the Prime. Fear not – if you do well, you may get to see me again.*" Excaliana raised her upper lip in a broken smile.

Saffron shrugged. "That sounds like something we can handle. What awaits us at this 'Rinn-Rhulian?' I'd like to know what we might be up against before deciding to sign on."

"*It is where the Spawn of Raug are trapped, if you must know, but you would only be facing other mortals. Before I tell you what Plane the job is on, however, I'm going to need a demonstration of your competence,*" Excaliana exchanged a glance with flame-face, "*and a guarantee of your loyalty.*"

"I am a fire-singer," Saffron offered more quickly than Be'naj would've expected. "I can summon flame to ravage my enemies. And Nokia, here, is great at extracting information – enjoys finding just the right amount of pain to get what she wants without leaving them useless."

"*Hmm, is that so?*" Excaliana looked Be'naj up and down. "*Neither of those would go very far here, of course, but mortals seem to be susceptible to both. Very well,*" she looked back to Saffron, "*show me your fire.*"

Saffron exhaled, and Be'naj was just as relieved that the request for verification had fallen on her. Singing in Begnari, Saffron extended her arm and a small blossom of red-orange fire began growing in her palm. While all eyes were on the conjuration, a huge creature emerged from the assembly grounds at the edge of the pavilion.

Saffron was just about to release her fire bloom when the creature stepped forward and snapped one of the poles holding up whatever passed for canvas in the Doomwait. The monstrous figure was taller than the bottom lip of the covering and hadn't ducked far enough, catching the material on its swollen body and nearly causing it to collapse. All the humanoids underneath jumped back at the commotion, and Excaliana seethed at the intrusion.

"What in the name of the Lord of Lies are you doing, you, you ... Hezrou?" she screamed, drawing a black blade from its scabbard.

"There are mortal souls here to devour, and I claim them as a True Tanar-ri!" the giant replied. The terrifying creature was a dozen feet tall and nearly as wide. Though standing on two legs with massive arms that reached almost to the ground, it also carried a tortoise-like shell on its back, covered with knots and spines. Its face reminded Be'naj of a horny toad, but with rows of serrated teeth filling its wide mouth. A stench, reminiscent of the ghast she slayed in the desert, seethed almost palpably from its body.

Be'naj saw Saffron's hand go to the hilt of her blade and acted similarly, though they stopped short of drawing their weapons.

"You cannot claim them, I'm on official Abyssal business, and these are my new associates!"

"Stand aside, bastard-fiend," the Hezrou commanded in its deep voice, *"or your soul shall perish first!"*

Impressively, Excaliana did not budge. *"My Matron is the Marilith Yugrina, The Lady of Anguish, and if you don't return to the Great Stair this instant, you shall not know another moment in your immortal life unkissed by torment!*"

Be'naj flashed wide eyes at Saffron. Neither of these individuals seemed like ones to cross, and she scrambled to figure how she and Saffron could extract themselves as quickly as possible without gaining the eternal enmity of either.

"Raaawrr," the gigantic Hezrou howled aloud in defiance, though it didn't advance. It flexed its tremendous arms in a show of strength, possibly deciding whether the significantly smaller fiend in front of it was bluffing. Excaliana unsheathed a second blade to bolster her threat.

"*Draw in defense of your new mistress,*" came a raspy voice that Be'naj could only assume belonged to the black-armored fiend. He was working around the table to their side, lowering his polearm to further discourage the Hezrou from violence. Instead, Be'naj took slow steps backward, hoping the fiends' attention would remain focused on their stand-off.

The fire-faced demon, however, took notice. "*Where are you going, coward?*" He turned, wheeling his weapon around to threaten Be'naj.

"*Whelp! You do not have the authority to command me. I am a True Tanar-ri!*" the Hezrou wailed.

"*As is my Matron!*" Excaliana countered, her back still to Be'naj.

"I thought it better not to get involved," Be'naj answered the fiend who accused her.

Saffron, however, gave her own answer. She grabbed the shaft of the fire-faced demon's weapon and yanked it down, creating leverage as she unsheathed her curved blade and sliced through the neck of the fiend in one movement. The Celestial weapon hummed with satisfaction at fulfilling its purpose, and its light flashed bright white as red flame spurted from the mouth-hole of the surprised demon.

"Run!" Saffron yelled and Be'naj turned quickly to flee, her thoughts prepared for the action. She looked over her shoulder briefly as she cut out from under the pavilion, making sure Saffron followed. She glimpsed the body of the black-armored fiend slumping to the ground and the expression of rage on Excaliana's face as she turned to witness the betrayal.

Be'naj wanted to give the Great Stair a wide berth, but wasn't sure whether cutting through Anarchiapolis would help them hide or only attract more attention. Not wanting to risk drawing more enemies, she opted toward the vast emptiness of the Doomwait, hoping they could outrun any pursuers to the Rift – assuming she could find it.

Once the lights of the settlement had faded and all was a dim grey, Be'naj made a quick right. She kept her wings tucked in but they slowed her as always, yet another reason she hated them. Her sharp breath and the pounding of her feet against the ground made it difficult to hear anything else. She didn't know whether they were even being pursued, but didn't dare stop running.

The brush of something against her wings startled her, but when she looked over her shoulder, it was only Saffron catching up. Be'naj wished she could use telepathy to ask Saffron if she was unhurt, for she couldn't spare the air to speak.

"*I will peel the skin from your delicious bones!*" came the Hezrou's voice in a perverse response to her desire. It was impossible to discern direction with her mind, and Be'naj worried they were going to be cut off. Still, she kept running straight because Saffron did.

"Just keep going – we should be able to see the Rift in a few moments." Saffron seemed in better shape, for Be'naj already had a stitch in her side and wasn't sure a few moments of running remained in her.

Inevitably, she started lagging, though she didn't want to. She was sweating profusely and her breath was ragged; she just wasn't able to keep the pace. Saffron drifted further ahead into the haze and Be'naj reached out, willing her friend to slow down, to not leave her behind. She didn't think she could manage to speak unless she stopped altogether – and imagined the giant, turtle-backed Tanar-ri only steps behind – so she kept running.

Be'naj thought she saw the Abyssal Rift in the distance – a spot of bluish color cutting through the foggy air – but couldn't go on without catching her breath. After a few more stumbling steps, she stopped and doubled over, resting her hands on her knees and gasping for air as the cramp pinched her side. Saffron had disappeared ahead of her, and Be'naj dared to peek over her shoulder while trying to normalize her breathing.

If she hadn't already been bent over, the huge talon swooping down from overhead would have snagged her. She caught the movement at the last second and dropped to the ground as the clawed fingers closed above her. Something akin to a giant vulture passed by and began climbing into the haze, its momentum carrying it past Be'naj.

"*You are mine, and there is no escape!*" came a new voice, higher-pitched than the Hezrou, but just as unpleasant.

Be'naj looked up, trying to trace the flight of the creature, but it had vanished into the smoggy sky. She forced herself to stand and draw her sword, its Celestial radiance a beacon she now felt forced to risk.

As she prepared to face another dive from above, the grey dimness was split by a streak of light and a clap of thunder. A pulsing sphere of white flashed in the sky, briefly illuminating Palomar, who'd struck a bird-like demon slightly larger than himself. The two adversaries hovered and circled in the air, vanishing and then reappearing with every blow of Palomar's sword, the majority of which were parried by the dark shaft of a jagged-tipped spear that seethed black energy.

Be'naj was mesmerized by the aerial battle and didn't notice Saffron's return until she'd looped an arm around hers. "Come, Be'naj, hurry!" Saffron yelled. Be'naj allowed herself to be pulled toward the Rift. Looking back, she saw the hulking shape of the Hezrou silhouetted in the haze, bounding toward her.

She forced herself to run, ignoring the protestations of her body as she headed for the dark-light of the Abyssal Rift. When she got close enough to see it clearly, she spied Thaelios and Dyphina, who stepped into the Rift as soon as they saw her. Saffron's arm had slipped forward until they were just holding hands, but she didn't let go, and Be'naj followed her into the crackling scar of energy.

The trip back to the Mountain was just as physically unpleasant, but it also came with a wave of relief. She was pulled forward by Thaelios and Dyphina as soon as she arrived on the other side, where they all waited for Palomar, hoping that the demons of the Doomwait decided not to cross as well.

Chapter 9

The Depths of Betrayal

Annoxoria's eyes snapped open and she sat up, narrowly escaping Sepathia's jaws as the Nightwing's sinuous neck lunged at her. She was in her bed, and the attack was only a nightmare – or was it? A sharp pain, originating in her stomach, spread through her as she sank back into her pillow.

She lifted the fur blanket that had fallen from her bare chest and carefully rolled it until her stomach lay exposed. Bandages of white linen encircled her abdomen, and memories of her quest for the Nightwing scale rushed back. She thought she had died in the forest on the slopes of the Wyrmsmoke Mountains, but here she was, alive in the bedroom she shared with Thuvian.

Daylight knifed through gaps in the curtains, and the polished ebony posts of her canopy bed glinted in its radiance. A cup of water rested on the nightstand, and she forced herself into a sitting position to reach it. She took a sip and glanced around the room, noticing not only that she was alone but that various features were out of place.

A number of decorative vases were missing, and a pictogram, drawn in some crimson pigment, defaced the smooth glass of the mirror her lover had gifted her. The wardrobe, standing against the wall beyond the foot of her bed, was chipped and scarred as if it'd fallen on its front face before being lifted upright.

The twin doors to the right of the wardrobe swung open and Thuvian burst through, dressed in a black tabard under his red cape, a sure sign he'd come from addressing royal business. "Ah, Nox, you're awake!" He crossed the floor in a few long strides to sit on the mattress beside her, then inspected the bandages across her midsection.

"I am," she said, taking one last sip of her water before replacing it on the stand. "What happened to our room? What happened in the valley?"

"I was afraid you'd left me," Thuvian said, his voice softer. He skimmed a clawed hand through her tight curls, and she leaned in to his touch. "And this," he drew back and gestured to the rest of the room, "is not nearly as bad as the rest of the castle."

"What do you mean? What is it?" Guilt seized upon her, for Annoxoria knew whatever she was about to hear was ultimately her fault.

"That fiend Izefet and his pet Aasimar betrayed us, as you suspected. They must have waited until I went after you, then set to ransacking the place. They paid no heed when the chamberlain forbade them from entering areas I'd restricted, then slayed the guards who were called to stop them."

Annoxoria heard the rising anger in Thuvian's voice, and one of his hands clenched a fistful of bedding. A lump grew in her throat, but she forced her question around it, "Did they take the Living Fire?"

He nodded, gravely. "They must not have wanted to risk facing me directly, for by accounts they didn't tarry long. But they stole all the Seeds of the Avatars we'd collected and did a good bit of damage in the process." Thuvian shoved his hands against the bed and stood, snarling to control his rage.

"All of my being screams to hunt them down and make them pay for this, but I can't abandon the castle until I learn what my sister is up to. It's been three days and I've had no word nor seen any signs. I know she can't abide your intrusion and subsequent escape. There will be a reprisal."

Annoxoria slowly shook her head, wishing to collapse inward until she ceased to exist. "I am sorry, my Lord. All of this is my doing. Let me help set it right."

"What you can do now is heal. I will need you in the weeks ahead, Nox, but not until you've mended." Thuvian peeked at her stomach again. "It looks like the healers got the bleeding stopped, at least, so you should recover. I'm amazed Sepathia's poison didn't finish you, but glad it didn't." He leaned over and kissed the top of her head.

Annoxoria could hardly stand him being so tender. It's not that she didn't enjoy his affection, but she knew it meant that he saw weakness – deemed her unfit to handle his usual rough edges.

"I've got to oversee the ballista preparations in case Sepathia attacks the castle directly. You should rest. I'll have the servants bring you food – you must be starving." Thuvian rose to leave, his deep red cape swirling in his wake. Annoxoria's mind cluttered with things to say, but she couldn't get any of them out before he closed the doors behind him.

Thuvian had mentioned that Izefet had taken the Living Fire, but she held onto hope that he hadn't found all of it. She whisked back the blankets and slowly rolled onto her side, being careful not to engage her core more than necessary. Annoxoria pushed her legs to the edge of the bed and then off, twisting until she stood.

The movement was painful, but not more than she could endure. No longer under the furs, her bare chest was cold. She hobbled to the stand where a black, silken robe hung. Slipping it on, she decided to look first for the satchel she'd taken on her journey, hoping it hadn't been lost in the fray with the Thralls.

She found it and her muddy clothes by the desk where she kept her make-up. Her heart in her throat, Annoxoria unclasped the satchel and searched through it, stopping when she came upon the rough, black scale of the Nightwing. She clasped it to her chest and exhaled. Though she still had no idea if the magic would actually work, at least her foray into the swamps hadn't been meaningless.

Her spirits higher, she dared to hope that the wards on her private chambers remained intact and were enough to thwart any members of the cult who had defaced her and Thuvian's shared quarters. She placed the scale on the desk and pressed her hands against furniture for support as she took short steps over to the hall.

Annoxoria felt like someone else had been here – had at least attempted to violate her personal laboratory and library. She exhaled sharply and prepared to walk without help; she'd run out of furniture to prop herself up with.

Using quick but abbreviated steps, she waddled down the short hallway to the door of her library. Stabs of pain marked her progress, but it didn't take long to reach the comforting wood, reinforced with bands of iron. She leaned against the door, then closed her eyes as she lowered a hand to the knob and turned – it was still locked.

Opening her eyes, Annoxoria took a moment to compose herself, then uttered the password and pushed the portal inward. Crossing the threshold, she executed a quick assessment of the room. Thankfully, nothing seemed disturbed. She limped to her desk, where some books were laid out, paying less attention to the discomfort of her stomach.

With effort, she sat in the comfortable chair and glanced over the books, still open to the sections she'd been reading before her journey. Annoxoria leaned down and opened a lower drawer on the right side of the desk. Another wave of relief washed over her. She withdrew the kraken sculpture Hadrian No More had crafted for her, still set with an inwardly lit jewel of Living Fire.

Its bright red glow leapt out to greet her, and a smile stretched her lips as she placed the statuette delicately on top of her desk. Sepathia may have poisoned her, and Izefet may have tricked her into cutting off a finger, but Annoxoria was going to have the last laugh. She was going to become what she was always meant to be, then she would destroy those who had wronged her.

She wanted to comb through her library and make sure she hadn't missed anything about transformation magic. Now that she had one of the Seeds of the Avatars specifically attuned to assist her, she had only to find the right spell to complete the job. If it didn't exist in her collection, she would have to find a library that would suit her needs. Perhaps she might even create an alliance with Cauzel Blackfeather – the notion made her laugh, which hurt her belly, so she pushed it aside.

It didn't matter. If she couldn't locate a spell to do what she wanted, she would simply have to experiment. She had plenty of slaves in the mines to work with. She would just have to be patient – not a particular strength of hers to be sure, but she could evolve. Whatever it took.

For now, Annoxoria was tired. Though she'd apparently slept for days, her body craved rest so it could heal. She wanted Thuvian to see her strong again, to touch her roughly, to desire her and take her the way she liked. She painstakingly rose from her comfortable chair and headed back to bed, making sure to seal the door on the way out.

"Annoxoria, are you awake?"

"Mmm," she responded, though her eyes remained closed and the soft touch of the pillow on her cheek defied separation.

"I've decided to send Pereen Guillory to Pasaxtree to gather information on what the Name of the Beast has been up to and see if we can get a sense of Izefet's whereabouts."

Thuvian's voice roused Annoxoria and she opened her eyes. It was night. The room was dark except for the three lit candles of a brass candelabra, clutched in Thuvian's left hand. "Have there been any developments?" she asked as she sat up. The ointment the apothecary had given her to smear over her wound was working better than she expected.

"None, and I tire of waiting," Thuvian said as he settled beside her. "I feel like prey: cowering in the Castle, waiting for my enemies to act. I need to hunt."

"I know he had to want all that Living Fire for something," Annoxoria offered, "and it certainly wasn't to help us."

Thuvian nodded. "I wanted to see if you had any information to pass along to the spymaster before he leaves. Anything that might be helpful for his investigation ..."

Annoxoria curled her feet back toward her bottom, bending her legs – a position that would have been impossible a couple days prior – and thought. Thuvian was far more familiar with Sepathia, and she'd leave it to him to figure his sister out. But what about Izefet: what did he truly want and where would that take him?

"The half-fiend belongs to this cult, if not leads it, but he's not local. He has connections in the east, and with the Dread Lich for that matter, so what was he doing here?" she asked herself aloud.

"He was after the Seeds," Thuvian said.

"That is true, but is that all? Yours could not be the only mine capable of harvesting them."

"But my mines are not yet well known. Perhaps he came here because he is trying to remain beyond suspicion from other forces? To influence matters without notice?"

"If that's all it is," Annoxoria reasoned, "then he might have other enemies. Perhaps Pereen should find out who they are? If we can bring some of Izefet's actions to light, we may find an ally against him that we hadn't considered."

"Yes," Thuvian nodded. "But what does he want? If his operations span Elisahd, might not his aspirations?"

"Master Guillory said he's been searching for Rinn-Rhulian," Annoxoria said, finally voicing what she hoped she wouldn't have to. It had been in the back of her mind since she learned of Izefet's betrayal, but she'd fought until now to keep it buried there.

"The eladrin ruins? Do you think he knows what's there?" Thuvian sounded worried, which made her even more uneasy.

"Do any of us, for certain?" She searched his eyes for absolution.

"Nox." He shook his head. "If the myths are true, mine would be the first kingdom to fall. We've spent too long building our future to lose everything because we lacked vigilance."

"Surely the Ellafous would warn us if the cult was lurking around," she reasoned.

"Would you wager on that?" he snapped, the shift in his demeanor unexpected. "They don't exactly relish the fact that we know how to gain entrance in the first place. I'm sure many of their order would prefer to remove us altogether."

Annoxoria reached out and touched her lover's chest to soothe him. "Which is exactly why I don't want you to go. There are too many who want us dead." She leaned back onto her pillow, searching the dark folds of the bed's canopy for solutions. "Let me gather my strength, my Lord, and I will go with you."

Thuvian opened his mouth and she placed a hand over it to silence his coming objection. "My magic will help us," she said firmly. *The gods know we may need it.*

Chapter 10

The Destination Rune

"Are you both all right?" Dyphina asked, gasping for breath from the trauma of traveling through the Rift.

Thaelios drew his Celestial dagger to add its light to the spear's. "Where's Palomar?" He felt that was the more pressing question, given the Aasimar had actually engaged in combat.

"I don't know!" Saffron cried. "Dyphina, the spear!" She snatched the weapon from the half-fey's grasp and leveled it toward the Rift while backing away. "Stay clear, all of you! We may have enemies pursuing."

Be'naj straightened and drew her sword. Thaelios's brain started cycling through the few spells he had memorized, but the crackling hum of the Abyssal Rift distracted him from finding anything useful.

"Hold a moment!" He shut his eyes and tried to block out the noice. "Palomar wouldn't let that creature through."

"What if he can't stop it?" Saffron argued. "Looked like he had his hands full."

Thaelios opened his eyes to stare at the scar of dark energy, waiting to see what emerged. He had no idea what kind of magic affected beings from the Lower Planes, and he settled on the *Mirrored Image* spell that had saved him in the Arena. His hand lowered to his ingredient pouch, ready to act if a threat came forth.

"Shouldn't we go for help?" Dyphina asked as the moments stretched on. "Back outside the Mountain?"

"Yes," Be'naj agreed. "We should fetch more Aasimar and see if they can assist Palomar."

"Palomar doesn't have that kind of time," Saffron argued. "You saw what was after us, Be'naj." She waited until the echo of her statement faded, then added, "I'm going back in after him." No sooner had she raised her spear than a shape materialized through the portal.

Thaelios had already murmured the first words to his incantation before he saw the white light of Palomar's weapon and realized it was the Aasimar. Saffron sprang forward and threw her arms around his neck, her feet lifting from the ground in the process. Thaelios released a sigh of relief.

"You made it!" Saffron exclaimed as she settled back on her feet.

"*Thanks to the Celestial armorers,*" he said, resting a hand on his breastplate. "*That Vrock would have impaled me had my protection failed. He withdrew once the Hezrou announced your escape, and I wanted to make sure they had no plans to follow before I crossed over.*"

"Do you mind if we fall back a little further to rest?" Be'naj asked. "The Rift makes me uneasy."

Saffron nodded.

"*Certainly*," Palomar agreed as they retraced their steps along the vast, empty tunnel. "*I am sorry you ended up in such danger, though the Lower Planes are fraught with it. Hopefully you were able to glean something useful from the ruse?*"

"I think so," Saffron replied. Once they had gotten far enough that the dark light and crackling of the Abyssal Rift were no longer detectable, they took seats in a wide circle off the main path. Saffron relayed as much of the interaction with Excaliana as she remembered, with Be'naj adding a few details.

"So this demonic family seems pretty deeply involved with the Name of the Beast, though we still don't know what they want," Saffron concluded.

"*It may be as simple as sowing strife on your world,*" Palomar mused ruefully. "*If this Marilith she referred to as the Lady of Anguish has half-human children, it could be that she was magically summoned to Elisahd sometime in the past. Many creatures harbor resentment at such intrusions, and she could hold a grudge because of it. Tanar-ri thrive on causing havoc and suffering and will always need targets for their incessant scheming.*"

"I found the mention of Rinn-Rhulian enlightening," Thaelios commented. "That's the name of an ancient eladrin citadel ransacked by humans during the Revenge of Arkmus. It's supposedly hidden on the slopes of the Wyrmsmoke Mountains just west of Ifelian. It shouldn't be too far from Pasaxtree, though I don't know why a fiend from another world would find it significant."

"I asked about that," Saffron answered, her voice achieving a higher pitch than usual. "Excaliana said it was … oh, something about the Spawn of Raug being trapped there."

"The Spawn of Raug?" Thaelios repeated.

Dyphina leaned closer to him. "Does that have significance to you?"

He shook his head. "Not personally. It doesn't sound Eladrin to me. I wonder how it fits with Rinn-Rhulian …"

"Are you jesting?" Dyphina laughed. She raised both hands in the air as if paying homage to a momentous occasion. "This is a glorious day in history! *I've* read about something the King of Books hasn't?" she said, placing a hand dramatically on her chest.

"Well, don't keep us in suspense!" Saffron prodded, unable to stifle a laugh of her own.

"Alright, alright." Dyphina calmed herself. "My father had this book of myths about the old gods he would sometimes read from at bedtime. My mother didn't really care for the stories, saying that the world was a better place for the gods' departure."

"Well, that's not a lie," Thaelios agreed under his breath, wondering if Dyphina actually had something helpful to contribute or if she was just taking the opportunity to capture an audience at his expense.

Dyphina glanced at him sideways but still had a smile on her lips as she continued. "Raug was one of the old gods – a terrible monster who burrowed into the deep places of the world, sowing destruction and bloodshed. He was fond of caves and causing terror, and the lore holds that he created numerous descendants that carried his foul nature. That's where the Rauglor, who whipped us in the mines, supposedly came from. And their smaller kin, the Rauggin."

"Ah, I was not familiar with these tales in Begnasharan," Saffron offered. "So why would Rauglor be trapped in an old eladrin city?"

"That's ridiculous," Thaelios interrupted, content that Dyphina's childhood stories were nothing more than speculative fancy. He might, however, benefit from a little more research on the banished Avatars once they returned to Ifelian. "Eladrin wouldn't abide such creatures nearby, and we don't keep captives. Furthermore, there is nothing about the aesthetic of eladrin society that Rauglor would find appealing."

"Would you just listen?" The smile had vanished from Dyphina's lips. "Rauglor and Rauggin are only the sapient descendants of Raug. There are many others, at least according to my father's book. The most terrible were simply referred to as the Spawn of Raug. These were huge, wild beasts that caused widespread destruction in the time of the Avatars. One story told how Eriane implored Raug to control his children, as they'd killed numerous mortals and smashed entire settlements in their wake."

"They sound awful," Be'naj said, barely loud enough for Thaelios to hear.

"They were," Dyphina agreed. "Raug simply laughed and refused to rein them in, so Eriane convinced Hurn the Hunter to intercede. Hurn's Avatar tracked them one-by-one, but they were too difficult to slay, so he drove them into a magical prison devised by Trigilas, the Father of Spells."

Thaelios thought it was an interesting tale, especially since they'd seen some of Trigilas's work firsthand, but he wasn't about to put full faith into eladrin history as told by an outsider. "And we're supposed to proceed on the merits of one of your bedtime stories?" he asked.

"I didn't say anything about what we should do next," Dyphina countered. "I'm all for finding a pleasant garden somewhere on Mount Celestia and lounging around for a few weeks of well-earned relaxation."

"I don't think it matters whether the story is completely true," said Be'naj, rising from her rocky bench. "Myths often contain a seed of history, and it's enough to at least make a connection in our case." She sheathed her arming sword, and the resulting shift in shadows combined with her blackened wings and hair to give her a sinister appearance. "We heard from Excaliana herself that the cult has plans for Rinn-Rhulian. It's clear to me just from what I saw in the Doomwait that we cannot sit idly while she enacts her plans. I just … don't know what we can do to stop her."

"*From Dyphina's story, it sounds like the Juda-cai – your old gods – at least knew what they were up against regarding the Spawn of Raug. Perhaps we should endeavor to seek their council? I know that Jaiden Luminere regularly communed with Criesha, and I served her cause while fighting beside him on Elisahd. She may be willing to hear our petition.*"

As preposterous as that sounded to Thaelios, Palomar looked eminently regal, standing in his brilliant armor with wide set feet. He had just held back a winged demon single-handedly and probably knew more about the workings of the cosmos than the rest of them combined. Perhaps it wasn't crazy to hear him out.

"But how would you go about asking her?" Saffron took the question from Thaelios's lips.

"Shecclad has spoken to me," Be'naj said. "I heard his voice in my trance-vision."

This time, Thaelios spoke up. "But have you ever directly asked him a question?"

Be'naj shrugged. "I offer prayers."

"The Doomwait has gateways to more than just the Abyss. The most prudent solution, though I'm hesitant to suggest it, may be to ask Ivaldi. He might know of a direct passage to Ishmere, the Plane of the Juda-cai."

Saffron visibly squirmed. "I don't like the thought of heading back there at all. What if Excaliana has set up an ambush?"

"I agree that it's too dangerous for the two of you to return," Palomar said, looking to Saffron and Be'naj. *"And I would likely draw the attention of any Tanar-ri, should they be waiting."*

That only left Thaelios and Dyphina, and he squirmed in his own skin at the premonition that he was about to be asked to foray into the Doomwait without any true protection. The question didn't come, and in the silence that followed, a small kernel of a voice, somewhere deep inside him, made him feel like a coward for not offering. He imagined Saffron would ultimately be willing to go, despite her recent experience. Was it his turn to step up, for Cauzel's legacy?

"I'll go back," Dyphina said meekly, breaking the silent staring contest. She shrugged and her voice grew surer, "I'll disguise myself, though it might help to have someone along who knew the native language …" She flashed her bright, moss-green eyes unabashedly at Thaelios.

"Well, you know me," he admitted, "any excuse to learn new things …" In reality, he was terrified, but everyone responded with enthusiasm and appreciation at his and Dyphina's decision, smiling and clapping them on the back. It was an unusual sensation – feeling needed. Thaelios found he quite liked it, and for the moment, some of his dread abated.

"It might be best to head back directly," Palomar mentioned. *"That way you can be out again before our enemies have time to formulate a plan, though that is not a specialty amongst Abyssal creatures."*

"Yes, I'm all for getting this over with," Dyphina agreed. They started back to the Rift, and Dyphina cast her alteration spell again, taking on the appearance of a sallow-skinned, sickly waif, almost mimicking a creature of undeath.

Before they stepped through the scar of humming energy, a thought occurred to Thaelios. "What do I do if Ivaldi wants more payment for his information? We have no Celestial feathers to bargain with," he said, gesturing to the decrepit Dyphina and himself.

Palomar shrugged. *"I doubt he will want more of the same."*

"You're a well-read sage yourself, Thaelios," Saffron encouraged. "Trade him information." She winked and Be'naj nodded, though he presently couldn't think of anything a creature like Ivaldi, living in the Doomwait, would find useful.

"Come on," Dyphina said, grabbing his hand, though he instinctively recoiled, due to her appearance. "If we don't just go, we'll no doubt find endless excuses not to leave."

Thaelios allowed himself to be pulled toward the Abyssal Rift, closing his eyes to ward against some of the disorientation as they stepped in. He only hoped he lived long enough to regret this decision.

As soon as he felt solid ground beneath his feet, he opened his eyes and became alert, looking and listening for signs of demonic presence. The background of the crackling Rift made the task difficult, but he was loath to move beyond reach of the portal. Everything looked uniformly dull as before.

"Are you all right?" Dyphina asked from beside him. Only then did he realize he was crouched and unmoving, his dagger clutched tightly in his hand.

Thaelios eased his posture and nodded, then without words – as both listened for trouble in the gloom – they started off in the direction they thought they remembered Palomar leading them before. The perpetual haze played havoc with his spatial orientation. No landmarks could be seen to reference – even up and down seemed to matter little, though he trusted his head remained above his feet.

What seemed like hours later, the ground asserted its claim to existence by shaking beneath their feet, accompanied by a low rumble seeming to come from deep below. Dyphina reached out and grabbed Thaelios's arm for balance, though his own knees were in danger of dropping him off his feet.

"What's going on?" she cried, panic clear in her voice.

Thaelios was sure the ground was about to crumble to pieces, when the shaking suddenly stopped, and he remembered what the sage had mentioned during their previous conversation. "That must be what Ivaldi referred to as a tremor-cycle," he laughed nervously. While he felt less apocalyptic than a moment before, his heartbeat was palpable in the tips of his fingers.

Dyphina released his arm and shivered. "I thought that was the end." She pressed her palms together, raised them to her lips, and exhaled. "Alright, at least we haven't been harassed by any locals. Do you think we're still going in the right direction? I don't see any lights, and it feels like we've walked for an eternity."

Thaelios frowned. "I was wondering the same thing. Is it possible we've not kept straight? I don't know how we can be sure …"

She sighed. "I suppose it doesn't help to guess – that's a quick way to get lost. I just hope we find something before something finds us."

They kept walking, and time stretched on silently until Thaelios could hardly stand it. "Perhaps talking will help, after all. At least it'll give our minds something else to do. For all we know, these demons can smell us from a mile away, anyway."

"I guess you're right," Dyphina answered. "What did you want to talk about?"

Thaelios's mind immediately went to losing Cauzel and how their lives would be different, even if they got back to Ifelian after all this. He wasn't sure how discussing that would make him feel, though, and shifted to a more recent loss that didn't sting so much. "That was too bad how Phaerim met his end. I wonder if he's got any family that Saffron could track down once this *quest* is over."

Dyphina's neck twisted quickly in his direction. Her mouth opened slightly and her brow furrowed as she stared at him, before looking away. "He's got two living parents and a younger sister in Pasaxtree, and I will tell them," she said.

The resoluteness in her voice surprised Thaelios. "Oh, I didn't ever hear him talk about his family. In fact, none of us talk very much about our families, do we? Do you think that's because thinking about such things would only make us miss them more?" He was the youngest of three, and had always craved the respect of his older siblings. It was the primary reason that he studied so hard and pursued Shaping in the first place. He was eager to show his sisters all he'd learned already. He watched Dyphina for her reaction, though given her current visage, his eyes practically begged him to look away.

She poked her tongue against the inside of her cheek before responding. "Saffron has a younger sister, Dhania, whom she helped rescue from the harem of a ruthless king. Phaerim takes – took – jobs as a merchant guard and always brings his sister, Jolea, a gift from whatever towns he visits. Be'naj is an only child who doesn't even know her own father, and I am the offspring of a kind Warden and a Wood Nymph, who fell in love despite their differences because they are wonderful beings with open hearts who taught me to be the same way." Dyphina had run out of breath, and when she choked on a sob, Thaelios noticed for the first time that she was crying.

"Has my question upset you?" he asked, confused at the outburst of emotion. Perhaps she was redirecting her fear of being nearly alone in the Doomwait – Thaelios certainly felt some of that as well.

Dyphina shook her head and wiped her eyes with the heel of her palm. "I just—" she sniffed loudly and didn't finish.

Uncomfortable at her sudden sadness, Thaelios looked straight ahead. "I ... How do you know so much about everyone?"

"I talk to them, Thaelios. While you're always reading, I talk to them, and we share our lives with each other. I could probably tell you a few things about Zygrim, too, if you wanted."

Thaelios's cheeks immediately grew warm. How much had the others seen? Did Dyphina overhear what Zygrim said to him on the day they left the Wolfspider's gladiator pens? "I, uh, don't really need to know anything else about Zygrim. He's in Zeblon – I don't know why I'd ever see him again."

Dyphina sniffed again, and he sensed her turning toward him. "Whatever you say."

He thought he heard a smile in her voice. Searching for a distraction, he stood in place and turned in a circle under the guise of gaining his bearings. To his surprise, almost directly behind where he thought they'd just come from, he saw a dim glow in the hazy distance. He sheathed his dagger to extinguish its light and create more contrast with their surroundings.

"Do you see that?" he asked as Dyphina swiveled to investigate what had drawn his attention.

She squinted, her half-human eyes not quite as sensitive to light as his. "Torches?" she asked.

"It's certainly something," he replied. "Should we head that way?" He turned back the way they'd been going and couldn't spot anything, not even a horizon.

Dyphina hesitated, still squinting. "Aaaahh, I suppose so. Even if it's not Anarchiapolis, maybe you can ask for directions."

Thaelios hoped it wouldn't come to that, now that he didn't have Palomar or Saffron around to back him up. He drew his dagger again, finding its white aura a comfort, and took longer strides than before toward the source of the light. With something to focus on, time didn't drag so much, and as they got closer, it seemed like they were approaching a settlement.

The shapes of the buildings were still irregular, and even if they were in Anarchiapolis, even in the right section, he wasn't sure how they were going to find their way around. He'd need to ask someone, but thought he'd wait until he found a creature unlikely to eat him. Thaelios kept his dagger out, weighing the deterrent of a Celestial weapon more important than the impression of neutrality. They still looked different from the fiendish population, either way.

Thaelios wandered the crooked alleys between buildings, waiting for wayward telepathic thoughts to alert him when they were nearer sentience. Dyphina kept close behind on his left side, one hand resting on the hilt of her undrawn weapon. They focused so much on looking for movement every time they turned a corner that Thaelios completely missed the leg strewn out before him until he tripped over it.

"Are you all right?" Dyphina asked, helping him to his feet. It was a small miracle he hadn't stabbed himself with his own weapon.

Looking back, he saw a man, almost human but something else, sitting with his back propped against a sloped structure. The nearest torch was a few body lengths away, and the buildings were angled such that the man was cast in shadow, until Thaelios's dagger illuminated him.

His eyes were only half-open, and he wasn't reacting to their presence in any way Thaelios could determine. He didn't seem dead, as his ruddy cheeks still held color and his head rolled slowly back and forth on his neck as if keeping its own record of time. Rows of small nodules lined the ridges of his face, but Thaelios wasn't sure if that was normal for his kind or a sign of sickness.

"Do you think we should leave him here?" Dyphina asked. "He doesn't seem like one of these fiends."

Thaelios waved his hand in front of the man's face, but got no response. When he snapped his fingers, however, the man's eyes opened wider and stared at him. "Do you need help standing up?" Thaelios asked in Illanese, unsure what other boon they might currently grant. The man didn't respond, so he asked again in Abyssal.

The man made a sound with his throat that might have been a decline of the offer, but Thaelios was unsure. Perhaps he wasn't a telepath.

"You know where Three Branches is? It is a tavern." He felt like it couldn't hurt to ask, though he knew his Abyssal was limited.

The stranger considered him, then the disguised Dyphina. "I'm ready for death," he croaked in the harsh tongue of the Plane. "Take me." He raised his arms as if expecting Dyphina to physically lift and take him somewhere.

She looked at Thaelios, shook her head, and took a step back.

"We not bring death, friend," Thaelios tried, prepared to give up. "Three Branches?" he repeated, holding up three fingers not far from the man's face.

To his surprise, the man used his thumb to gesture at the wall behind him. Thaelios looked up at the building he was leaning against, but couldn't see any defining characteristics. "Very well," Thaelios nodded, rising from his crouch. "I hope you find what you're looking for, sir."

"I don't think there's anything we can really do for him," he said to Dyphina, switching back to Illanese. "Let's go." He interlocked their elbows and led her away from the stranger, whose arms sagged along with his eyelids. Figuring it couldn't hurt, but not expecting it to help, he went the direction the man indicated. After two more crooked blocks, Thaelios heard voices in his mind.

"If you don't give me that ingot, I'm going to carve out the hollow of your chest and birth a grim worm in the cavity—"

"I'm not sure we want to go this way," he said to Dyphina, trying to remember that the words likely weren't directed toward him.

"No, look!" Dyphina pointed further down the street to where a long branch with a head dangling from it emerged from the wall of a building. Their approach was from a different angle than before, but it looked as if they'd found the tavern!

Thaelios saw movement near the front of the building as they drew nearer, but before making it to the next major thoroughfare, a creature flew across their path from a side alley. After crashing forcefully to the ground, four spiderlike arms bent downward and pushed it back onto anthropomorphic feet.

No sooner had it stood than a second creature lunged from the alley, tackling the first and straddling its body. The aggressor had bladelike protrusions extending at an angle from its forearms, and viscous fluid dripped from its unhinged jaw.

Paralyzed by a combination of fear and indecision, Thaelios watched as the violence unfolded a few steps away.

"Come on!" Dyphina yanked him by the arm, restoring his mobility as she ducked and sped past the brawl, heading for the front door of The Three Branches. Swept up awkwardly in

Dyphina's wake, Thaelios barely avoided a wayward appendage as he slipped by.

With no song from Palomar to ward their minds, a flood of telepathic chatter assaulted Thaelios as he followed his fellow apprentice between the large, oddly shaped bodies loitering in the tavern's entryway. He wondered how the telepathic natives managed to not become overwhelmed. Could they selectively disregard or enhance particular voices they were more interested in? While Thaelios desired to discover more about the subject in the future, all he wanted at the moment was to avoid the crowds and finish their mission so they could leave this realm of distraction and danger.

As before, the chatter in his head cut off once they reached the bar. He followed closely behind Dyphina as she climbed the irregular stairs, heading for the same table where they'd first found Ivaldi. Luckily, the sage was still there, the brim of his green hat shielding his face as he pored over an open book set on the table in front of him. Dyphina checked the neighboring booths for danger, though without their Celestial companions, none of the locals seemed to be paying them any mind. They pressed forward to the edge of Ivaldi's table.

"Are you going to ask a question, or are you just interested in casting a shadow across my page?" the sage asked without raising his head.

"My apologies," Thaelios answered. "We would not interrupt your research if it weren't important."

Dyphina nodded, her sickly visage adding an element of desperation to their plea. "We need to know how to get to Ishmere," she added.

At the mention of the Juda-cai homeworld, Ivaldi slowly raised his head. His snoutish nose wrinkled as he considered his guests. "You again," he stated calmly, laying his quill flat across the parchment he'd been making notes upon. "You seem to have lost your more ostentatious friends. I hope not to an untimely demise."

"Of course not," Thaelios replied. "May we sit?" He slid onto the bench across from Ivaldi even as the sage nodded. The sullen-looking Dyphina glanced over her shoulder once more before taking her seat.

Thaelios swept back some of the silver hair that had fallen over his pointed ears. "I'll get right to it, so as not to waste your time. We have need of information and figured you'd be the best source. Is my assumption correct?" A little indirect flattery shouldn't hurt, he thought.

Ivaldi tapped his fingers upon the pages of his open book. "I do deal in the acquisition of knowledge – but hopefully you remember that I don't share it for free."

Thaelios nodded, running over what facts he could broker with that would be of interest to a sage in the Doomwait. "And what would it cost me to learn the quickest way to travel to Ishmere?"

Ivaldi pulled back to rest flat against the support of his bench. He interlaced his idle fingers and turned his attention to Dyphina. "You look different than before. I see you learn quickly. This visit has earned you much less attention. That is also the way I prefer things."

Dyphina spoke up, "Do you have an answer for us, or are you stalling?"

Ivaldi snorted and shifted his eyes back to Thaelios. "Why do you want to go to Ishmere? I'm not sure you have what it takes to survive there."

So he does know something about it, Thaelios mused. "Let us worry about that, friend. How do we get there?"

The sage sighed and crossed his arms. "In order to share this with you, I will need something useful." Ivaldi took stock of the denizens sitting at the nearest tables, checking to see if any were listening in. "You're obviously from elsewhere, and Plane-walkers have usually seen interesting things. What do you know about Mount Celestia?"

Thaelios chewed on his lower lip, deciding how to respond. He was unsure he'd picked up anything valuable to Ivaldi during his brief time on Palomar's home world, but if he had, would sharing it constitute a betrayal of their Celestial guide? Was there anything else he could offer?

The sound of tankards toppling to the floor and the screech of benches being pushed back drew Thaelios's attention across the upper story of The Three Branches. A pair of fiendish creatures stood in confrontation on opposite sides of a table.

"Give me that Soulstone, or by my True Name, I will scorch the ground beneath your corpse!"

A third creature, bulky and tall enough that it had to duck to keep its horned head from scraping the ceiling, pushed toward the stand-off from a far corner. It had faceted eyes like an insect, and held a massive, black trident in both hands. "Sit down before I skewer you both!" it commanded in raspy Infernal. "Or take your argument outside."

Thaelios watched the instigator consider the new threat, then slowly pull the wayward bench forward to retake his seat.

"Never a dull moment," Ivaldi chimed.

Something about the initial fiend's curse triggered Thaelios's memory. "I have something even better for you," he declared as he turned back to the sage. "On my home world, there is a stone tablet containing the True Names of a dozen fiends. That should be worth something, no?"

Ivaldi's eyes narrowed. "You're lying … if you had access to that kind of power, you wouldn't be here, dealing with me."

Thaelios shrugged. "The tablet has been split in two. I only have access to one half. But the other exists, and if the right entity was to find both, they could extort a bevy of mighty beings into servitude."

Uncrossing his arms and leaning forward, Ivaldi whispered, "And you're going to tell me where your half is, is that it?"

"Once you tell us how to reach Ishmere …"

The sage's eyes narrowed again and his fingers resumed their tapping. "I suppose I shall trust you, then. I will hold you to your end of the bargain, though I can't imagine you're going to like what I have to tell you."

Dyphina exhaled sharply. "Don't worry, we're used to bad news."

"Alright, then," Ivaldi continued. "See how this compares. Of course, there are a number of ways to travel from world to world, but only one I'm aware of that will get you where you want to go. The Juda-cai are not to be trifled with. They are usually the ones visiting other realms – I've never heard of anyone else going to or returning from Ishmere."

Thaelios nodded. "We understand. You won't be held responsible for our safety." He was ready to get what they needed and get out of the Doomwait before one of these fiends decided to bring them trouble.

"Very well," Ivaldi continued. "The Doomwait holds an interesting position in the cosmos, creating an equilibrium between the realms of positive and negative energy. A number of wounds, if you will, have been opened by the stress of its adjacency to the Upper and Lower Planes, and you can reach the first layer of many striated worlds from here." The sage licked his lips and swallowed with more effort than usual. "Alas, Ishmere is not one of them."

"What?" Dyphina asked. "I thought you knew something useful. Don't tell us about all the ways that aren't helpful—"

Thaelios shot her a stern look. "What my friend means to say, Ivaldi, is that we're in a bit of a hurry and would like to be on our way as soon as possible." It was true – he had no idea how much longer Dyphina's disguise was going to last, let alone which demon forces might be assembling to cut them off from the Rift.

"I understand," the sage replied, though he didn't seem in any rush to reach the end of his exposition. "Luckily, or not, depending on your view, there is a stairway near here that leads to the top layer of the Abyss. The Abyss is a fascinating place, comprised of infinite layers. Connecting all of them is the Chaos Cyclone. I can only describe it as an enormous whirlpool of shadow and despair – you will have no difficulty recognizing it."

Dyphina shook her head. "You're right, that doesn't sound good."

"If one were to descend through that whirlpool, the Chaos Cyclone would normally deposit you on a random layer of the infinite Abyss. However, the Lords of the Abyss have devised a way to send their minions to specific locations through the use of Rune Magic. Though the most powerful Tanar-ri can navigate from one realm to another through their own Gating abilities, lesser beings can navigate through the Chaos Cyclone by carrying a Destination Stone that anchors travelers to a particular realm."

Thaelios thought he saw where the sage was headed. "And can these 'Destination Stones' be tied to a plane other than a layer of the Abyss?"

Ivaldi nodded. "There is an archive, a repository of Destination Stones connected to the smithies where the Rune Magic is forged. In theory, the Chaos Cyclone could take you to any negative energy plane, including Ishmere. You would have to find the correct stone in the archive, however."

Thaelios shrugged. "I'm sure they have some system of cataloging them."

"I must warn you," Ivaldi said. He looked toward the neighboring booths before continuing. "Only the Lords of the Abyss have the authority to assign Destination Stones. To get what you need, you're going to have to break into the repository and steal it."

"Do you know what's guarding them?" Dyphina asked. "The Stones?"

Ivaldi shrugged. "Demons? Worse? Rune Magic is time consuming and difficult. The Stones are very valuable."

Thaelios nodded. He understood nothing about this would be easy, but he wanted to make sure he knew everything he needed to before reporting back to the others. "Would each of us need one, or would one do for a group?"

"I cannot guarantee a Destination Stone for Ishmere will be on-hand, but there likely wouldn't be more than one." Ivaldi sighed. "As I said, it's almost unheard of for anyone who is not a Juda-cai to travel there. However …" he continued even as Thaelios opened his mouth to reiterate the question, "as long as anyone wishing to travel is in an unbroken chain of contact to the bearer of the Stone, they will be transported along with him."

"Good," Thaelios responded. In fact, this was all far from good, but he felt like he could at least present the information soundly enough for their group to come to a decision. He quickly shared enough about the Hall of Doors and the location of the Tablet of Broken Names back on Elisahd to fulfill his part of the bargain, then he and Dyphina slipped out of The Three Branches just as her illusion wore off.

His thoughts were so occupied by what was to come that the journey back to the Abyssal Rift seemed shorter than the first time. No Tanar-ri ambushed them, but Thaelios felt far from relieved as he shared the news of what they were up against in order to reach Ishmere.

Chapter 11

The Chaos Cyclone

"This sounds extremely dangerous," said Saffron.

Thaelios didn't disagree with her assessment. He certainly wasn't going to push for entering the Infinite Layers of the Abyss. "Are we sure we want to pursue this course? We don't even know that finding the Juda-cai is the best way to protect my people from whatever danger is to come."

"To be fair," Dyphina interjected, her natural beauty returned, "it does seem that the Juda-cai would be aware of the Spawn of Raug – he is one of them, after all."

Saffron and Be'naj both nodded, leaving Thaelios to turn to the Celestial for support. "What do you think, Palomar? Your kind can appreciate the perils of the Abyss better than the rest of us."

Palomar set his jaw and furrowed his brow. "*If we are aware of a threat to the innocent, we should not sit by and allow it to become manifest. That said, the five of us attempting to infiltrate an Abyssal repository of Rune Magic is unveiled folly.*"

Saffron looked surprised and started to object. "But—"

Palomar shook his head, "*Fire means nothing to demons, and even the lesser Tanar-ri are physically stronger than any of you ... which is why I shall ask one of the Celestial Marshalls for aid.*"

Be'naj smiled and nodded. "Do you think the other Aasimar will help?"

Palomar shrugged. "*I spent long spans battling Abyssal invaders under Illicurus. I know a few veterans from that campaign still assigned to protect Vilonia. I will ask and hear their answer.*"

"So, are we headed back to the settlement? I would be happy to get out from under this mountain," Thaelios said. He was sure having a contingent of Aasimar accompanying them would make him more comfortable, but uncertain whether abandoning this course altogether might ultimately be best.

They left the crackling, dark energy of the Abyssal Rift behind and strode in pensive silence to the surface. The blue sky above and the warmth of sunshine on his face were fresh air to Thaelios's suffocating soul. Only under the canopy of the heavens did he appreciate the unseen oppressiveness of a Plane saturated by negative energy.

"*Perhaps you should wait here, friends*," Palomar projected as they reached the armory. "*My conversation with Khanarme demands privacy. I shall return as soon as I can.*"

Thaelios didn't mind the break and sat down on the black soil to wait.

"It is difficult to measure time, here," Be'naj mentioned. "I cannot tell if the sun has moved since we arrived. When was the last time you slept, Saffron?"

"I have no idea, but now that you mention it, I'm exhausted."

Dyphina followed up with an unrepentant yawn. "I wonder if they have anywhere comfortable to sleep."

"I don't think Aasimar require rest, to be honest," Thaelios postulated. What he'd gleaned during his linguistic studies of the Lower Planes suggested that creatures without finite lifespans generally lacked the baser needs of mortals.

"I could use a break to trance, myself," Be'naj added. "Perhaps Shecclad will send me a message if he knows I'm trying to reach him."

"And how would he know that?" Thaelios asked. "Even if he normally watched your every move on Elisahd, which I highly doubt, that doesn't mean he could follow you here to Mount Celestia."

Be'naj's wings twitched. "How do you know how it works? I've received these visions most of my life and still can't explain it."

Saffron placed a hand softly on Be'naj's shoulder. "I don't think we're going to decipher the mysteries of the cosmos anytime soon. Why don't the two of you trance now while we wait, and I'll keep watch for Palomar's return. I have a feeling it could be a while."

Thaelios followed her gaze across the training field to where a retinue of Aasimar practiced aerial maneuvers. He had no doubts that the moment they were in meditation, Saffron would wander off to investigate. Calculating they'd be safe enough regardless, he gave in and slipped into alternate consciousness. When Saffron roused him, Palomar had returned.

"Khanarme was sympathetic to our plight but understandably demanded guidance from Hiruth Jeshu, May His Light Shine Forever, before organizing a raid into enemy territory. I apologize for failing to anticipate your weariness; I have already forgotten so much since returning to Mount Celestia from my time with mortals. We shall find you proper shelter and comfort in the Ulimar village."

"Will I be able to speak with Rhazine?" Saffron asked. "I'd like to make plans for her should we fail to return."

"Of course, but do not fear. As Hiruth Jeshu said, May His Light Shine Forever, He can send you to Elisahd whenever you wish."

Back in the village, Rhazine embraced Saffron as soon as the door to her host's abode opened, though Thaelios calculated it less than a day since they'd parted. The two Begnari women went inside, chatting vibrantly as Dyphina and Be'naj followed in their wake.

Palomar seemed to be carrying on a telepathic conversation with the Ulimar who lived there as they stood near the entryway, staring silently at one another. Thaelios breathed deeply, deciding to stay outside and enjoy the natural splendor of Mount Celestia's bottommost layer. It wasn't Ifelian, of course, but he couldn't count on any such scenery where they were headed, and the old-growth trees just beyond the settlement looked spectacular. He wandered toward them, making sure to bring some rations and the book taken from Trigilas's quarters.

He would have plenty of time to indulge while the humans slept. At the edge of where civilization touched the wilderness, Thaelios found an enormous tree unlike any he'd ever seen. Its trunk was broad, ribbed, and folded so that it resembled the throne of a giant. Its long limbs extended from both sides and were weighed down by heavy green leaves that bowed them toward the ground.

Similar specimens led into a thicker forest, but they were widely spaced given the girth of their foliage. Thaelios gently rubbed the bark and found it smooth. The limbs twitched slightly at his touch, and he had a sensation that the tree was somehow aware of his presence. Such an odd feeling. Checking to make sure he was alone, Thaelios sat upon the low curve of the trunk and nestled back against its flatter rise. The nearest limbs bent slightly toward him, but once he was satisfied that no harm was meant, he cracked open Trigilas's book and started to read.

The breadth of magical knowledge demonstrated by the Father of Spells within this single tome was staggering – doubly so, knowing everything else Trigilas had accomplished. One of Cauzel's first lessons to his new apprentices had been about the necessity of finding a specialty. It was nearly impossible, he'd said, to become adept within all areas of magic. There was simply too much to learn and too much variance in the structure of the schools. Building upon learned concepts, once you'd mastered them, was the most efficient way to expand proficiency.

Thaelios closed his eyes and breathed in deeply. What was *his* calling? What kind of magic was *he* best at? Early on, he'd found illusions useful and they came easily to him. Apparently, Cauzel had a talent for them as well, given how he'd fooled everyone into believing he was human. But was Thaelios going to create a legacy through trickery? It seemed unlikely.

He thought about the trapped devil, M'thenzor, and how Trigilas had used the knowledge of supernatural beings to his advantage. Summoning could be an accelerated path to power, but also dangerous. Thaelios was never going to banish Avatars from Elisahd, but he'd now seen firsthand the impressive nature of the Outer Planes and those who lived there.

Something brushed against Thaelios's face and he opened his eyes to find the limbs of the tree curling in upon him, almost in an embrace. He reached out and stroked a broad, green leaf. Doing so created a tinkling sound similar to a wind-chime, and Thaelios felt a soothing peace fall upon him. A sudden urge to reenter his trance and meditate would not be denied, even though he'd wanted to make some progress on *Gradations of Immortality*. The book could wait, Thaelios decided. The humans would have to sleep longer, anyway, and he'd certainly have plenty of time to read before Palomar received any news.

"There you are," Palomar projected as he pulled aside the curtain of green-leafed branches that had cocooned around Thaelios. *"I see you've discovered the comforts of the cradling ilyho."*

Thaelios realized that the tree he sat upon had curled in to the extent that he was almost entirely hidden from view. "How long was I trancing? It appears my lucidity was compromised."

"*I cannot answer truthfully, for I know not when you began. Marshall Khanarme has returned, and the others are rested and preparing for the mission ahead.*"

"Your friend got permission from Hiruth Jeshu to enter the Abyss?" Thaelios felt a twinge of disappointment.

"*May His light shine forever – yes.*" Palomar's pearlescent face was painted with a look of satisfaction. "*My just Lord seems keen to protect our mortal friends. If I were to guess, I'd venture He's been impressed by the ingenuity and courage your troop has shown. It is rare for those native to the Primes to ever find their way here, after all.*"

Thaelios stood and the tree's limbs receded to their initial position. "So he didn't think our venturing to the Nether Realms was foolhardy?"

"*Quite the contrary. He has decreed a full company of Celestial soldiers should guard the four of you.*"

Perhaps this could be done, Thaelios thought. He already held enough trust in Palomar to pity any enemy unfortunate enough to face a collection of determined Aasimar.

"*Come.*" Palomar waved as he turned toward the village. "*We should join the others.*"

Thaelios wasn't sure how large a company of Aasimar was, but a dozen armed Celestials waited at the cave leading into the base of the Mountain, Arinome among them. The enormous Seraph stood with arms folded across his armored chest, his four wings intermittently shifting in hypnotic synchronicity. The Aasimar wore shining silver mail, their uniform perfection made distinct only by the varying colors of their hair and the feathered tips of their wings. Saffron, Be'naj, and Dyphina huddled closely and looked out of place, dwarfed by the surrounding Celestials.

Be'naj looked more calm and resolute than he remembered, and had acquired a polished shield that glistened in the slanting rays of Mount Celestia's sun. Dyphina, in contrast, appeared anxious. She chewed on a handful of what looked like dried fruit, reminding Thaelios how famished he was. He approached to see if she'd be willing to share.

"We haven't been into the Doomwait in some time," a crimson-haired Aasimar projected as he stepped forward and clasped Palomar's wrist. Thaelios guessed it must be the Marshall. *"The biggest threat from the Tanar-ri is their numbers, so stay in formation and obey my orders,"* he continued as he looked over the company. Khanarme locked his gaze momentarily on Palomar. *"Don't expect them to fight fair."*

Palomar nodded. *"After we push our way through the Abyssal Stair, the real resistance is likely to begin. I will guide the mortals to the Runestone repository to search its archives for our Destination Stone. Hold the demons back as long as you can, but you should retreat once we're safely on our way."*

Arinome's deep voice resonated in Thaelios's mind, *"We can only expect plans to hold together for so far ... we're entering the realm of Chaos, after all."* Many of the Aasimar nodded.

"The Light of Hiruth Jeshu will see us through," Khanarme said and set a pace into the cavern beneath the Mountain. *"Use your songs and trust your brethren."*

The Celestial company filed after their Marshall, with Palomar taking the rear. The mortals followed, and Thaelios had to hustle to keep up with the Aasimar's naturally long strides.

Dyphina took his book and placed it in her backpack with Cauzel's spellbook as they walked.

"I hate to put a damper on things," Thaelios mentioned between breaths, "but how are we supposed to find the archives?"

"The Abyss is a dark place, Thaelios, for demons do not require light to see." Palomar looked back briefly to acknowledge the question. *"Rune Magic requires forging, however. The light of the fires should serve as a beacon."*

"We're going to stick out like bats in a bird's nest, aren't we?" Dyphina asked.

Palomar turned his head again and smiled. *"We will not escape attention, for certain. You should not be surprised if word of our coming reaches the Tanar-ri even before our arrival. Also, Saffron, your fire magic will likely be ineffective, as most demons are immune to the element. Concentrate on your martial training."*

Saffron nodded. "What else should we know about them? What should we prepare for?"

"Tanar-ri are devious and cruel. They enjoy inflicting pain and will sometimes avoid slaying an enemy outright if they think they can safely incapacitate them. To this end, many employ venom or carry disease, so even the smallest wounds should not be neglected."

"They sound as horrible as they look," Be'naj reflected.

"You must do whatever you can not to perish on their plane, even if that means fleeing," Palomar continued. *"For if a mortal dies within the Abyss, their essence will be trapped. They will be reborn as the lowest form of demonic spawn and tortured for eons."*

Thaelios's feet ceased propelling him forward. "This is more than I signed up for."

"Have faith, my kin," Be'naj encouraged. "We have a dozen Celestials to keep us safe."

"I'm not sure an army would make me feel secure, given the stakes." The shadow of the Mountain already lay over them, and Thaelios stared at the dark triangle that formed the mouth of the tunnel beneath. The Aasimar marched on, though his fellow apprentices and Be'naj held back with him.

How is it that they were all so ready to risk their eternal souls while he hesitated? Was it a lack of courage on his part or an abundance of reason? Were they aware of what was on the line and still deemed their mission worthy?

Saffron looked at him with soft eyes and laid a hand upon his shoulder. "I understand your fear – it's completely natural. Only a year ago, I too would have questioned our sanity. But I learned from the Order of the Rising Moon, as much as I'm loath to admit it, what it is to struggle on behalf of something greater than the self." Her gaze was unfaltering. "I saw men giving their lives because they believed in providing security for others. And though they paid the ultimate cost, their sacrifice succeeded in creating the world of their vision."

Was it that simple? After what he'd seen in the Doomwait, Thaelios wouldn't deny that sinister forces sought to harm his people. Eladrin history was already marred by so much hardship; they didn't deserve whatever might be coming. He thought of Zygrim, the man he'd barely known, yet who knew him better than any other, and how the gladiator had risked his life to spare Thaelios's, almost as if it was instinctual.

"I see what you mean," he replied to Saffron, not because he was certain he did, but because of the sudden sense of loss that clutched at the organs in his chest. He wanted to disappear, though would settle for the group returning to their march.

Thaelios started moving again and the others mirrored him. The progression of Aasimar had never ceased, and the mortals had to hustle to catch up. One of the Celestials hummed a tune that produced a halo of light around the company. It swelled and receded with the amplitude of the song, keeping the crushing darkness of the overhead mountain at bay.

When the company reached the Abyssal Rift, Khanarme turned to address his followers, his crimson hair streaked with intermittent flashes of electric blue. *"When we enter the Doomwait, we'll be flying swiftly for the Abyssal Stair."* His telepathy temporarily blocked out the incessant droning of the Rift. *"Aasimar will carry the mortals, with Arinome leading the way to discourage confrontation. Once we enter the Abyss, we can expect the battle to come to us. Palomar will take charge of our guests while we occupy any Tanar-ri."*

"It's been eons since I've smote demon scum!" Arinome's deep voice resonated.

Khanarme flashed him a piercing look but didn't address the comment. *"You are each responsible for the Aasimar beside you. Defend first – we're here to assist the mortals in their mission, not start the next Blood War."*

The heads of most of the Aasimar nodded in agreement.

"Those not carrying mortals … weapons out!"

All but four of the Celestials drew blades that shone with holy, golden light, Khanarme included. One of the remainder stepped behind Thaelios and placed a pearlescent hand on his shoulder. Others did the same to his friends.

One-by-one, they all stepped into the Rift, vanishing in a series of crackling flashes. When it was Thaelios's turn, the sensations of crossing to another world were no less jarring for having previously experienced them. The gloom of the Doomwait once again numbed his spirits, as if an ancient sadness weighed upon him. A moment later, he was lifted into the air, supported by strong arms wrapping around his shoulders from underneath. The flapping of feathery wings and the euphoric sense of weightlessness distracted him from the cloying miasma.

Even with his keen sight, Thaelios could see nothing beyond the backs of the few Aasimar directly in front of him. The perpetual haze muted everything else, even the ground, so he had no idea of their altitude. The Aasimar must have had a better sense of direction than he, for the halos of distant torches soon heralded their approach to Anarchiapolis. Thaelios found relief that no attacks came while he dangled from such a height.

The sudden descent of white wings in front of him briefly preceded his own, and the accompanying rush of air felt refreshing in the stagnant atmosphere. Denizens of the Doomwait scurried to make room for the Aasimar arrival, and even before Thaelios stood firmly on his own feet, he registered a barrage of telepathic curses heaped in their direction. Despite the crudeness of thought, the accompanying aggression failed to manifest. Thaelios didn't know how to differentiate an actual Tanar-ri from the other abominations stalking this Plane, but the glow of Celestial blades seemed enough deterrent for the moment.

The Aasimar shifted into an outward-facing circle with the mortals at its center, cutting off much of Thaelios's view. Arinome continued hovering above them, his powerful quartet of wings beating as quickly as Thaelios's pulse.

A piercing, physical roar split the air, and Thaelios ducked in response. He couldn't see the originator, but it sounded big. The circle shuffled in a uniform direction, causing those within to move along the same path.

"We claim the right to justice!" Khanarme shouted.

"Who-ah," the Aasimar answered, raising their shields and shifting their feet into a protective stance.

Thaelios stretched onto the tips of his toes to see what was happening beyond his living enclosure. Two more roars, from opposite sides of the circle, exploded close enough that he covered his ears in shock. Thuds and the *whoosh* of swinging weapons followed, the perimeter swaying as several Celestials responded with swift violence.

Wails of pain followed, answered immediately by song, and then the circle began moving again. Thaelios stumbled as they started down a series of wide, stone steps, each nearly as broad as he was tall. The hum of the Aasimar's weapons strengthened in response to the singing, and Arinome flew further down the steps, beyond sight.

"Prepare for the Abyss."

Thaelios thought the voice was Palomar's, though he couldn't be sure. He searched for Saffron's face, but an unnatural darkness suddenly cast everything in deep shadow. Continuing down the stair, he became enveloped in a cascading grey mist, like passing through a sinking thundercloud.

The ground leveled off, and the Aasimar stopped moving. All was pitch black, save the Celestial weapons and armor, whose glow reflected off their owner's pale skins. The air was difficult to breathe and stank of unsavory fumes.

"*One got away*," Arinome shared as the Aasimar spread into a line. "*It no doubt Gated to raise the alarm. Expect company.*"

With the circle broken, Thaelios could at least see back in the direction they'd come, though the shining metal only illuminated so much. Movement gave some shape in his mind to the dark curtain they'd passed through, a semi-solid downward flow of void.

"Which way do we go?" asked Saffron, the first mortal to overcome the stagnation of their transition. She held the glowing tip of her spear aloft, trying to use its radiance to track something out of the oppressive blackness.

"*There!*" Palomar finally said, pointing.

"I don't see anything," Dyphina said.

"I see it!" Be'naj's voice sounded hopeful. "The faintest red glow."

A sudden rumbling like distant, sustained thunder dimmed the momentary satisfaction. The Aasimar spread a body's length apart from one another.

"*Inrohim, Leator, watch the portal*," Khanarme ordered. "*We don't want to be caught from behind.*"

Two Aasimar spun to face the curtain of void, but Thaelios's eyes were trained on the emptiness of the Abyss beyond the line of Celestials, straining to put an image to the rising noise he could already hear. What sounded like many running feet was joined by a series of snapping *pops*, similar to rapid rain on metal. Concurrent with the cacophony came flashes of rectangular mist, dull grey but infinitely brighter than the surrounding darkness. These flashes were instantaneous but provided glimpses of huge shapes striding through them, as well as numerous smaller forms swelling around them at speed.

Arinome took several steps forward from the formation and raised an open palm to the unseen sky. With a low, bellowing note, a flare of golden light shot upward, exploding at great height into flashing streamers of Celestial energy that cascaded slowly downward. The resulting illumination was quickly subdued by the Abyss, but it allowed a better view of the oncoming horde.

Dozens of sinister bipedal forms raced toward them. They were roughly human-sized, char-black, bearing twisted thorns across lithe limbs. Thaelios estimated they'd be overrun within moments. Joining the mass of similar creatures were a handful of larger demons with grotesque bodies, closer in size to Arinome.

One had a great horned head like a scaled bull, with massive arms ending in crab-like pincers. Another was shelled and bloated like some sort of upright turtle, only with nightmarish teeth and claws.

There were others, but Thaelios didn't have time to examine them before his Aasimar neighbors broke into numerous harmonies. Their music was both invigorating and ominous, and the Celestials took slow, anxious steps forward while awaiting the charge.

Thaelios felt a sudden urge to relieve himself, struggling not to while absently trying to recall the words to any spell at all. His lips trembled but nothing emerged.

"*Come, quickly!*" Palomar urged, though it was Saffron who yanked Thaelios's arm. "*Sheathe your weapons.*"

Dyphina and Be'naj did so, but Saffron's spear lacked a covering. Whether disadvantageous or not, its light provided some comfort as Palomar rushed the mortals away from the imminent conflict. Thaelios heard battle cries and the clashing of weapons behind him, but didn't dare look to see if they were being pursued. All he could do was follow the bobbing of Saffron's spear-tip and try to breathe through the heavy air.

The screams and curses were horrible but dimmed to nothing as they ran. Thaelios could not even see the plane he tread upon. Luckily, the terrain seemed level, though as soon as he celebrated that fact something tripped him and he skidded face-first across the ground. No one else noticed, and Saffron's light drifted frighteningly distany.

The surface was ice-cold as Thaelios pushed his hands against it to rise. The comparative silence, now that he wasn't running, astonished him. Only his labored breathing countered the surrounding quiet. He thought about calling out to the others to stop, but the realization of where he was prevented him – what if something else heard?

He tried to resume running, but a few steps confirmed that the terrain was no longer smooth, and a sharp pain in his right knee protested against supporting his full weight. He could see it now, though. Gazing toward the invisible horizon, the red glow of distant fire provided a beacon he could at least make for. Saffron would have to realize he wasn't with them before long and return. He cursed himself: how would she find him? Her light was already so dim, nearly swallowed by the darkness.

Thaelios hesitated, then drew his own blade. The Tanar-ri could see through the blackness, after all. With the light of his weapon, he saw that the ground was littered with debris, resembling broken pieces of whatever the hard floor was made of. He headed for the fire-light, though managed only a brisk walk. Anything faster brought too much pain.

He'd lost sight of Saffron's spear but forced himself to believe they'd find one another along the route. It was the only way he could keep moving. For what it was worth, the red glow seemed to be growing. After what could have been an hour, Thaelios heard the shuffle of shifting debris. He stood still, wondering if he'd kicked a loose piece, though he knew deep down the noise came from further off.

Holding his blade high, he turned in a circle, staring into the unfathomable layers of shadow, looking for movement while hoping he saw none. He heard the noise again and snapped toward the direction it came from. Something stood motionless at the edge of his light. Had it been there before? He took a tentative step closer and the object moved, looking like a rotten, stunted tree come to life. It growled like a small dog and then charged, sending Thaelios into a stumbling back-step.

"*Impecto!*"

The familiar voice seized Thaelios's attention just in time to catch streaming shards of blue energy fly from Dyphina's outstretched hand, her silhouette illuminated by the curved blade of her Celestial sword. The magic arrows streaked past him, striking the aggressor with a snap like cracking wood. It fell to the ground, still, and by the time Thaelios could look up again, his fellow apprentice was nearly crushing him in a one-armed embrace.

"Why did you leave us?" she asked, her question muffled by his tunic as she pressed against him. She sounded scared, but he hadn't yet found his own voice. Dyphina drew back, and when the glow of her weapon was lowered, he saw the others approaching, their own blades unsheathed.

"What spell was that?" Thaelios managed to ask. He'd never seen Dyphina use such magic before.

She snorted incredulously, then smiled and shook her head. "It was in Master Cauzel's spellbook, you ring-tailed lemur."

"Thaelios!" Saffron cried as she drew closer. She bent forward once within a few strides, struggling for breath. Be'naj and Palomar approached more slowly.

"My friend, how did you get separated?" Be'naj asked. "We thought we'd lost you."

Momentarily out of danger, he was touched by their concern. "I fell and became lame. I didn't dare cry out."

"*It is my fault,*" Palomar said. "*I pushed too hard and should have taken the rear position.*"

Saffron stood tall and shook her head before settling her gaze on Thaelios. "We were getting close before we realized you weren't there. Can you still move?"

"Not quickly. I can walk."

"*I shall carry you the rest of the way,*" Palomar stated. "*We are not far from the repository but should be quick about it.*"

"Do you know what happened to the other Aasimar?" Thaelios wondered aloud, though he knew the battle was unresolved when they left. Just this once, he wished someone would lie to him.

"*Khanarme is an experienced Marshall; I expect he found a way to overcome the odds, or lead his charges safely home. I look forward to greeting him upon my return to Mount Celestia.*" Palomar hooked his arms around Thaelios's from behind and took to the air. They flew slower than in the Doomwait, and Thaelios wondered if the air was indeed thicker in the Abyss. He still struggled to breathe normally.

As the red light grew brighter, it revealed hints of the building they intended to enter. Palomar landed a good arrow shot from the nearest forges, leaving Thaelios a few moments to take in their destination while the women caught up.

Unearthly smiths toiled at a dozen forges set at the tips of a six-pointed star, outlined by a trough of molten lava. The clang of hammers on anvils punctuated the near constant push of air from giant bellows at each station. In the center of the star rested a black spire, the top of which was concealed in darkness far above. While the smiths were obviously not of any mortal race, they didn't look strictly demonic, either.

"Do you think we have to climb that?" Dyphina asked, stepping in close behind Palomar and peeking around one of his broad arms.

"*We will only know once we're inside.*"

Saffron walked a few steps closer to take a better look. "How exactly are we supposed to get past those forges? Just walk in like we're not from another plane?"

"*Those don't look like Tanar-ri. My guess is, the smiths will stick to their work unless we interrupt them. I worry the repository itself will be better guarded.*"

"Shall we, then?" Saffron asked. "If Khanarme had to retreat, there's no telling when demon reinforcements might arrive."

Palomar nodded and walked purposefully toward the dark spire, but swiveled his head between forges to prevent any surprises. Be'naj laced an arm under Thaelios's shoulder and offered to support him.

"Thank you," he said, accepting her help even though he wasn't sure he needed it. They doubled their staggered steps to keep up, until Saffron called out.

"Look up!" she cried, extending her spear to point toward the peak of the spire.

Two of the vulture-like Tanar-ri Palomar had struggled against in the Doomwait dove toward them from the darkness. Without hesitation, the Aasimar drew his greatsword and sang, causing his radiant blade to crackle with additional energy. Be'naj untangled from Thaelios and drew her weapon, preparing to smite the demons should they attack.

This time, Thaelios kept his wits. He'd been studying a new illusion from Cauzel's spellbook and felt confident it was close enough to his *mirrored image* that he could pull it off. He placed a hand on Saffron's back and recited the spell.

The demons let loose their evil mockery of a bird-like shriek as they drew near, angling their flight to strike at Saffron and Be'naj with their talons. A moment before impact, Thaelios's spell took effect and Saffron appeared to shift positions without actually moving. The demon altered his path but merely clutched at vacant air while Saffron drove her spear upward into its belly.

Be'naj simultaneously lifted her shield and sword to both ward off and wound her opponent, but its talons knocked her off-balance and she couldn't follow through. Palomar took advantage of Saffron's blow by leaping into the air, rising above the staggered Tanar-ri, and slashing downward. A thunderclap peeled through the thick air as Palomar's sword sundered the flesh between the vulture-like demon's wings.

The creature crashed to the ground with a horrid death-wail, leaving Thaelios to search the sky for the second fiend. It had soared past Be'naj and disappeared into the darkness, though he still heard the beat of its wings high above. Then suddenly, the flapping stopped with a sharp *pop*, accompanied by a flash of grey mist.

"*He's gone to fetch others*," Palomar warned. "*We should be swift.*" He landed, sheathed his heavy sword, and jogged toward the spire once again, leaving the others to follow.

Thaelios kneeled to help Be'naj off the ground, sending another surge of pain up from his knee. "My thanks," she said, putting the tip of her blade into the hard ground and using its leverage to stand.

He winced but said nothing, taking note that the smiths at the nearest forges had stopped their work to stare. Their black faces appeared stern but none had moved closer. "I think we've attracted too much attention."

"Hurry!" Saffron called back at them. She and Dyphina had covered nearly half the remaining distance to the dark obelisk.

With Be'naj helping support him, Thaelios joined the others before a tall crease in the obsidian façade of the spire. It may have marked a doorway, but the panels on either side were flush with the upward slanting face of the protrusion. Once his fingers found purchase, the muscles in Palomar's arms and back bulged as he struggled to force the heavy panels open, but they wouldn't budge. When he relented, Saffron wedged her spear into the crack to pry it open but had to surrender lest the shaft snap in two.

"Perhaps there's another way in?" Be'naj tilted her head back to get a more complete view of the spire. "Maybe a window higher up?"

"Oh, Thaelios!" Dyphina shouted as she clasped her hands together. "What about that spell you cast to unlock our chains in the mines?"

He shrugged. "It's worth a try." The metallic sounds of the smiths hammering away at the forges had returned, and looking around, Thaelios saw that they were again being ignored. Maybe the workers were slaves and lacked the Tanar-ris' interest in eliminating everything not of their realm. If so, would Saffron demand that they stop to free the smiths?

Wiping the thought from his mind and concentrating on the crease he hoped was a doorway, Thaelios summoned a portion of his power and spoke, "*Otreritus penicul.*" To his pleasant surprise, the sound of grinding stone murmured back from underneath the panels' smooth, black surface. When the grating stopped, the doors popped forward the span of Thaelios's little finger.

"*Wonderful!*" said Palomar before he reached between the panels and slid them open along the length of the outer wall. The space beyond was pitch black, but Saffron's radiant spear provided enough illumination for Thaelios to spot a surprised Abyssal denizen staring back with vacant sockets from behind a chest-high partition on the far side of the entry chamber.

The creature looked like a humanoid skeleton wrapped tightly in red, leathery flesh. A rim of small horns adorned the crown of its head, and its body wept with clinging droplets on the verge of dripping to the floor.

As recognition flooded its features, the demon dashed toward a serrated glaive propped against the back wall where it met the partition. Palomar moved just as quickly, drawing his sword as he raced forward, and slamming its tip into the wall as the demon reached for its weapon.

"*Intruders!*" it howled telepathically as it yanked its hand back. "*Intruders in the Pit of Runes!*"

Thaelios had no idea over what distance a creature from the Outer Planes could project its thoughts, but he worried reinforcements were on their way. He stepped into the spire after his companions had flooded past him. By the white light of their Celestial weapons, he saw the rest of the room was empty except for a small winged creature the size of a monkey. It screeched at them from its perch in the left corner of the room.

Palomar had turned his blade toward the humanoid demon and backed him off with a threatening step forward. "*You know what happens if I slay you on your home Plane, don't you, Babau?*"

The demon snarled and snapped its bony jaws. "*What do you want here, Aasimar?*"

"*Where are the runestones kept?*" Palomar asked, failing to mask his urgency.

Thaelios kept an eye out for the appearance of new adversaries, knowing it was only a matter of time. The winged creature in the corner kept up its annoying racket, and Thaelios realized it was probably a Quasit. He'd read about ambitious Shapers summoning such Abyssal fiends to serve as magical assistants. Given his current experience, he doubted such a pact could be worth it.

The demon Palomar had called a Babau reluctantly pointed toward the only other door in the chamber. Across the partition from the creature's glaive, the panel was similar to the outer doors – smooth and dark – though it did bear a simple metallic handle.

"*Open it!*" Palomar demanded.

While the demon lumbered from behind the partition, its expression undeniably malevolent, Thaelios peered over the obsidian divider. Open upon the counter on the other side was some sort of mighty ledger, its massive pages inscribed with columns of Abyssal runes.

Liquid dripped from the Babau as he snaked his way to the door, a *hiss* accompanying the droplets that struck the floor. The demon spared a second look at Palomar's gleaming greatsword before reaching out and pulling the handle.

The panel looked heavy but slid to reveal a rectangular compartment barely big enough for them all to squeeze into. They smushed even closer together to make sure no one came in contact with the demon. In the pale light of the Celestial's sword, Thaelios barely made out the reflection of numerous runes lining the walls, their dark surfaces slicker than the surrounding material.

"*Is this some sort of trick?*" Palomar accused upon assessing the dimensions of the compartment, which had no other exits.

"I think it's a transport," Thaelios offered. He recognized many of the runes as numerals, followed by what he guessed were location categories. He boldly stared down the Babau. "Take us to where the Destination Stone for Ishmere is kept."

The demon snarled, indignant that a mortal would dare to command him, but the flat of Palomar's blade pressing against its chest held it in check. *"Do as you're told,"* the Aasimar ordered.

Taking stock of the number of radiant weapons in the compartment, the Babau relented, pressing his palm over one of the runes in the wall, which glowed a sickly green at his touch. The room shook and then started moving downward, the sensation of dropping causing Thaelios's stomach to tighten uneasily. As they descended, the air grew so hot that perspiration broke out across his body. It only took a few moments to reach their destination, but when the door opened again, the Babau seized the opportunity and bolted.

Be'naj lunged to grab it by the arm, but immediately released it in a gasp of pain. Thaelios could hear the skin of her hand sizzling. "Come back here!" Saffron yelled as she gave chase, though the darkness of the room created a disadvantage for her. Palomar followed.

While Dyphina checked Be'naj's injury, Thaelios stepped out of the transport chamber. He had no desire to run down a demon. The space they'd entered was cavernous, and rows of shelves nearly twice his height created aisles between them. True to the Abyssal schema, instead of being neatly lined, the rows were offset, creating a labyrinth of turning corridors.

Saffron, Palomar, and the Babau became lost to him in the maze, and the glow of their weapons with them. Thaelios unsheathed his dagger for light, though the massive room's deep emptiness threatened to swallow it.

"There must be something magical about this place," he marveled aloud. "Its darkness is almost palpable."

"Can you bring that closer?" Dyphina asked, squinting to better see Be'naj's palm.

Thaelios obliged, meeting the women half-way as they exited the transport compartment. Be'naj's hand was bubbling slightly, and Thaelios's side twitched with the memory of Gullagion's acid melting his flesh. Her burns didn't appear nearly as deep, though still clearly agonizing. Be'naj was biting her lower lip to cope.

"What we need is a quick drink from that Celestial Spring, though we'll have to settle for our waterskins." Dyphina ducked behind Be'naj to dig into her backpack. "We've got to rinse this so it doesn't get worse, even if it hurts."

Be'naj winced, grasping her right wrist to manage the pain. Just as Dyphina started pouring water over Be'naj's hand, a snarling scream made Thaelios jump in his skin, nearly causing him to drop his Celestial blade.

"Saffron! Are you all right?" Be'naj called out, though the sound hadn't seemed human in origin.

"*We're safe*," Palomar responded, still beyond sight, "*though we're now short a guide.*"

"Not that we could trust that one," Dyphina noted under her breath. She replaced the waterskin and rummaged through Be'naj's pack to find the bandages. "I don't think you're going to be able to grip your sword for a while, Be'naj. At least not comfortably."

Be'naj nodded but stared at Thaelios, communicating her intention to remain useful, while Dyphina wrapped her hand.

White light, piercing gaps in the shelves, announced Saffron's and Palomar's return. It took several minutes for them to navigate the twists and turns of the stacks before coming into view themselves. "This place is endless," Saffron said, slightly out of breath. Stray curls of her dark hair made her appear as frazzled as she sounded.

"How *are* we supposed to find what we need?" asked Dyphina. She looked back at the transport chamber. "We don't know that we're even on the right level."

"I believe we are," Thaelios countered. "I can still read Abyssal, even if my conversational skills have atrophied. The glyphs that lit up roughly translate as 'Extra-Abyssal Planes, Rarely Traveled.' That seems accurate for Ishmere."

Saffron walked to the nearest row of shelves and propped her spear against it. It was lined, just like the others, with fist-sized, cubicle bricks of a stone similar to the outside of the spire. She lifted one from its resting place and hefted it.

Thaelios moved closer and saw that, like the wall of the transport, the surface of the stone was marked by a second, smooth material in the shape of an Abyssal rune. "Torimath," he read. The rune lit up, its radiance soft and blue.

"Is that the name of a Plane?" Saffron asked.

Thaelios shrugged. There were more Destination Stones on this level of the repository alone than he had memories in his head – bookworm or no, there was no way he could be familiar with all of them. "I would postulate so."

Saffron replaced the stone on the shelf. "So is there some sort of indexing, or do we have to wander this entire structure trying to find a singular brick amongst this?" She extended and slid her palm through the air to indicate the vastness before them. "The entire Tanar-ri army is likely to be outside by the time we succeed."

"*I have an idea,*" Palomar said. He sheathed his sword. "*That stone responded to its rune being called out. If we sheathe our weapons and make it completely dark, I can use my song to project my telepathy beyond its normal range. If I fly above the shelves, calling out for* Ishmere, *I should be able to pick out its light in the darkness."*

"That's brilliant, Palomar," Be'naj said, patting the Aasimar's shoulder with her left hand. Thaelios nodded his agreement as the others murmured theirs.

"Put away your weapons, please – the darker the better." Everyone did as asked, and Palomar began singing.

Goosebumps pricked along Thaelios's arms, for Palomar's voice had a haunting quality in the utter blackness. Its sound was joined by the flapping of wings, both of which receded as Palomar rose toward the ceiling, high above. Silence resumed as the singing ceased – the Aasimar was too far away to hear his flying. Then, piercing the stillness, the repeated echoes of *"Ishmere,"* blossomed in Thaelios's mind. All he could do was hope and wait. Worry about what might be gathering on the surface had just started to creep in when the telepathy changed.

"It worked. I found it!"

One of the women hissed, "Yes!" but Thaelios couldn't tell who it was in the dark. In another few moments, the flapping of wings and the soft blue glow of the Destination Stone heralded Palomar's return. Saffron uncovered the tip of her spear, which had been hidden beneath her shield on the floor.

"That's the one, right?" Dyphina asked.

Thaelios took a closer look as Palomar held out the cube. Already, its rune was fading, but sure enough, it read 'Ishmere.' "That's it," he nodded. Without need for another word, they packed into the transport chamber and Thaelios scanned its walls for the glyph that would take them back to the ground floor.

As soon as the panels opened again on the ground level, a peeling screech from the Quasit greeted them. It leapt from its perch and flew out of the main doors into the heavy Abyssal air beyond. The forge fires cast their eerie red glow upon the nearby landscape, and when Thaelios reached the exit, he found his earlier fears weren't baseless.

Silhouetted by the firelight were a quartet of demons: presumably the Vrock who escaped, a pair of additional Babau, wielding glaives, and a hulking monstrosity three times Thaelios's height. This Tanar-ri was not only tall, but thick, looking almost squat despite its height. It had wide horns like a bull's, strong arms that ended in sharp, serrated pincers, and a pair of proportionally tiny humanoid arms in the center of its chest, as if an unlucky mortal had lost its limbs only to have them sewn near the demon's heart.

Thaelios had seen something like this from afar when the battle began near the Abyssal stair, but up close the sight incited panic. The ground shook when this giant took a step forward, for the demons had clearly spotted their prey.

"*Glabrezu,*" Palomar stated, his tone tinged by awe. "*We should run. Run!*" he yelled, his voice more urgent than his usual serenity suggested possible. The Aasimar tossed the Destination Stone to Thaelios, pointed to his left, then drew his weapon and faced the demons.

The others obeyed, sprinting in the direction Palomar had pointed, though Thaelios quickly fell behind. His knee throbbed, and though he struggled to block out the pain, it slowed him nevertheless. He glanced over his shoulder to check on the singing Palomar, who had taken to the air and was now enveloped in a cocoon of white light. A blow from the Glabrezu's massive pincer nearly knocked the greatsword from the Aasimar's hand, but Thaelios had to return his attention to his footing, lest he trip again.

He was past the forges, heading back into the darkness, with the clang of metal and snaps of thunder exploding behind him. As sure as he was that Palomar was a force to be reckoned with, Thaelios felt certain the Celestial was overmatched. He had the sinking feeling the recent past was playing out again as the light of Saffron's spear grew more distant ahead of him.

He switched the Stone to his left hand and drew his weapon, determined not to sprawl to the ground a second time. The short blade created a swirl of disconcerting shadows as he ran, its movement making him dizzy. The pain in his knee was getting worse, and his breath grew ragged as he pushed himself to his limits. And still, Saffron's light grew dimmer.

Sparing a look back, Thaelios noted the red glow of the forges was now far behind, painting a nightmarish horizon, but Palomar's white was gone. "Thank you, friend," he said aloud, though no one was around to hear him. The futility of trying to keep up seized him, and he realized that if the demons used his light to pinpoint him, they may be able to teleport instantly to his side. As much as it felt like suicide to do so, he stopped running and sheathed his weapon.

A blood-curdling screech from somewhere above startled him as he tried to catch his breath. He looked upward but could see nothing. Panic caused him to take off again, but after a few steps he stopped, sure that his leg would fall off in protest should he continue. The weight of the Destination Stone in his hand compelled him to squeeze it. His own despair was heightened by the realization that, without this artifact, none of his companions would have a chance to escape, either. The calm of resignation slowly replaced his dread. They were all doomed.

As a last act of frustration, he lifted the Stone above his head to smash it on the ground. Before he could, a *swoosh* of air and a startling impact lifted Thaelios from his feet. Only, he never hit the ground.

"*I've got you,*" Palomar grunted, the flapping of feathery wings proving he was real through the blackness.

Thaelios struggled to keep from dropping the Stone, which was still extended awkwardly. "How did you find me?" he asked after managing to tuck the cube against his chest.

"*I too can see in the dark, though not as far as the Tanar-ri.*" His voice was clear but sounded strained. Though concerned, Thaelios was too frightened to question why.

"Were you victorious?" he asked instead.

"*My legs are broken, my sword as well, but I've bought us some time. It should be enough … behold!*"

Thaelios felt ashamed for his complaints, albeit unvoiced, but after looking toward the ground ahead, all that was forgotten. In the near distance, lightning danced between unseen clouds, and beneath it swirled an enormous whirlpool of animate chaos. Grey caps highlighted the dark matter of its shadowy substance. From the air, the phenomenon looked to be a mile or more across.

At the closest edge, Thaelios spotted the white lights of his friends' weapons, all drawn. Palomar descended toward them, the sound of a mighty wind reaching Thaelios as they approached the Chaos Cyclone. The women looked up in surprise when Palomar got close enough for them to hear his wings, but relaxed when they recognized him. The Aasimar set Thaelios gently upon the ground, but continued to hover.

Dyphina skipped forward and threw her arms around Thaelios. "I was so scared we'd lost you again!"

"How did you escape, Palomar?" Saffron asked, relief coloring her words.

"*There will time for tales, later,*" he replied. "*We should leave the Abyss as soon as possible.*"

"What do we do next?" Thaelios extracted himself from Dyphina, hoping to help along the process.

"*As there is only one Destination Stone, we must create a chain of contact to its holder. Join hands.*"

Keeping the Stone clutched firmly in his left hand, Thaelios sheathed his weapon and extended his other arm. Dyphina's expression sobered, and she put away her weapon before locking her fingers around his wrist. Saffron's face went grim before she dropped her spear and shield, then held Dyphina's open hand. Next came Be'naj, and lastly Palomar, who had to stretch to reach her while staying aloft.

"*Now, Thaelios, activate the Stone by speaking its rune, and we should all enter the Cyclone on the count of three.*"

"Ishmere," Thaelios uttered. The Destination Stone lit up, its blue light adding a ghostly tinge to his skin. He took a deep breath and counted down, "Three, two, one."

Together, they jumped into the swirling shadow. The sensation was similar to leaping into a tall pile of sand. Thaelios sank immediately past his knees, then slowly descended further as they were whisked away along the rim of the spinning Cyclone. It seemed to be moving much faster than it had when observed from above. Palomar was still higher than the others, only into his knees while the rest had sunken to their waists.

Thaelios continued to hold the Stone up high, though he wasn't sure he needed to. The churning became nearly deafening and the spinning disorienting. He had just closed his eyes to see if that would bring some calm when he felt the Destination Stone lifted from his hand!

His eyes shot open to see the Quasit from the obsidian spire flying across the Chaos Cyclone, their only hope for survival securely in its grasp. He looked in panic to Dyphina beside him, but her whipping green hair hid her face. Thaelios could see, however, that she'd released Saffron and extended her free arm toward the miniature demon.

A trio of illuminated bolts launched from her fingers and struck the Quasit, who dropped the Destination Stone into the Cyclone before crashing down itself. Thaelios struggled in horror to pull himself free from the Abyssal shadow, but could manage to lift only a finger's length before continuing to sink. The Destination Stone seemed to momentarily float on the surface of the Cyclone, a handful of body lengths away, taunting him. Though not physically far, it might as well have rested back on Elisahd for all he could reach it.

At the end of the line, which Thaelios could see as they curved along the spiral of the Chaos Cyclone, Palomar was also fighting to break loose. Not yet as deeply submerged as the others, and able to use his furiously flapping wings for leverage, the Aasimar pulled free and flew to where the Stone had now sunken beyond sight.

Palomar plunged back into the churning waves of Chaos, reaching beneath the surface to grasp for the Destination Stone.

Thaelios was now down to his armpits, watching helplessly as Palomar struggled to retrieve what he had lost. Finally, with a triumphant stretch, the Aasimar hoisted the rune cube high over his head.

His wings were now caught, however, and more of Palomar's body lay hidden beneath the surface than was above it. He struggled briefly, then relented. The noise of the spinning maelstrom filled Thaelios's ears, and he doubted he could have heard himself speak, but Palomar's telepathy cut through clearly.

"*I cannot get free, my friends. I will toss the Stone, and one of you must catch it. It has been an honor to know you, and I will not truly be lost if you remember me.*" With that, Palomar hurled the Destination Stone in their direction. Thaelios could see hands reaching for it, but was nearly submerged himself and wasn't sure what happened. He felt Dyphina's hand tighten around his wrist, and then he was beneath the surface.

Thaelios instinctively held his breath. His ears popped, then all became completely calm, like he was weightless in an endless sea.

Chapter 12

Ishmere

I n an instant, Be'naj's body was crushed so thoroughly that she almost didn't recognize it drifting away beneath her, drawn by a weight she no longer felt. She didn't feel anything, she realized, though the lifeless sacks of her companion's crumpled forms joined hers in a relentless journey toward the bottom of some unfathomable sea.

Be'naj's consciousness continued, though she experienced it differently without a corporeal anchor. She concentrated on projecting her cogitations, wondering if perhaps that was how Palomar expressed himself.

"Can anyone hear me?" she thought. *"Is this real?"*

Not all sensory input had vanished. Without understanding how, she witnessed three translucent spheres floating beside her. Pale, golden light defined their surfaces, the reflected gleam of bright sparks suspended in their centers. Beyond their auras, the world appeared midnight blue, rapidly darkening to solid black with distance.

"*Be'naj, is that you? What is happening?*"

It sounded like Saffron, though Be'naj assumed the thoughts came from one of the nearby spheres of light, as they were the only things visible. Did she share that fate?

"*It appears the transition to this world has resulted in a replacement of our physical forms ...*"

Be'naj witnessed one of the glowing globes, clearly Thaelios, pulsing in time with his thought-speech. She could still see, but did so from inside this bubble that now encased her consciousness.

"*Dyphina, are you here, too?*" Saffron said.

Before Be'naj heard a response, her mind turned to Palomar. Only three other spheres were present, so what had become of their Aasimar companion?

"*I am, but gods if this isn't strange,*" Dyphina answered.

"*Did anyone see what happened to Palomar? Did he go under?*" Be'naj didn't expect her companions to have an answer, but she wasn't ready to accept a reality where they'd lost him completely.

Thaelios answered after a short silence, "*I'm sorry, friends. I lost the Stone – it's my fault he's gone.*"

"*We're not doing that,*" Saffron said. "*Neither laying blame, nor giving up. We're going to find Palomar.*"

Be'naj loved Saffron for her certainty. Of course, Thaelios couldn't let it stand.

"And how are we supposed to find anything?" he asked. *"We don't even have bodies."*

From a great distance, further than Be'naj had any right to see, a pulse of light, small but steady, flashed like a lighthouse beacon. *"Do you see that?"*

"See what?" Dyphina responded. *"Besides us, everything is darkness."*

"There it is again!" Be'naj was sure, now. *"Some sort of blinking, very far away. I think we should head for it. It's calling to me."* She felt the same sense of guidance that came with her trance-visions. She was confident that they should follow, but wasn't sure how to move.

Putting all her focus toward reaching the beacon, Be'naj's mind-sphere started moving, or at least it seemed to, relative to the others. *"You just have to concentrate. Try to follow me,"* she said, unsure she should feel quite as pleased as she nevertheless did.

Be'naj found she could look in any direction without it affecting her movement, and soon the others had mastered propulsion as well, gliding through their environment with mental effort alone.

"Is this Ishmere?" Saffron asked. *"Can the gods live in such a desolate place?"*

Thaelios responded, *"Little is known of the Juda-cai, beyond what we've extrapolated from their Avatars in ancient times. What we need to figure out is how we're going to get our bodies back."*

"*Shecclad will help us*," Be'naj stated, growing ever more confident as the beacon grew larger. If this was the world of the gods, then it must be the Sky Lord calling to her. "*Surely you can see it now?*"

"*The space around us looks turquoise, probably because of our light,*" Dyphina answered. "*But that quickly fades to black, Be'naj, and I don't see anything more than a few body-lengths out. Well, the length of what our bodies used to be. What will I do if I can never touch again?*"

"*It's there, I promise you,*" Be'naj said, ignoring Dyphina's last question. "*Even if I'm the only one who can see it,*" she said more softly.

"*I trust you,*" Saffron said. "*We cannot have come all this way for nothing. Perhaps your god can help us.*"

Had Be'naj had lips, she would have been smiling. All she wanted was a chance to share with Saffron some of what she'd felt since she was a young Eladrin, back in the Mystic's shrine in Gilsage. If Saffron gave her a chance, Be'naj could show her the blessings of Shecclad were real.

Time was difficult to track with no actions to fill it. It stretched on and on, but the beacon grew ever closer. At last, the pulsing stopped and the light began stretching toward her, expanding as it did until all the darkness was brightened. Once the radiance washed over her, it blinked out of existence. In its place, filling her entire frontal visual field, was a mind-sphere similar to hers, only significantly larger.

"*Where did that come from?*" Dyphina exclaimed.

"*Are we in danger?*" Saffron added.

"*It's ... Shecclad,*" Be'naj answered, somehow sure of it.

"*Yes, my Chosen. You have found me at last.*" The voice was male, strong yet reassuring. Be'naj realized she'd been waiting most of her life for this feeling of acceptance. This was more than just hearing a mysterious voice. With the remainder of her being, she felt a presence joining with her. She welcomed it.

"*We have traveled through much to be here, my Lord. We come seeking answers.*"

Saffron's persistence had not perished with her body. "*Pardon my intrusion ... Shecclad, but we have lost much,*" she said. "*Is there anything you can do to restore us to our former state?*"

Shecclad's mind-sphere remained still and silent, worrying Be'naj that Saffron had offended him with her request. At last, though, he answered, "*I have watched you alongside my Chosen, fire-singer. You have a part yet to play. Each of you do, but none so important as the daughter of Celestia.*

"*What you do not understand is that you exist now because I saved you. The pressure here is too much for corporeal figures, for we dwell far beneath the surface of Ishmere. I preserved your essences when your bodies could not survive.*"

"*So you don't have a body, either?*" Saffron asked.

"*I have no need of one. Not in this realm, at least. I create different forms when visiting other Planes. All of the Juda-cai do.*"

Thaelios made a sound like he was clearing his throat, though of course at the moment such a gesture seemed ridiculous. "*If you don't mind my asking, your Lordship, why do you live here if the depths cannot support physical life? Why not go to the surface?*"

"Because bodies can be destroyed by numerous means. We used to live above, but learned our lesson when a pair of nearby stars collided. Everything we'd built was wiped away in an instant. But now, here, without bodies, we have nothing left to lose. Nothing others can take."

"I'm sorry if I seem simple," Dyphina interjected, *"but isn't life without a body* boring?"

Once again, a pause left Be'naj nervous. Her friends seemed to be asking all the wrong questions.

"Our passions play out across the cosmos, little one, which brings us to why you are here ..."

Be'naj was unsure if she was supposed to offer an explanation, or wait to be told.

"Conversations might be easier if you felt more at home." With that, Shecclad's huge sphere raced toward them, and Be'naj braced for an impact she only partially realized she shouldn't feel. A moment later, she was her old self, standing near the peak of a mountain.

The air was fresh and cool, blowing her long hair from her shoulders while the sunlight played its soft warmth upon her skin. Low clouds created a blanket further down the slope, concealing the true altitude, though she felt it must be significant.

Saffron, Dyphina, and Thaelios all stood nearby, looking over their own bodies as if they belonged to strangers. Be'naj smiled and threw her arms around Saffron's neck, nuzzling her soft hair and inhaling her sorely missed scent: lavender and sage.

A shadow passed over them and Be'naj looked up to see a huge bird diving toward the peak. Like a giant eagle, but with two extra pairs of eyes down its neck and wearing a halo of miniature blue stars, it circled once, then landed upon a twisted, windblown tree that clung almost sideways to the mountainside.

"Is that better?" The voice was still Shecclad's, but it seemed physically audible, coming from the bird though its beak never opened.

"Much," Dyphina replied, nodding and running her fingers over the bare skin of her arms. She wore a seafoam colored dress that flowed outward below a fitted bodice.

Noticing the change in clothing, Be'naj looked down at what she was wearing. Though it didn't seem to carry the weight she associated with iron alloys, she was adorned in a silvery breastplate also fitted to her form. Complete with greaves and gauntlets, it more than rivalled the Celestial armor worn by the Seraph.

"Is this real?" she asked.

"Not yet," Shecclad replied. "For now, you all exist within the creation of my mind, though I have the power to grant you physical bodies again. Alas, doing so now, you would lose them again instantly. But the armor is my first gift to you, Chosen. It shall protect you even from fiends of shadow, for whom steel is no barrier. "

"I have done nothing to deserve it, but I thank you." Be'naj found it difficult to speak further, so thankfully Saffron stepped in.

"Mighty Shecclad, we are all grateful to have your audience. Indeed, we risked our lives …" Saffron swallowed before continuing, "as did others, to reach you. We believe there is a deadly threat to the Eladrin on our world, and that it has something to do with your kind."

Shecclad laughed sardonically. "The Eladrin have a history of thinking *my kind's* very presence is a threat to them," he boomed. The eagle turned its head so that all three sets of eyes stared at Thaelios simultaneously. "That's why your ancestor, Trigilas, had us banished, no?" The monstrous bird's sharp talons tightened against the tree trunk, which crackled under the pressure.

Thaelios wilted under the intense stare, which relented soon after this achievement.

Saffron, however, did not. "Your pardon, Shecclad, but the threat I speak of comes from something called the Spawn of Raug. Does that mean anything to you? Is Raug not one of your people?"

Shecclad lifted his wings and took a moment to clean his feathers before responding. "Raug is one of the Juda-cai, yes." He sounded almost disinterested. "He has many progeny, for Raug has a strange proclivity for mating with numerous mortal species. It is a desire I don't quite understand."

Saffron visibly shook off his digression. "What about the Name of the Beast? They are the ones plotting against the Eladrin, and seem to have Abyssal ties."

"Yes," Shecclad replied with certainty. "I have been watching their development and now realize what they are. You would do well to remain vigilant against this cult, for their true power comes from beyond your Plane."

"What can you tell us, my Lord?" Be'naj asked, eager to finally receive an answer.

"Long before you were born, my Chosen, a human Shaper used an ancient elwise portal, abandoned by the firstborn, to summon a fiend well beyond his capacity to control. She was a

Marilith, but instead of smiting the Shaper immediately for his insolence, she mated with him, and passed his sorcerous blood to a set of twins – half-fiends who were free to travel between worlds."

"I think we met one of them in the Doomwait," Be'naj said.

"Excaliana?" Saffron responded.

Be'naj nodded, then turned back to the giant eagle on his perch. "Please, my Lord, go on."

"Unlike most of the Tanar-ri, Mariliths tend to be patient. I have no doubt she's long had plans to corrupt the world of the mortal who dared summon her all those years ago, and they are finally coming to fruition."

Thaelios took a step forward. He was dressed in a fine blue tunic, decorated with silver embellishments that played off the tone of his metallic-colored skin. "So, the Spawn of Raug are real?"

Shecclad stretched his neck. "I have no doubt my brethren has left dangerous progeny behind wherever he visits, but I don't have knowledge of the specific threat you speak of."

Thaelios's eyes and lips tightened pensively. "I think we should seek out Rinn-Rhulian to get to the bottom of this."

"But Raug is not the Juda-cai you should now be most concerned with. Indeed, while I have been concerned with the Name of the Beast and wished to warn you of them, I have become aware of a more subtle but insidious plot.

"Before I reveal it, I have a proposal for my Chosen." Shecclad stared straight at Be'naj. "I have tested you for many of your years, Be'naj, knowing you would one day seek me out." The eagle lowered its head in her direction. "You are unique, and I would have you as my Champion, if you accept."

Be'naj could hardly believe it. Of course she would be his Champion! The Sky Lord had spoken to her for years, had guided her steps toward protecting the vulnerable ... and yet, before now, he'd always been so cryptic. Doubt crawled up Be'naj's insides, expanding from her stomach. If Shecclad knew of the peril they'd journeyed so far to stop, why had he not simply communicated what she needed to know back on Elisahd? If he truly wanted to join with her, could he not have decided to do so without placing her friends in danger?

Be'naj bowed her head, partly to hide her trembling. "I have always trusted your guidance, my Lord. I would be proud to fight for you, back on my world or upon others. But before I accept this great honor, might you allow me to ask one question?"

The eagle's various pairs of eyes blinked, though disconcertingly not in unison. "What would you know?"

"Could you not have communicated al this in a vision?" Be'naj brought a hand to her mouth, dismayed at the truth of her blooming realization. "Don't get me wrong, I am awestruck to be in your presence – but others are lost now because of the journey here, and they are so for trying to help me. That is a heavy weight to carry."

"I am sorry you have suffered, but you must stiffen, for there is more to come. Once I learned what Luprak was up to, I knew time was short and you must be tested more directly. The vision I bestowed was purposefully unclear because you needed to take the precise journey you did."

Be'naj shook her head, feeling bewildered. "I don't understand."

"Luprak already has a Champion on Elisahd, and you have heard of him: The Dread Lich himself, Hadrian No More. Even now, they are working to cast Elisahd into eternal Shadow."

"What does that mean, 'eternal Shadow'?" Dyphina asked.

Saffron had told Be'naj that the ghast she'd fought in the desert was one of Hadrian No More's lieutenants, and she'd heard frightful bedtime stories about the mad lich when she was a child. He was not an adversary they could take lightly.

Shecclad answered, but Be'naj interpreted his tone as waning in patience, "Elisahd, the Prime Material Plane you dwell upon, is connected to the Prime Elemental Planes of Air, Earth, Fire, and Water. They each shaped its creation, and that connection is maintained through the Touchstones – sites brimming with the power of those elements. Each Touchstone is attuned to one of the elements – for now. Luprak, through Hadrian No More, is attempting to realign the Touchstones to the Plane of Shadow. The Touchstones are intended to secure balance; if all four were attuned to the same Plane, it would merge with the Prime Material. In this case, Elisahd would be cast in Shadow. Your days would be dimmed and the nights darker. Plants would die off, and most of life would follow."

"Why would he do such a thing?" Be'naj asked aloud, though the thought was intended for herself.

"Because the undead thrive in shadow," Shecclad answered, "and Luprak is obsessed with bringing night and doom upon all worlds."

"So what do we do to stop them?" Saffron asked, her voice more demanding than Be'naj thought appropriate.

The great eagle fluttered its wings and turned its head until all four mortals met its gaze. "Changing the alignment of a

Touchstone is not an easy thing. A mortal alone cannot do it – the power required is too great. The Juda-cai can affect such a change, but only through our Champion; only the favored bond is strong enough for that much Channeling. That is why it is imperative for you to agree to become mine, Be'naj.

"Furthermore, the Champion must be properly attuned to the Plane they seek to realign the Touchstone to. You see, I needed you to drink of the Celestial Fountain to attune yourself to another Plane, Be'naj, and prove you were worthy through your resourcefulness. Not just any person can handle the burden of being a Champion of the Juda-cai."

Be'naj's head spun with all this new information. How was she supposed to re-align these Touchstones and stop the Name of the Beast at the same time? She looked to Saffron. No matter where she had to go next, she didn't think she could bear it if Saffron could not go with her. Returning her gaze to the Sky Lord, she summoned the courage necessary to speak, afraid of what would come next. "I will become your Champion, Shecclad, though I still require guidance. How do I reach the Touchstones?"

Shecclad dipped his feathery head, his halo of blue stars swirling faster with the movement. "Their location is unknown to me, for I can only see through the eyes of my faithful. Trigilas's spell has closed the Veil of Nessus between our worlds, and I cannot send you home. I can transport you elsewhere, but returning to Elisahd and locating the Touchstones are tasks you must undertake."

Be'naj nodded. "If you return us to Mount Celestia, Hiruth Jeshu can send us home."

"That would be best," Saffron agreed, placing her hand upon Be'naj's shoulder guard. "We must report Palomar's fate to the Celestials. Perhaps they will have a way to find him."

"I will make these bodies real upon your departure from Ishmere," Shecclad announced as he stretched his wings to their full, impressive length, "but there is more about the Touchstones. Immediately after changing their alignment, one has a momentary window to lock the connection against future tampering. The mechanism to do so exists on the Ethereal Plane, however. Should you find a way to lock the Touchstone, it would prevent Hadrian No More from coming behind you and changing it again for a millennium."

Saffron hadn't removed her hand. "Changing the Touchstones and dealing with the Name of the Beast seem too difficult to do at once," she said. "I think we could use help, and I just had a crazy idea as to where we could find it."

"Ooh, this sounds promising," Dyphina cooed. "Do tell."

"You are not the only Champion of the Juda-cai I know, Be'naj."

"What do you mean?" Thaelios gave voice to Be'naj's own confusion.

"In the war against the King-priest, I fought with the Order of the Rising Moon. Their Grandmaster is the Champion of Criesha. Perhaps if we pay a visit, we can convince her to mobilize Jaiden toward our cause. More than the Eladrin are at risk from the Spawn of Raug, after all."

"Do you think he would do it?" Dyphina asked.

Saffron shrugged. "He would if Criesha asked. Or, more likely, commanded. Convincing her is our true obstacle."

Be'naj's heart seized upon the news. The more help they received, the more likely Saffron would be able to stay by her side. "Sky Lord, would you be able to send us to speak with Criesha?"

"We are not unfriendly," he replied, his tone suggesting interest at the development. "I could send your mind-spheres to her, and she could create physical bodies for you from the images I deliver. Give me a moment to inquire as to her amenability." All six of the eagle's eyes closed, and the halo of stars pulsed above his head. "She has agreed," he said as his eyes reopened. "Before I send you on your way, I have one last gift for you, Be'naj."

She fell to one knee, separating from Saffron, and bowed her head. "I do not ask for anything further, My Lord. I am forever blessed by being in your presence now, and this armor is already a boon beyond my deserving."

"Nevertheless, my Champion, this final gift seals our bond."

Be'naj felt a peculiar invigoration coursing through her wings, and when Shecclad said nothing further, she lifted her head. She looked in time to see them still expanding, their white and brass feathers lengthening as the bones supporting them did likewise. They stretched on, not stopping until the tips were further away than she would have been able to reach had her arms doubled as well. Her mouth fell agape, and she turned to Saffron to see her friend's eyes wide as they lingered upon Be'naj's wings.

"Go on, use them," Shecclad boomed. He flapped his own wings, rising from the perch of his tree trunk into the thin mountain air.

Be'naj's imaginary heart beat so quickly she thought it would burst, but Saffron was now smiling and nodding at her, and with a few mighty thrusts, Be'naj's wings carried her aloft. She continued gaining altitude, rising higher until she had cleared the peak. Shecclad circled not far above, and with previously unused muscles, she pivoted the angle of her wings, beating them to rush forward into the growing wind.

Joy threatened to consume her as she turned again to follow the great eagle, looking briefly at the ground far below while wishing this feeling would last forever.

Chapter 13

Starlight
and Waterfalls

Eventually, Be'naj had to come down, though her wings felt strong enough to fly forever. The others waited for her upon the mountainside as she descended, no doubt eager to continue their journey. It seemed like a lifetime since she'd last seen the hot springs at Skywatch Haven, and she imagined her companions suffered at least a twinge of homesickness, too.

Shecclad reclaimed his perch once Be'naj landed, the wood crackling under the pressure of his mighty talons. "Are you ready to visit Criesha?"

Be'naj looked to Saffron, hoping things hadn't changed between them because of her elevated status, and received a nod in response. A glance at Dyphina produced a similar reaction, but Thaelios timidly tapped his foot as if he had a question.

"Is there any chance you've recreated the spell books Dyphina stowed in her pack?" he asked the giant eagle.

"Oh, I completely forgot," Dyphina said. A backpack instantly appeared and he slung it from her shoulder to check the contents. Sure enough, it contained all of the previous pack's contents, including Cauzel's and Trigilas's books.

"Satisfied?" Be'naj asked.

Thaelios grinned. "Just wondering."

Her confidence brimming with her new gifts, Be'naj faced the Sky Lord. "We are ready."

"Very well, my Champion. Succeed on your quests, for there is much I look forward to achieving upon your world." Shecclad stretched his wings once more, and as soon as he flapped them, the mountain and the sky collapsed in on itself, disappearing to leave Be'naj standing in a dark, endless void.

Her friends were still with her, but they all drifted as if weightless. "Did something go wrong?" she asked.

"I don't know," Saffron answered. "I feel fine."

"Look!" Thaelios exclaimed, pointing into the empty space before them.

Only, it wasn't entirely empty anymore. The twinkle of distant stars began populating the void until it took on verisimilitude of the night sky. A bank of thin gray clouds swept in, carried on a sudden wind, to form a misty carpet under their feet. Heavenly bodies, nearer than the stars, crowded from above until planets, moons, and comets completed the illusion that they were somewhere beyond the normal pull of the world. While Be'naj was mesmerized by the scenery, a shaft of pale green light shone upon the clouds a dozen paces in front of her. Just as quickly as it had appeared, the light started fading. In its place stood a woman of undeniable, yet otherworldly, grace.

Her hair was dark and drawn up in a style of precise loops and curls, adorned with bands of silver set with emeralds. She wore a sleek blue gown, with extra fabric draped down the low-cut front. Her skin was luminescent, shaded slightly green like the shaft of light that brought her there.

Be'naj couldn't deny her immediate attraction toward the woman and felt guilty for it a breath later. She reached out and took Saffron's hand.

"Are you Criesha, then?" Saffron asked, apparently not nearly as impressed as Be'naj.

"Of course I am. You know that, just as I know who you are, Lady Saffron." The woman took slow steps toward them, her dress clinging to her thighs. "I must say, when Shecclad told me you were among a troupe seeking to petition me for aid … well, I cannot remember anything so unexpected." Criesha halted, close enough for Be'naj to see that her eyes were an unusually dark shade of blue – like the sea near the horizon when she took the ship to Zeblon.

"You, you're stunning," Dyphina murmured, a hand absently raising to her lips.

"Thank you," Criesha said, bowing her head slightly at the compliment. "I don't believe we've been introduced …"

"This is Dyphina and Thaelios," Saffron said tersely, "and I presume Shecclad mentioned his Champion, Be'naj."

Criesha smiled. "The Sky Lord mentioned each of you, but that is not the same as an introduction, now is it? You are *all* welcome to my realm." She extended her palms in a gesture to the night sky.

"Thank you," Thaelios, Dyphina, and Be'naj echoed while Saffron stood mutely, arms crossed over her chest.

"Now that we've been properly acquainted …" Criesha said, folding one hand over the other. "I know I'm immortal, but the suspense is just about killing me." She gave a sly smile, and Be'naj looked from her to Saffron, noting their eyes were locked upon one another.

Clearly, something odd was going on, but Be'naj couldn't fathom what kind of history Saffron could possibly have with a goddess. She'd never talked about anything remotely pious before. "My Lady," Be'naj began, trying to break the tension and hoping that Saffron would come around, "we have learned of several threats to our homeland recently and are in search of aid."

Criesha broke her stare with Saffron and angled her head toward Be'naj. "And what sort of succor were you seeking from me?" No sooner had she spoken than her gaze returned to Saffron.

"We—"

"I want her to ask," Criesha interrupted, gesturing toward the stoic Begnari.

Saffron huffed and uncrossed her arms. "I know you have some influence over Jaiden Luminere. We— I, was hoping you could convince him to help us stop a plot by the Name of the Beast. The cult is seeking to free a destructive force that would threaten Elisahd."

Criesha looked to be weighing Saffron's request for a few moments before answering. "See," she said, her features and posture relaxing, "that wasn't so hard, was it?" She walked closer to Dyphina and bent down to draw up a handful of cloud. Dyphina appeared nervous but didn't move, and Criesha gently blew on the grey vapor in her hand. It dispersed into a fine mist that encompassed the half-fey's head before disappearing entirely. "You have a secret," the Juda-cai said nonchalantly, letting her eyes trail down Dyphina's body before turning back to Saffron.

"So you want my Champion to fight beside you against great odds and at significant peril to himself and my cause ... and do you offer anything in return?"

"No," Saffron answered, as if she could barely be bothered. Her hands moved to her hips. "If I have things my way, Jaiden and I will be nowhere near one another. I don't know what *your* cause is, but Jaiden loves his homeland and would be protecting that. Though yes, there would likely be some risk. But as you would surely attest, your Champion is quite capable, yes?"

Be'naj could hardly believe her ears – Saffron was not nearly this irreverent to Shecclad, or at least not that she'd noticed. Was her friend going to put their cause in jeopardy simply because of *whatever* was between her and Criesha?

Thaelios stepped forward to salvage the situation. "What I think Lady Saffron is trying to say, honorable Criesha, is that our desires most likely intertwine. By all accounts, the Spawn of Raug are formidable creatures, and we have no way of knowing how many we may face. Preferably, we would stop the cult before they set any loose. But we have more than one imperative task to complete, and if I've read my friend's statements correctly, she intends to go with Be'naj on another quest," he glanced at Saffron, "leaving Dyphina and I to deal with the Name of the Beast." He strode calmly over to the half-fey and rested both hands upon her nearest shoulder. "As you can probably ascertain just by looking at us, martial prowess is not our strength. Until we learn otherwise, we should consider the entirety of Elisahd in danger, which means, like it or not, your Champion and all else you hold dear there. Confounding the cult quickly – before the situation grows more dire – seems our best course."

Criesha tilted her head askance as she considered the silver-haired Eladrin. "I had a long and mostly kind relationship with your people in the centuries prior to the Banishment."

Thaelios nodded slightly. "I have read many poems honoring your gifts, Lady Criesha."

"Ironic, isn't it, that I provided magical inspiration to the Eladrin when they first learned to create spells, only to have it used against my kind in the end."

Thaelios remained motionless and silent, and Be'naj worried once again that their hopes were slipping away. "I think our history with the gods is complicated," she said, hoping her intervention could smooth things over. "Even after the Banishment, the Eladrin continued their faithful worship of Eriane, and the Shrine of Shecclad in Gilsage has seen continual use as well."

"Yes, Be'naj." Criesha took a step back to get a better look at all four. "Some have remained pious, for sure." Her gaze came to rest on Be'naj after considering the others. "You are unique, aren't you? I have a feeling it was the Sky Lord who was blessed by your joining and not necessarily the other way around. So, a winged mortal and three Shapers. However this turns out, I shall have to keep an eye on each of you."

"And how will this turn out?" Saffron asked. "It's your decision, is it not?"

"Clearly your manner had nothing to do with why Jaiden pined so long for you. Hmm, I suppose you must have other *talents*, though obviously they weren't sufficient."

What was this? Be'naj thought her heart stopped beating for a moment. Had Saffron been in a romantic relationship with this other Champion? Did she still have feelings for him and that's why she was being so short with the goddess?

Saffron seethed but bit her tongue, then took a step closer to Be'naj and grasped her hand. "Jaiden missed out on something he never deserved, but it doesn't matter now. I've found the one I'm supposed to be with …" She punctuated this last statement with a squeeze of Be'naj's hand.

Confused emotions pulled Be'naj in different directions. She needed some time to work through everything but didn't think she could do so while still in the presence of this goddess. "Lady Criesha," she said once she found her voice, "can we count on you to intercede on our behalf? We would be most grateful – all of us." She looked into Saffron's dark eyes, strong and fiery, then down at their intertwined hands.

"Of course," Criesha said with a gentle smile, all the challenge removed from her tone. "I was already aware of the danger posed by this cult, and quite honestly, I think Jaiden is better motivated by a challenge. We can all use allies, after all, and I'm confident none of you will forget this."

Her last words lingered in the air until Be'naj punctuated them with her own voice. "Excellent. Then would you do us the further kindness of sending us back to Mount Celestia?"

"With these bodies, of course," Saffron added.

Criesha shook her head slightly, and Be'naj worried once again that all their plans were about to unravel. "Even the Juda-cai cannot Gate directly from a Lower Plane to an Upper one."

"I thought Shecclad said you could send us back?" Dyphina squeaked.

Criesha shut her eyelids at the high-pitched sound and sighed. "No, but I can send you as far as the Doomwait," she said as she opened her eyes, "and I trust you can make it from there. I doubt you would have ever reached me if you could not."

"That will be sufficient, thank you," Be'naj replied, willing the others to remain quiet long enough for them to be on their way. She was dying to find a peaceful spot to trance, with so much to consider.

Criesha nodded. "I will let Jaiden know to expect you soon, and look forward to our shared successes…"

"Thank you, my Lady." Be'naj bowed slightly.

"A pleasure to meet you," Dyphina shared, mirroring her bow. Thaelios mimicked her but had enough sense to remain silent.

Saffron did not. "I appreciate your help," she said, never letting go of Be'naj's hand.

Be'naj was pleasantly surprised and hoped the gesture mitigated the possibility that Saffron would reach their destination with some sort of physical deformity – Criesha would be the one granting them new bodies, after all.

Without responding, Criesha's body was suddenly enveloped in a green moonbeam and vanished. Be'naj and Saffron looked at each other, but before either could speak, the night sky collapsed on them in a rush. An instant later, with a rumble like thunder, the gloomy gray of the Doomwait replaced the void, and the four companions found themselves at the edge of Anarchiapolis.

"Is everyone all right?" Saffron asked. She still appeared like her normal, perfect self: long, dark hair, fiery eyes, and smooth, tanned skin.

In a flash of concern, Be'naj extended her wings and peeked to either side – they remained long and powerful, and already she yearned to fly again.

"Yes, and you?" Dyphina answered.

"We should make for the Rift with haste, given our lack of weapons and Be'naj's new physique," Thaelios added.

"Indeed," Be'naj agreed. "Perhaps I should fly ahead so as not to draw attention to the rest of you?"

Saffron shook her head. "I don't think it's necessary we split up."

"Perhaps not necessary, but possibly wise," Thaelios mentioned. "She does look more like an Aasimar than ever, and we know the reaction they tend to cause."

"Yes, I don't wish to put you in danger." Be'naj checked over each shoulder to see if she'd already drawn unwanted attention. Not seeing any Tanar-ri in plain view, she clasped her warm hands over Saffron's and leaned forward until their foreheads rested together. "Be swift, and I'll meet you at the Abyssal Rift."

Saffron licked her lips and nodded, caressing Be'naj's skin. After backing away to gain room, Be'naj leapt and, with a great flap of her wings, thrust into the gloomy air, taking silent enjoyment in her new ability.

Trusting Saffron would find a way to keep the others safe, she tested her wings to see how fast she could fly. Without scenery rushing by for context, it was hard to tell, but she felt as if she could keep pace with the birds that migrated south from Ifelian for winter. The crackling, bluish energy of the Rift appeared before she was truly ready and she circled above it a few times before landing. It would be foolish to tire herself before reaching the safety of Mount Celestia.

Waiting beside the Abyssal Rift was trying. Not only did its buzzing give her a headache, but time crawled and Be'naj started second-guessing herself. Had she been selfish to leave the others or was it truly for their own safety? She was about to head back toward Anarchiapolis when movement in the gloom caught her attention.

Be'naj resisted calling out, aware of the consequences if these were not allies. Soon enough, she caught the red flash of Saffron's kank-hide armor and was able to distinguish the group of three as they drew closer. She released the breath she'd been holding and rushed forth to greet her friends.

"Did you have any trouble on the way?" Be'naj asked, still fearful her choice had led to some unforeseen negative outcome.

"No, we're fine," Saffron assured her.

"It did seem longer than before, now that we weren't flying, too," Dyphina added. "But at least we remembered the way."

"I am eager to leave this place behind," said Thaelios, looking over his shoulder. "Might we step through and talk later?"

Be'naj nodded and took Saffron's hand. Together, they stepped through the Rift, its unsettling effects leaving Be'naj disoriented when they arrived in the tunnel underneath the Mountain. Once they'd all appeared, it hit her harder that Palomar wasn't with them. They'd returned to his home without him, and even though she knew the way, she missed his guidance.

"We have no weapons," Saffron noted. "No source of light."

It was true. Though the Rift itself crackled with blue and midnight energy, casting an eerie glow about them, Be'naj remembered the heavy blackness of the walk through the rest of the Mountain. There was no way they could navigate it in the dark.

"I can cast Cauzel's light spell on something," Thaelios said. "Give me a moment." Luckily, Criesha had faithfully re-created Be'naj's pack, and after foraging through it for a moment, Thaelios retrieved a drinking bladder. "*Lucemi*," he chanted, and the waterskin emitted a soft, white glow.

"Lead the way," Dyphina coaxed. Though he'd been hesitant to do so prior, Thaelios sighed and took the forward position. Perhaps they all felt the heaviness of Palomar's absence.

They walked the span of the tunnel in near silence. Be'naj's own somberness was reflected in the joyless faces of her companions. She tried preparing what to tell the other Celestials when she saw them, but fitting words eluded her.

The cave entrance and corresponding triangle of daylight lifted her spirits somewhat, and the eventual breath of the warm

Celestial wind upon her face carried a sense of solace with it. Though she experienced sadness at Palomar's loss, she didn't want to ascribe emotions to his brethren. Perhaps the Aasimar had ways of dealing with such things that she could learn from. Part of her belonged here, and she decided to pay closer attention to the ways of her previously mysterious heritage.

The training fields were busier than she'd seen them, and worry that their excursion had brought on dire circumstances gnawed at her gut. As she hesitated, Saffron passed her, heading determinedly toward the armory. As Be'naj followed, she noticed a crimson-haired Aasimar standing near the building with a pair of others and wondered if it might be Khanarme.

When they got closer, she recognized the Aasimar Marshall, who turned to face the mortal foursome as his companions dispersed. Be'naj had no doubt he'd noticed who was *not* with them.

"So, you survived your trek through the Abyss! I'm glad to see it," Khanarme said when they'd closed to within a dozen paces. *"Where is your guide, Palomar?"* he asked, crossing his arms over his thick chest.

Saffron kept moving and didn't answer until she'd drawn to a comfortable, conversational distance. "Marshall, I'm glad to see you alive as well. We succeeded in our mission, but also bring sad news." She hesitated and swallowed before continuing. "Palomar was separated from us and swept into the Chaos Cyclone without a Destination Stone. Is there something you can do to find him? I will go back to the Abyss myself if it will help."

Khanarme's face fell. *"That is grave news for Palomar, for there is no way of knowing where the Cyclone might send you."*

"What about Hiruth Jeshu?" Saffron asked.

"*May His Light Shine Forever, He might be able to discern Palomar's whereabouts, but we have pressing issues to deal with. Our own foray into the Abyss was not without losses, and violent incursions like this are always met with retaliation. You should leave this strata before the Tanar-ri arrive.*" Khanarme gazed beyond her toward the cleft in the Mountain, as if he expected to see demons rushing out at any moment.

The Marshall's lack of motivation to assist his fellow stunned Be'naj. "Don't you want to at least search for Palomar? He is probably stranded and alone, and we should help him!"

"*I assure you, Be'naj,*" Khanarme said as he uncrossed his arms and placed his fists on his hips, "*we feel the loss of every Aasimar, but the defense of Mount Celestia is paramount. If we do not see to it, there will be more losses, and Palomar would not want that.*"

She was impressed that the Marshall actually remembered her name. His expression softened while still managing to look grim. "*You should not hold out hope for your friend's return. The Abyss is infinite and full of enemies. Even if we could find Palomar, there is little chance he would survive that long. I will mourn him with the others when the time comes ... and you should do the same. It would be foolish to imagine otherwise.*"

"There is always hope!" Saffron interjected. "Perhaps if you knew Palomar better, you would remember that." Despite her words, Saffron's face crumbled and tears started to flow.

Be'naj couldn't stand it and cradled Saffron's head into her neck. She glared accusingly at Khanarme, who shifted his stance uncomfortably.

"*Have it your way*," he finally said. "*I must convene with the other Marshalls, but you should heed my words and leave as soon as possible. A battle with the hordes is not something I would expect mortals to survive.*" He stalked off, heading purposefully toward the center of the training field.

Saffron sniffed heavily and pulled back from Be'naj when he was gone. "I'm fine," she said, tear streaks still marking her cheeks. "We should find Rhazine and seek an audience with Hiruth Jeshu."

"May His Light Shine Forever," Thaelios added reflexively. He shrugged when Dyphina shot him a look and rolled her eyes.

The group marched toward the Ulimar village and located the house of Rhazine's host in short order. The Begnari girl seemed pleased to see them again, especially Saffron, and excitedly gathered her belongings when told it was time to leave. Saffron spent some time conversing with Rhazine in their native language, and it tickled and warmed Be'naj's heart to see Saffron's motherly instincts on display. She was patient while listening to the girl, who clearly had a lot to say, and Saffron even quickly braided Rhazine's hair to keep it from falling across her face during their upcoming walk.

"How do we reach Hiruth Jeshu?" Be'naj asked Grennald as Saffron helped Rhazine strap into her pack.

"*May His Light Shine Forever, the Bright Lord lives on the sixth peak. You must climb the Mountain.*" The Ulimar gestured toward the looming giant in the distance behind them, its higher reaches obscured by thin strips of wispy cloud.

"How long will that take?" she responded. Mount Celestia seemed very tall indeed, and she was not strong enough to carry her companions in flight.

"I will take you as far as I can, friends of Palomar," Grennald offered, "though I cannot ascend beyond the first peak."

"Oh, well we would certainly appreciate that," Be'naj replied, the unexpected gesture putting her somewhat at ease. She had no idea how easily one might become lost along the slopes. Grennald nodded, went inside his abode, and returned with a walking staff. The six of them started their hike toward the base of the Mountain.

They were taking a different path from the one that led to the tunnel beneath, and an idea popped into Be'naj's head as they drew closer to the Mountain. "Don't wait for me, I'll catch up," she said to Saffron, not pausing for a response before taking to the air.

The air was much fresher than it had been in the Doomwait, and even the mild sunshine granted a wider range of vision. She'd already seen that the avenues they'd walked upon were lined by trees, but the vast stretches of green she saw from above reminded her of Ifelian. The top of the canopy was highlighted by golden streaks of sunlight, the cleared spaces few and easily noticeable by contrast. The flight back to the Celestial armory was brief.

Be'naj didn't like the idea of their party being weaponless once they left the safety of Mount Celestia, and suspected that Hiruth Jeshu would not begrudge her borrowing from the Celestial stores. She could always return what she took if he objected. Not wishing to be greedy, she selected an arming sword for herself and a spear for Saffron, figuring the others would prefer to rely on their magic anyway. The Aasimar passing her on the way out nodded in recognition of her presence, but didn't question it.

Be'naj resumed flight and aimed for the direction the others had been heading. She spotted them before they reached the slope and rejoined them. Saffron appreciated her gift and used the spear as a walking stick as they gained elevation.

The path was smooth stone, wide enough for them to walk in pairs, but the incline left the tendons around Be'naj's foot sore. "How long do you think our climb will take?" Saffron asked the Ulimar after they'd been ascending for a while.

Grennald shrugged. *"You are mortal – our sense of time differs. What would you call the duration of our climbing so far?"* He glanced back as he asked his question, but continued walking.

"I would guess it's been about an hour?"

The Ulimar nodded, the dark curls on his head contrasting against his pale, luminescent skin. *"Then we will reach the first peak in perhaps ten hours."*

"The *first* peak?" Thaelios asked, slightly out of breath.

"Yes, the highest point that I am able to go. Mortals are not restricted, so you can continue from there."

"But, where would we go once we've reached the top?" the eladrin Shaper queried.

"Beyond," the Ulimar answered. *"You will see."*

Be'naj recalled the rapidity of their descent and wondered what the opposing experience might be like. They continued climbing in a spiral up the outside of the Mountain. Tall conifers dotted the slope during their ascent, blocking much of the view that would have validated their progress.

Saffron gasped and grabbed Be'naj's arm as they rounded a corner. The path dipped and widened onto a slightly bowed shelf at least a dozen paces across. A narrow meadow of wildflowers grew upon the soil-covered terrace, tucked away in a pocket of slanted sunlight, filtered green by the leaves of the surrounding trees. The blanket of violet, white, and gold petals reminded Be'naj of a miniature Skywatch Haven.

"May we take a moment?" Saffron called ahead to Grennald while already striding toward the blossoms.

"I think my feet could use a rest," Dyphina mumbled, skipping to join Saffron, the skirt of her pale green dress billowing in her wake.

The Ulimar didn't speak but took a seat on a rock, leaning forward on his staff with both hands. Be'naj took this as consent and strolled toward the middle of the meadow. Her armor was so light she could barely feel it, and she sat cross-legged amongst the flowers, tilting her head upward to catch the sun. She wasn't sure there was time to trance, but she assumed the familiar pose, wondering if Shecclad might visit her with a vision anyway.

Rhazine looked awestruck as she slowly wandered the perimeter of the meadow, gazing at the flowers and trees like they were precious works of art.

Dyphina giggled as Saffron tucked a tiny bouquet of flowers behind her ear, drawing Be'naj's attention. Saffron wore a similar arrangement, and a butterfly, appearing to be made of blue and clear crystal, fluttered about her hair.

"Ooh, look at that!" Dyphina gasped, pointing at the creature. "It's so beautiful." She reached out and extended her index finger, which the butterfly promptly alighted on.

"I think it feels the same way," Saffron said, smiling as she leaned in to get a better view.

Be'naj closely watched the two of them together. Was there something there she hadn't seen before? She shook off the sudden sting of jealousy. After all they'd been through together, it was only natural that Dyphina and Saffron had developed a tight friendship.

"As marvelous as the scenery may be," Thaelios interrupted, "I am eager to return to Ifelian. Do you think we might be on our way soon?" He'd walked up behind Be'naj, but she could imagine his dour expression without seeing his face.

Dyphina sighed. "Off you go," she said to the butterfly as she tossed it upward off her finger. It flew to another flower, unconcerned with the visitors' impatience. Saffron stood and offered her hand to Be'naj, who took it and rose as well.

Grennald was already a few paces further up the path as the others fell into line, and their trek continued. In what felt like a few more hours, judging by the fatigue of her legs, Be'naj spotted the peak of the Mountain at last. They were almost as high as the lowest clouds now, but the temperature had not noticeably dropped. As serene as it was, she wasn't sure how she'd take to living in a place where the weather never changed.

"*We will be there soon*," their guide stated.

As they climbed higher, they ascended to where they became level with the direct rays of the sun, which painted the surface of the mountainside a soft, golden color. They'd nearly reached the end; the summit touched the sky only a few body-lengths above the path's terminus.

Be'naj was about to ask where they were supposed to go from here, when she heard a tinkling sound, like distant chimes carried on the wind. A few steps further revealed shimmering air at the end of the path – a few more gave the faint, bending light a definite shape. A space resembling a wide, arched rectangle undulated with calm energy, leaving a completely different impression than the Abyssal Rift underneath Mount Celestia.

"This will take you to the next layer, my mortal friends. Would you like me to pass along a message to Palomar when he returns?"

Be'naj's stomach tightened uncomfortably at the mention of the lost Aasimar. She looked to Saffron, who knew Palomar longest and had already given news to Khanarme.

Saffron took a breath to steel herself, then simply replied, "When you see Palomar, give him our love."

The Ulimar nodded and stepped aside. Given that walking beyond the end of the path would result in a precipitous fall if the portal failed, Be'naj stepped quickly to the fore. "I'll go first," she volunteered, stretching her wings to prepare for flight, if necessary. "Thank you, Grennald, for taking us this far." She walked forward and stepped into the shimmering archway of air.

Unlike the Rift, the passage between strata was instantaneous and without disorientation. When she appeared on the other side, Be'naj was standing on the wet, sandy shore of a small lake, the majority of its circumference enclosed by sloping rock walls. The roar of numerous waterfalls of different heights and widths filled her ears, speaking of a tremendous water source higher up the mountain. Indirect light reached the cove from a large gap in one section of the rock-domed sanctum, leading to what she assumed was the surface of Mount Celestia.

Saffron, Thaelios, Rhazine, and Dyphina appeared one-by-one beside her, and Be'naj couldn't hide her smile as she turned to face them. "Have you ever seen such a sight?" She had to raise her voice to be heard over the crashing water, which filled the lake lapping at the beach just paces away. Be'naj turned back to the reservoir and took a few steps toward it, her feet sinking in the wet sand. She kneeled and touched the surface of the water with her palm. It was cool and looked clean. Leaning closer, she drew some of the liquid into her cupped palm and took a drink. "It's refreshing," she said over her shoulder before taking another sip.

The others joined her on the shore, slaking their thirst with cool water from the lake. "I don't know how long we've been traveling, but I'm guessing we could all use a rest, no?" Saffron asked.

Dyphina nodded. "I could sleep for a week."

"This seems like a perfectly good place to make camp," Saffron continued. "Look." She pointed across the lake toward a large, hollowed-out area beneath a wide waterfall. "I bet we could all fit in there."

Thaelios shrugged. "It's not like we've seen any predators on this plane. I would assume the whole area is safe."

"Just because the Aasimar live here doesn't mean that its animals don't still hunt," Saffron admonished.

Dyphina had already grabbed the hem of her dress and was lifting it up her body. "I haven't had a bath in weeks," she said. "Sorry, Thaelios, but you don't mind, do you?" Though she'd asked, Be'naj noticed the half-fey didn't wait for a response to finish removing her dress. Apparently Shecclad had gifted her silky undergarments to go with the outfit, but Dyphina quickly shimmied out of those as well.

"You haven't even had that body for two days," Be'naj pointed out, watching for Saffron's reaction to Dyphina's nakedness. "How dirty can you be?"

Dyphina ignored her and splashed into the water, shrieking as she went. "It's cold!" she yelled, but that didn't stop her from diving in head-first.

"Come on," Saffron said, turning her gaze to Be'naj. "It looks like fun, and it may help with aching muscles." She winked before starting to unfasten her armor.

"I'll … just explore a little," Thaelios said, already walking around the edge of the lake to give the women privacy.

Rhazine conversed with Saffron in Begnari, then started disrobing as well. Be'naj sighed, torn between being left out and exposing herself to the others. She'd been naked with Saffron before, sure, but they were alone and connected in a way she'd never experienced. Finally, once the other women were all in the water, she turned her back to them and removed her armor and underclothes.

Now that her wings were longer, Be'naj found she could wrap them forward to partially conceal herself. She did so until waist-deep and able to push forward to swim. The water *was* cold, but Be'naj found it refreshing, and her body acclimated after a few moments.

She folded her wings behind her as she swam, but they still created more resistance than she liked, and making headway was a chore. She made the effort to swim toward Saffron, who'd managed to nearly reach the center of the lake. The water was dark that far away from shore, and Be'naj imagined the reservoir was quite deep, perhaps fed by some underground aquifer.

"See, wasn't this worth it?" Saffron asked as they treaded water. She looked around, and Be'naj followed her cue to take in the array of surrounding waterfalls. The view truly was spectacular. Saffron took a deep breath and submerged, quickly swimming beyond Be'naj's sight in the deep water. Rhazine and Dyphina were slowly making their way over, laughing as they playfully splashed one another. Be'naj wasn't used to seeing the foreign girl smile.

Just when Be'naj started to worry about Saffron's lack of resurfacing, she felt a hand grab hers and Saffron's head thrust above the water like it'd been shot from a bow. Saffron huffed in fresh air but was smiling, and shook the water from her face before wiping her eyes with her spare hand.

"It's really far down," she yelled over the sound of the waterfalls. "I couldn't touch the bottom."

"I'm not sure you should try," Be'naj said, happy to feel the touch of Saffron's skin.

"So, I feel pretty much the same, but how do you like your new body?" Saffron asked. "I mean, you can *fly* now. That must be pretty great."

Be'naj thought about it and couldn't keep from smiling. "Yes, Shecclad gave me a great gift." She was going to expound but Dyphina and Rhazine had drawn near, their splashing and shrieks making the space seem even more crowded.

The four of them tread water for a while as Saffron taught Dyphina and Be'naj a few words in Begnari, so Rhazine could feel included. After they'd successfully learned to pronounce *waterfall, fish,* and *swim,* Be'naj suggested they move back toward the shore so they didn't completely tire out and drown.

Saffron swam back next to Be'naj, and when it became shallow enough that they could stand and keep their heads above water, Saffron took hold of Be'naj's hips under the surface and guided her thighs wider until Be'naj's legs wrapped around Saffron's waist.

Be'naj wasn't sure what to make of it, but didn't say a word. The look on Saffron's face was so intense that she dared not question her and wrapped her hands around the back of Saffron's neck to keep stable as Saffron supported her by the buttocks.

"Being in the water reminds me of the first day I met you," Saffron said just loud enough for Be'naj to hear.

Be'naj found it suddenly took more effort to breathe, and her heart beat faster, joining a tingling sensation that expanded from somewhere beneath her belly to between her legs. "I ... I remember," was all she could manage. Saffron was gently raising and lowering Be'naj, whose sex was pressed against Saffron's belly. The tingling was getting stronger.

"I think I'm going to get out and dry," Dyphina said, making splashes as her knees broke the surface of the lake. Rhazine followed suit.

"Do you want to get out, too?" Saffron asked, her voice huskier than usual.

Be'naj let out a breath, then swallowed, searching to find her voice as the pulsing in her nether regions intensified. She was worried she might explode if it continued and didn't want to embarrass herself. "I, I think we should," she finally managed to say, unwrapping her legs from Saffron's middle.

She proceeded out of the water without looking back at Saffron, folding her wings around her again for modesty, and headed for her pile of clothes. Be'naj kept her head down as she donned her armor, noting how light each piece felt, but unable to concentrate on anything but the image of Saffron's beautiful face, framed by dark wet hair, and how her body had reacted to their embrace. When she finished and turned back to the lake, she saw that Dyphina, Rhazine, and Saffron were all still naked, leisurely reclining on the sand, propped up on their elbows.

"Mmm, that swim was just what I needed," Dyphina said, working her toes into the course, wet grains. "You know, I could fall asleep right here."

"I'm guessing that's not *all* you needed," Saffron joked from where she lay across from the half-fey. She smiled and wrestled Dyphina's toes with her own, then stared up at Be'naj and bit her lower lip as her expression grew more serious. It was like she was daring Be'naj to match her gaze, to see her body willingly exposed and still maintain the reserve not to act—

"I'm going to trance," Be'naj announced, trying to push such thoughts from her head. "The rest of you should sleep as long as you need to recover, then we can continue up the Mountain." She left the three women to dry out and enjoy one another's company, instead searching for where Thaelios had gotten off to.

Be'naj found him sitting cross-legged under the fronds of a giant fern half-way around the lake. She headed for him, stopping at a respectful distance so as not to intrude, then assumed the position herself and started to clear her mind.

Be'naj's subconscious mind never strayed far from thoughts of Saffron as she tranced. By the time she emerged, she realized that her earlier behavior was only running from something that she wanted because she was scared. She had crossed a continent to find Saffron, and loved her, and now it appeared that Saffron wanted to be with her as well. She was no longer an adolescent, and Saffron wasn't the eladrin boy who'd played such a hurtful trick on her.

Summoning her courage, she arose and headed back to the beach. Thaelios was no longer nearby, but she didn't bother looking for him. Instead, she walked to where the women had fallen asleep on the sand, both relieved and perhaps disappointed that Saffron had dressed again before nodding off.

Be'naj knelt and gently shook Saffron awake, then held a finger to her lips when Saffron started to ask a question. Not wanting to wake the others, Be'naj boldly took Saffron's hand and led her toward the waterfall with the carved-out hollow behind it.

The crushing weight of the falling water grew louder as they approached, but she wasn't sure that it made more noise than the rapid beating of her heart. After looking back to make sure the others were still asleep and they were unnoticed, Be'naj led Saffron carefully over the wet rocks and behind the waterfall.

It was too loud now for talk, but she sensed that Saffron understood her intent. They stood facing each other for a couple of deep breaths before Saffron pulled her hand from Be'naj's grasp to cup her cheeks in both palms. Saffron leaned forward and pulled Be'naj's face toward her.

Be'naj was led willingly, and closed her eyes just as her lips parted slightly to meet Saffron's. The instant they touched was electric. A latent hunger took over, and they kissed desperately as if afraid the moment would never come again. Be'naj's hand found its way into Saffron's hair, and she used it to push Saffron's head forward, as if somehow they might find a way to melt into one another. They kissed deeply until both ran out of breath.

Be'naj breathed raggedly when they finally parted, wanting to express how this moment had instantly made the rest of her life make sense, but her head was spinning and she couldn't find the words, and then suddenly they were kissing again.

Saffron's hands went down to Be'naj's armor and Be'naj's did likewise to Saffron's. They both struggled blindly finding a way to disrobe the other, unwilling to break their kiss again. The attempts proved futile, so they eventually parted, simultaneously deciding it would be easier for them to each take off their own armor.

"Ah-ahem!" The unnaturally loud sound of Thaelios clearing his throat came from deeper in the cave along the bending waterfall. The Eladrin soon appeared from his concealment, walking closer to make himself known. "I was, uh, just exploring the falls earlier and I, well, didn't want to see something I shouldn't."

Be'naj felt her face bloom with the heat of a thousand suns. She quickly looked herself over, making sure her body was not accidentally exposed.

"I noticed from my vantage that the others had risen, and thought it might be time to be on our way?" Thaelios continued, shouting to be heard over the deafening water.

"Of course," Saffron replied, recovering her wits. "We should probably discuss our plan for when we return to Elisahd, no?" She looked to Be'naj as if including her on the discussion would erase the sight of their carnal pursuits from Thaelios's mind.

Be'naj managed a nod, then waited her turn to step carefully across the slippery rocks as they exited from behind the waterfall. An awkward silence hung over their walk back to the others, mitigated by the roar of liquid descent.

"There you all are!" Dyphina said as Be'naj, Saffron, and Thaelios rejoined them on the beach. "Investigating the falls, huh? This place is from out of a dream, yes?" At least she didn't seem to have any suspicions about what they'd been up to, which relieved Be'naj.

"Before we go," Saffron said, "this might be a good time to talk about where we're headed when Hiruth Jeshu sends us back to Elisahd."

Thaelios murmured agreement.

"As Shecclad explained, we've got more than the cult to worry about. While they certainly must be stopped, it sounds like Be'naj is the only one of us who may be able to thwart Hadrian No More's plan to descend our world into permanent Shadow.

"We've been through a lot together," she continued, looking specifically to Dyphina and Thaelios, "but I keep coming back to the same answer: in order to save Elisahd, we're going to have to split up."

Be'naj watched the faces of her companions as Saffron's words sank in. One at a time, Dyphina and Thaelios nodded, though the former kept her head down afterward.

"I've been preparing for that since we left Ishmere," Thaelios admitted.

Saffron placed a hand on Dyphina's shoulder until the woman raised her eyes. "I wish it weren't necessary, but there's simply too much ground to cover. Be'naj needs to find the Touchstones, and I'm going to stay by her side."

Dyphina forced a smile. "You should."

"We'll take on the Name of the Beast," Thaelios assured with unusual certainty. "Once we're back at Blackfeather Perch, I have no doubt we'll be able to strengthen our cause. Even Iliana might be willing to help." He smirked.

"I do think you should return there, but not until you've gone to Selamus first," Saffron said. "Criesha promised to enlist Jaiden Luminere to our cause, and he has plenty of resources at his disposal to give you aid. Willem the Shaper lives in the palace as well and might be a valuable ally – he corresponded with Cauzel, after all."

"So that's it, then?" Dyphina asked. "I'm going with Thaelios, and I suppose Rhazine will stay with you and Be'naj, seeing as how you're the only one she understands."

Saffron nodded. "I'll make my way back to the Perch as soon as I'm able."

"We're not saying our goodbyes yet!" Be'naj asserted, feeling the early sting of oncoming tears. "Come now, we've got a mountain to climb. Four more times," she added with a laugh.

She gathered her pack and let Saffron lead the way toward the break in the rocks that would bring them outside the Mountain. The flora looked different at the base of this layer – more like a jungle. Numerous birds called back and forth, and Be'naj caught sight of their colored plumage as well as some curious, monkey-like creatures amongst the high canopy.

The change from one peak to the next kept the journey from being monotonous, even though it felt like they were continually starting over. The view was different each time they ascended the slopes of Mount Celestia: one layer held a golden metropolis sprawling across the valley beneath, another hosted a great sea, stretching to the horizon. On the fifth layer, the clouds acted like prisms, casting rainbows across the sky at numerous angles. Finally, after stopping to sleep a few more times, they reached the temple of Hiruth Jeshu, built into the mountainside of the sixth layer.

It was the only time they had encountered any structures upon the slopes. Indeed, they had not even seen another Celestial since leaving Grennald on the first layer, until they neared the temple. Aasimar stared at their approach, but none confronted them. Upon the stairs, they were greeted by a violet-haired Aasimar who bowed before addressing them.

"Fair returns, mortal guests. I am Athendra, servant to Hiruth Jeshu, may His light shine forever. He sensed your presence and bid me bring you to Him." Athendra was slim, but well-muscled and fair, just as all the Aasimar.

"We are honored to have another audience with your Lord," Be'naj replied and bowed. She followed Athendra into the temple and her friends came behind. The sound of string instruments, far-off yet omnipresent, hung in the air as they approached the Sanctum. A pair of Aasimar, flanking the double doors, each opened one of the portals, allowing a blindingly bright light to escape into the greater chamber.

Be'naj continued following Athendra but had to shield her eyes until she entered a smaller room where the radiance suddenly became bearable.

From his throne, Hiruth Jeshu gazed upon her with kind eyes. She remembered that others had seen him differently, but she saw an ebony-haired man with smooth, caramel skin. His eyelids and fingernails were painted bright silver, and when he moved his arms, they trailed vibrantly colored motes of light.

"I, I can see you now!" she exclaimed. "Before, your visage was blinding."

"Something within you has changed, my child. I wonder, did you find the answers you sought from the denizens of the Lower Planes? I hope the patrol of Celestials I dispatched on your behalf facilitated your quest."

Though he seemed to be speaking to the group, Be'naj felt like his eyes were trained solely on her. "Yes, my Lord," she responded. "Arinome and the Aasimar gave us the protection we needed to infiltrate the Abyss. We are sorry for the losses suffered on our behalf – there is one in particular who has fallen beyond our reach that we were hoping you could help recover."

"Speak your request, Child of the Mountain."

Be'naj swallowed the lump rising in her throat. "Our friend, Palomar, was sent to an unknown layer of the Abyss by the Cyclone. He is very resilient and I'm sure he's finding a way to survive, but could use help. Is there any way you could send him succor, my Lord?"

Hiruth Jeshu stood, clasped his hands together, and descended the few steps down from his dais before responding. *"Alas, Be'naj,"* his voice became even more calm and soothing. *"I have no power over the nether realms. The Abyss is beyond my reach, and I can no longer see Palomar."*

Saffron stepped forward. "Is there nothing that can be done?"

"His soul is sacred and will be honored, just as every Celestial lost. We will look to others to rise and take his place, as is our way."

"But he's *Palomar*. No one can take his place," Saffron objected.

Hiruth Jeshu eased into a toothless smile. *"I do not expect you to understand – we do not stress the importance of individuals here. We are interested in the improvement of souls and can celebrate Palomar's achievements while not losing sight of those who remain."*

Be'naj couldn't believe what she was hearing. She assumed the Aasimar might hold a wisdom to help deal with loss, but this sounded like they'd forsaken one of their own. It felt like her chest was constricting around her heart. Was Palomar so unique among the Aasimar? She was certain he would not cease searching for any of them until he knew they were safe. But she didn't see how they could find Palomar on their own, nor stop the threats against Elisahd while crusading on the Aasimar's behalf. She envied Rhazine, who was at least mostly unaware of Palomar's sacrifice.

Saffron's face was also painted with disbelief – if she had any more words, she was keeping them to herself. Dyphina stepped over and wrapped her arms around Saffron, leaning in until their heads rested against one another. In the silence that had taken hold, Hiruth Jeshu returned to his throne.

"I'm afraid I have more unwelcome news for you, Be'naj. The soul of the one who fathered you is no longer upon Mount Celestia. He most likely perished in battle against the Tanar-ri or Baatezu. I am sorry you did not get to meet him.

Be'naj was already so bewildered, she wasn't sure the news changed anything. "I see."

"If you found what you needed, I presume this audience includes a request to return home. Have you given thought as to where on your world you would like me to send you?"

After no response from Saffron or Be'naj, Thaelios cleared his throat. "We were actually thinking we'd like to split up." He looked to Saffron, who nodded, before continuing. "Dyphina and I would like to visit the palace in the human city of Selamus. And the others ..." Thaelios deferred to Saffron again.

"We would travel to the mansion of the Circle of Twelve in Zeblon," she said, straightening and stepping out of Dyphina's grasp.

"But we promised the Wolfspider we'd never return. Won't that put you in danger?" Dyphina asked.

Saffron remained resolute. "We'll have to risk it. Without Cauzel to lean on, they seem the most likely to know something about the Touchstones. There are twelve of them, after all."

Thaelios raised his eyebrows and tilted his head.

Be'naj had only heard stories of the Wolfspider from the others, but she was confident she'd be able to protect Saffron from the ruthless guilder.

When no one else added anything, Hiruth Jeshu raised his hand. *"Very well. Join hands with those you are traveling with. Have you been to these places before?"*

"I have," Saffron answered. She took stock of the others as she reached out to Be'naj and Rhazine. "But I'm the only one who's been to both."

"Then close your eyes, Lady Saffron, and picture the palace." Hiruth Jeshu waited as she obeyed. *"Good. Now, imagine the abode of this 'Circle of Twelve.' Excellent. That should do nicely. You may open your eyes. Are you ready to go?"*

Saffron twisted her head to address the other group. "Don't worry, we'll see one another soon. I believe in you and wish you success."

"Yes, may you all stay safe and bring safety to Ifelian," Be'naj added.

"Don't take too long," Dyphina cried back. "And take care of each other."

"Good fortune," was all Thaelios uttered.

Then, after a final nod from Saffron, the stonework of the vaulted Celestial temple disappeared.

Chapter 14

The Ruins of Rinn-Rhulian

Annoxoria knew that, if Thuvian had to wait even a single day more, he might literally start climbing the walls of the castle. He'd tried to practice patience while waiting for her to heal, but the combination of Sepathia's overdue vengeance and Izefet's unanswered treachery had left him paranoid and anxious.

Though still sore, Annoxoria's own seething at the half-fiend turncoat's betrayal seemed to have fueled her recovery, and she was confident in her ability to travel after several weeks of rest. The downtime had provided an opportunity for her to parse through a number of scenarios in her mind, as well as for the laborers to repair the damage to Nightwing Castle.

It was obvious all along that Izefet had coveted the Living Fire, but she'd never been able to determine for certain why. After lying in bed, however, reflecting on the sum of their interactions, she finally started piecing things together.

Izefet had admitted, even flaunted his connection to Hadrian No More, and after seeing Gullagion in Thuvian's throne room and the dweomercraft of the Living Fire kraken statuary, she believed it. The relationship he hadn't been forthcoming about was the one with Sepathia. With the thralls they'd already encountered in the valley, she had to consider that the two had been working together for Thuvian's demise and maybe more.

Pereen Guillory, the spymaster, had found evidence that members of the Name of the Beast had not only infiltrated Pasaxtree, but had been operating within Drachenmark. She knew one of their agents had wormed his way into Cauzel Blackfeather's tower as well. Although she found the idea revolting, she'd acknowledged that the cult had probably found a hold inside the castle – all the more reason to employ misdirection going forward.

Izefet the Damned had tried to change the subject when she'd brought up Rinn-Rhulian, and his body language betrayed his professed ignorance. Annoxoria didn't typically pay credence to ghost stories, but she knew of the legends surrounding the ruins and didn't dismiss that there was something to them. She'd felt the power of the place personally, and knew the Ellafous considered the site sacred and watched over it, though none lived there. Perhaps Rinn-Rhulian held more secrets than they had already discovered.

Investigating the ruins would give them something to do instead of waiting for Sepathia or the half-fiend to act. Like Thuvian, she favored conquering over cowering. She'd nearly finished packing for the westward trek into the next valley, where the ruins of the abandoned eladrin city lay well-hidden by the undisturbed growth of ancient trees. Reaching Rinn-Rhulian would take a couple of days, for the way was too steep for a conjured steed, and crossing the mountain was never easy. She wondered what had possessed the Eladrin to choose such a spot in the first place.

Annoxoria'd stowed a couple changes of clothes and enough food to get them by, but she knew Thuvian could hunt or forage if they needed more. She entered her private study to retrieve a few spell components, but stopped when she saw the Living Fire statuary sitting on her desk. It seemed to stare at her, the imbued ruby winking with a knowing light. Obeying her impulse, she grabbed and stuffed it into her pack before buckling its top and vacating the room.

She hurried down to the courtyard where Thuvian waited for her, yet taking care on the numerous stairs so as not to aggravate her injury. Leaving before dawn, they planned to keep their journey as secret as possible lest a spy leak news of the Castle's vulnerability. Only a few chosen individuals had been told, and they'd been left with a list of excuses to give others who inquired about the Lord and Lady's whereabouts.

Grellock, her most intelligent and loyal ogre, stood with Thuvian and two of his best Rauglor hunters. Lord Skullreaver favored secrecy as well, but asserted that the deviousness of his sister demanded added protection. Annoxoria's lover wore steel bracers and shoulder guards fastened by chains, but otherwise trusted in the natural resistance of his scales.

The smell of the Rauglor was something she could do without, but she held her tongue, instead using it to greet her Lord with a kiss. She'd dressed sleekly in black leather, including her clawed gloves, and was confident she could disappear into the shadows upon any sign of danger.

"The sooner we get moving, the sooner we'll reach the cover of the trees," Thuvian said after breaking their kiss.

Annoxoria nodded, knowing Sepathia was his most urgent concern. Thuvian led the way, gripping Viper's Kiss with both hands, though he'd also strapped his powerful horned bow to his back. The Rauglor flanked him a few steps behind, carrying bows of their own, used to the formation of their hunts.

Annoxoria went next, moving more briskly than she was used to in order to keep up with the half-Nightwing's long strides. She was proud that he didn't need to slow on her account. Grellock took up the rear, his heavy steps shaking the ground, and his large form covering Annoxoria's profile from behind.

Within half-an-hour, they reached the first copse of evergreens along the back slope of the mountain leading away from Nightwing Castle. They were using the game paths she knew Thuvian was intimately familiar with; she trusted in his guidance, and for most of the trip, they had little to fear from the skies.

When they did break cover, their pace quickened until the trees were overhead once more. The rest of the group had excellent night vision, and they traveled well past sunset. After twilight, Annoxoria kept close to her mate, whose twin enchanted blades glowed with a dim blue radiance. Even so, she tripped on enough roots and stones to be glad the dark hid her embarrassment.

The climb over the ridge of the next mountain proved the most challenging part, and Annoxoria was exhausted by the time she went to sleep each night. She was glad to do so in a tent with Thuvian, however, which made it all worth it. He made love to her more savagely than he had during her time healing in the castle. It brought her bliss, and she made no effort to stay quiet or conceal their activity from their underlings.

The full light of day had not yet painted the morning after their second night of camp when Annoxoria started seeing tell-tale signs that their destination was near. Stone markers with weathered and moss-covered eladrin runes stood waist-high at irregular intervals along the path. Every now and then, she heard disturbances among the trees – twigs snapping or leaves rustling – but whenever she looked, the only movement she spotted was the vegetation itself.

"The Ellafous?" she whispered ahead to Thuvian.

He nodded without looking back. "They are watching."

Annoxoria had expected as much and found the idea somewhat comforting. She and Thuvian had been here before and realized they were not alone on that trip, either. Still, the half-eladrin, half-human guardians had not shown aggression, and she hoped they wouldn't as long as they were not provoked. Thuvian suspected they recognized his eladrin heritage – though Annoxoria saw only dragon – and felt some rules of kinship applied even if they looked nothing alike.

They were, indeed, close. The path they'd been following ended, and Thuvian commanded Grellock to hack through the underbrush with a machete. Annoxoria remembered how the growth encircling the ruins was unusually thick. She suspected ancient magic had enchanted the surrounding woods. When they'd cleared through two dozen paces of vines, low branches, nettles, and entangled leaves, a clearing lay beyond.

Only the grey stone carved from a nearby mountain quarry remained, so old was Rinn-Rhulian. The foundation and crumbled walls of the eladrin citadel sprawled across the field ahead, encroached on all sides by old forest. The elwise had lived here before the Gift of Arkmus and were mostly slaughtered when the God of Battle set humanity against them.

Thanks to his involvement in the construction of Nightwing Castle, Thuvian was able to spot an anomaly the last time they were here. One section of wall, decorated by carvings with an archway motif, looked significantly less weathered than the adjacent stone. When Annoxoria had cast a spell to detect enchantments, she discovered an illusion had been placed upon the area and found a corresponding eladrin inscription set with warding glyphs.

A locked doorway had been hidden in the stone wall and would only open when one of the Ellafous touched the glyphs, or so the inscription read. Thuvian had guessed that his mixed heritage might also suffice, and sure enough, a passage had opened for him.

He and Annoxoria returned to the enchanted doorway, giving orders to the Rauglor and ogre to keep watch and enter only if a threat manifested. She wondered if Izefet was after what was beneath and felt a tightness in her stomach after she cast her spell to reveal the illusion. Had the half-fiend already been here? Would the Ellafous allow that, or were they perhaps unable to stop him?

Thuvian reached out and lay his hand upon the largest glyph, which came to life at his touch, glowing brightly. Once again, the stone slid aside to reveal an open archway with narrow stairs leading down. Annoxoria grasped his muscular forearm with both hands, calmed by the texture of his glossy scales.

Only a sliver of sunlight reached the passage, and it didn't extend beyond the first few steps. Thuvian glanced down at her and then clasped Viper's Kiss with both hands. "Ignite," he ordered, and the blue glow of the blades surged to a brighter green. A sizzle accompanied the change, for the weapon's ends had become enveloped in magical acid.

Annoxoria released Thuvian's arm so he could lead the way downward. She followed a couple of paces behind, allowing space in case he had need to swing his weapon. The room below was as she remembered it, vacant of life and hauntingly beautiful. Veins of a silvery material in the walls and ceiling reflected the light of Viper's Kiss. Against the wall directly across from the base of the stairs stood an ornately carved, wooden stand. Unlike the ruins above, everything in this room was perfectly preserved and looked new.

The stand had small, metallic braces that supported a staff of polished wood. The staff was a shade taller than Annoxoria and possessed a paler grain than the stand. Runes spiraled around its circumference from the base to its head, which held a green crystal set into a tight hollow. She knew from her previous visit that it also held an enchantment, though she'd yet to decipher it.

Given the Ellafous were watching, Thuvian had forbidden her to take it, but she doubted Izefet would show the same courtesy. Was the staff what he'd been searching for, or was it a way through the door? Lord Skullreaver turned right once the steps met the floor and walked over to a stone pedestal, set between two columns that melded into the back wall.

The slanted top surface of the pedestal was divided into a matrix of polished marble plates, each about the size of a hand. On the wall above the pedestal was a warning, written in Eladrin. Thuvian lifted one end of his weapon closer to re-read the passage:

"Of the many Dooms we have escaped, one is locked within. The way to the Door can be guessed, but only a fool would do so, for another Doom awaits the impatient. Knowledge leads to our Salvation, and ever will. It can be passed down or granted by a well-planted Seed, though Wisdom does not come with it."

"I can't tell if that's poetry or just poor writing," Annoxoria derided. Why couldn't the Eladrin, or Ellafous, or whoever was responsible for the message, just state things plainly. It was a puzzle, and one that had stuck in the back of her mind since she saw it, though she hadn't memorized all the words.

"But what do you think it means?" Thuvian asked, turning his attention from the inscription to the pedestal.

She tasted the air, stirred by magic, without need for a spell to inform her of its properties. The marble plates radiated power, and she possessed enough arcane knowledge to realize touching them would have consequences. She'd studied magical traps and was wary about setting one off with careless experimentation.

"I think we're right not to touch them without knowing more," Annoxoria replied. She suddenly remembered that she'd brought the Living Fire Izefet had given her. Removing her pack, she searched for the kraken.

"What is it?" her lover asked.

"The Name of the Beast has been searching for this place, and Izefet stole the Living Fire we'd already mined. He wanted it for something …" She grasped the black metal statuary and her forked tongue extended in unconscious acknowledgement. "Perhaps that's what 'Seed' refers to in the riddle: the Seeds of the Avatars."

"Yes, that is what the elwise call them." Thuvian's tone suggested he'd caught on. "I didn't know we had any left."

"This was locked up in my study when the fiend ransacked the castle. They couldn't get in." Annoxoria was actually quite pleased with herself for outwitting Izefet. Not knowing what difference it might make, she carried the obsidian statuary over to the pedestal.

The Living Fire's red light sparkled and grew in intensity, acting like a dim, infernal lantern in the darkness. Thuvian held back Viper's Kiss so the hues wouldn't compete. As if written in invisible ink, runes appeared upon each of the marble plates as Annoxoria passed the light of the Living Fire over them.

"Look at that!" Delight in her discovery stretched Annoxoria's lips in a wide smile.

"Ingenious," Thuvian murmured. Then, a moment later, "What are we supposed to do now? Spell out something?"

Annoxoria was in the midst of contemplating the options when a coarse shout from her ogre carried down from the top of the stairs.

"Arrows!"

Thuvian shared a look with her and then was off, bounding up the stairs as she stuffed the Living Fire back in her pack. Doing so left her in complete darkness, save the rectangle of dim light marking the exit. She was familiar enough with her spell components that she could identify them by touch, and forced herself not to rush until she'd extracted what she needed from the pouch at her waist. Whoever was attacking would suffer the melting sting of acid for their trouble.

Annoxoria took short steps over to the stairs and used her hands to feel their edges before working around to ascend. She paused at the top, took a deep breath, and was about to surge into the open until she heard Thuvian's voice. He was conversing, not emitting feral battle cries. Curious, Annoxoria emerged into the morning light.

Grellock and the Rauglor had fanned out on either side of Thuvian, the latter holding their bows with arrows nocked as their heads swiveled, looking out into the trees. She saw a green-feathered arrow piercing the trunk of a nearby mountain hemlock that had broken through a floor of crumbling stone.

Given that aggressions had been thus far contained, Annoxoria risked joining her Lord to get a better sense of what was going on. She nudged her ogre aside to stand next to Thuvian and saw that he spoke to a man she assumed was an Ellafous.

"—reason to disturb the secret chamber?" The man who asked the question was wrapped in a green, hooded cloak, fringed with intricate designs, and held a recurved bow. Yet his golden, eladrin eyes drew her attention. He had an arrow drawn, though she presumed he had not fired the first shot himself. He would be a fool to address a superior force in the open if there were not others behind him, hiding in the trees.

"We have the same concerns as you," Thuvian explained, "for we suspect others seek to uncover the secrets buried here."

"You do not appear Eladrin, yet were able to enter the chamber – how do we know your intentions are honorable? You have been here before, after all," the Ellafous stated.

"And we have not taken your treasure," Annoxoria asserted. "You are addressing Lord Thuvian Skullreaver, ruler of Drachenmark, and are yourselves standing on land within his domain. Who are you to question us?"

"Nox—"

"Do you not see the remains of our city around you?" the Ellafous archer asked. "This has been our land since before your first ancestor was born. And there are dangers beneath that would spell Doom for us all if unleashed. It is our sworn oath to make sure that doesn't happen."

"Friend, we have no intention of probing your secrets further. To answer your question, I have eladrin blood, too. At least part of us is kin." Thuvian emitted a draconic snarl, as if his own body desired to demonstrate how clearly the other half was not related. "I am glad to know of your oath and fully support you honoring it. Consider this a shared warning, then, for others may come soon for your secrets."

"I appreciate your warning, though must still ask you to vacate and never return to this site. If you come again, I will have no choice but to assume you speak falsely of your intent."

Annoxoria opened her mouth to object, but Thuvian grasped her wrist tightly, cutting off her speech. She looked up at his face and he shook his head slightly before addressing the Ellafous once more.

"We will take our leave, but use care that your defense of this location does not widen further into my territory. I am crafting a nation, and I expect my sovereignty to be respected." With that,

Thuvian turned and pulled Annoxoria with him, heading north, the way they'd come. Her ogre rumbled at the lost opportunity to bash in skulls but followed without a word, and the Rauglor came after.

"I spotted at least a dozen more at the tree-line," Thuvian whispered as they reached the trees themselves. "I didn't appreciate his presumption either, but it wasn't worth the possibility of losing you."

Annoxoria had been prepared to argue, but his words disarmed her. She was still hot at the audacity of these natives but decided to save her aggression for the tent.

Chapter 15

The Eight Hills

Thaelios had just long enough to wonder whether this was the last time he would ever travel from one plane to another before he appeared on the stone steps of yet another magnificent building. He knew he was no longer on Mount Celestia by the chill that immediately set into his exposed skin.

"What trickery is this?" a man yelled before bounding down the first few steps in Thaelios's direction, extending his glaive as he came to a halt. A second man, dressed in a similar white tabard emblazoned with a purple crescent moon, joined his partner, though he remained a few steps further back and didn't brandish his weapon.

"What is it, Uther?" the second man asked, staring hard at the newcomers. Thaelios couldn't determine if the man's question was in reference to him or the reason for his partner's outburst.

"These two just appeared out of thin air!" Uther explained. "And the one in front looks strange – must be Shapers. Should we warn the Grandmaster?"

The guards spoke Illanese, so Thaelios assumed Hiruth Jeshu deposited them in the right place. "We are, in fact, Shapers," Thaelios stated, lifting his palms to show his empty hands, "but we mean you no harm."

The second guard lowered the angle of his glaive and crouched when Thaelios spoke. Perhaps reassurance would be better received from Dyphina? Thaelios glanced over his shoulder at his elegant companion in her new, green dress created by the gods.

She seemed to understand and a beguiling smile broke across her face as she stepped forward to draw the guards' attention. "Gentlemen," she started, clasping her hands together, "please don't be alarmed. We have traveled far to visit Grandmaster Jaiden Luminere, who is expecting our arrival. Would you be so kind as to escort us to him?"

"Sorry, m'lady," the unnamed guard responded, though his firm stance softened and the shaft of his weapon rose. "We cannot allow entrance to the palace simply on your word."

Dyphina pouted and straightened her posture, lifting the cleavage exposed by her bodice.

"But, um," the man stuttered, his eyes trained precisely where Thaelios felt his companion intended. "Allow me to speak with the chamberlain, and if you are indeed expected, I would be more than happy to escort you to the Grandmaster's court." He turned to his partner. "Uther, stay with the visitors and await my return."

Uther hesitated at the command. "Well, yes, certainly," he finally decided, drinking in Dyphina's full form. He lifted his glaive and planted both feet on the same step, adopting a neutral posture.

"Wonderful," Thaelios said under his breath. "I suppose we'll just wait here to be shown in." He lifted his head and gawked at the extravagance of the palace. The façade was striking in shades of white and gold, with rose-colored windows at various heights. Several spires stretched high enough to remind him of Blackfeather Perch. He couldn't imagine the expense of building such a large structure out of stone.

Spinning on his heels, he took in the even grander view as Dyphina flirted with the remaining guard to entertain herself. He stood at the top of a high hill, overlooking a city, vast beyond expectations. The sight of Zeblon twinkling below during their excursion to the mansion of the Twelve was breathtaking. Witnessing the full splendor of Selamus during daylight was undeniably awesome.

It dwarfed the coastal city – crowded buildings seemed to squat upon one another, competing for breathing room among the surrounding hillsides. Though positioned on the tallest, other peaks rose nearby. Both they and the valleys between were filled by the sprawl of human construction. Thaelios was in the midst of approximating Selamus's population when hands clasped his shoulders from behind.

"Isn't this exciting?" Dyphina squealed. "We're going to be staying in a palace!"

"With hundreds of people who look more like you than me," he responded. Thaelios knew she would never understand the anxiety that being the only Eladrin in a human city summoned. Dyphina's ancestors, at least on her father's side, had likely helped wipe out most of Thaelios's.

"Aw, but look at this view ... I bet it'll be even more impressive once spring takes hold." Dyphina's enthusiasm was not curbed by his lack of it.

"Hopefully we'll be far from here by the time it does," Thaelios said, turning back toward the palace at the sound of new footfalls upon the stone steps.

"The chamberlain says you should be admitted," the returned guard announced. "Erm, sorry for the delay," he added, sounding unsure whether he should apologize.

"Wonderful!" Dyphina skirted up the steps past Thaelios and wrapped an arm around the elbow of a surprised Uther.

The guard who'd apologized stared sternly at Thaelios as he ascended after Dyphina, though made no move to follow. Thaelios let Dyphina draw attention to herself and thus, away from him. Between her natural beauty and escalated exuberance, she was doing a fair job of it. Courtiers stared as she vibrantly pointed and *oooh*ed at features of the palace as they progressed to meet the chamberlain.

Thaelios wasn't immune to being impressed, either. The entryway bore an extravagant array of pools, with fountains and falls of moving water. The hall beyond was wide and bright, its rose-colored glass casting streams of tinted light along their path. Most of the stone was a polished white, and high ceilings showed off a set of winding stairs that branched toward the series of towers above.

Descending those steps, and nearly to the bottom, was an agèd man with a dusting of white hair on his head and a short beard. He used a tall staff to help him navigate the stairs, though his eyes rested firmly on Thaelios. His gaze was kind – not the judging stare of the guard they'd left behind. He wore pristine white outer robes over a vest of green and waved at Uther with his empty hand.

"One moment, one moment. Don't make me run, lad!" The elder man nevertheless quickened his pace once he'd reached the ground floor. Uther stopped and Dyphina withdrew her arm from him, turning to assess the newcomer.

Thaelios caught up and stood beside Dyphina with his arms crossed, still scanning the periphery of the great hall to see if everyone else was staring at him as well. People seemed to be carrying on their own conversations, but he spied a few glimpses in his direction.

"What have we here?" the white-haired man asked a little louder than necessary, coming to a stop and leaning heavily on his staff a few paces away. "An Eladrin in the prince's palace? Although, I suppose there is no longer a prince in the palace. Have you come to see me, I hope? Or are you bound for an audience with the Grandmaster?"

Thaelios was about to answer that he hadn't any idea who the man asking him was, but was cut off before he could get a word out.

"And oooh, what a beauty you are, m'lady." The man had already shifted his attention to Dyphina, who extended her hand at the compliment.

"Why, thank you, kind sir."

The talkative fellow stepped closer to accept her hand and leaned forward to plant a kiss on her knuckles. "An exotic look, you have. I've never seen hair … in such a color." He turned back to Thaelios. "Both of you are quite striking, really."

"And, who might you be, sir?" Thaelios asked, suddenly less confident in his Illanese.

"Ah, of course! Where is my sense of decorum? My name is Willem, though some simply know me as the Shaper of Selamus. And who might I have the honor of speaking to?"

Dyphina withdrew her hand and placed it on her throat while straightening her posture. "I am Dyphina, this is Thaelios, and we're also Shapers!"

"You're Willem the Shaper?" Thaelios asked. He remembered the name from what Cauzel shared of his correspondence. Was this a human he could actually trust?

"I am," the man responded with a smile. "I take it you've heard of me? I suppose that puts me at a disadvantage, but I am absolutely delighted to make your acquaintance!"

Uther the guard coughed to gain their attention. "Master Willem, I am escorting these guests to the chamberlain. Shall I leave them with you instead?"

"Of course, of course," Willem squinted his eyes shut while waving his empty palm. "I suppose everyone has something better to do than stand around and chat with an old magpie like me. I will take them the rest of the way if you are eager to return to your post, sir."

Uther bowed slightly at the Shaper of Selamus, then to Dyphina, and headed back toward the palace entrance. Thaelios watched him recede before realizing that Dyphina and Willem had already continued onward, speaking softly to one another as they walked with arms entwined. With some distance now between them, Thaelios heard the chatter of the humans around the room more clearly.

"I think it's an Eladrin. What is he doing here?"

"Is this an ill omen?"

"Are we preparing for war again? I'll send those devious elwise back into their forest holes."

Some of them openly pointed at Thaelios as well, and he felt like the once vast hall was closing in on him. His breathing became ragged, and he scurried to catch up with Dyphina.

"And you traveled here all the way from Ifelian? How is that old boy, Cauzel, doing these days?" Willem was saying as Thaelios drew closer. Dyphina looked over her shoulder at his approach, her eyes wide with doubt on how to answer the question.

Thaelios felt more at ease within proximity of Dyphina, but still oddly claustrophobic. He didn't possess the clarity necessary to guide such delicate matters. He shrugged, leaving it up to her to handle the situation.

She stopped walking and turned to face Willem, placing the hand of her unencumbered arm atop the Shaper of Selamus's. "I am sorry to be the bearer of such news," she said, all of the previous mirth drained from her voice. "Our master, Cauzel Blackfeather, perished in the desert outside of Zeblon."

Willem drew a sharp breath and his brows fell. "Oh my. I was not expecting such news." He looked to Thaelios with glassy eyes. "I am so sorry for your loss." His attention returned to Dyphina. "Both of you. Cauzel was a good friend and a great teacher. I am certain you have a solid foundation in Shaping if you learned from him." He cleared his throat and cast his gaze around the hall. "I do not wish to detain you from your business, and I have some letters to write. But it would please me greatly if we might have another conversation soon. I trust that, after your long journey, you will be staying a while?"

Thaelios had not yet considered that, for all its splendor, he would be happy to leave this city as soon as possible. "We are not sure how long we might be here. I suppose that depends on our audience with the Grandmaster."

"Well, at least for the night, yes?" Willem nodded for them. "Why don't you join me for breakfast in the morning? The stairs are good for the constitution. I'm up at the top," he pointed upwards, "and will make all the arrangements."

"That would be lovely," Dyphina answered. "We'll look forward to it."

"Excellent, my dear. Now, the chamberlain is just ahead." He pointed again, this time across the intersection of another wide hallway, at a middle-aged man with short, brown hair. He wore a crisp suit of blue with gold embellishments and was in the midst of explaining something to a servant carrying a covered tray of polished silver. "My task takes me in the other direction, and you'd save me some steps if we parted now," Willem continued.

"We'll be fine," Dyphina assured him. After another pat on his hand, she untangled their arms and waved back as he parted down the adjacent hall. "He seems nice," she said absently.

"Well, he might be the only one," Thaelios replied. "I don't think anyone here has seen an Eladrin before."

Dyphina considered him with an empathetic look. "Perhaps you better understand Cauzel's decision to wear an illusion? Come along, the faster we get this meeting over with, the sooner we can return to Ifelian." She locked elbows with Thaelios as she had Willem, and led them toward the chamberlain.

Thaelios felt an odd sense of protection in her closeness, and wondered if she had some lingering enchantment cast that he hadn't noticed before. Whatever the case, the chamberlain looked up when they were within a few paces and his eyes grew wide.

"Ah, yes," he said, doing an excellent job of concealing his surprise at Thaelios's appearance. "You must be the delegation from Ifelian. Grandmaster Luminere is expecting your arrival, but I'm afraid it came sooner than we thought. I apologize for not having the proper preparations in place to receive you."

"Oh, that's quite alright," Dyphina answered, her previous enthusiasm returned. "We look forward to meeting the Grandmaster."

"Of course. He's finishing up an audience with the Countess of Goldenshire, but I can escort you to the throne room and he shall be with you as soon as he's concluded business with the Countess." With a bow of his head, the chamberlain proceeded toward the end of the hall with a stiff gait. Two pairs of guards, draped in white tabards, stood at attention on either side of a set of wide doors with bright metallic handles toward their center.

"What do you think Jaiden looks like?" Dyphina whispered. "Saffron knew him, but didn't seem to want anything to do with this visit."

"He's probably a terrible bore," Thaelios whispered back. "With warts on his face," he added as they paused for the chamberlain to crack open the door.

Dyphina giggled at his comment but stifled it when the chamberlain waved them into the throne room. She gasped when they entered, taking in the scene before them.

The central portion of the room had a domed ceiling, which was painted to look like the night sky. The mural was interrupted by four slender windows extending most of the way to the top of the curved ceiling, allowing ample light to bathe the floor. A dais in the center of the space rose in several graduated steps, with a white throne perched upon the top level. A young man, not far into adulthood, sat upon the throne, surrounded by a sphere of glimmering, golden-green light. His dark brown eyes matched his thick hair, and trained intently upon a woman speaking from beyond the edge of the dais.

To either side, short antechambers branched off, ending in a series of doors. A dozen or so courtiers crowded together in the antechambers, watching but keeping a respectful distance from the throne. The Grandmaster did not have a face covered in warts. In contrast, it was smooth and attractive, leaving Thaelios to wonder how one so young attained such a prominent stature.

Grandmaster Luminere was dressed in a white tabard bearing the same purple crescent as those donned by the guards. His clothes beneath the tabard were dyed the color of the moon upon his chest, but weer not otherwise remarkable. A golden chain hung from his neck, but he wore no crown or other obvious symbol of power.

The woman speaking to him, however, was dressed in an expensive-looking gown of a bright, golden hue. Tiny crystals were beaded upon it in intricate designs, causing the entire outfit to shimmer as her body moved with her speech. "… and for this reason, as well as the many others I've discussed with you previously, I believe I am the best choice to help this province further heal from the wounds of recent war."

"Lady Goldenshire, you make excellent points, and I shall take them all under consideration before making my recommendation," Jaiden replied.

"And when might that be, Grandmaster? I feel as if all of Dawn's Edge has been holding its breath, awaiting your decision."

Jaiden allowed a short laugh. "Believe me, Countess, I don't want this choice hanging over me any longer than necessary." His gaze passed above her head and landed on Thaelios. "I am just about to receive guests who may be able to facilitate a conclusion."

Countess Goldenshire turned at his remark and laid eyes upon Thaelios as well. So did the rest of the gathered courtiers, it seemed, for a rush of whispers filled the pause in the primary conversation. The Countess did not address anyone else, turning back to Jaiden before speaking. "You are putting this decision, so integral to the people of your homeland, in the hands of outsiders?"

Thaelios felt the symptoms of claustrophobia return with the attention and wondered if he might just slip back out of the throne room, unnoticed.

"Not at all," Jaiden responded, undaunted. "These are emissaries from my Goddess, and I will always trust Criesha to guide me. Certainly, there are no doubts about her affection for the Seven Provinces after she helped deliver them from the grasp of Chelpa?"

Dyphina crossed her arms defiantly and whispered to Thaelios, "Ooh, nicely done."

Thaelios had to admit the Countess was placed in a tough position, even if he didn't appreciate her original take. His anxiety at the previous scrutiny lost its traction as his focus shifted to Jaiden Luminere stepping down the dais in his direction. The globe of light stayed with him, and Jaiden advanced close enough to the Countess to take her hand.

"I am grateful for your visit, my Lady, and do hope to have an answer for you soon. If you will excuse me, now, my other guests have been through much to reach me, and I must give them my full attention." Jaiden bent to kiss her palm and she acquiesced.

"Of course, Grandmaster," she replied, a slight sense of defiance still tinging her voice. "I will await your endorsement." Countess Goldenshire withdrew her hand and lifted the skirt of her gown as she walked toward the antechamber on her left. A pair of attendants separated from the crowd to join her, and once they did, the group moved back toward the main entrance.

Thaelios and Dyphina stepped further into the room to give the entourage space to exit. "Here, why don't you let me take that?" Thaelios said as he helped remove the pack from around Dyphina's shoulders. "You look more ladylike without the encumbrance."

"Thank you," Dyphina whispered.

After Thaelios put it around his shoulders, the pair stepped closer to the Grandmaster, who waited for them with his fingers intertwined. Thaelios was wary of stepping within the circle of light, but he didn't feel any differently after doing so.

"Welcome to Selamus, my friends," Jaiden said in a conversational tone, quieter than he'd used to address the Countess. "Criesha told me of your coming, and that you had need of my abilities." He thoroughly assessed each of them in turn, but didn't give away any of his conclusions. "If you prefer, we can have a more private conversation in one of the council rooms…" Jaiden said, gesturing to the sets of doors to his right.

"Yes," Dyphina answered, blushing as she dipped into an abbreviated curtsey. "That may be better for everyone."

Thaelios shrugged. He didn't object to getting out of the view of gawkers, but suspected Dyphina had other motivations for getting the Grandmaster behind closed doors.

"Excellent." Jaiden smiled. "Please, follow me."

Once they were inside the adjoining room, which held a long, narrow table of polished wood, surrounded by a dozen, high-backed chairs, Jaiden closed the door behind them. He offered them seats and they took a moment to introduce themselves.

"I'm sorry for that business out in the throne room." Jaiden sighed and put his face in his hands. "With the prince gone, the other dukes are demanding a new Duke of Dawn's Edge be named to maintain balance. They want me to choose between the local nobles since I still hold the good-will of the people. But seeing them preen and parade and squabble is exactly why I don't want anything to do with it. No matter who I pick, I'm guaranteed to make enemies."

Dyphina looked at Thaelios, then rested a hand on Jaiden's shoulder. "I'm sure you'll do a fine job."

Thaelios coughed and gave his best look of disapproval to his companion. He should have known she'd try to flirt her way through their interview. "Might I ask what enchantment surrounds you, Grandmaster? Is it some sort of protection magic?"

Jaiden lifted his head and looked around as if searching for what Thaelios spoke of. "Oh, you mean this?" he finally said, lifting his palms slightly above his shoulders. "It's an Aura of Truth – keeps people from lying to me. I use it when I'm holding court to put people in a forthright mood. Before they caught on, I heard plenty of interesting things." He looked at Dyphina and she mirrored his mischievous smile.

"Oh, well now that's a handy trick," Thaelios admitted.

"*I* won't lie to you," Dyphina offered. "Go ahead – ask me anything." She uncrossed and re-crossed her legs under the skirt of her dress.

Thaelios rolled his eyes. "I don't know how much your Goddess has already communicated to you, but we came to ask for your help on a very important quest."

Jaiden nodded and adopted a more sober look. "Criesha told me to expect a pair of foreign Shapers, who would come asking my assistance. She said I should hear you out, but that the decision was ultimately mine." He paused to frame his next words. "So let me start by asking a question of you: we've never met, and you're not from the Northern Provinces, so why me?"

"Saffron said you were the most capable person she knew, and she hoped you would help us," Dyphina blurted before Thaelios could form an answer.

"You know Lady Saffron? What else did she say?"

"She said she'd rather milk a goat until her hands blistered than have to travel with you all the way to Ifelian." Dyphina covered her mouth as soon as the words were out and her eyes became saucers.

Jaiden chuckled and shook his head. "Well, I suppose we know the Aura still works."

Dyphina dropped her hand and gave a toothy grin. "I'm sorry, I didn't mean to offend you."

"None taken," Jaiden assured her. "You've removed any doubt that you indeed know Saffron."

Thaelios sighed. "Grandmaster, we were apprenticed with Saffron under the same Shaper, but we have very little in the way of martial skills. We're trying to stop a cult, led by fiends from the Abyss, from releasing the Spawn of Raug, which were responsible for widespread destruction before the Banishment." He had to pause to catch his breath and wondered if the Aura of Truth was causing him to try and say everything at once.

Jaiden was looking at him with a blank face. "I only understood about half the words you just said, though your Illanese is really quite good," he added. "So, if I were to come with you, where are we going and what are we up against?"

Thaelios and Dyphina shared a glance, and she gave a deferring shrug.

"First, we need to return to Blackfeather Perch in Ifelian," Thaelios began. He stood and started pacing as he imagined the logical steps toward the successful conclusion of their quest. "It would be prudent to locate Rinn-Rhulian and determine what magical precautions have been taken to keep the Spawn hidden. The Eladrin were involved, so of course there's going to be some advanced sorcery." He stopped and stared at Dyphina, who already followed him with her eyes.

"There are a few obstacles and adversaries we need to be wary of: Annoxoria, the witch who threw us into her dungeons, anyone who might belong to The Name of the Beast, and quite possibly the Dread Lich, Hadrian No More."

Dyphina squinted and nodded, "Oooh, we really need to do something to get *that* bitch back!"

"Weeell." Jaiden drew out the word in a higher pitch as he also stood. "How did you two manage to gain so many enemies?"

"Oh, come on," Dyphina challenged. "If you knew the people on that list, you'd be sure we must be doing something right. In all seriousness, if the cult succeeds in their plans, thousands will die. And I can guarantee coming with us is going to be a lot more exciting than spending your afternoons sitting on some throne talking to nobles."

Jaiden twisted the shape of his mouth. "I hate to say it, but things have been fairly boring since the war ended." He chewed lightly on the end of his thumb while he considered. "Ah, but I have to decide on this Duke issue." Jaiden snapped his head sharply toward Thaelios. "Who would you choose?"

Thaelios shrugged. "That's easy – whoever offers you more."

Dyphina gasped in disbelief.

"Oh!" Jaiden pointed at Thaelios and looked at Dyphina. "I think he's on to something." He offered his hand to the half-fey woman and helped her to her feet. "I'll tell you what. I'll have the chamberlain escort you to some vacant guest apartments in the palace, and I'll sleep on your offer. Keep your things packed; if I decide to go with you, we'll leave in the afternoon."

"Well, I hope to see you again tomorrow," Dyphina mentioned. "Please let me know if there's anything else I can do to help make up your mind …"

She smiled, and Thaelios put his hands onto her shoulders to steer her out of the room. He wanted to get to their quarters and away from curiosity seekers as quickly as possible.

As nice as it was to trance in the solitude of his private room, Thaelios felt like any rejuvenation he'd attained overnight had completely dissolved during their climb up the nearly endless stairs. He'd gotten used to Blackfeather perch, but this seemed much worse. For one thing, he had to take all the steps without a break, and for another, there was no railing to keep him from falling a hundred feet to his death on the stone floor of the palace.

"Whew, almost there," Dyphina said. She seemed to be in a good mood, but Thaelios wondered if that would change once she realized how much she was "glistening" from their hike up to the top tower. When she reached the landing, she peered over the edge, then immediately turned her head. "Don't look down," she warned.

He disobeyed and instantly regretted it. The spiral of their ascent had tightened once they rose above the level of the vaulted ceiling and into the interior of the highest tower, but only open air awaited between his vantage and the impossibly distant marble below. The lack of spatial reference led to a loss of balance, and Thaelios started to teeter before Dyphina pulled him back and steadied him.

"I just told you not to look!" Dyphina sighed, and they both straightened their posture and the fresh clothes the palace servants had laid out for them this morning. A single door with a sturdy knocker offered the only way to continue, and she wrapped upon it three times. The sound echoed over the chasm behind them until overpowered by Willem's voice.

"Ah, yes, come in. The door is unlocked."

Dyphina entered ahead of Thaelios, once again drawing attention while he got a chance to assess his new environment. Willem sat at a small, round table in the middle of a quaint apartment, bathed in light from the large tower window that curved along with the sloped wall to their left. On the far side of the room was a study with a desk and bookshelves. A large, white and yellow bird sat on a perch in a gilded cage that hung from the ceiling, a little too close to the table supporting their morning meal.

"Welcome to my little corner of the palace," Willem said with a smile, not bothering to stand as he greeted them. He gestured with the napkin in his hand to the pair of empty chairs around the table, then promptly tucked the cloth inside the collar of his grey wool shirt.

Thaelios and Dyphina took the offered seats. The plates at each setting were already stacked high with hot cakes and butter, fresh fruit, thin slices of pork, and a fried egg. Thaelios found the meal extravagant and well beyond what his hunger could accommodate. He was unsure of where to start.

"I know it's more than necessary," Willem supplied upon seeing his hesitation, "but I was as a loss as to what what you might prefer and guessed that meals on the road may have been a bit sparse. I hope you don't mind." He was already stabbing a slice of melon on his plate, which he looked eager to consume.

"It's wonderful, Willem," Dyphina responded, spreading butter over her hot cakes with a silver knife. "I'm starving."

Willem winked and passed a small crystal bowl full of powdered sugar. "So, where exactly have your travels taken you? You said that Cauzel fell in the deserts outside Zeblon, which is far enough from Ifelian but no closer to here. What caused need of such a journey?"

Cauzel clearly had a relationship with this Shaper, but Thaelios was still hesitant to share their quest with just anyone who asked. "We came here to seek an audience with the Grandmaster," he replied.

"Ah, yes my boy, but why?"

"I probably have fifty years on you, Sir. And we came to him asking for help." Thaelios bit off a chunk of pork to chew on in order to keep from saying anything he would regret.

Willem stared at him for a few heartbeats, then set down his knife and fork. "I apologize for being too familiar, Thaelios. I'm used to being older than everyone else, you know?"

"We're trying to stop the Name of the Beast," Dyphina supplied, breaking the awkwardness. "They're a cult, led by demons. We think they're trying to free the Spawn of Raug."

Thaelios shot her a hot look. Was she even capable of exercising discretion? "We don't know precisely what they're up to, but they seem to intend the Eladrin harm."

"Hmm, is that so?" Willem said before stuffing a forkful of egg in his mouth. "And is that how Cauzel fell? Fighting against this cult?"

"He died fighting a rock troll. Well, a troll and a lieutenant of Hadrian No More," Dyphina added.

"My word! The Dread Lich is involved, too?"

Dyphina shook her head as she concentrated on slicing her cakes into thin strips. "It's a long story. But we went to Mount Celestia and saw the Aasimar, and then the Abyss, oh, and don't forget Ishmere! Now we're here, trying to get Jaiden's help before we return to Ifelian. Do you suppose he's going to aid us?"

"Whoa, slow down a moment, my Lady." Willem once again set down his utensils. "How on Elisahd did a pair of Cauzel's apprentices travel to the Outer Planes? I'm near the end of my career and have never mastered extra-planar travel."

Thaelios shrugged. "The Hall of Doors." If Dyphina was going to tell him everything anyway, he might as well set the facts straight. "I managed to retrieve a book written by Trigilas himself from his quarters in Ancient Tarmuth."

"The Father of Spells?" Willem certainly sounded impressed.

Thaelios puffed up his chest a bit and nodded. "It's a treatise on roads to immortality, with a collection of powerful spells he created himself."

Willem placed his hand on his chin and his eyes lost focus. "Mount Celestia, you say? It is quite a path you've traveled already, friends. We actually hosted a flight of Aasimar here at the palace, during the war against Chelpa. They've all gone, now," he added, wistfully. "I found that, despite their heavenly origins, they were as varied in purpose as any collection of humanity."

Dyphina shook her head slightly. "Palomar was brave, selfless. A true diplomat for his kind."

Thaelios's head swam with memory. "But there was an Aasimar in the mines, don't you remember? Obviously, we'd never seen one before at the time, but it put us to sleep when we tried to escape. It was working for … them."

"Palomar, you say?" Willem asked. "Oh, he was a fine one. You met him on Mount Celestia? Astounding! He perished in battle, here. Turned into a ball of ethereal light when he died, from what Jaiden told me." Willem stood from his chair and shivered visibly before clasping his hands behind his back. "That Illicurus was another matter, though. Cold and calculating."

Willem walked toward the bright window, putting his back to the table. His pet bird gave a couple of screeching calls as he passed its cage. The Shaper of Selamus stopped when his forehead was almost flush to the curved glass. "After I recognized his disposition, I began to worry what might happen if the Aasimar turned from allies to enemies. They are Shapers in their own right, you know," he said, turning his chin toward his left shoulder. "They use Harmonic Manifestation, which led me to start experimenting."

Thaelios wasn't sure how the conversation had turned toward magical theory, but he wasn't disappointed. He finished chewing a piece of fruit and slid his chair back from the table to face the wrinkled Shaper.

"I was looking for a way to combat their song, should the Aasimar eventually turn on us."

"And did you succeed?" Thaelios asked.

Willem turned from the window to look at him, his eyes flashing with excitement. "You know, I think I did, after a fashion." He crossed the room and bent behind his desk, opening a couple drawers and searching through them. "Aha!" he cried, then rose to his full height. He walked back to the breakfast table, dangling a square, green pendant from a thin chain.

"What is that?" Dyphina asked, reaching out her cupped hands to receive the trinket.

Willem shrugged. "I've taken to calling it my Music Box, but more accurately, it is a talisman of discordant melodies."

Thaelios nudged closer to Dyphina to get a better look. "How does it work?"

"Whenever someone in relative proximity begins to Shape through harmonics, my Music Box adds strains that mimic the singer, influencing the outcome of the spell. Usually, that means no coherent effect is created."

"Fascinating!" Thaelios replied, plucking the pendant from Dyphina's hands by its chain. "You should try it, Dyphina. Sing something."

"Well ..." A knock at the door interrupted Willem. "Come in," he called.

The door opened, and a young man in a white surcoat with the purple crescent of the Order poked his head in. "Sir, I apologize for the intrusion—"

"You can enter, young man. I'm not going to turn you into a toad," Willem said in a not-quite-comforting tone. After a brief hesitation, the man crossed the threshold.

"Grandmaster Luminere sent me to find his visitors, Sir," he said, glancing at Thaelios but not maintaining eye contact. "He wishes them to meet him at the stables in an hour, prepared for travel."

Dyphina looked at Thaelios. "Does that mean he's helping?" She started to smile.

"Thank you, son," Willem said. "I'll make sure they get where they're supposed to be."

The messenger nodded and disappeared, shutting the door behind him.

"Well, it sounds like your journey is far from over," Willem continued. "While I find your company endlessly interesting, I know you have preparations to make."

Dyphina stood. "Thank you for breakfast." She leaned forward and gave Willem a hug.

"Yes, thanks for your hospitality," Thaelios added. "It is not entirely common." He extended the pendant to return it, but Willem shooed him with his hands.

"Keep it," he said. "Cauzel was a dear friend, and it is the least I can do to repay him by helping his pupils in some small way."

"You are too kind," Dyphina said softly, placing her hand over Willem's.

Thaelios bowed. "It is a worthy gift."

Willem shrugged. "If you ever feel like taking up Cauzel's correspondence, I would be happy to write about any number of topics. I mostly enjoy the isolation of my tower, but it can get a bit lonely with only Lydia around."

The bird squawked at its name.

Dyphina giggled. "Certainly."

"Good luck dealing with the cult," Willem called out as Thaelios and Dyphina exited. "I am glad you have others to fight beside you."

Return to the Circle

B e'naj had just enough time to wonder whether she'd truly ever see Cauzel's apprentices again, before she appeared upon a smooth stone landing, looking up at a rocky cliff. She felt the sun behind her and heard the undulating roar of waves battering the cliff beneath her. The smell of salt was thick upon the air, and humidity's prickling caress danced over her skin.

Saffron still held her hand, and Be'naj knew that was sufficient to get her through anything. Rhazine stood on the other side of Saffron, face painted with wonder as she stepped forward. She turned in a slow circle and Be'naj followed suit, their view opening up to a distant horizon with the sea far below. Be'naj shielded her eyes from a glaring sun, whose warmth was harsher than the glowing orb on Mount Celestia. Fierce wind rushed up the side of the cliff from the ocean, tousling her long hair and ruffling her wing's feathers.

"*Ishu ete carabits fhellon Zeblon!*" Rhazine exclaimed.

Even with her eyes still on the sea, Be'naj sensed joy in the young woman's words.

Saffron turned to Rhazine. They held a conversation in Begnari, which blunted Rhazine's enthusiasm until she eventually cast her gaze downward. After their exchange, Saffron addressed Be'naj in Illanese. "I brought us back to Zeblon. The path upward will take us to the Circle of Twelve's mansion."

"You think they will help? Didn't they fail you before?"

Saffron exhaled noisily and clapped the butt of her Celestial spear against the stone. "They did. But there are twelve of them, and we only need one with the knowledge to help us. These were the best odds I could think of."

Be'naj nodded. If Saffron thought this was the right way to proceed, then it probably was. "What did you say to Rhazine?" Glancing over Saffron's shoulder, Be'naj saw that their companion's head was bowed, her left hand clasped onto her right forearm.

Saffron shook her head slightly. "Once she recognized where we were, she wanted to see her father. That's impossible right now, but I told her we'd revisit the topic after our meeting with the Twelve."

As if summoned by her words, Ayez the Many-Colored approached from the path that led to a door in the hillside. "Spinning seasons of Nerris! I confess I didn't think to see you again so soon, Lady Saffron. And, Be'naj, was it? You look different than when I last saw you. You succeeded in finding your friend, yes?"

Be'naj nodded and was about to thank him for his previous help, but Saffron was first to form words.

"Ayez, is the Circle of Twelve truly dedicated to thwarting the Dread Lich?"

It was not the greeting Be'naj would have offered, but she took great interest in the response. Saffron clearly had more of a history with this Shaper than she.

Ayez squinted and took a few steps closer, using his orb-tipped staff to gain purchase up the path's incline. "I can see we have things to discuss, Lady Saffron," he said once close enough for his casual tone to be heard over the steady wind. "But shall we go inside to do so? The house is warded against scrying."

Saffron stared at Ayez for a moment, her grip on the spear tightening, then relaxing. "Lead the way," she finally said, stepping aside to let the man pass.

"Of course," Ayez responded, though his glance passed to the glowing tip of Saffron's spear before he started up the path. The winding trail, cut into the rock, was narrow enough that they were forced to walk single-file, but it was a short trip to the plateau above.

The large house waiting for them there was familiar from Be'naj's previous visit, though the gargoyles stationed along the lower portion of the roof still unnerved her. Ayez led them through a door that matched the rest of the exterior, into a sunlit room dominated by a large table of polished wood. Be'naj recognized the sphere of swirling colors at its center that had created the map they used to locate Saffron in the desert.

"Has Cauzel taken a female disguise, or is this a new companion?" Ayez asked, assessing Rhazine as she passed him to get further into the room.

"This is Rhazine, the Wolfspider's daughter," Saffron said unapologetically as she claimed a chair at the table.

Ayez stood agape, and Be'naj suspected Saffron took pleasure in his reaction. "Cauzel didn't escape our struggles in the desert, I'm afraid," Be'naj explained. She folded her wings tightly behind her back and pulled the chair next to Saffron far enough from the table to accommodate her.

"I'm sorry to hear that," Ayez managed, though he was paying closer attention to Rhazine.

Probably used to being ignored when folks spoke Illanese, she obliviously wandered around the perimeter of the room, looking at the bookshelves before discovering the full-length mirror set in the corner.

Deciding to let things be, Ayez took a seat on the opposite side of the table, facing the northern windows. He propped his staff against the dark-grained table and placed both hands on its smooth surface, leaning forward so he could speak softly. "I was worried when we learned you'd been taken into the desert. I can't imagine it was for friendly purposes, but I was glad to know your friends were going after you." He was looking expectantly at Saffron, who regarded him coolly.

"Is that supposed to be some kind of apology?" she asked. "Your cabal employed me for their own purposes and then didn't live up to their side of the bargain."

Ayez sighed in exasperation. "We just needed more time. We didn't expect that the Wolf—" He looked over his shoulder at Rhazine, then quieted his rising voice, "that the Wolfspider would seek to be rid of you so quickly after our meeting. Which only makes me wonder if someone may be feeding him information. Do you really think it's wise to have his daughter here?"

"Rhazine's just another victim of her father's unscrupulous dealings." Saffron made no attempt to stifle the volume of her voice, and Rhazine turned her head toward them, though only for an instant, after hearing her name. "She was being sent as a requested offering to Hadrian No More, and the Wolfspider needed us to intervene."

Ayez raised his eyebrows. "I imagine the Wolfspider has at least an inkling of what the Dread Lich is capable." He sat back in his chair and took another deep breath, relaxing with the exhalation. "Very well. You have your freedom, I see." Ayez extended a flat palm toward Saffron. "Why then have you returned to us?"

Be'naj worried that Saffron wasn't ready to let her grudge go and decided to ensure the direction of the conversation. "Shecclad has informed us of Hadrian No More's true agenda," she blurted. That seized Ayez's attention. "As the Champion of Luprak, he is attempting to bring Elisahd in concurrence with the Plane of Shadow."

Ayez stifled a humorless chuckle. "What does that even mean? I've been working against the corrupting influence of the Dread Lich for many years now, but I have no idea what you're talking about."

Be'naj folded her hands together and placed them on top of the table. "I am the new Champion of Shecclad, the Sky Lord. We spoke to him directly on Ishmere, and he informed us that Hadrian No More is the active Champion of Luprak."

Ayez puffed his cheeks and shook his head slowly. "I admit, I am not well informed of the pantheon beyond those gods vying for influence in Zeblon. But are you suggesting you visited the realm of the gods?"

"We did, Ayez," Saffron calmly confirmed. "We entered Ancient Tarmuth and used the portals there to travel to other worlds. You should listen to her."

Be'naj gave Saffron a grateful nod before continuing her narrative. "Luprak is the God of Night and Inevitable Doom. There was once a prominent faction of his among the Eladrin, and my people all know the story of how his followers were banished from the forests and sought refuge in the darkness, underground."

"This is very heady, Be'naj," Ayez said, though he didn't look away.

She continued. "There are four Touchstones on our world, and each is attuned to one of the Elemental Planes – that keeps us connected to them and enables their material to be present in relative balance. Channeling Luprak's power, Hadrian No More seeks to realign those Touchstones to the Plane of Shadow. If he is able to change all four, that Plane would envelop us completely. Who knows what dire consequences that would bring?"

"We need the Circle of Twelve's help. Be'naj can alter and lock the Touchstones, but we don't have a clue where they are," Saffron added. "For all we know, Hadrian No More is working with a significant head start."

Ayez clicked his tongue. "This sounds like a serious issue, but I admit ignorance of anything like these Touchstones you mention." He straightened in his chair and placed his hands flat upon the table. "That doesn't mean much, however, for my focus is Chaos Magic, and this is far from that. We should bring in Ezmina – she's the Twelve's archivist and a talented augur to boot. I'd wager if it's mentioned in a book, she's come across it." He stood. "She's likely in the library right now. Why don't we move to the parlor, and I'll see who else I can round up?"

Be'naj and Saffron stood, following Ayez out of the room and into the great hall. Rhazine lingered at the mirror, checking herself out in various poses.

"You can make yourselves at home, through there," Ayez said, pointing to the open doorway on the opposite side of the room. "The library is upstairs. I'll gather whoever is available and join you in a few moments." He started up the curved staircase toward the balcony, and Saffron led the way to the parlor.

The floor of the sitting room sank toward the center, and a couple tiers of fur-lined couches ringed the depression. Wide windows on two of the walls allowed ample sunshine to fill the space, with the southern panes set upon hinges and opened to let in a pleasant ocean breeze. A hallway, leading deeper into the house, split the remaining wall.

Saffron propped up her spear, then selected a position on a lower couch that provided a view of the great hall. She sank back into the cushions, looking exhausted. Be'naj unbuckled the scabbard of her Celestial sword and sat close beside Saffron. She placed the sheathed sword across her lap and a hand on Saffron's knee.

"Is there anything I can do to help?" she asked. "You seem a little tense. I thought returning to our world would at least bring some comfort."

Saffron straightened her posture and smiled. "It does, Be'naj. And having you with me helps more than I can put into words. It's just, dealing with these people again ..." She shook her head. "And now that we're here, I don't think I can leave Zeblon without trying to free the gladiators who fought beside me. We have a key to the collars; it wouldn't be right to leave them."

Be'naj squeezed Saffron's knee and nodded. "I'll fight beside you if that's what it takes – I'm with you, no matter what." Be'naj turned her head at the sudden sound of footsteps.

Rhazine skirted hastily to the couch and sat beside Saffron. Leisurely entering the parlor behind her was the tiefling Be'naj had met briefly during her previous visit. Her skin began itching as he drew near, an effect similar to what she experienced when in proximity to the Tanar-ri in the Abyss. More important than her discomfort was the fact that he wore the Living Fire pendant around his neck!

"Ah, so it is true," Sirran said nonchalantly. "When I heard that the Crimson Scorpion had returned to our house, it was something I had to see with my own eyes."

"Where did you get that jewel?" Saffron demanded.

"What, this?" Sirran answered, extending his slender, long-nailed fingers as his hand passed over his chest. "I found it in the Desert of a Thousand Regrets. It was lying in the sand near the buried city of Tarmuth. Your tracks led to the door, but I couldn't find a way in myself."

"The Living Fire belongs to Saffron," Be'naj interjected as Ayez and a few others filed into the room past the stoic Sirran.

"Lady Saffron!" exclaimed an alluring woman with a mix of human and eladrin features. She stepped down to the room's center to greet her guests. Saffron stood and the two women embraced, though Saffron's engagement lacked warmth. "None of us were sure when we'd see you again after the Lodestone didn't work, but we worried when you vanished into the sands. And this must be Be'naj!" The woman's white dress was expertly tailored to enhance her already regal appearance. She extended her arms expectantly, and Be'naj succumbed to the pressure by standing to hug the stranger.

"Ezmina, this is Rhazine," Saffron said, gesturing to the still-seated Begnari.

"Yes, the Wolfspider's daughter, no less?" Ezmina stated as she withdrew from her embrace of Be'naj, though she offered no additional greeting to her final guest. "How wonderful," she added, forcing a smile before taking a seat on the sofa across from Be'naj. Unsure of what the proper protocol was, Be'naj awkwardly waited to sit until Saffron did so.

"Well, yes, I suppose brief introductions are in order," Ayez said, turning his head to account for everyone present. "I am Ayez the Many-Colored, and seated with you is Ezmina Skysilk, our Archivist. Here we have Sirran, our Unseen Seer, Groilen, our Illusionist, and I don't think you've ever met Resasha, our Pact Shaper."

Resasha, who appeared to be Begnari, nodded. Her dark-painted lips and multiple facial piercings, combined with her black leather suit, gave her an aura of intimidation.

"I've briefly shared with Ezmina and the others what you said about the Touchstones," Ayez continued, "but I wanted them to hear it from you directly, as I'm hardly the expert and couldn't supply many details."

"I have read some on the Touchstones," Ezmina took over, "but would appreciate hearing exactly what you've told Ayez. It might help me select the best resources."

Be'naj looked at Saffron, who nodded her assent, and then explained in greater precision everything she'd gleaned about Hadrian No More's agenda from their conversation with Shecclad. By the time she finished, the faces of the Circle of Twelve looked as if they were attending a funeral.

Groilen shook his head. "I knew his evil was far-reaching, but this is beyond anything I'd conceived."

Ayez nodded his agreement. "It's clear we cannot let the Dread Lich's plan come to fruition."

"It would mean disaster for all of Elisahd," Saffron reiterated. "That's why we need your help. Be'naj has to reach these Touchstones before Hadrian No More, and we have no idea where to find them."

"What do you think, Ezmina? You say you've come across tomes regarding these sites?" Ayez asked.

She nodded while staring vacantly ahead, her face pale. "My people, the Ellafous," she started without any hint of emotion, "became the guardians of many eladrin secrets and ancestral knowledge when the firstborn retreated after the Revenge of Arkmus. Though I have read of the existence of the Touchstones, I'm aware of only one source that details their precise location and magical properties."

"And you're familiar with the book?" Be'naj asked, cautiously hopeful.

Ezmina snapped out of whatever reverie had claimed her, and her eyes softened as she turned to Be'naj. She nodded as she spoke, "The Grimoire Precario." Ezmina looked over her shoulder at Ayez, who was sitting on a higher-tiered seat. "It is a famous book – Icharnius the Black stole it from Luin-menel nearly three centuries ago."

Ayez shut his eyes and exhaled heavily through his nose.

"Of course he did," said Sirran the tiefling, the hint of a smile in his voice.

"Who is Icharnius the Black?" Be'naj asked, wishing Shapers in general would do a better job of explaining to the uninitiated.

Resasha hummed, almost like a purring cat. "He was the renowned necromancer who apprenticed Hadrian No More. An absolute master of the Darker Arts." She sounded as if she held this necromancer in great esteem.

"And what became of him?" Saffron pushed, an edge of irritation reflecting Be'naj's own faltering patience.

Groilen cleared his throat. "Hadrian No More ended him when he discovered his master's plan to sacrifice him in order to achieve Lichdom."

Be'naj lifted her eyebrows and inwardly shrugged. That seemed like a fair response on the part of their adversary. "So, we're assuming Hadrian No More now has the book?"

Ezmina smiled wanly and nodded. "It makes the most sense. Especially if he's already pursuing the Touchstones."

Saffron shook her head. "That doesn't matter. We still have to do something. All your combined magic has to be good for *something*."

"We can steal the book ourselves," Sirran responded dryly. Groilen looked at him like he was insane. "I don't imagine the Dread Lich would expect such a course," the tiefling added.

Groilen snorted. "Damn right he wouldn't, because he lives in the Iron Fortress, surrounded by a thousand corrupted souls that do his bidding."

"Where is Hadrian No More's Fortress?" Be'naj asked, wanting to give Sirran's proposal a fair chance.

Groilen snorted again while crossing his arms across his chest. "In the Plane of Shadow."

"Do you know how to get there?" Saffron asked, undaunted.

"We know the Shadow Gate his lieutenants use," answered Sirran, the Living Fire casting an eerie red glow upon his horned chin. "It's on the western side of the Fire-Wall Mountains."

"Three hundred miles away!" Groilen scoffed. "Across the desert."

"One could sail up the River Chelhos, almost to Lucnere," Ayez admitted. He shrugged when Groilen stared at him. "It wouldn't be too far overland from there."

"I've been there," Be'naj mentioned meekly, though no one acted as if they'd heard.

"How would we get the book from him?" Saffron asked.

"Not by force, certainly," Sirran said, tapping the tips of his ruddy index fingers together in front of his lips. He still remained near the entrance of the room with Resasha, and started pacing as he spoke. "We would have to use subterfuge – either complete non-detection or some sort of distraction. The undead don't sense my life force the same way they would the rest of you."

"A *blessing* of the Lower Planes," Groilen derided.

"So, you're coming with us?" Be'naj couldn't keep from asking. She didn't look forward to itching for weeks on end.

"Hadrian No More was particularly interested in acquiring Rhazine …"

"Saffron!" Be'naj exclaimed. "We're not using her as bait."

Saffron held up her palms. "I'm just thinking out loud. Maybe we can use it to our advantage?"

Ayez sighed and leaned back upon the couch, fixing his gaze to the ceiling. "If you were to parlay with the Dread Lich, and I can't believe I'm even stating that as an option, you would need a quick avenue of escape. Otherwise, you're all risking fates worse than death." He leveled his eyes at Groilen, who winced when he caught Ayez's meaning.

"Oooh, Myalyssa's not going to like that," he said, shaking his head. "Those Teleportation Runes cost a fortune and took her almost two moons to create. Each!"

"But what better use for them?" Ezmina added. "We're talking about warding off eternal dimness upon Elisahd."

Groilen lifted his hands. "As long as I'm not the one that has to tell her …"

"So, we'll need passage on a ship to Lucnere as well as these Teleportation Runes. Now, who is coming with us?" Saffron asked.

The Circle of Twelve dropped silent, and the parlor was filled with downcast eyes.

"Sirran?" Saffron asked. "You sounded eager for this challenge."

"You *would* be the best choice," Ayez added. "*Unseen Seer* and all."

The tiefling fixed a stare at Ayez that might have been peering into his soul.

"No one else, then?" Saffron asked. "Alright, when can we leave?"

Be'naj gasped. "I think we should ask Rhazine how she feels about entering the presence of a powerful necromancer who wants to ritualistically sacrifice her." She knew Saffron wasn't keen on sitting idle, but that wasn't an adequate excuse for placing others in danger.

Saffron shut her eyes briefly and shook her head. "Of course. I'm sorry. She should absolutely have a say – though I don't see how we're going to get close enough without her," Saffron added under her breath. She turned to Rhazine and started speaking quickly in Begnari.

Be'naj watched the young woman's face closely, holding her breath as she awaited Rhazine's decision. Saffron was right – they hadn't come up with a second option on how to get close to the Dread Lich's bookshelves.

A few nods from both Begnari women ensued as their conversation stretched, until suddenly, Saffron leaned in and embraced Rhazine. "She'll go with us!" Saffron reported, "But she wants to see her father again afterward."

"Is that wise?" Be'naj asked, feeling nevertheless relieved.

"Probably not," Saffron shrugged. "But that was the compromise. She wanted to see him now, and that could be disastrous."

"Indeed," Ayez said as he stood. "Well, I am going down to the workshop to speak with Myalyssa. Sirran, I'm sure you have arrangements to make, and I can tell our guests want to leave as soon as possible."

Groilen pushed out from the couches to make room for Ayez to get by. "I'll go down to the docks and see about the next available passage to Lucnere." Sirran was gone when Be'naj looked around, likely slinking back to wherever he'd initially emerged from. At least she wasn't itching anymore.

Ezmina, Saffron, and Be'naj stood as well, though Rhazine remained planted on the couch. The Ellafous Shaper cleared out first and headed back toward the stairs. "I'll see if I can find anything even a little helpful about the Touchstones."

"Or the Plane of Shadow," Saffron called after her. Then she whispered to Be'naj, "Can you stay with Rhazine for a moment? I need to have a quick word alone with Groilen."

"Of course," Be'naj replied, though she wondered why she couldn't share in the conversation.

Saffron smiled. "Thanks. I won't be long." She hurried out the front door to catch Groilen.

Be'naj decided not to refasten her sword around her waist just yet, returning to take a seat as close as possible to one of the open windows. Perhaps she might catch a few notes of Saffron's conversation on the breeze …

Though she heard the sounds of both participants' voices escalating in pitch, the intermittent phrases the wind allowed to reach her didn't add up to anything coherent. It sounded like they were arguing, though that didn't surprise her. Rhazine had set to braiding thin rivulets of her hair, unconcerned by Be'naj's attempted eavesdropping. After what might have stretched into a quarter of an hour, the talking ceased and heavy footsteps preceded the front door's reopening.

Be'naj shifted in her seat to no longer face the window, hoping her intentions weren't obvious. "How did it go?" she asked as casually as she could muster after Saffron dropped her weight heavily onto the cushions.

"Some of these Shapers are stubborn," she replied.

"You don't say?" Be'naj played along. "What were you two talking about?"

"Oh, I was reminding Groilen how the Circle of Twelve still owed me for a favor I did them, and I wanted to ask one in return."

"What was it?"

"I persuaded him to get day passes for Zygrim and Wemic, the other gladiators I fought with during my captivity. And to book passage for them to Lucnere, too." Saffron made the statement as if it was a small thing, but stared at Be'naj with expectant eyes.

Be'naj chose her words carefully, torn between praising Saffron's compassion and admitting jealousy at having to compete with others for her attention. "That doesn't sound like it comes cheaply."

Saffron blew at a strand of hair that had fallen across her face. "No doubt. But I can't leave them in there to die for the sport of others when I have a key to their collars – and the Twelve *do* owe me."

"Well, I guess we'll have more company on the boat." Be'naj wasn't sure what else to say. She recognized it might be nice to have others to talk to besides Sirran. "Are we staying here tonight, then?"

"Oh yes," Saffron added. "Groilen said they had room for us at the cottage across from the stables, since the Twelve come and go from this house at all hours. We should be able to enjoy some quiet there."

"Perhaps we should retire, then? I know the two of you can't have slept in half-an-Age, and I would like to try communing with Shecclad."

"I wouldn't mind some sleep, though I'd like to be awake when Groilen gets back." Saffron stood and extended a hand to assist Be'naj to her feet. She gave a quick explanation to Rhazine, and then the three of them headed to the cottage to get some well-earned rest.

Chapter 17

Morning's Shimmer

T haelios gazed over the deck railing at yet another sunrise painting gold upon the western horizon. As beautiful as the light dancing off the water was, it felt like the trade barge Jaiden had put them on crawled up the Morning's Shimmer River at the pace of an infant. No doubt riding along while others toiled at the oars was easier than cutting across the river valley on horseback, but it seemed to be taking forever. Certainly, the Name of the Beast would be on to the next phase of its diabolical plan before they ever reached Blackfeather Perch.

Still, the trip gave him time to devour nearly everything in Trigilas's book. The Father of Spells was undoubtedly an even greater genius than eladrin legend boasted. *Gradations of*

Immortality contained magic beyond Thaelios's acumen, though just glimpsing the ambitious feats Trigilas pursued convinced him. While human Shapers who sought to prolong their existence often devolved to necromancy, Trigilas had taken an entirely different approach. He'd obviously gotten inspiration from dealing with immortal entities from the Outer Planes, and sought to mimic their constitution.

While he'd not found a way to bestow true immortality, other options to extend life had proven promising. One particular ritual that fascinated Thaelios involved Shaping a new body and transferring one's life source into it. There didn't seem to be any requirement that the new body matched the old, though it was unclear if the Spark that allowed one to Shape magic in the first place would be transferred.

Thaelios turned his back to the rising sun and sat upon the gently sloping prow of the vessel. The raised lip of the hull shielded him from the cold wind coming off the water, though indirect rays of sunlight still reached him. He'd have to remain content to read for at least another day, it seemed. Though the crew's uncomfortably long stares had mostly faded over the week of travel, he'd not grown comfortable enough with any of the humans to engage in idle conversation. That included Jaiden, for whom the opposite seemed to be true in regards to Dyphina.

The fey portion of her nature had been on full display, practically since they'd boarded in Selamus. She'd been at Jaiden's side nearly every time he saw them, laughing or flipping her hair from one shoulder to another. Thaelios wondered whether she could even help herself – talking to strangers seemed to come easily to Dyphina – but realized her flirtatiousness had its advantages. It took attention away from him, to start, and he was thankful for that. She could also be persuasive in a manner beyond his capability, and he'd never put much effort into learning charms.

He pushed thoughts of his fellow apprentice from his mind, settling in against the chill morning air to give his full attention to the page. He was rereading the Selective Reincarnation ritual to learn as much as he could about what bound a body and spirit together. Thaelios was so absorbed that he lost track of time and didn't notice Jaiden and Dyphina until they stood on either side of him, peering over the bow.

"Looks like a storm's rolling in from the north," Jaiden announced.

Dyphina shivered visibly. "It's getting colder, too. I'll have to get my cape from below."

Thaelios realized she was right. Goosebumps covered the silvery flesh of his arms. "I should do the same, I suppose." He marked his place in the book with its thin, golden cord and closed it before standing. "Thank you for the extra clothes and supplies," he mentioned to Jaiden after a pause. Expressions of gratitude were no exception to the reluctance he felt addressing humans.

Jaiden waved him off. "Don't mention it. I knew you two were traveling light, given the ground you covered. It's a shame Lady Saffron couldn't make this final part of the journey as well."

"I'll get yours too, Thaelios," Dyphina said, stepping toward the cabin hatch, consigning him to face alone whatever awkward conversation was about to unfold.

With the wind blowing against them, the sail of the single-mast vessel had been lowered and the steady rhythm of the oars plunging beneath the surface of the water stood out in the momentary silence.

"Yes, a shame," Thaelios eventually responded. "She and Be'naj had an equally important mission elsewhere, but she spoke well of you and was confident you'd give us aid."

"She did?" Jaiden leaned his elbows against the railing and faced the wind. The curls of his thick, dark brown hair peeled back from his face. He turned to Thaelios so the breeze didn't steal his words. "Well, I don't know of anyone more capable. If it's important, I'm glad she's the one taking care of it."

"Indeed," Thaelios replied. "I wish I had the same confidence in our success as we both have in hers."

"So, what's in that book you're always carrying around?" Jaiden asked, nodding toward the tome cradled in Thaelios's hands. "Is it a history or something?"

Thaelios shrugged. "I suppose one could describe it as such. It was written by a great scholar of my people, who is no longer living."

Dyphina emerged from the hatch with a heavy cloth cape draped around her shoulders. She carried another, folded in her arms, which she handed to Thaelios. The capes were white, emblazoned with purple crescents at their center, matching the tabard Jaiden wore over his tunic.

"I bet this country will be beautiful come spring," Dyphina said, looking toward the southern shore as Thaelios fastened his cape.

"Aye, I imagine it will," Jaiden answered. Dyphina took up a spot against the railing much closer to Jaiden than necessary and gazed up at him. He considered her and opened his mouth, but paused and turned to Thaelios instead. "I wanted to let you both know we'll be disembarking in the next few hours. I convinced the captain to skiff us to shore before they reach Koriskon. Better to not announce our arrival to an entire city, I think."

Thaelios nodded. "That seems wise."

"Will we be on foot, then?" Dyphina questioned, her pitch high.

Jaiden smiled. "I suppose, but we've got bedrolls and plenty of hard rations for it. I also brought silver. We could hire a wagon or buy ourselves horses in a village if we need to. There should be opportunities as we near the Ifelian Corridor."

"Hmm," Thaelios considered. "Yes, but we can't vouch for the safety of the Corridor, given past experiences."

"Well, we can take things as they come. I'm sure Criesha will be looking out for us."

"Does she … always?" Dyphina asked, not breaking eye contact and sliding her hand along the railing until it touched Jaiden's arm. "Look out for you, that is."

Thaelios wished he had half of Cauzel's skill and could take the shape of a caterpillar so he might simply crawl away. Instead, he decided to put Dyphina in her place. "Did I hear correctly that the knights of your Order swear a vow of celibacy?"

Jaiden clenched his teeth in an expression somewhere between a grimace and a smile. "Well, uh, yes, they do now, but that's a somewhat recent development."

"Is it?" Thaelios played along, not truly interested in the details.

"Criesha requires my complete devotion as her Champion. The most devout within the Rising Moon have taken on a similar oath as a way to show their dedication to our Goddess and the cause."

Dyphina turned her head slowly to Thaelios and smiled, then just as deliberately returned her attention to Jaiden. "That must be so *hard*, having to give up the needs of the flesh." She shifted to assume a position that mirrored Jaiden's, her elbows nestled firmly on the railing. Dyphina arched her back and her chest thrust out as a result. "I'm not sure I could give all that up so easily."

Jaiden licked his lips and swallowed, his eyes taking in the half-fey's reclining body. "Oh, I never said it was easy ..."

"Alright. Good talking to you," Thaelios interrupted. "I'm just going to go finish reading somewhere else and look forward to disembarking." Not waiting for a response, he made for the aft of their ship.

He just couldn't understand why people felt compelled to act in such ways. Thaelios didn't have a problem with sexuality, specifically, but it was something best expressed behind closed doors. Though he'd fought hard not to linger on them, memories of Zygrim taking him into the private chamber within the Den of Sin surfaced.

Thaelios walked nearly blind past a pair of sailors headed in the other direction and settled into a corner on the opposite end of the ship from Dyphina and Jaiden. He was too busy remembering how, despite his impressive musculature, Zygrim had so delicately undressed him. They had both been drunk, Thaelios justified to his own subconscious – buying enough leverage to indulge his memories a little longer.

Up until the point it actually happened, there was not a moment during his six decades of living that Thaelios had contemplated sharing such intimate experiences with a *human*. Like many Eladrin, he grew up thinking most humans would just as soon slit his throat as hold a conversation. Cauzel had changed that, though it turned out his mentor was Eladrin after all.

He'd been trying to keep the memories of that evening in the Den of Sin locked away – what good could come from dwelling on them? And yet, he didn't think the intoxicating heat Zygrim had filled him with was something he could ever forget.

The rhythmic crash of the oars upon the water suddenly stopped, drawing Thaelios's attention back to his surroundings. "Drop anchor!" the captain shouted from the bow. Finally, Thaelios could focus on something else – like planting his feet on dry land.

He closed the book he hadn't even started reading again and made his way to the hatch to gather his belongings. Thaelios didn't bother saying farewell to the sailors, who he assumed would be glad to see him off their ship. Jaiden had emerged from below deck wearing a suit of polished plate armor, the silvery metal accented by the same purple as his tabard.

"Are you sure you don't want to wait until we're ashore to don that?" Thaelios asked. "If our boat were to tip, you'd sink like a stone."

"I trust my balance," Jaiden responded. "Besides, the alloy is feather-light. I can march at full speed while wearing it, without tiring."

By the time they stepped off the skiff into the ankle-deep water that lapped the southern shore of the Morning's Shimmer River, the rolling clouds had blanketed the sky and a light snow began to fall.

Dyphina thanked each of the rowers with an embrace while Jaiden transferred their packs from the boat to the beach, one by one. Thaelios found his and checked to be certain Cauzel's spellbook and Trigilas's tome were both present and secure. Reassured by the sight of his now prized possessions, he hoisted the heavy pack onto his back and waited for his fellows to do the same.

"Are you sure you're going to be able to manage in that armor?" he asked Jaiden once more. He was almost tired just thinking of walking around while encased in metal.

Jaiden chuckled. "I promise I'm fine. Willem enchanted it." He watched the skiff returning to the cargo ship for a moment before facing Thaelios. "Are we ready, then? If we continue following the tree line west, we should eventually reach the Corridor."

"Then let's get started," Dyphina added merrily, holding her hand out to catch falling snowflakes. "Moving might help warm me up."

Jaiden nodded and led the way, heading inland just enough to get off the soft earth along the riverbank. His metal boots left clear imprints in the ground, and Dyphina seemed to be making a game of walking exactly where he stepped.

Thaelios flexed his fingers to test their circulation, taking up the rear as his mind wandered to the new spells he'd been focusing on from Cauzel's spellbook. His old master, while not as gifted as the Father of Spells, displayed an impressive ingenuity and had clearly possessed a passion for transmogrification magic.

Thaelios worried about the possibilities of taking the wrong shape or getting stuck in another form, and didn't have much desire to learn the same kinds of tricks. Having thought back on his recent experiences and his expanding grasp of the types of adversaries he was likely to have confrontations with, he was leaning toward a specialization in abjuration. Though the Celestial fountain had healed him, he could not forget the pain of Gullagion's acid eating away at his flesh. Preventing such harmful effects seemed a prudent course of study.

In the thick of his considerations, Thaelios wasn't sure if the ragged sound of a horse exhaling somewhere behind him was real or imagined. He looked over his shoulder to be sure, and stumbled into Dyphina as his feet reactively hastened him forward.

Four feral-looking humanoids sat atop chestnut steeds a good stone's-throw away, but moved with a slow gait toward overtaking them. The gently falling snow obfuscated their appearance, but Thaelios saw enough to know they were neither human nor Eladrin. "Jaiden, we're not alone!" Thaelios called.

When it was clear they were noticed, the riders stopped. Two of them held short, curved bows, and Thaelios spied spiked shields and fur-wrapped scabbards on the flanks of the horses. An uneasiness passed down his throat into his stomach and his fingers started twitching, eager to assist in casting.

Jaiden strode a couple of steps past Thaelios and Dyphina, interposing himself between the Shapers and the mounted quartet. "Orcs," he said quietly. "We've had problems with them in the Black Hills, but that's far from here. I've not found them to be friendly." He placed his hand on the hilt of the sword, sheathed at his side, but did not draw.

For a long moment, both groups remained rooted in place, assessing one another. In his head, Thaelios went over the chant for the new shielding spell he'd been practicing, anxious to see if it truly worked. Without a word, the lead orc spurred his horse into a gallop and the others mirrored him – the two armed with bows raised them and nocked arrows as they approached at speed.

Jaiden rushed forward to meet them, creating more distance between the initial point of attack and where Thaelios and Dyphina stood. Thaelios extended his elbows sideways, freeing them from the overlap of his cape. "Stay behind me," he said to Dyphina without looking back. He felt her shifting position but put all his concentration into Shaping.

The first pair of arrows were foolishly fired toward Jaiden. Without hope of penetrating his plate protection, they nevertheless deflected before striking its surface, as if some invisible hand had swatted them away. Thaelios ducked as one of the projectiles ricocheted past.

The grandmaster had lowered the visor of his helmet, which was set with an ivory, spiraled horn resembling a unicorn's. He'd also drawn his sword, and its blade shone with a pale green light. The archers had slowed their steeds to draw again while the other two orcs, curved falchions in hand, bore down on Jaiden.

Finishing the words required for his spell, Thaelios felt ready for the next round of arrows. A shimmering disc of force, about an arm's length wide, floated a similar distance in front of Thaelios's chest. It moved in accordance to his hand gestures, just like he'd practiced, but he had yet to test its strength against any substantial impact.

The first arrow approached on target, heading straight for his torso. He didn't need to make any adjustments and watched as the arrowhead snapped off its shaft, which spun into the air, harmlessly redirected. The second arrow was an overshot, but Thaelios had no way of knowing if Dyphina was in danger. He slid the disc quickly up and to the right, catching the arrow before it whizzed past him, likewise separating the metal from wood.

No sooner had he successfully deflected the missiles than Thaelios had to refocus on the other orcs. Their sword-wielding enemies had overrun Jaiden, who split their approach. One of the orcs fell from his saddle as he passed, a victim to Jaiden's prowess, but the other bore down on the Shapers.

He pulled his horse to a stop as he came alongside Thaelios, who must have seemed an easy target, weaponless and unarmored. As the orc warrior's sword sliced in a lethal arc toward his head, Thaelios shifted his shielding disc to interpose. The force of the blow, absorbed by the spell, was strong enough to knock the weapon from its wielder's hand.

The orc's surprised eyes suddenly shifted behind Thaelios, who had no idea what Dyphina might be up to. With a guttural shriek, the orc dropped the reins and lifted his hand to cover his face. A couple of breaths later he pulled it away, and Thaelios could see his eyes were covered with a white film.

The moment's distraction spelled the rider's end. He gasped horribly and spit out blood as the glowing tip of Jaiden's sword exited from his belly, having pierced both crude armor and flesh.

Another volley of arrows whisked Thaelios's way. He blocked one with his spell, though a sceond stuck into his cape, just beneath his left arm. The orcs reached for new arrows, but Jaiden wasn't going to leave them unchallenged. After removing his sword from the impaled orc, he grabbed its lifeless body and pulled it down from the saddle. The horse snorted an objection to the shifting weight, but allowed Jaiden to replace its former rider.

One of the archers noticed the development and began wheeling his horse around to flee. The other, however, was too focused on his shot. Thaelios was ready and easily blocked it, though shortly after the arrow flew, the orc noticed a mounted Jaiden bearing down on him.

With not much time to maneuver, the orc dropped his bow and tried to draw another weapon to defend itself. It never got the blade from its sheath. Jaiden caught up and, in one fierce slice, severed the creature's arm above the elbow. Another blow quickly followed, ending the screaming howl of the injured.

Thaelios scanned the beach for the final archer, but it had a significant head start. He dropped his spell and turned to make sure Dyphina was alright. Her body hummed with a residual radiance, the intensity of her beauty almost frightening. "You blinded him, just like in the Arena," Thaelios surmised.

Dyphina nodded. "This time I was still afraid," her voice shook, "but it was intentional. I called upon it." She exhaled deliberately. "And what about you? I've never seen that spell before."

Thaelios cracked a satisfied grin. "Well, perhaps you'd have picked up some new spells if you weren't paying so much attention to our young friend."

Jaiden rode up leading a spare horse, then lifted his visor and dismounted. "They must have stalked us. Someone isn't too keen on our association."

Thaelios agreed, though he didn't know how their enemies could have found out where they were so quickly. He kneeled over the dead orc lying nearby. "There," he said, pointing to an inscription etched into its dark hide armor. "It's the same as on the Mystic in the animal pens. Saffron said that was the mark of the Name of the Beast."

"It's the same group responsible for the death of the Prince," Jaiden said. He peered at the thick mass of trees to the south, perhaps to make sure no more orcs awaited them. "We'll have to stay alert as we travel."

"But at least now we have horses," Dyphina added.

"Their swords may be a little heavy for you, but we'll check the steeds. Perhaps they stowed smaller weapons you could arm yourselves with."

"I'm decent with a bow," Thaelios mentioned, looking back to where the archer had fallen. "What about the bodies?"

"We don't have time to bury or burn them," Jaiden responded. "Perhaps the snow will conceal them if enough falls. We should start moving; we may be able to keep ahead."

Dyphina lifted herself into an empty saddle. "Do you think there are more?"

"There are always more enemies."

Thaelios claimed the bow the dead archer had discarded and redistributed some of the supplies from his pack to his animal's to lighten his own load. A thin layer of white covered the bodies of the fallen by the time they were on their way.

By noon, the snow had stopped and they reached a small town at the northernmost point of the Ifelian Corridor. The road continued north toward Koriskon, but they were thankfully moving south, back into the forests of Thaelios's homeland.

They ate their midday meal in a field on the outskirts to avoid attention, but Dyphina convinced them to let her visit a tavern and gather what news she could. Thaelios agreed it was worth the risk, not knowing what had changed in the last few months, especially in Cauzel's absence.

She returned two hours later with a loaf of fresh bread and a general sense of unease from the townspeople. Raids upon merchants and even regular folk had increased, seemingly concentrated along the northern side of the Corridor. Fewer suppliers were willing to make the journey down to Pasaxtree, and that created a shortage of goods from the Northern Reaches. With that grim news further urging their sense of caution, the three companions made their way to the road and were soon under the bare winter boughs of the Ifelian forest.

Thaelios counted them lucky not to have passed another soul heading north along the road, though he recognized it was unusual for what Cauzel had described as a well-traveled thoroughfare. Had the humans really become so fearful of using their own road? The Eladrin would normally welcome such abandonment, but Thaelios doubted it was a good omen.

"So, what else have you learned from Cauzel's spellbook?" Dyphina asked after they'd ridden for some time in silence.

The sun was hidden behind a layer of low clouds, and the dusting of snow had rendered the land in an austere pallet. Normally reluctant to share arcane knowledge, Thaelios thought the backdrop appropriate for secrets. "Our master had been working on a spell for elemental resistance, not unlike what the Temple of Eternal Flame used for protection against Saffron in the Arena. Only, his would simultaneously guard against fire, frost, lightning, and acid."

"That's impressive." Dyphina's face was obscured by the hood of her cape, but he could hear the sincerity in her tone. "And you've learned how to cast it?" There was the doubt he expected.

"Not yet," Thaelios answered. "Cauzel never finished his formula, but I can tell where he was headed from his notes. I'm attempting to complete the spell, but I need access to his full research. I hope to work on it once we reach the Perch."

"Criesha has granted me a few powers that I would call miraculous," Jaiden chimed in. "But I'm clearly just a vessel. How do regular people, like Willem for instance, learn to do magic?"

Thaelios shook his head. "Not everyone can. I know scholars from different cultures debate this, but eladrin tradition tells us the presence of the Avatars filled the world with what we might call, 'magic potential.' Some creatures have a trait, a bloodline if you will, that allows them to feel the presence of this potential. Anyone possessing that Spark is capable of Shaping, but that is not enough. You still have to learn to manipulate the energy into a useful arrangement. Practice helps."

"So, it's kind of like swordplay?" Jaiden replied. "I mean, anyone can pick up a blade, sure, but the combination of balance, strength, and dexterity … not to mention instinct – some people are just born with it. Regardless, I practiced every day for years to get where I am today."

"Sure, it's sort of like that," Dyphina offered.

Thaelios smiled. Jaiden probably couldn't tell from her tone that the half-fey was teasing him. "The hour is getting late.

Should we set up camp away from the road?" He would have liked to keep going, but he knew the humans needed sleep to be at their best, and it was prudent that Jaiden remain alert.

They camped west of the road, far enough off and behind a grove of evergreens to be shielded from view. Dyphina cast an enchantment to mask their scent while they slept. Thaelios kept watch for a while, reading in Trigilas's book until it grew too dark. He'd been pleased with his casting of the shielding spell and was eager to continue learning. At last he tranced, leaving enough time to replenish and still start breaking down camp before the others awoke.

"We should follow the road until it's time to camp tonight," he said, once they got moving. "Tomorrow morning, we'll cut southeast through the forest toward Blackfeather Perch."

They rode at a leisurely pace, watering their horses at the tributaries that fed into the swamps of Ergilad to the east. The beasts nibbled at whatever shrubs they found, though Dyphina bemoaned the lack of adequate food for their steeds. Thaelios promised they'd receive ample nourishment once they reached the stables at Cauzel's tower.

The woods were quieter than Thaelios could ever remember, even in the heart of winter. With no traffic along the road and no sign of wildlife other than the occasional small mixed flocks searching for seeds, it didn't seem exactly like coming home. Thaelios felt like this was just a quasi-real approximation of the forest he grew up in.

Finally, in the dead hours of the afternoon, he saw the first sign of other travelers. A wagon lay askew on the western edge of the road, half of it sloped down the embankment that led to a wide pool of reedy water. The Wyrmsmoke Mountains rose up shortly past the pond. No obvious sign of the horses that had been pulling the wagon could be seen, but his keen eladrin eyes did catch movement on the other side of the vehicle.

"Look, there!" He pointed to what seemed like bundles of cloth lying on the road in front of the wagon. From this distance he couldn't be sure, but his guess was they were dead bodies. He stopped his horse and turned to the others to hear their assessment.

Instead of being cautious, Jaiden urged his horse into a trot, riding forward to investigate. Dyphina shrugged and followed suit. Thaelios exhaled his frustration and reached for his spell component pouch, searching for inspiration. He felt uncomfortable repeatedly entering situations without time to prepare. Cognizant of how far the others were ahead of him, he sped forward as well, still holding the pouch in one hand lest he need it.

"Hello!" Jaiden yelled as he drew nearer, hoping to get the attention of whoever was behind the wagon. The response was a chorus of hisses, which caused Jaiden to halt his approach.

Out from the concealment of the tilted, wooden side panels stepped a mixed quartet of creatures. Thaelios recognized two of them immediately from an earlier encounter – Thralls of the Nightwing. The other two were reptilian lizardfolk, like the ones who had helped that witch Annoxoria kidnap them from Cauzel's training grounds. None of them brought up pleasant memories.

One of the lizardfolk held a heavy chest in both arms, and they all seemed to be taking account of the newcomers, especially the armored Jaiden. After another round of throaty gargles and hisses, the group broke into movement. One Thrall scrambled up the side of the wagon with the nimbleness of a squirrel, while the others all darted back behind the wagon, running for the water.

"What do we do?" asked Dyphina.

Thaelios was unsure. He didn't like the idea of criminals getting away, especially since it appeared these creatures had murdered the wagon owners, but he was also hesitant to initiate a confrontation. Following their progress toward the pond, he saw that a couple additional lizardfolk were already swimming across to the far side with stolen goods.

Jaiden, however, didn't hesitate for long. He dismounted and drew his sword, then charged down the road toward the sloped bank of the pool. He caught the last of the Thralls as it noisily splashed into the pond, hacking it across the back of the shoulder with his glowing blade before it could escape. It crashed face-first into the brackish water, but the others were already beyond reach. Jaiden looked at the fleeing creatures, then down at his own feet, already obscured in ankle-deep liquid and mud. "Cowards!" he called, but the lizardfolk paid his insult no mind.

Thaelios and Dyphina nudged their mounts forward as Jaiden trudged back from the edge of the pond to the road. He looked down at the slain wagon drivers with a creased brow.

"Are you alright?" Dyphina asked, her voice thick with compassion. "Did you know them?"

Jaiden shook his head. "Of course not." He looked up at her. "But someone did. Some children's fathers will never come home now." He returned his view to the water as the last of the creatures rose from its icy grip. "What are those things?"

"We've run into them before," Thaelios answered. "Annoxoria, the Shaper who put us into servitude, used lizardfolk in her raiding party. The others, though, used to be human. They're Thralls of the Nightwing, so I don't know why they'd be working for a sorceress."

Dyphina shrugged. "Perhaps they're not. More than ever, we need to regroup at Blackfeather Perch and get a better sense of what's going on."

"I agree," Thaelios said. "I worry that when we get there, with Cauzel gone, we may end up with more questions than answers." Though after all this time, he would gladly give a month's wages to see another familiar face, even if it belonged to Iliana.

Chapter 18

Reaping What You Sow

Annoxoria wasn't sure how to feel after returning to Nightwing Castle from Rinn-Rhulian. She and Thuvian had been insulted by the Ellafous, though she was grateful that the site had protection. While not her original goal, now that she'd discovered another clue to the mystery of the ruins, she was seized by a compulsion to investigate. Whatever Rinn-Rhulian protected, it was Power.

On top of the emotions stirred up by their excursion, she was also painfully aware of Thuvian's impatience for his spymaster's return. Her Lord was a man of action, and she knew that, sooner or later, he would act. She preferred his choice be strategic.

For the time being, he kept busy preparing the castle for a direct attack from Sepathia, though Annoxoria suspected his sister's retaliation would take a more subtle form. Wanting to stay occupied herself, she decided to conduct an impromptu inspection of the mines. Even if Izefet and the Aasimar had made off with all the collected Living Fire, more probably existed beneath the castle.

She had one of her ogre lashers escort her through the deepest section of their operation. If the Aasimar were already directing the laborers toward the Seeds of the Avatars when they abruptly left, it made sense that those were the areas to concentrate on exploring.

Irritation at the slowing of production in recent weeks needled Annoxoria. Since Thuvian had ordered an end to their merchant raids along the Ifelian Corridor, she no longer had as many new workers to replace those who perished. At least she hadn't had any troublemakers like those apprentices she'd kidnapped from the Blackfeather estate. There'd been no news regarding Hadrian No More's ghost lieutenant, nor anything of the Shaper, Cauzel, for that matter.

Of course, ceasing their ambushes along the Corridor had been part of the plan. With the leadership in Pasaxtree and Korus hesitant to recognize Drachenmark and grant Thuvian a seat at the table, his promise to make the Ifelian Corridor safe again for merchants had given him a chance to earn their respect. Following through had been easy, but came at its own cost.

The Rauglor were eager as always to push around their subordinates, and redirecting slaves to explore the desired veins proved a satisfying task. By the time it was completed, Annoxoria was ready to leave the stifling heat of the mines.

She decided a cool bath was just what she needed, and had her servants draw one. Lowering herself into the water and lying back, her fingers played over the rough texture of her stomach wound. Annoxoria swore she would find a way to pay Sepathia back for the stinger injury, though at the same time, she fantasized about what it would be like to have such a powerful weapon innately part of her being.

Was a magical solution to freeing her imprisoned soul beyond her capabilities of Shaping? Surely, the Living Fire would provide the amplification she needed. Or perhaps, she would have been wise to cultivate cooperation with Cauzel Blackfeather instead of dismissing him as an adversary. What if he possessed the arcane expertise she required?

That thought caused her to hold her breath and duck her head underwater. She couldn't start second-guessing her decisions now. Her instincts led her to where she was – consort-queen of the mighty Thuvian Skullreaver was an achievement she wouldn't dismiss. But what if she could still benefit from Cauzel's repository of knowledge?

She quickly broke the surface of the bath, taking a deep breath and sitting up straight. It was a long shot, but she still might have a way to access the library at Blackfeather Perch. Eager to give it a try, Annoxoria washed quickly, then hastily toweled off and slipped into a soft, black tunic.

Annoxoria grabbed her jar of expensive scrying sand, gathered from the lair of a basilisk, along with a pitcher of the water her servants had used to fill her bath. She sat in front of the gilded basin stowed in the corner of her laboratory. Her hands shook slightly as she poured the water, anxious to see if her notion bore fruit.

Next, she scattered a spoonful of the rose-colored sand into the water, chanting a scrying spell as she concentrated on the novice who'd briefly served as an intermediary between the Name of the Beast and herself. Would he be near enough to his scrying device to receive the summons? Would he even answer if he was?

She didn't have to wait long to find out. The surface of her pool began to vibrate, creating ripples that suddenly revealed a new reflection in place of her own. When the trembling subsided and the water stilled, Annoxoria was staring down at the image of a young man's face. He had light brown eyes, strawberry blond hair, and a stubble-covered jaw.

"I must say," he began speaking with a cocky tone, not waiting for her to address him, "I am surprised to find you calling. Surprised, but curious."

"Is that because you know your master, Izefet, has betrayed me?"

"Izefet is yet another humble servant to our greater cause … a cause he serves well."

"And what cause is served by gaining my enmity and that of Lord Skullreaver? Are you certain the path you're pursuing isn't merely foolishness, disguised?" Aware she would eventually need to ask for a favor, Annoxoria first wanted her adversary to squirm and second-guess his allegiances.

"The Name of the Beast is rising, whether or not you can fathom it, Annoxoria Nefzen," the man replied. His bravado had clearly swelled since their last conversation. "Why is it that the Lady of Drachenmark has called upon me?"

Annoxoria paused – she had to play this just right. "I know what Izefet desired the Living Fire for. And seeing as how he so rudely tried to dispose of me, I'm going to make sure he doesn't get what he wants … unless I get something I want in return." The expression on the young man's face stiffened, though he tried to appear unchanged.

"Your resilience is impressive, My Lady," he finally said. He turned his head to check over his shoulder before continuing. "While we all serve the same purpose, we are not all the same. I'm willing to hear you out."

"Good. Perhaps you shall not share the fate of Izefet for betraying me. You are one of Cauzel Blackfeather's apprentices, no? I presume you have not yet been exposed and still have access to his tower?"

The man opened his mouth, then closed it. "I have … been inside the Perch, yes."

She felt uncomfortable revealing what she was about to, but for all she knew, Izefet had found out her secret and already shared it. "I need any magical research your unsuspecting master has collected on transmogrify – transformation magic. Can you bring it to me?"

Annoxoria's scrying partner pouted as he considered her request. "I might be able to do that. Cauzel has left Ifelian on a journey, or at least I'm fairly certain he has. But if I were to risk theft against the most powerful Shaper in Ifelian, I would need the reward to be mine, more than merely a promise not to thwart Izefet."

"So, you do care more for yourself than your cause." It didn't really matter what this pawn desired in return. She knew now that allegiance to this cult was simply an excuse for self-serving cowards to hide behind the cloak of anonymity. Still, she would play the game and ask. "What is it that you want?"

"One of your slaves," he replied without hesitation. "The dark-haired apprentice you captured. I want you to release her to me, but in such a way that she knows I rescued her."

That was not at all what Annoxoria had prepared to hear. It didn't matter that the slave in question was a thousand miles away and probably dead. "That can be arranged, if you deliver what I'm seeking."

"Well, then," the young man said, his tone smarmy and pleased, "I shall contact you about the exchange once I've succeeded."

"I'm sure you will," Annoxoria replied. She reached down and dipped a finger into the water, disrupting its surface and ending the magical conduit. She had little confidence this initiate would actually come through, but it was a possibility, nevertheless. The thought left her energized, and she decided to spend the rest of the afternoon in bed, warming herself up for Thuvian.

A few days later, Pereen Guillory returned from his mission to Pasaxtree. Thuvian called for an audience immediately upon being informed of his arrival, and Annoxoria joined him in the throne room. She was hungry for any news of Izefet – preparing to hear the worst yet still eager for what she might learn.

"My apologies if I kept you waiting, My Lord and Lady," the spymaster offered in a sullen tone that cast his genuineness in doubt. Still, he kept his head respectfully low. "I imagined you'd be otherwise occupied when I returned."

Thuvian's throat rumbled before he ever opened his mouth. "Don't compound it with empty pleasantries, Pereen. What did you learn of this cult's plans in Pasaxtree?"

Annoxoria crossed her arms and stared unsympathetically at the spymaster, who looked vexed by his Lord's reprimand.

Pereen cleared his throat. "The Name of the Beast's influence is … intricate, to say the least. Conflicting rumors accuse different members of the City's Council and merchant guild as being loyal to the cult. None of the actions that can be traced back clearly demonstrate such allegiances, though I have my own suspicions. Not even my operatives have found anyone who claims to know of, let alone personally met, Izefet."

"So the demon-spawn is content to lie in the shadows?" Thuvian stood from his throne, stepped down the dais, and paced. "But for how long? Crafty as he is, he must still know he alone cannot overcome the Ellafous. If he wants access to Rinn-Rhulian, he will need help."

"He has the Aasimar," Annoxoria mentioned. "We don't know how many. We only saw one or two at a time, but there may be more."

Pereen cleared his throat again, this time to reclaim attention. "There is more news from Pasaxtree, I'm afraid."

Thuvian stopped moving. "What is it?" he hissed over his red-caped shoulder.

"Their Council is displeased with the raids along the Corridor."

"I know, that's why I stopped them," Thuvian spat. "It was the price of our treaty and trade agreements. Come spring, the influx of goods will help my kingdom flourish."

"Only, they haven't stopped, My Lord. They've reportedly grown in frequency as of late."

"What?" Thuvian spun on his heels. "I haven't authorized an ambush in weeks."

The spymaster interlaced his fingers and licked his lips. "And yet, according to the Merchant Guild of Pasaxtree, there have been more casualties than ever."

Thuvian looked dead at Annoxoria, his nostrils flaring. "Is this the cult, or Sepathia?"

Pereen kept talking, even though he was no longer being addressed. "Pasaxtree thinks it's you. They recovered rubies from your mines on one of the slain lizardfolk, or so it is claimed."

Despite her lover's perturbation, Annoxoria felt oddly calm now that she was finally receiving clarity. "It's probably both. We know Sepathia has influence over lizardfolk, and Izefet stole from us before abandoning Nightwing Castle. He could have planted the rubies. Now we know why your sister hasn't attacked … she's trying to get a human army to do it for her."

Thuvian growled at the mention of Sepathia. "I will not have all my efforts unravel because of my sister's lies. Besides that, we are not looking for war with Pasaxtree."

Annoxoria shrugged. "What do you want to do? We can destroy whoever we have to." She felt her draconic blood coming to an ecstatic boil at the thought of all-out conflict, though she knew such a choice was unwise. Would that she were living in the right body.

Even as her emotions started to simmer, Thuvian's seemed to cool. "No, not yet, though that time may come. We need to convince the humans of another course." He looked back to

Pereen. "Perhaps it is time for the Lord of Drachenmark to address the leaders of Pasaxtree in person."

The spymaster nodded once, then bowed. "As you wish, Lord Skullreaver."

PHILLIP M. LOCEY

Phillip studied Creative Writing at the University of
North Carolina at Chapel Hill and earned a Master's in
Library and Information Science from the
University of South Florida.
Weaned on the fantasy genre from a young age,
he spent decades creating the imagined world of Elisahd,
where the majority of his tales are now set.

Visit elisahdbooks.com for more stories,
artwork, and news about books to come!

Want More?
Join my mailing list at the website above and
receive a free book set in the same world as this series.

The Saga Ends with
"A World in Shadow," Book 4 in The Chain of Living Fire.

www.ingramcontent.com/pod-product-compliance
Lightning Source LLC
Chambersburg PA
CBHW071046250626
47159CB00002B/386